THE LEGEND
OF
WAHKAN

MELISSA SHARMAN

authorHOUSE®

AuthorHouse™
1663 Liberty Drive
Bloomington, IN 47403
www.authorhouse.com
Phone: 1-800-839-8640

Published by AuthorHouse 02/06/2014

ISBN: 978-1-4918-3679-8 (sc)
ISBN: 978-1-4918-3678-1 (hc)
ISBN: 978-1-4918-3677-4 (e)

Library of Congress Control Number: 2013921213

For my friends and family who never stopped believing in me, and for my husband who supported me from beginning to end.

Acknowledgements

I WOULD LIKE TO THANK JENNIFER Coleman and Debbie Arbelo who both encouraged me to write this story. It would have never come to be without their persuasion and enthusiasm.

I WOULD ALSO LIKE TO THANK Eric Sharman, David Coleman, Cindy and James DeVaughn, Betty and James Coleman, Phyllis and William Sharman, Isaac Bellflower, Jackie Coltrain, Laura Dorning, Megan Goodman, Bryan Sarfaty, and Jimmie Rogers.

"One thing I learned from my elders…
Never doubt a spirit."
– Dena

PROLOGUE

THE RAIN WAS POURING HEAVILY as second shift neared its end. The locker room was beginning to quiet down as officers were rushing to get home. A few other officers were walking in, about to begin third shift. Alyssa was grabbing a few items from her locker, ignoring the commotion as she hurriedly shoved the items into her bag. She didn't want to get caught up in a conversation with the other women who took their time dressing and putting their belongings away.

Alyssa zipped her bag and stood, tossing the strap over her shoulder. She refused to look back as she walked around the corner and pulled the door open. It made a soft screech as she stepped into the hall and halted, allowing the door to close gently behind her.

"So is it true?" a young man asked.

Alyssa took in a deep breath and rested her body against one side. She stared at her former partner and sighed. He was a great friend but at times he could be quite a nuisance.

"Kevin, I really didn't have much of a choice," she replied.

He walked to a nearby window and leaned against it. "We've been partners for a couple of years now, right?" he asked. Alyssa nodded and remained standing near the door. "I really hate what you are going through, but I don't think I am ready to find a replacement."

"Look, this was really hard for me to decide, but my doctor suggested it," Alyssa stated and glanced down the hall, hoping no one was around to hear.

"What are you going to do?" Kevin asked.

Alyssa approached him. "My father thought it would be best for me to come and stay with him and my mother, which means I'll be breaking my lease, but you know it just might do me some good. I think my father is finally going to try and give me…some answers," she replied hesitantly.

Kevin looked a bit confused. Alyssa cleared her throat and glanced at her watch.

"Answers to what if you don't mind me asking?"

"You know it's been a difficult topic, and it's very hard for me to explain and go into detail without you wondering if I'm going insane. Besides, I need to get moving. With these few tremors we've experienced today, I'd hate to get caught up in a panic with the residents while trying to get to the highway."

Kevin nodded and pushed himself away from the window. "I understand. I'm sure these tiny quakes are nothing to be concerned with," he said and looked at Alyssa. He was going to miss having her alongside him in the patrol car. "Well at least give me a call sometime if you want to go grab a beer. We're going to miss having you around here," he added.

Alyssa smiled and leaned towards him, giving him a friendly hug. "I'll definitely stay in touch. Just remember that this is temporary, okay? I need to figure some things out right now," she said and Kevin patted her back.

"Alright. Well, take care," he said and watched Alyssa walk down the hallway.

"I will. Bye," she said, looking back at her former partner.

"Bye," he responded and stood there as Alyssa disappeared around a corner. Millions of thoughts raced throughout her mind, questioning her decisions and the possible consequences as she approached the lobby. She wasn't sure if it was going to be the right choice. She was nervous and afraid, her heart fluttering away, but she knew that it was a done deal. There was no turning back now.

"You remember what I said, Alyssa…"

Alyssa's thoughts were interrupted as she glanced up to see the chief of police standing near the exit, smiling back at her. He was a happy, good-hearted person, a close family friend of her father's. He had been around long before she was born.

"You come back when you are ready," he added.

"I will. Thank you so much for everything," Alyssa replied. She knew she would miss Robert and the rest of the precinct. They were all close, a family of their own.

"You're welcome. You just take care of yourself. We'll see you again soon I'm sure," Robert said and opened the door for her.

"Of course. I'll see you guys later," Alyssa replied and waved to the secretaries behind the counter.

"Bye honey! We'll miss you," one said, looking up from behind her computer, waving. It was Kristin, the only secretary to acknowledge her since the accident. Alyssa never knew why the others kept quiet.

Alyssa smiled after saying her goodbyes and stepped outside. The door carefully closed behind her, and the rain began to kiss her face gently. The weather was finally beginning to calm down, and she could remember what a relief that was...

CHAPTER ONE

NIGHT WAS SOON TO ARRIVE and the fatigue was already setting in. It was the daily routine Alyssa dreaded the most, sleep. The frequent underworld and haunting town she seemed to visit every night became certain, a ritual almost. They were to be expected...

She could recall the constant night terrors and awakening to sweat on her face and chest, her heart beating rapidly, and her breaths panting as if it happened moments ago. The images were too difficult not to dwell on. They quickly crept into her mind the moment she sat on her bed to prepare herself for what was to come later that evening. Alyssa was extremely nervous about this one, and it had nothing to do with the nightmare that was sure to torment her. It was actually her father, James. He had been extremely difficult to talk to since the accident, but she believed tonight was going to be different. There was a change coming. She could feel it.

Alyssa sighed softly and pushed away the thoughts as she continued to sit on her bed, staring at the luggage in front of her. One bag was prepared for the five day trip that she reluctantly decided to take with a few friends. The others were for her stay at her parents' house. She wasn't quite ready to move all of her belongings there permanently. She still held onto the glimmer of hope of possibly returning to her home. She was dreading the idea about moving back in under the same roof as her folks, but she was also thankful at the same time. How many other parents would allow their twenty-five year old to move back in, especially after a doctor stated that he was concerned about their mental health?

At least the doctor listened and gave me advice, a possible diagnosis, and a referral. He never turned his head or walked away like my father always does...

Alyssa closed her eyes and took in a slow, deep breath, clearing her mind once more until she felt a buzz beside her, a loud chiming ring following afterwards. She opened her eyes, her body shaking from the startle.

"Goodness..." she murmured and reached for her phone, grabbing it and pressing answer on the touch screen.

"Hello?" she asked and began to smile, the thoughts of sand and sun now appearing in her mind. The thought was able to rinse away all of the depressing images.

"Hey! Are you about ready?" an excited but soft voice asked. It was Kayla, a childhood friend of Alyssa's and the only one she could truly confide in.

"Almost. I just have to stop by my parents' place to drop some things off there first, but I won't be long," Alyssa said and stood up. She walked to her dresser, thinking about a couple of items she wanted to take with her.

"Okay, cool. We are ready over here. Just call me when you're headed this way," Kayla responded and Alyssa smiled, looking at a picture of her and her father that was taken at the shooting range years ago.

"I will. Thanks again for inviting me. I'm really looking forward to this," she replied, picking up the picture and stuffing it into her back pocket.

"No problem. It just wouldn't be the same without you. I'll see you soon, okay?" Kayla stated as Alyssa opened a trinket box that sat on her dresser.

"Okay. See you in a bit."

"Bye."

Alyssa tossed her phone onto the bed and gently pulled a necklace her father had given her out of the trinket box. She sighed softly, staring at the unique piece. The red, odd shaped stone embedded in a white gold pendant always had a way of mesmerizing her. She thought it would be a nice piece to wear during the vacation regardless of its history.

I should bring it with me. My father has a lot of explaining to do, and I know this piece has something to do with the accident. Perhaps when he sees it again, he can recall everything.

Alyssa gently secured the necklace around her neck and tucked it under her white t-shirt. She patted it, assured that it would stay, and turned to grab her phone, gently picking it up. She then turned and grabbed her luggage that sat by her bed and tossed the long strap to one over her shoulder. Mixed emotions were already building within her as she carried her bags into her small kitchen and living room. Alyssa glanced at the windows and noticed the evening light was already piercing through the blinds, touching the floor softly. She had allowed too much time to pass. She needed to get herself together and get moving if she wanted to have this talk with her father before leaving.

I cannot go until I have tried...My father has to understand that I need this. It could give me the peace of mind I have longed for since all of this began.

She quickly sat her bags down by the front door and turned to retrieve her purse from the kitchen counter, looking around at the same time to make sure all the lights were off. As she picked up her purse, she searched through it to make sure she had everything she was going to need while away from home. She wasn't going to risk any possible delays if she could prevent them. Her friends knew her best. She was bound to forget something.

Alyssa smiled and tossed the strap of her purse onto her shoulder. She hurried to the front door and felt her phone vibrate in the palm of her hand. She looked at the caller ID and groaned.

"Oh not now Kevin," she murmured, hitting ignore.

I wonder about him sometimes. Good guy, but damn...He knew I was going to have a busy evening. I've got to get going or I'm going to make us all late.

Alyssa grabbed her bags and opened the front door to her single wide mobile home. She stepped out onto the deck and took in a deep breath of the fresh mountain air. The warm, late August breeze that whistled around blew her dark, blonde hair off her shoulders as she placed her phone inside her purse and grabbed her keys. Alyssa gently closed and locked the door before turning to walk down the steps to her black Chevrolet Silverado. The old, wooden deck creaked with every step she took, something that always rattled her nerves now-a-days. She ignored them and fought back the fears that were brought on by her imagination, rushing to get to her truck. Once she reached it, she tossed her luggage into the bed and glanced back at the property. It was hard to let go of. She was going to miss the luxury of living in her own home. She had moved out at nineteen, maturing quickly. She couldn't help but imagine how it was going to be living back in the same house she grew up in, although most of these memories were pleasant ones. But then again, everything had dramatically changed with the passing of her brother when she was only twelve years old.

Alyssa's smile faded and she quickly shook the negative images away.

Such a long time ago...I had almost forgotten...

She looked back at her truck and reached for the door handle, suddenly jumping in fright. A deep, scratchy growl disrupted her thoughts. It was heard in the distance behind her, awakening her deepest fear. Alyssa released a low gasp, her heart skipping wildly within her chest. She quickly turned around to examine the large front yard, her eyes wide. It appeared vacant. The sun was beginning to hide behind the acres of trees as its light was slowly fading. The wind still blew around gently, pushing a few leaves across the grassy terrain. Alyssa took in a deep breath, releasing it slowly, scanning the area one last time.

That really didn't sound like a stray. Maybe I'm hearing things. I guess I shouldn't be too surprised...Seems like I get worse every day.

She turned back towards her truck and opened the door, tossing her purse into the passenger seat as she climbed in and sat down.

Alyssa carefully closed and locked the door, glancing back at the mobile home and the trees that surrounded it. She thought once more about the strange sound and the bizarre events that began in the city just a couple of days before she put in her medical leave of absence.

It's just so odd...All of these strange things they say that happened in Rockdale Valley, not to mention the earthquakes. Virginia has always been a stable area. Maybe my father will know more and at least be willing to talk about that. Hopefully things in town will smooth out while I'm gone.

Alyssa took in a deep breath and pondered the conversation she was planning on having with her father as she started her truck. She was still anxious. She wondered how her father was going to react with this unexpected visit. Due to the way he had been lately, she couldn't predict how he would respond.

Alyssa slowly turned her truck around and drove down the hills of her driveway, preparing herself as best as she could. Once she reached the secluded street beside the property, she cleared her mind and carefully turned right, making her way west toward the mountains and the setting sun.

CHAPTER TWO

THE TWELVE MINUTE TRIP TO the Bennett's secluded home seemed more like a half hour drive. Alyssa had finally turned onto the gravel driveway that led up a hill and into a lush, green field with a few oak trees.

"Finally," she whispered.

She parked her truck beside a tree that stood near the red brick house and switched off the engine. Alyssa opened the door eagerly and stepped out onto the gravel. She turned to retrieve her purse and stopped once she noticed her mother's car was the only one that sat under the carport. Her father's truck was gone. Alyssa mumbled to herself and looked at the front door of the home. It hung slightly open and appeared to have been damaged. There were pieces of wood fragments and splinters scattered around it. And then her eyes focused on the carport as she noticed the disruption in the gravel from her father's pickup.

Odd...How did I miss this when I pulled up?

Alyssa climbed back into her truck and opened the glove department, her sense of eagerness fading to suspicion. She gently picked up her Berretta 9000 S 40 caliber handgun and slammed the compartment door shut. Slowly sliding out of her truck, she held the pistol up close and watched the area cautiously. She hoped that she wasn't being too cautious. The area seemed safe.

Alyssa closed the door as quietly as she could and walked toward the entrance of her parents' home. She couldn't shake the feeling that was erupting within her. Her instincts were warning her of possible trouble, the adrenaline beginning to pump rapidly into her veins.

Alyssa slowly stopped once she reached the broken door and held her pistol steady. She glanced at the debris that lay around her, the wood and glass crunching under her boots.

"Goodness..." she whispered and slowly pushed the damaged door open.

"Mom?" she asked and her mouth slowly dropped, her heart sinking deep within her chest. She took in deep breath and tried to focus on the disaster in front of her. Furniture and electronics were scattered on the carpet, torn and broken as shreds of fabric and pieces of equipment lay on the floor. Shredded books and newspapers lay close to her as she cautiously stepped inside the wrecked house.

I can't believe this. What could have happened? I had just spoken to them earlier today...I should get back in the truck and call for help...

Her police training took over instead as she remained standing inside the house. The difficulty of the matter was overwhelming. She couldn't imagine her parents being hurt or worse...

Just stop...I can't think like that...

Alyssa took in another deep and steady breath through her nostrils, trying to remain calm. She scanned the living area thoroughly and noticed her family portrait crushed on the floor. Alyssa frowned and slowly kneeled down beside the broken frame, realizing that the shattered glass was stained in red. She touched it gently and her heart began to flutter uncontrollably. The blood was fresh, loose under her fingertips. Alyssa quickly stood up and glanced at the hallway that stretched to the back of the house.

No...This can't be happening...Who could have done this?

She exhaled heavily and focused her attention towards the hallway. Something was imprinted in the carpet, a red smear. Alyssa held her pistol out in front of her and slowly approached the peculiar mark, keeping an eye on the other rooms down the hall. Many thoughts raced throughout her mind once she reached the stain. It was a track, a footprint. Alyssa was trying not to allow the fear to get the best of her. She stared at the strange print, examining every detail.

These don't belong to a human...or to any animal that I am familiar with for that matter...

Alyssa looked further down the hallway and decided to check the rest of the house. She had to ignore the fear and anxiety that continued to build within her. She had to make sure her parents were not in the house.

Alyssa held her pistol out steadily once more, focusing towards the first room on the right. She cautiously approached it, ignoring the negative thoughts that tried to creep into her mind as she quickly stepped into her parents' dining room. She took slow breaths, moving her pistol across the room swiftly. The small dining room was untouched. A large table sat in the middle of it and a French cabinet stood at the end against the wall holding her mother's favorite china.

Maybe they were able to escape...They just had to...

Alyssa carefully stepped back into the dimly lit hallway and looked towards the last two rooms in the back. She continued to hold her pistol out in front of her and approached her parents' bedroom. The sounds of her soft footsteps and exhale of breath were all she could hear as she focused on the room she slowly stepped up to. Her heart continued to thump wildly, the sweat pushing from the pores on her face, accumulating on her forehead. It was almost too much for her to overcome.

Please...They had to have escaped...

Alyssa held her breath once she reached the door frame and stepped into the devastated bedroom, slowly lowering her pistol. Her mouth dropped in pure shock and fear. Blood covered most of the floor and bed as glass lay strewn around the shattered window. Pillows and pieces of the comforter were torn and thrown around the room, and a couple of lamps were knocked off the end tables, cracks spread throughout them.

Alyssa breathed heavily and stared at what looked like large gashes carved into the wall. There were four large tears etched deep into the sheetrock, drywall and dust covering part of the once blue carpet.

Alyssa slowly approached the large gashes, ignoring everything else around her.

What on earth...

She gently touched the tears and thought about the track she saw in the hallway. A sudden flashback of her reoccurring nightmare quickly flashed before her eyes as she heard the loud, wicked scream that haunted her in her restless dreams. The dark underworld, the hellish creatures filled her vision as she released a low gasp and closed her eyes. Her hand slowly dropped to her side, the fear erupting inside her, rushing throughout her body and sending her into panic. Alyssa opened her eyes and quickly turned around, looking back toward the hallway. Her eyes were wide and full of concern. At least the underworld she was so familiar with was now no longer in her view.

I've got to get help now!

Alyssa ran back into the hallway, holding her pistol close. She carefully watched her surroundings as she began to run towards the front door. She pushed through all the debris and ran out of the wrecked house, refusing to look back. She ran to her truck and didn't stop until she reached the driver's door. She feared a possible encounter with a monstrous animal. It could still be lurking near the area, waiting to spring on its next victim.

A monster? What else could have caused that much destruction, leave those kinds of tracks and gashes?

Alyssa gasped for air, breathing heavily as she grabbed the handle to her truck and pulled the door open. She jumped into the seat and shut the door, continuing to exhale loudly as she locked it and sat her Berretta in the passenger seat. She decided to take one last look at her parents' house before retrieving her phone from her purse, questioning the reason of how and why something like this could happen in such a remote area. Did anything that created those tracks and gashes actually exist? Her only guess was a bear though the tracks didn't quite fit and bears were not known to break down front doors.

And I don't believe a black bear has claws that large.

Alyssa's frustration and anxiety elevated. The atmosphere around her was gloomy and calm which made the situation extremely tense, but she felt somewhat safe in her large truck. She just needed to clear her racing mind in order to focus. She took in a deep breath and looked at her phone.

I barely have service...Odd...

Alyssa unlocked her phone and opened her keypad, pushing 911 as quickly as she could. She placed the phone to her ear and waited. A scratchy ring was heard, but then it suddenly stopped.

"Hello?" Alyssa asked, her heart beating rapidly. She received no response. Alyssa sighed and looked back at her phone, realizing she had a voice mail from Kevin. She pushed play and placed the phone to her ear. Static echoed from it as she tried to listen carefully. "A... lyssa...The...is...crumb...part...Get...ut..."

"Ugh!" she gasped and threw the phone in the passenger's seat. She quickly switched the engine on, realizing what she had to do.

I don't know what the hell is going on, but I must get to Rockdale Valley and fast!

Alyssa sped her truck around and drove down the driveway, gravel and dirt slinging out from under her tires. She slowed just enough to see down the street, clearing it of any oncoming traffic. She pressed harder on the gas pedal and sped out onto the pavement, straightening out the curves of the road that would eventually take her to Rockdale Valley's main highway. She took in a few deep breaths, attempting to calm her nerves as she examined her surroundings. The few street lights that stood in the area were now on and shone dimly on the pavement as darkness began to stretch across the sky. It wasn't going to be long before the night settled in, and her friends were sure to start questioning her whereabouts soon.

They are going to have to leave without me...

Alyssa drove around each bend of the road until she reached the mountains near Rockdale Valley's main highway. She slowly stopped her truck once she reached the dark, secluded road and glanced at the large field that sat across from it. The horses that once occupied the field were nowhere to be seen. The area was silent. Alyssa bit her lip and looked toward the highway that was shaded with acres of trees and mountainous terrain. It stretched far north east and around multiple descending bends.

I must remain strong for my parents. My dad's truck was gone so they must have escaped. But what about those tracks? And the marks on the wall? I've got to stop. I need to focus...

She prayed and hoped for her parents' safety as she pressed down on the gas pedal, turning onto the small highway that would take her to Rockdale Valley.

Alyssa knew the lonesome drive to town was going to seem endless. She couldn't help but dwell about her parents and what may have occurred at their home as her heart continued to ache heavily. With all of the blood and devastation, could they have gotten out? She shook her head and looked out her window, fearing the worst. The sky continued to darken, the sun's last remaining glow slowly fading away. The trees that stood around her stretched their branches toward her and the dark sky as she glanced at them, bewildered from the situation.

Maybe this is just another dream...

She groaned, knowing this nightmare was a reality. A little relief seemed so close, but now so far away.

Alyssa soon turned a sharp corner and glanced up ahead, releasing a low gasp as she put her thoughts to the side. There around the bend was the Sheriff's car on the side of the road. Its front door was open, and its lights were flashing brightly. A few orange cones were left sitting in front of the vehicle, their fluorescents shining brightly from her headlights. Alyssa carefully pulled off the road once she reached them and glanced at the white car.

Thank God...

She quickly opened her door and stepped out onto the pavement.

"Sheriff?" she called out and jogged to his door.

A bit of hope began to grow within her as she approached the vehicle, relief washing over her. Alyssa stopped once she reached the door and glanced inside, noticing that it was empty. She looked around and examined her surroundings. The atmosphere was quiet except for the whistles of the wind that continued to blow through the trees. No one was in sight, the area dark and calm. Alyssa began to breathe deeply once again, the frequent fear beginning to push away the little hope she had just regained.

"Sheriff!" she called out again and looked past the trees in the distance.

Where could he have gone?

Alyssa released her breath slowly and looked back into the Sheriff's vehicle. She noticed that his radio receiver was sitting in the seat and she quickly reached for it. Alyssa sat down and pressed the call button.

"This is Officer Bennett with the Rockdale Valley Precinct. I'm off duty and I'm on Highway 29 near Fairview Lane. I need assistance. Over," she said and waited patiently. As the seconds went by, her anxiety quickly grew.

"This is Officer Bennett. We have an emergency. Please respond!" Alyssa exclaimed. Her patience was wearing thin.

Come on...Why aren't they answering!

She sighed in frustration and dropped the radio, glancing outside. The wind had begun to pick up, alarming her.

Forget it...I need to hurry.

She quickly stepped out of the Sheriff's vehicle and jogged back to her truck. Alyssa took one last look around, feeling hopeless. She placed her hand on the door handle once she reached her truck and froze. The sounds of helicopter blades were suddenly heard in the distance, getting louder with each passing second. Alyssa looked up toward the sky, keeping her hand on the door handle. A Chinook helicopter was making its way towards Rockdale Valley as Alyssa thought to herself and opened the door, slowly sitting down in the seat. It wasn't the first one she had heard and seen today. She gently pulled the door shut and wondered if there was more going on than she was probably aware of.

Could it really be that serious? And why wouldn't anyone respond at dispatch? I should have just answered Kevin's call...Damn it!

Alyssa switched the engine on and carefully drove around the Sheriff's car, taking one last look at it. She was disappointed in herself. It would have taken only a few seconds to answer the phone call from her former partner. There was some alarm to the odd, broken up message.

Alyssa sighed once more and looked back at the road ahead, ignoring the negative remarks in her mind. A few tears slowly began to fill her eyes. There was an uneasy feeling lingering in her gut that she was unable to shake. She couldn't comprehend it, but she wasn't going to allow it to slow her down. She quickly wiped away the tears that fell onto her cheeks and focused on the quiet street. She grew more afraid after the flashing lights disappeared. She had made a turn around one of the sharp, descending bends, one that would soon lead her to the valley.

As minutes slowly crept by, Alyssa turned another sharp bend and noticed the hill ahead that would overlook the southern portion of Rockdale Valley. The wooded area and mountainous terrain began to dissipate into a field with only a few patches of trees. Thick, green grass covered most of the ground and was shaded in some areas by large branching arms of oak trees. She was close to town and only minutes away from the station once she recognized the welcome sign ahead. Alyssa began to pray some more, her anxiety level elevating. She was never much for prayer in her past, but she felt that it was the only option she had left now.

I can't seem to get there fast enough. If only my...

Alyssa's heart jumped as her phone suddenly began to vibrate.

"Oh, thank goodness!" she exclaimed, the adrenaline burning in her veins. She lost her thoughts and quickly grabbed her phone, looking at the caller ID.

That's strange...

All it read was incoming call. Alyssa became confused. Her signal was still low as she noticed one small bar in the top left corner of her phone. She mumbled to herself and looked back at the road, her mouth quickly dropping. She had reached the top of the hill, but the road up ahead was completely destroyed. Trees were lying across the ground and the pavement, their roots sticking out of the soil. The earth and pavement were split and crushed and appeared to have been pulled deep below into the trees and wilderness that was a part of Rockdale Valley. Large boulders and rocks sat near the steep ledge of the drop-off and debris cluttered the street.

Alyssa gasped loudly and stomped on the breaks, swinging her truck off the road. She yelled in fright and closed her eyes tightly as the corner of her truck slid into a large oak tree, blowing out one of the front tires. Her head slammed into the steering wheel from the sudden impact, her body held tight behind the seat belt's firm grip. Alyssa groaned once the truck settled and her body slowly slumped back into her seat, darkness blanketing her eyes peacefully.

CHAPTER THREE

"**A**LRIGHT MEN, WE WILL BE landing in the city in approximately three minutes," Kyle Smitherman said as he looked back at everyone on board the Chinook helicopter that flew towards Rockdale Valley. He was the Captain of the 9th Army Special Forces Group on board with him, and he always carried a firm look on his tan, aging face. His thick, ashy blonde hair laid flat against his head as beads of sweat were already making their way onto his forehead. He was confident. Almost too confident compared to the other soldiers who expressed unsure feelings about the mission.

The soldiers quickly nodded and got prepared as each held their primary weapon, the M4 assault rifle. A few had the M203 grenade launcher attachment. Their secondary weapons consisted of M67 fragmentation grenades and an M9 9mm pistol.

"So what do you think is wrong with this place?" Specialist Alex Morton asked as he looked back at his closest friend, Sergeant First Class William Thompson. They had become good friends after Alex joined the group a few years back.

Will looked at Alex and shrugged. "They're just earthquakes, but the severity of this does seem a bit odd. The only thing that makes me so unsure is how the residents have described them, and let's not forget the other things they've said which I'm finding difficult to believe," he said and Alex mumbled to himself, looking at the other soldiers.

"Well you know how people can get in chaotic situations. They over exaggerate, and what exactly could be under this town? This is a search and rescue mission, but we're also here for something else and we don't even know what it is," Alex said and took in a deep breath.

Will slowly nodded. "Well I'm prepared for whatever the hell it is," he replied.

Alex smiled and looked back at him. "You and me both, brother."

Will took in a deep breath and looked towards the front of the helicopter. He began to recall the news report he saw yesterday evening. It was one that had truly disturbed him...

The wind was lightly brushing against the windows of his small apartment as the night sky covered the city. Will was sitting at his table looking through files when the TV caught his attention. The evening news had breaking information regarding a small, remote town far west in Virginia as he picked up the television remote and quickly turned the volume up.

"Yet another large earthquake followed by frequent tremors has struck Rockdale Valley. Reports have been pouring into the studio, and it appears to be worse than we had imagined. We now have live to report, Miss Heidi Balentine," the newscaster stated as the view switched from the studio to a live helicopter coverage above Rockdale Valley.

"Hi Rick. As you can see, we are just above the south side area of Rockdale Valley. A few of the buildings in this area have collapsed and most of the streets have suddenly split open. Due to the extent of the damage, it's going to make it impassable for the residents who are still trying to flee this side of the city," Heidi Balentine stated and her cameraman scanned the area below them. The image looked like a war zone. The area was completely destroyed. Debris and trash littered the streets as a couple of police cars sat at intersections with their lights flashing brightly. There were residents abandoning cars and running in all directions as panic began to flood the town.

"We can definitely see the extent of the damage. This is truly unbelievable and very difficult to watch. Do we know if Cathy Woods received any word from authorities or the residents?" Rick asked as the camera now focused on Heidi's concerned expression.

"No Rick. We had contact with her earlier, but we are having difficulties now with the satellites. I'm sure we will make contact with her very soon and get back with you on that," she stated as the view switched back to Rick.

"Okay. Thank you Heidi Balentine. As we stated earlier today, it appears peculiar events have been reported by the local residents. Just the other day, there have been multiple reports of missing persons and quite a few animal attacks. A mandatory evacuation order has just been given and authorities have made it clear to relocate immediately until an investigation has been completed. We will have more coverage on this story when we return..."

Will shook the image away and looked at Kyle who was now standing up. Reality quickly set in as the news station faded to the sound of blades chopping the air and the smell of hydraulic fluid.

Kyle examined the faces of the soldiers onboard, attempting to read every one as he spoke up. "Listen carefully. You have already been briefed about this operation, and you know that we've heard some crazy shit about this place..." Kyle paused and scanned their faces once more. "But it's our duty to correct it if at all possible. You all have been supplied with a radio, a GPS device, and a city map. You've also been given the coordinates to the operations center. We determine what the hell is going on, if anything, and what may be causing the destruction while we rescue the residents who may have become trapped or ignored the evacuation order. We fear that it could very well be terrorists. That's why we need to be ready," Kyle firmly stated and paused, looking into the eyes of the twenty soldiers around him before continuing, "I do not care how bizarre it is soldiers. We've been warned of strange things that might be lurking around this town, and I don't care how crazy it does sound. I need you all to be cautious and alert."

The helicopter slowly came to a stop in mid air, hovering over the city. Will cleared his throat and prepared himself. His long night was about to begin.

Kyle balanced himself as the helicopter slowly began lowering itself to the pavement. Will glanced at Alex, feeling a bit of anxiety growing within him.

This mission isn't going to be like any other. This gut feeling of a death trap just waiting for us will not go away. I don't see how the local residents would make up stories about the incidents that have occurred here.

Alex glanced at the other soldiers as they were all talking amongst each other about the operation.

"I'm kind of looking forward to what we may run into," Private Matthew DeRamus said as he patted his rifle.

"Look man, it's probably nothing so don't get all hyped up. We're probably just going to get the idiots that decided to stay behind," Specialist Travis Tidwell replied.

Kyle raised an eyebrow and cleared his throat. "This is a very serious operation, soldier. I wouldn't take the information we were given lightly unless you really want to end up getting yourself killed," he stated, and the helicopter touched the pavement carefully.

"Yes sir," Travis replied.

Will glanced at Alex. "Why do I get the feeling as if he knows more than we do?" he asked quietly while the other soldiers stood up, checking their vests and weapons.

"It's all politics brother," Alex replied, shaking his head as he stood up and followed the other soldiers out the back of the helicopter.

Will watched him as he tried to put his thoughts away. He quickly stood up and followed the others onto the trashed and deserted pavement.

All the soldiers stood amongst each other as Kyle slowly made his way in front of them. He was examining their surroundings and was quite astonished at all the destruction that surrounded them. Hearing about the incidents that occurred during the past couple of days didn't compare to being placed in the middle of it. Everyone had a sense of uneasiness as they scanned the area. The helicopter had made its touchdown in the middle of a small shopping center parking lot. The pavement was cracked and fractured in some locations as an abundance of debris lay scattered about. A few small fires engulfed a nearby newspaper press and drug store, their crackles whispering through the night. The dark sky was spotted with gray clouds as a light breeze gently blew around them. The small valley resembled a ghost town.

Kyle stood firmly in front of the soldiers and examined their expressions. A few seemed stoic while others seemed eager.

"Alright men, we're all going to split up and do a clean sweep of the southern valley. If any of you reaches extreme danger, don't hesitate to contact the other teams in the area. Also, if you encounter anything suspicious, contact me," Kyle said and the soldiers nodded.

"You've been given instructions of your team assignments and the whereabouts you'll be searching. You know your mission, soldiers. Let's move out!" he exclaimed and a few soldiers replied, "Hooah!" while the others grouped with their teams. After a few soldiers shook hands and wished each other luck, they quickly made their way to their destinations as they looked over their maps and discussed their strategies.

"Okay, it looks like we have a lot of places to explore," Private Chris Davis said as he examined the western area of the city map. He was their team's young medic and still expressed boyish features. Will and Alex stood beside him as Specialist Broderick Coleman jogged to where they were standing.

"Alright guys, I'm here," Broderick said and took in a deep breath.

"Well how about we start here," Will said as he looked towards the press and drug store.

Alex nodded and they all began walking towards it. Chris stared at all the wreckage they were approaching, carefully making his way down the deserted street. A few cars had flipped onto their sides as glass and debris surrounded the pavement. Small trees in the area leaned down as a few of their roots stuck out from the earth. Street lamps and power lines were lying on the ground and a few signs were hanging from their posts, swaying back and forth with the wind. The atmosphere was tense. It was unsettling. It didn't take long for the suspense to build within the back of their minds.

"It's so strange, isn't it? Everyone seems…gone," Chris said, feeling anxious.

"I know. It's odd," Alex replied and glanced at the abandoned vehicles.

Will cleared his throat and responded, "Let's just stay focused, okay?"

"Yes sir," Chris replied as Broderick approached a damaged car that sat near the sidewalk. He peered inside it, shaking his head in disbelief. No one was inside the vehicle which was a promising sign.

Alex approached the door to the Rockdale Valley Press, stepping around debris as Will examined the street and the other buildings that stood in the distance, carefully following him. Chris searched another car that had been pulled into the earth, clearing it of any signs of life. He searched around the vehicle, hoping there were no injured civilians.

Broderick glanced down the street, stepping away from the vehicle he was examining. It didn't take long for his anxiety to rise though he hid it well. He was determined to complete the mission. It was just that part of him that was extremely nervous. It was his first field mission as a Green Beret.

"Maybe they all got out in time," Broderick stated as Alex and Will pulled the damaged door to the press open.

"I'm shocked at all the damage. It did look horrendous on the news report they were able to get, but I didn't think it was going to be this severe," Will said and carefully stepped inside the lobby of the press.

"I don't think anyone knew what to expect," Alex added and stepped over broken glass that had been thrown to the floor around the door. Broderick and Chris followed them inside as Will looked around the trashed room. Glass split and cracked under their boots as they stepped into the quiet lobby. Newspapers and magazines were scattered on the floor as a phone receiver hung from the counter in the back. A couple of couches remained intact, sitting slightly off center in the middle of the room. A door stood to their left and a set of stairs sat in the back corner.

Alex walked to the counter and picked up a newspaper, reading the first article on the front page. Will carefully approached the stairway, looking at the others. "I'm going to check up here. I believe the fire is towards the very back. There could be survivors," he said as Chris and Broderick walked to the other door that stood to their left.

"I'll come with you," Alex stated and carried the newspaper article with him.

"We'll search down here," Chris said and Broderick opened the door, stepping into an office.

Will nodded. "Don't be a hero, Private. If the building is unstable or the fire larger than expected, get out and meet us across the street," he stated.

"Yes, sir," Chris replied and followed Broderick into the office.

Will turned to make his way up the wooden stairs, taking in a deep breath. The wood creaked after every step he took as Alex carefully followed him. The building already seemed unstable. Will began to doubt his decision and became even more nervous. His heart was already speeding up, the perspiration intensifying. Alex didn't appear to be alarmed. He was too focused on the article in the paper.

"Check this out, man. Wicked night skies, strange earthquakes, and spine chilling noises or *voices* underground. Could the end be near?" Alex said, reading from the article. They passed a window that overlooked the alley in the back as Will glanced out it. "Locals are quickly leaving and some seem to be disappearing. The local wildlife appears to be acting strange as vicious attacks are also being reported. This small, once peaceful town is beginning to fall apart at the seams. Will there be any answers after the destruction? Will there be anything left to salvage? These are just the few questions that the civilians of Rockdale Valley want answered..." Alex paused and looked away from the article. Will stopped once they reached a dust filled hallway and looked back at him.

"I can't read any more of this. Maybe Satan is under this town," Alex said and rolled the newspaper up.

"Let's not joke about this," Will replied and approached a room to the left. The door hung open as he looked inside, clearing it quickly.

"I'm sorry. It just seems a bit absurd," Alex replied and followed him into a large copy room.

"I know," Will said as he approached a table that sat in the middle of the room. Alex sighed and rested his rifle up against his shoulder, carefully placing the newspaper on a desk next to him.

Will picked up an article that was a couple of days old and scanned through it.

Mandatory evacuation is highly possible as an investigation to the third earthquake is being done. It has been advised that if you have a place to seek refuge to please do so as the investigators feel another earthquake is imminent...

Will slid the article out of the way and read another one that was lying under it.

There have been multiple reports of brutal attacks caused by what appears to be large animals of some type, possibly bears. Everyone is to be advised of the curfew that has been put into place starting at 7:00 PM. Due to the tremors and quakes, investigators feel that the local wildlife is on the move...

Will shook his head as he pushed the article to the side and stared at another that had a picture of a young woman standing by an older gentleman. It was dated three days ago.

Rockdale Valley Precinct wanted to thank former Officer Alyssa Bennett for her hard work and dedication to this city as...

"Did you find anything?" Alex interrupted and Will glanced up at him. He was now standing by a few computer terminals as Will responded, "Oh, no. Just a few articles."

Alex nodded and looked towards the hallway as the sound of glass shattering was heard below them. "What the hell?" he asked and gunfire suddenly erupted below.

"Shit! Come on!" Will exclaimed and pulled his M4 and sling over his head. He dashed out of the room and back into the hallway. Alex followed him and gripped onto his M4 tightly. He wondered what they could possibly be firing at. The area seemed desolate.

Will carefully ran down the weak, dusty stairs and back into the lobby as the gunfire ceased. He stopped and held his M4 carefully, the adrenaline rushing into his veins. Alex ran up beside him, breathing heavily as he stared at the room they last saw Broderick and Chris enter. The door hung slightly open and Will raised his M4 towards it. The screams of death still echoed through his mind as he remained calm and vigilant.

Thunderous footsteps were suddenly heard in the room, inching closer to the door. They sounded monstrous as Alex stared in fright, his eyes wide.

"I don't like the sounds of this," he said softly.

Will refused to hesitate. "Alex, get your radio and contact Kyle," he ordered and glanced at Alex. Alex was still breathing heavily, but he nodded. "Okay," he replied and pulled his radio out from its holster as the door to the room suddenly shattered off its hinges. Alex shook in fright as Broderick and a large animal dove into the lobby in front of where they stood. Dust and wood splinters slung in all directions as Broderick and the broken door slammed against the floor. Will's eyes widened as the large, demonic beast that landed over Broderick's body slowly looked up at him. It was about as tall as the average human and bulky in size as each step it took shook the floor around them. The creature's teeth shown over its curled, angry snout as its devilish reptilian-like eyes glared back at them. Its large, dagger-like claws were long and jagged on its hands and feet. A set of thick, curvy horns protruded out the side of its face above the jawbone and blood covered parts of its thick hide, its wounds unveiled.

"Oh my God..." Alex whispered and gripped onto his radio.

"Contact Kyle, Alex! Now!" Will yelled and began firing at the creature. It released a loud scream and slung its head back. Fear overwhelmed Alex, his hands trembling on the radio. He took a few steps back and pressed the call button. A little static began to echo from it as Alex ignored it and continued to hold the button down.

"Kyle! We need emergency backup now!" he yelled and the devilish beast suddenly dashed toward him. Will gasped and dove out of the way as Alex screamed in horror. The creature swung its bulky head and curved horn into the left side of Alex's face, knocking him to the floor quickly. Alex lay motionless as the creature looked back at Will. Drool spilled from its lower jaw, and it slowly slid its large talons across one another, their dreadful screeches striking agonizing fear deep within Will's body. He slowly stood up as the beast growled and lowered its head, glaring into Will's helpless eyes.

"Hell no," he whispered as he grabbed a grenade and turned to run back up the stairs behind him. He heard the beast scream, the loud footsteps echoing behind him. Will gasped and jumped into the hallway, dropping the grenade behind him. He quickly leaped into the copy room and crawled under the table as the explosion of the grenade shook the floor and tore through the walls. Dust and debris filled the hallway and parts of the room Will hid in as he slowly opened his eyes and stared out into the cloudy hallway. He began to breathe heavily, hearing the beast's spine chilling scream.

What the hell is this thing!

The fear began to overwhelm him as he held his M4 tightly. The loud, monstrous footsteps returned, shaking the floor once more. The wood creaked even louder now. It sounded as if it was going to give way after each step the beast took in the hall.

"Group......Where...your position?" Kyle's scratchy voice echoed from the radio and into the room. Will quickly grabbed it, fumbling with the button.

About damn time!

"West side area! The small newspaper press!" Will shouted into the faulty radio. His heart sank once the devilish beast slowly stepped into the room. Its loud exhaling breath sent a chill down his spine as he sat the radio down and reloaded his rifle. The beast growled and stared at the table Will hid under, breathing deeply.

"Fuck it." Will whispered and rolled out from under the table. He didn't care anymore as he ignored the thoughts that were telling him to hide. He quickly stood up and fired his rifle at the beast's chest. All he could think about was his group as the creature screamed and took a few steps back. Its weakened body trembled from the injuries.

"Die you son of a bitch!" Will yelled and kept pulling the trigger.

The creature bolted toward him with its last bit of energy, pushing through the streams of bullets as it released a piercing cry. Drool spilled onto the floor around it and Will gasped as his gun ceased to fire, his magazine emptying. Many thoughts hit him instantly, but he was too late to react as the beast smashed into him. Will dropped his rifle and his body slammed against a large copy machine. He could feel the buckle on the chinstrap to his helmet break as the helmet quickly slid off his head. Will collapsed to the dusty, wooden floor and heard the static and fading voice of Kyle echo from his radio.

"Hold tight....We're......our way."

Will's lifeless body rested on the floor and no more sounds were to be heard. Darkness crept into his eyes and the image of the large beast slowly faded away.

CHAPTER FOUR

ALYSSA WAS STANDING IN THE *middle of the street, fire consuming every building and tree around her. Some of the buildings looked familiar, but then there were a few that seemed to have appeared from another town. It didn't make sense. She had no escape route.*

She stared, turning her body to examine the hell she was in, hoping to find some way around the flames. The intense heat was brushing against her skin and clothing, singeing the hair on her arms and scalp. Alyssa coughed and gasped as the flames rolled closer, the smoke spilling into her lungs. She was running out of time...

Alyssa's eyes began to flicker as the scent of smoke and gas began to fill her nostrils. She took in a deep breath and started coughing profusely. She quickly covered her nose and mouth, hoping that would be rid of the fumes that continued to push into her lungs. She had to get out of the truck as quick as she could, but the pain began to ache in her head and back as soon as she tried to move her body.

"Damn," she choked and placed her free hand on her forehead. A little blood was beginning to dry near her hair line as she gently patted her head for injuries. She quickly, but carefully unbuckled herself and searched for her belongings, letting go of the hell she was just in.

The earthquakes actually did all of this?

Alyssa held her breath and grabbed her pistol and billfold from her purse. She then opened the glove department and grabbed a small side-pack and a box of ammunition. Smoke rose from the engine and toward the night sky as Alyssa quickly pushed her door open, gasping for the fresh air. She slid out of the truck and fell to ground, dropping everything but her pistol as she gripped it tightly. She collapsed on the grass, pain continuing to spread throughout her body as she coughed and sucked in the air. She didn't want to be near the truck for too long.

I can make it...

Alyssa slowly sat herself up, getting herself together. After taking a few deep breaths, she carefully picked up her billfold and ammunition and placed it inside her side-pack. Her hands trembled. She couldn't help herself as she fumbled with the zipper, pulling it towards her to close the small bag. Alyssa sat against the back of her legs and looked at the wrecked truck, surveying the damage and the area carefully. The hood of her truck had crippled inward, the smell of gas and smoke congesting the area.

Alyssa sighed heavily, rubbing her head gently. She had to keep pushing forward. It wasn't safe to be anywhere near the truck, and the darkness was already making her nervous. She knew she had to get into the valley somehow, no matter the extent of the damage.

It could have been a lot worse...I can't believe the damage around here. There's got to be some relief in Rockdale Valley...

Alyssa took in a deep breath and attached the side-pack around her waist as she pushed herself to her feet. She looked at the deserted road and slowly made her way towards it, cautiously examining the debris in the area.

I was lucky...

Alyssa stopped once she reached the road and looked toward the cliff. A little fear began to build up within her as she slowly walked toward it. The only light that lit her way was from the moon above, but something seemed mischievous about the night. She wasn't prepared for what she was about to see over the ledge, but her body pushed forward. It was the sudden, strange feeling that struck her briskly as if her mind and body were coaxing her, pushing her to walk towards the ledge. Alyssa gently climbed over a few fallen trees and shielded her face from the barely naked branches and limbs. They slid their way against her skin and clothing, snapping back into place after she passed through them. She was still breathing heavily, ignoring the pain that continued to ache throughout her body.

What is this? I've never felt this way...

Alyssa stopped herself and looked towards the atmosphere above. The moon and stars were shining through some of the dark clouds, sparkling dimly.

Alyssa took in a deep breath and continued toward the cliff. She stepped over more debris from the pavement and climbed over another tree before reaching the ledge. Alyssa stopped a few feet from it and looked toward the debris below, her mouth slowly dropping. The pavement had been crushed as hard soil protruded out from under it. A lot of the trees near the cliff had fallen as branches and limbs were scattered about. A few power line poles had fallen in the distance, their wires strewn across the ground.

Alyssa stared at the calm, gloomy wilderness below her, overtaken by the vast devastation. She glanced toward Rockdale Valley and saw a few familiar landmarks in the distance. At least they were still standing from what she could tell. She hoped the damage wasn't near as bad as what she was witnessing in front of her. The area was unrecognizable.

Alyssa released a low sigh, and her chest began to ache. She was so close. The burning anxiety was building up within her as she continued to gaze upon the town. She was full of thought and lingering emotions, almost numb to the dull aches that pulsed throughout her body. Dirt dusted and smudged her face and arms from the tree limbs and brush she had crawled through. She was beat and battered, but she couldn't put too much thought into it. It was just the awkward feeling that still possessed her, overpowering her. It made her gaze upon the wilderness and debris below, increasing her heart rate.

What's wrong with me? Have the night terrors really taken such a toll on me?

Alyssa took in another deep breath and suddenly, her body stiffened. A cool chill ran down her spine and the hair on her arms quickly stood on end as soft, eerie whispers slowly began to flow around her. She stood still and listened carefully. They were almost too soft to hear as she held her breath, catching the end of the gentle, yet unpleasant sound. They slowly faded away into the distance, disappearing into the wind. Alyssa breathed as quietly as she could. She hoped they wouldn't return as she slowly looked around, relaxing herself from the sudden fear. But before she could turn to look behind her, a soft earthquake began to rumble below her feet, startling her once more. The dirt and damaged pavement around the steep ledge began to fall as Alyssa gasped and quickly stepped back. She glanced towards the unstable ledge, her heart pounding uncontrollably as she watched pebble and rock crumble and fall. Alyssa released a low gasp as the earth's tremor stopped and the whispers returned, speaking softly into her ears. She covered them with the palms of her hands and tried to shake the awkward feeling that continued to possess her.

What is this!

The whispers ceased once again, disappearing slowly into the wilderness. Alyssa clenched her teeth and lowered her hands, breathing heavily. The adrenaline that was rushing through her veins began to overcome the dull aches. She took a step back and her heart dropped as she heard another low, scratchy growl behind her. Alyssa spun around and scanned through the debris and trees that still stood in the distance. Nothing was in sight. The agonizing fear was overwhelming as her heart raced away. The blood rushed quickly through her veins, and the heat pushed out from the surface of her skin. Sweat was accumulating near her hairline and the pits of her arms as Alyssa's mouth hung open, gasping for breaths.

That growl...Why does it seem so similar to the one I heard back home...

Alyssa's thoughts were interrupted as the earth began to shake and crack once more. It rattled violently, crumbling the loose soil and damaged asphalt under her feet.

"No!" she gasped. The ground around her split and gave way. Earth and debris fell around her as she hit a few protruding mounds of soil and rock. She yelled in pain as she slammed against a small branch of a tree, feeling a burning sensation within her ribs. The branch cracked as splinters and leaves fell on and around her. Alyssa continued to plummet into mounds of soil until one finally pushed her toward the ground below. She rolled a few feet down before stopping in a soft bed of cool grass. She yelped and immediately turned onto her back, gasping for air. The intense pain rushed all over her body as she continued to choke, unable to catch the wind that was knocked out of her lungs. She closed her eyes tightly and prayed for the pain to stop as she tried to catch her breath. All she could think about was the possibility of being stranded in the debris with no one to help her. That's when she suddenly realized that she had forgotten to retrieve her phone from the wreckage.

Oh no...

Alyssa groaned and gasped loudly once more, attempting to calm herself down using the techniques she was taught. She began taking slow and deep breaths until the pain eventually started to subside into uncomfortable, dull aches.

This was a mistake...What was I thinking! Oh God, I can't die out here! What if something was following me? I've got to recollect myself...Think Alyssa...

She took in another deep breath and moved her arms around. She then wiped the dirt and sweat away from her face, feeling the pain in her back and side.

I've got to lie here for a moment...

Fear and anxiety still swept throughout Alyssa as she tried to remain calm. She allowed a few more minutes to slowly pass before gently sitting herself up. Once her breathing became more relaxed and stable, she looked herself over. Dirt and dust covered most of her clothes and body as she examined the cuts, scrapes, and contusions on her arms. Blood trickled down some of the wounds on her forearms as she ignored it, carefully moving her legs. The pain continued to ache and throb. Alyssa clenched her teeth, attempting to fight through it. She suddenly gasped once more and relaxed her muscles as she lay back down on the cool grass. She sighed heavily and looked back toward the ledge. Dirt and pebbles continued to roll down it as Alyssa turned her attention to the wilderness that surrounded her. She had missed the pavement to the road that continued to town. It sat about ten feet from her. Most of it had been crushed from the collapse in the earth as concrete and hard soil littered the area closest to the ledge. A few small trees and leaves were lying by Alyssa, but some of the oak trees still stood in the distance. A light breeze began to push through them, its cool touch brushing against her face. It was very calming. She closed her eyes, allowing it to soothe her body.

I've got to try and get up...I've got to remain strong...

Alyssa carefully sat herself up and tried to ignore the pain. She clenched her teeth and carefully forced herself to her feet, her muscles trembling. She breathed heavily and the pain continued to throb as she stood as carefully as she could. Alyssa remained standing, ignoring her battered state and looked toward Rockdale Valley. She wasn't going to allow anything to slow her down. Her parents were all she had left.

The precinct isn't too far from here...I can make it...

Tears began to accumulate in her eyes as she closed them, refusing to allow one drop to fall. She wasn't going to give up yet.

Alyssa carefully dusted her shirt and pants off, the pain beginning to intensify once more. She groaned and placed her hand over her necklace that lay under her shirt. She had forgotten about it until she felt the stinging sensation on her chest. She felt the warmth of blood on her shirt and sighed, pulling the necklace out from behind it, fearing that it may have gotten damaged from the fall. Alyssa examined the stone carefully. It was still intact, embedded in the pendant snuggly. She let it rest on top of her shirt and slowly unattached the side-pack that was around her waist. It was torn and battered. She could hear the stray bullets rolling around in the pouch. Alyssa sighed and opened the small side-pack. Her billfold was still intact as she pulled it out. She retrieved her cash, driver's license, and credit cards and placed the billfold back into the pouch. She stuffed the items she retrieved into her back pocket and then looked around the ground for her pistol. Alyssa groaned as she scanned the area for her Berretta. It wasn't in sight and she sighed in frustration.

Damn...I've got to get moving...

Alyssa decided to leave her side-pack behind. It was one less thing she had to carry. She wasn't fond of carrying purses let alone handbags. She preferred to travel light.

Alyssa gently placed her side-pack on the ground by a fallen tree. She dusted her hands off and carefully started walking through the brush and debris. The pain ached even more with every step she took, but she continued to fight through it as she slowly and carefully made her way through a small patch of trees. A few areas of the earth around her were jagged, and a large pit ripped through part of the ground and pavement ahead. The atmosphere remained calm, and the gentle breeze continued to push its way around her. Alyssa began to ponder her thoughts as the whispers she heard earlier crept back into her mind.

I've got to be hearing things...or maybe the doctor was right.

She shook the thought away and walked out of the small patch of trees, suddenly stopping herself once she noticed all the destruction that surrounded her. Alyssa couldn't help but gaze in astonishment. A few cars were left abandoned in the street as some appeared to have been sucked into the earth below. The pavement was cracked and segments of it were pushed upward into jagged ledges. A few of the buildings still stood and showed minor signs of damage while others that once stood in the area had collapsed. Concrete and brick lay strewn around, resembling the aftermath of a natural disaster.

Oh my God...What the hell happened...?

Alyssa examined the parking lot of the Rockdale Valley Shoppette. It was a small shopping center that stayed busy on the weeknights and weekends. Now it was destroyed and abandoned as a strange feeling lingered the area. It was unsettling. She could feel it within the pit of her stomach. Alyssa sighed in disbelief and stared at the once lively shopping center.

It's too quiet. No one seems to be here. No officers on duty to protect the city and residents from looters...No emergency crew. This is so odd...and just depressing. I've never seen such devastation.

Alyssa looked towards the small street that would take her to the Rockdale Valley Precinct. She noticed a few fires that engulfed a couple of buildings that still stood intact, their bright blazes illuminating the street.

I didn't realize that it was going to be this severe, but it cannot be vacant. There has to be someone here...There has to be an emergency crew. I've got to keep moving.

She pushed her way through the pain as she carefully walked towards one of the town's small business districts. The buildings sat neatly rowed beside one another. Alyssa glanced at the small fires in the area. They danced and lit up the night, their whistling crackles awakening the calm atmosphere. She watched them and wondered if Kevin and the others were going to be at the station. She then realized she had no idea what the time was as she also wondered how long she had been out in her truck. She couldn't have been unconscious for too long. She must have drifted off. It would explain the hell she visited again.

Hell indeed...Absolute hell.

Alyssa mumbled to herself and pushed her thoughts to the side. She was unsure, but she hoped it wasn't that late.

Alyssa slowly stepped up onto the sidewalk by the small newspaper press and looked down the deserted street. The road was cracked and torn in some areas as pieces of concrete and brick had crumbled to the pavement from some of the buildings near her. More power line poles and street signs had fallen in the area and a couple of cars sat next to the sidewalk. One car had been pulled into the earth. Alyssa slowly approached it, peeking inside the broken passenger window. Glass lay strewn around the seats and floorboard as her eyes moved to the deployed air bag.

This is so awful...

Alyssa turned her attention back to the road. Her expression was full of disbelief as she thought about the spirit of the once peaceful community. There were parades, city festivals, and all sorts of fun activities throughout the year. Everyone was friendly and rarely did Rockdale Valley suffer any crimes.

Now this place resembles an apocalypse.

Alyssa took a few steps down the sidewalk and gasped as she heard glass shatter in the distance followed by a loud thud. She stopped in her tracks and carefully stepped away from the street as she looked across it towards a small boutique and diner. Loud footsteps echoed in the distance, sending Alyssa's heart rate skyrocketing.

I don't have my pistol...Damn it!

She slowly stepped towards the newspaper press as the heavy footsteps seemed to get closer. The adrenaline continued to pump through her veins as she carefully stepped inside the building and stood by the broken window. Glass cracked under her boots, breaking into smaller shards as she attempted to be as silent as she could. Alyssa stood carefully and watched a large animal of some kind step into view from the alley beside the boutique. Its loud exhale of breath made Alyssa quiver. Her eyes widened in fright. The animal looked almost reptilian with its rough hide and sharp, dagger like claws. Its teeth were hanging over its bottom jaw as the animal stood and sniffed the air.

Alyssa covered her mouth and took a few steps back.

Oh my God... What's going on in this town! What is that thing!

Fear overwhelmed her as she turned around and limped around the couch and to the desk that sat in the back. A phone was hanging off the receiver, catching her attention as she quickly snatched it up and placed it to her ear. No dial tone was heard and she began breathing heavily as she slowly placed the phone on the counter and looked back towards the broken window. Alyssa carefully inched her way towards the stairs, keeping her eyes on the window and road. The heavy footsteps returned as her attention suddenly turned to the floor in front of a room near her. Blood was smeared across it and a broken door was lying near the coffee table. Alyssa's heart dropped and she turned to make her way up the stairs.

I've got to hide!

She continued to breathe heavily, carefully making her way up to the hallway. The floor creaked and cracked, frightening her even more. It didn't take long after suffering from her chronic nightmares to ignite her imagination in the worst possible ways. All it took was a sound or even a smell to erupt the fear that became a part of her everyday life.

Alyssa stumbled in the hall she had reached and stopped, noticing the tremendous damage to the walls and floor. Fragments and char covered parts of the wall as a sweet scent faintly lingered the area. The floor had a few large tears in it as the wood seemed like it could give way at any moment.

This doesn't look good...What if this person was fighting the thing that I saw? The blood downstairs...Oh no...What the hell did I get myself into!

She carefully stepped over the weak, wooden beams and into a room on the left, the fear within her intensifying. Alyssa grabbed the door and closed it gently, trying not to make a sound. She did not want to come face to face with this monstrosity. She took in a few deep breaths and turned to examine the room she was in. It was small and full of computers and copy machines. A few pieces of copy paper and newspaper articles lay strewn across the floor and a couple of tables sat in front of her as she walked to the window in the back of the room, her mind on one thing. The blinds were open as she peeked through them, gazing at the pavement below. The thing she saw earlier was nowhere to be seen. The small road and alley were vacant.

What if it's tracking me...What if it's in this building right now!

Her fear became too overwhelming to bear as her heart pumped rapidly.

I need to stop...I am only making it worse! This thing could have very well walked the other way...whatever it is.

Alyssa turned her attention back to the room, examining it closely. It didn't appear out of the ordinary until her eyes focused on the floor. There were large bullet casings near one of the tables. She walked to them slowly and kneeled down to pick one up, keeping a watchful eye on the door near her. The achy pain in her body returned once she pushed herself back up to her feet, stretching up her back and into her ribcage. Alyssa groaned and rubbed her side, examining the bullet casing.

5.56mm NATO...M4...M16...What the...

A soft groan was heard on the other side of the room, startling Alyssa as she fell back and caught herself on the table behind her. Her heart thumped rapidly once more as she tried to catch her breath.

Someone is here...Someone is actually here...

She was nervous, but hopeful as she slowly walked around the table towards a large copy machine that sat against the wall. She had suddenly forgotten about the thing outside as she kneeled down beside a young man in a digital military uniform. Blood was drying on the side of his head, his short brown hair sticking to it. His helmet, its strap torn, was lying near the copy machine, and his M4 carbine was lying on the floor near him. Alyssa glanced at the assault rifle. She looked back at his uniform and read his name and insignia.

Thompson...Army...He's an E7...How come he is the only one here? Or...was he left behind?

Alyssa thought about the blood she saw downstairs as the young man moved his head to the side. She gently placed her hand on his shoulder, and his eyes slowly opened.

"Are you okay?" she asked.

"What...Where the hell am I?" he asked as he looked around.

"The Rockdale Valley Progress. It's the local newspaper press," Alyssa responded, looking at him concernedly.

"Oh shit...Alex..." he said and carefully sat up. Pain rushed through his head and back as he gasped, closing his eyes.

"Easy now," Alyssa said, and the young man took in a deep breath and looked at her. He seemed to be deep in thought as Alyssa remained calm and patient. She looked back towards the door, thinking about the creature she saw earlier.

Could he have seen this thing too?

"Who are you?" she asked calmly, turning her attention back to him.

He was examining the room carefully as his eyes eventually met back with hers. "I apologize. I'm William Thompson. Army Special Forces. We were deployed here for a search and rescue mission as well as to rule out any possibility of terrorism."

"I guess that explains why this town is so empty," Alyssa replied and looked away, a bit upset for not keeping up with the news.

How could have been so blind to all of this? I've allowed my suffering to take over my life...

"Are you alright? You look hurt," Will said, looking at the blood on Alyssa's arms and shirt as well as her battered clothing that was covered in dirt. Alyssa also looked at herself, not realizing how bad she appeared to be.

"Oh...I had an accident trying to get here. I wasn't even aware of how serious the situation was, but I had to come and get help. I totaled my truck. The damage around here is unbelievable. The roads are inaccessible..."

"What happened? Why would you come here to find help?" Will interrupted, confused.

Alyssa took in a deep breath. "I came because something had happened back at my parents' place just over the mountain. I don't know if someone broke in, but the place was trashed. I don't even know if they are still alive. My father is captain of the precinct for this town, and I figured this is where they would have come to if they were able to get out," she said and thought about the wrecked house. Grief began to strike her as Will examined her concerned expression.

"I sincerely apologize and I hate to say this, but I'm not sure what kind of help you are going to find around here as far as law enforcement. They will be too busy here, but I'm sure we can get you the necessary help that you need for your wounds, and we will also let my commander know about what may have taken place at your parents' residence."

Alyssa nodded. "Thank you," she said softly and looked into his green eyes.

"What is your name? You look familiar," Will said and carefully pushed himself to his feet.

Alyssa stood up as well and responded, "Alyssa Bennett." She couldn't help but look at Will's handsome face even with the dust and blood that was covering parts of it.

"Okay, now I remember. You were in an article on the table over there. Former cop?"

Alyssa nodded. "Yes," she replied and refused to say anymore.

Will nodded and rubbed the back of his head, glancing at his helmet.

"What happened here?" Alyssa asked and Will looked back at her, thinking about the devilish creature and his team. The beast's bright, evil eyes and vicious, sharp teeth flashed in his mind as the thought of its loud shriek made him shutter a bit. He remained calm however as he picked up his rifle and helmet.

"There's something lurking around this place. It's not human and it's not an animal we are familiar with," Will stated and placed his helmet on his head.

Alyssa's eyes widened as she quickly responded, "You've seen it too..."

Will nodded and checked his rifle, replacing the magazine. "It attacked my team," he said, pulling back the charging handle. He carefully approached the door to the hallway and looked back at Alyssa, taking a deep breath. She could sense his pain by the way he moved, but he hid it rather well. She admired his determination.

"We can't stay here. It's not safe. I need to salvage what I can downstairs and get a hold of my commander to let him know what has taken place. You need to come with me so we can get you out of here," Will added and Alyssa stood still. She was expressionless.

"I'm not sure if I want to go back down there. What I saw outside..." Alyssa paused as she tried to figure out what it was.

"I understand...Trust me," he said and opened the door slowly. He looked out into the hallway. It remained empty and quiet.

Alyssa slowly stepped up to him as he stepped into the hallway. He carried his rifle close, carefully making his way down the hall.

"Be careful. The floor could collapse," he whispered as Alyssa carefully followed him to the stairs. The floor creaked loudly as they stepped past the damaged wood floor and onto the stairway.

"Where is your commander at by the way?" Alyssa asked softly as they carefully stepped down the stairs and into the lobby.

"He was going to be north of here. All I have is a GPS device and a map now that my radio got destroyed. I hope he didn't cross paths with one of those things too," Will replied as he stepped into the lobby and stopped. He looked at the broken door and debris that lay on the floor before turning his attention to the blood that was smeared across it and into the room that Broderick and Chris had entered. Alyssa stepped up beside him and examined the debris as well. She remained calm and watched Will approach the room cautiously.

"Alex?" he called out and received no response. He peered into the room and stopped in his tracks. Alyssa stood still and could see the horror in Will's face. She was sure that he just got his response, one that he was hoping not to receive.

The bodies of Alex, Broderick, and Chris were slumped on the floor lifelessly, their blood covering most of the floor around them. Broderick received the most damage. He was torn down his torso.

Will slowly approached his friend and kneeled down beside him as Alyssa stepped up to the doorway. The strong scent of blood filled her nostrils and weakened her gut, but she remained calm.

"Alex..." Will whispered and placed his hand on his friend's shoulder. Alex had received a hard blow to the side of his face, a large hole just above his cheekbone. Blood had dried under his eyes and ears.

"I'm so sorry, buddy," Will whispered once more as he patted Alex's shoulder and carefully removed the ammunition cartridges to his M4.

Alyssa watched him carefully as he retrieved an M9, a holster, and a few cartridges from the other two soldiers. Will looked back at Alyssa and held up the M9 and the hip holster.

"Here. You may need this. I really don't know what else to expect in this place so we better be safe than sorry," he said as Alyssa approached him, gently taking the pistol and holster from him. Will looked back at his friend one last time and stood up. Alyssa noticed the grief within his eyes, feeling bad for him.

"The residents were obviously not making up the stories about the incidences that have occurred here. I'm sure everyone had the same reaction as the others did. It just sounds like nonsense, but you and I have seen the thing with our own eyes," Will stated and looked at Alyssa. "There could be more going on. We must stay alert until we get to the operations center," he added and turned to walk back into the lobby. Alyssa took one last look at his fellow soldiers and sighed in disbelief.

What is happening here...Why would hell erupt in this beautiful town?

Alyssa took in another deep breath and turned to follow Will to the lobby. She remained quiet until they stepped out of the newspaper press and back into destruction that was now Rockdale Valley.

CHAPTER FIVE

WILL WAS CHECKING THEIR SURROUNDINGS to make sure everything was clear as he and Alyssa stood close to the sidewalk near the damaged street by the press. He tried to remain focused on his objective, not noticing Alyssa examining his stressed expression.

"I'm really sorry about your team, William," she said.

Will turned his attention to her as he pulled his GPS device out of his vest pocket. "Please, call me Will. Thank you, though," he said somberly and thought about Alex and the others. "They were good men," he added.

Alyssa slowly nodded and attached the hip holster to her belt. She didn't want to say anymore. Seeing someone grieve deeply affected her as if she knew the one who had deceased personally. Alyssa cleared her mind and carefully secured the M9, turning her attention toward the boutique and diner. The atmosphere was quiet as a light breeze continued to push trash and leaves across the ground. Will looked through his GPS, trying to familiarize himself with locations and street names. Alyssa decided to give him a moment even though she knew the valley like the back of her hand. This gave her time to think about Kayla and her friends.

I wonder if they have tried to contact me...I'm sure Kayla has. Would she bother to come look for me? I can't see them just leaving... not without knowing what happened to me.

Alyssa became sad the more she thought about it. It was their last chance to enjoy themselves before the cooler season came in. Her life had been extremely hectic the past few weeks, and the chance to truly relax was going to be missed. After the persuasion from her father, she had become very excited about it.

Alyssa slowly shook her head, but all of these thoughts quickly vanished when a little anxiety began to build within her chest. The strange, overpowering sensation soon followed, striking her once again. It crept slowly throughout her, intensifying as Alyssa tried to focus on it and remain calm.

No...Not again...What is causing this?

The soft, wicked whispers also returned, traveling through the breeze around her. Alyssa released a low gasp and glanced at Will. He seemed unaware as the whispers became louder, speaking in an unknown tongue.

"What is that?" Alyssa asked concernedly, looking around anxiously.

Will lowered his GPS and noticed Alyssa's frightened expression. He quickly checked their surroundings again but saw nothing except the empty streets and debris.

"What's wrong, Alyssa?" he asked, turning his attention to her. Her expression was alarming.

"You don't hear that? Those...strange sounds?" Alyssa asked.

Will stared at her for a moment until a soft tremor began to quake beneath their feet, quivering the ground gently. Alyssa suddenly gasped and fell to her knees, burying her face into the palms of her hands. The haunting scream that occurred in her nightmares appeared once again in her mind as the dark visions of her hellish underworld flashed before her eyes. Alyssa yelled in fright, seeing the frightful images of the demonic creatures and the hot, bright fire overtaking the valley. Will knelt down beside her and grabbed her arm gently, placing his GPS back into his vest pocket. He tried to keep her as well as himself steady until the ground stopped shaking. Tears were streaming down Alyssa's cheeks as she lowered her hands. The whispers vanished, and the earth slowly settled, becoming calm.

"What is going on?" she choked, trying to shake the wicked thoughts from her mind. "Please tell me you heard them too?" she added as she looked into Will's concerned eyes.

He shook his head quickly. He couldn't understand what was happening.

"No, I didn't hear a thing," he said as a loud, dreadful shriek erupted behind them.

Alyssa and Will quickly looked toward the drug store as the creature they saw earlier was now standing there. It was breathing heavily, staring at them with its wicked eyes. Its hide was coated with wounds and thick blood, its teeth appearing over its angry snout. A low, growl rumbled from its throat and through its quivering lips that curled above its sharp, stained teeth.

"Oh my…" Alyssa said as her heart dropped. Will quickly pulled her to her feet and stared at the creature that killed his close friend. The pavement around them began to split as he shouted, "Come on!"

Alyssa gasped, stumbling on the ground as Will began pulling her to the street that sat between the press and shopping center. The creature screamed ferociously, lowering its upper body as the ground began to shake once more.

"Shit!" Will yelled.

Alyssa lost her balance and fell to the cracked pavement, landing on her side, gripping the asphalt with her hands. Will stumbled forward and lost his balance, falling to the ground as well. He landed a few yards away, his helmet thrown to the pavement. Alyssa was breathing heavily as she watched the asphalt in front of her rip open. Parts of the ground around them began to split and collapse as Will rolled onto his back and aimed his M4 at the devilish creature that suddenly appeared behind Alyssa. He could tell it was severely weakened from its body language. Its muscles quivered and its loud, thunderous step took an extra effort, but the beast wasn't ready to abstain from the fight yet.

The creature growled and opened its large mouth, releasing another high pitch wail that echoed passed them, piercing their ears. Alyssa clenched her teeth, sitting herself up as the earth stopped shaking. She could feel the ground around her trying to give way. It felt weak and loose. She released a heavy gust of air and tried to pull herself away with all the strength she had left.

Will was watching her closely, glaring at the weakened creature that stood near her. He placed his finger on the trigger of his rifle, about to pull it towards him until a shot from a pistol slammed into the creature's side. Will glanced behind him, hearing the creature scream once more.

"Patrick!" he shouted and Alyssa looked behind her, witnessing the earth and pavement collapsing. The demonic beast leaped over her as dirt and pavement fell below. Alyssa's reflexes quickly responded as she grabbed a hold of the ledge in front of her, holding onto it as tightly as she could. Her body dangled above the dark trench. She had no idea what was below her as it intensified her fear, pushing more adrenaline into her veins.

"Look out!" Patrick yelled as he continued to run towards them. Will pushed himself to his feet. The blood covered beast had landed in front of him as Patrick continued to fire at it.

"Will!" Alyssa gasped, gripping onto the ledge. She could feel the jagged edges of the pavement and concrete tear into her palms as she fought to ignore the pain that shot throughout them.

"Hold on!" Will yelled and took a few steps back, aiming his rifle at the creature's bulky chest. Drool spilled around it and onto the torn pavement as it took a thunderous step towards him. Its large body shook the earth and its gurgling growl shot fear throughout Will's body as he stared at the beast's haunting eyes and teeth.

Another quake slowly began to rattle beneath them, but that didn't stop Will from firing more rounds at the beast's flesh as he pulled back onto the trigger, firing a few bursts of ammunition at a time. The earth and pavement began to split in more areas, and the gunfire echoed obtrusively around them.

Alyssa was now losing her hold as the earth continued to quiver, loosening up her tight, achy grip from the ledge. She gritted her teeth and began to groan. She couldn't let go. She refused to become trapped in the pit below. The eerie whispers slowly returned to torment her, flowing around her softly. Alyssa released a low gust of air, trying to shake away the sudden thoughts that crept into her mind. Not even the constant gunfire or the beast's dreadful scream would interrupt the haunting images that flashed before her eyes.

Just stop...Just go away...Please...

The ledge she held onto suddenly gave way, tearing away from the rest of the earth and pavement as she and parts of the crumbled street fell below into the pit of darkness. Alyssa yelled, closing her eyes until she hit the bottom, landing on her side, feeling the tight, achy pain erupt within her ribs. She immediately covered her head, awaiting the debris that was going to fall below. Dirt and soil rained down on her, dusting her clothing and bouncing off of her skin. She could hear the loud thud of asphalt hit the ground near her and collapse onto what sounded like concrete or brick. Alyssa continued to cover her head until the earth stopped shaking. The whispers slowly ceased, and she lowered her hands away from her face, opening her eyes carefully.

What the hell is causing all of this! I do not want to die here... not like this!

The loud, thunderous footsteps and vicious screams of the creature were still heard above her as the gunfire continued to erupt. Alyssa breathed heavily and sat up, looking towards the street above. More pain began to stretch across her body, but she was beginning to feel numb to it thanks to the endorphins that continued to run throughout her. Her breaths came and went rapidly, and she eventually turned her attention to the corridor she was sitting in. Alyssa realized that it was a section of the city's sewer system. Parts of its brick walls were still intact, suffering only minor damage. One side of the wall however, had been pushed back extensively and stretched as far as the eye could see. Sections of the floor had also been crushed. Concrete and brick lay strewn around the side of the damaged wall as steam pushed its way out of cracks and crevices. Very little water covered the ground. Most of it had drained into crevices and back into the earth.

Alyssa had landed on a large mound of dirt as she glanced at the crushed brick floor that was located just a few feet from her. She was lucky.

The asphalt that fell would have killed me for sure...

Alyssa took a deep breath, releasing it slowly as she turned her attention back to the corridor. A few of the oil lamps that were left intact on the undamaged wall were still lit and glimmering as she looked at parts of the brick that had collapsed from the earthquakes. The corridor she was lying in stretched far into the distance. Once her eyes finally adjusted to the dim light, she noticed another corridor to the left. She breathed steadily, the fear continuing to torment her.

Will...The other soldier...

Alyssa looked back up towards the street, realizing the shouts from Patrick and Will were beginning to fade away in the distance. The beast's scream and footsteps were also beginning to fade, and the silent atmosphere was slowly returning around her. Alyssa carefully pushed herself up and stood steadily.

"Will?" she called out. The adrenaline began to flush into her veins once again, the rush of heat erupting inside her. The last remaining screams of the beast slowly disappeared, and Alyssa was now left alone.

Oh no...What am I going to do? What happened to them? Maybe I could reach the ledge...

Alyssa tried to jump and grab the ledge above, but missed each time. It was too steep to climb as she sighed and took a few steps back. She looked down the corridor, the atmosphere calm and quiet.

There's got to be another way out...I'm sure I can find a ladder and a manhole cover somewhere. I'm just afraid at what I could possibly run into down here. It's so dark...

Alyssa cleared her mind and slowly walked down the dingy corridor. The smell of contaminated soil and dirty water made her stomach cringe as she stepped over brick and concrete. The little light in the area shone dimly from the small fires of the oil lamps that burned slowly. They gave her just enough light to see.

Alyssa focused on the path ahead and rubbed her sore, achy arms. Most of the pain subsided into dull aches, becoming very bothersome. It made it difficult for her to focus on the situation that she was now facing alone.

I came here on my own...I can finish this on my own. But that thing...Where could that monster have come from? Is it the results of a bio-weapon? Is the Government even aware of its existence? What is the world going to say once they find out what has happened here?

Alyssa took in a slow, deep breath and looked at the large cracks and crevices of the ground and pavement above her. She could see the night sky and stars shining down upon her. Alyssa prayed and looked back down the corridor, carefully stepping over more brick and debris. She had to find a way out from the dark underworld.

Alyssa took in a deep breath and began to listen to the calm sounds around her. Water was dripping into the distance, echoing softly throughout the corridor. Warm steam whistled and hissed around her as it pushed its way out of cracks and crevices from the floor and walls. The temperature felt a bit warmer. Alyssa was having trouble breathing in the humidity. Sweat was already accumulating on her forehead, some of it slowly dripping down the sides of her face. She gently wiped the trickling beads of sweat away and suddenly stopped in her tracks as a soft shift in the ground was felt below her feet. Something had moved. It was felt in the earth as it shifted once more. Dirt and soil began to fall from above, sprinkling down upon her and the wet brick.

Not again...Oh please...

Alyssa was breathing heavily, staring deep into the corridor. It seemed clear and vacant as she scanned through the darkness. Silence filled the area, and the fear completely immobilized her. She decided not to take another step.

What was that?

Alyssa stiffened as a loud and warm exhale of breath touched her back and sent a chill down her spine. It had pushed her hair off her shoulders and against her face as pieces of her hair stuck to her clammy cheeks. The hair on her arms quickly stood, goose bumps spreading across her body as she listened to the lungs of something large behind her.

Oh no...This is it...

Alyssa slowly turned around to face what was behind her, the fear rushing throughout her body. She carefully placed her hand on her M9 and looked into the corridor. It was now covered with darkness. There was nothing in sight. Alyssa held her breath and squinted her eyes, her heart thumping wildly within her chest. The seconds crept by and her eyes gradually adjusted, focusing on a large object. The image slowly began to appear as the gentle moonlight that slipped through the tears above began to illuminate its features.

Alyssa's heart sank deep within her chest, her body feeling faint as she realized that she was now in direct opposition with the force, the *being* that had been causing all of the destruction in Rockdale Valley. Her eyes widened and her mouth slowly dropped. It was her ongoing nightmare...

What appeared in front of her was the face of a mythical creature. Its long snout protruded from its face, and its large, yellow eyes with a single streak down the middle glared back at her. A few teeth hung over its bottom jaw, its nostrils flared. It released a loud exhale of breath, the warm air rumbling through the corridor. It pushed past Alyssa and brushed her hair back as she stared at the dragon. She couldn't make out the rest of its snaky body. It took up most of the space that made up the tunnel. Alyssa realized the cause of the major damage to the sewer walls. The large beast in front of her had been pushing through the earth, destroying the valley's foundation.

What...what is this...? I must be dreaming. I have to be!

Alyssa slowly took a few steps back, staring in fright. The dragon hissed and the wicked whispers surrounded her once again, clouding up her mind. Alyssa lost her breath and suddenly fell to her knees, closing her eyes tightly. She covered her face with the palms of her hands and clenched her teeth, a sudden vision rushing into her mind...

Alyssa's eyes opened up into what appeared to be a hospital room. Her father was standing next to her.

"Dad?" she asked as she looked at him.

"Hey Honey...How do you feel?" James asked and patted her hand gently.

Alyssa thought for a moment. She felt no pain at all. "I think I'm okay. I just can't remember anything. Dad...what happened?" Alyssa asked concernedly.

"There was an accident..." James replied and sighed as the image slowly faded to a trail in the middle of a forest. Alyssa and her father were hiking up the mountains near Rockdale Valley, one of her favorite outdoor activities.

"We're not too far from this cavern. The others should already be there. Excited?" James asked and looked back at Alyssa. She was trailing behind him, looking through the wilderness. She nodded quickly as a smile rose upon her face. She knew it was going to be an evening she'd never forget...

The images suddenly faded as Alyssa's eyes opened wide. She gasped for air and sat on her hind legs, placing her hand on her chest. Her heart was beating rapidly; her breaths were short and fast. She was confused, awestruck.

Alyssa took a deep breath and slowed her breathing, realizing that she was still face to face with the mythical creature as she looked back into its large, haunting eyes. She felt a trickle of warmth slide gently down from her nose, closing in on her lips. Alyssa gently wiped the blood away and glanced at it.

What just happened?

The dragon hissed and continued to stare at Alyssa while she managed to push herself back to her feet. She gazed into the dragon's eyes once again and thought about her nightmares as well as her father. This was the beast she was unable to see but could always hear in her vicious dreams. Now she was facing it in the town she had grown to love and cherish, and it was ripping it apart.

"So...it's you...You are the one that's been haunting me...in my restless dreams..." Alyssa stated softly and wiped the blood on her pants, keeping a watchful eye on the beast in front of her. The dragon remained still and quiet as Alyssa continued, "I really don't know what I…or possibly my father…has done…" She paused as the dragon hissed once more.

What are you trying to tell me…?

Alyssa gazed into the dragon's glowing eyes and watched the fire dance around its large, black pupils. Silence filled the tunnel and she tried to remain calm, taking steady breaths.

"*Who* are you?" she whispered and trembled. The dragon narrowed its vivid eyes. The wicked whispers slowly returned, and Alyssa closed her eyes, listening to them carefully. The unknown tongue suddenly sounded familiar.

…Uktena.

The dragon slid its hand out from under it and placed it in front of Alyssa. Its large talons slid across the brick as it pulled its way closer to her. Alyssa opened her eyes, her heart beating rapidly once more.

What am I doing? This is insane…Run Alyssa…Run!

She spun around and ran down the rugged corridor as fast as she could push herself, hearing the dragon snarl and suck in a deep gust of air. Alyssa gasped in fright, feeling the sudden force from the beast's bellow as it pushed past her. She stumbled, but continued to push herself forward, focusing her attention on the other corridor that stretched off to the left.

Oh God…Give me the strength to get out of here! I just need the extra strength…

The adrenaline was pouring into her veins, flushing throughout her system as Alyssa breathed heavily. The earth around her began to shift with the tug and pull that Uktena forced upon the tunnel. The dragon was coming after her.

What have I done! What does this thing want from me!

Alyssa was still awestruck. The reason behind the violent earthquakes that had ripped apart the valley was right here, pulling through what was left of the town's sewer system. She couldn't fight away the images of her chronic nightmares and how they have erupted into reality, consuming the once tranquil town as if it were a vengeance.

Alyssa could still hear the dragon trailing behind her. Its rapid movements, its large, snaky body, pushed through the tunnel and continued to shift the earth. Alyssa glanced behind her as she jumped over a large crevice in the broken brick. She heard the rumble in Uktena's chest, the deep breath she inhaled into her lungs. Something sounded different about it. Alyssa had reached the other corridor and heard a whisper in her mind, urging her to make a leap for it. She gasped and quickly dove into the next passageway. She had a feeling of what was about to happen next.

Shit!

Alyssa yelped as her body fell against the rugged brick. Pain shot through her ribcage, spreading into her chest. She moaned through tightly clenched teeth and looked behind her, watching the hot flames pass by, illuminating the area brightly. She could feel the intense heat as it pushed against her and the surrounding brick walls. Alyssa shielded her face with her hand and looked away, the heat brushing harshly against her skin. She pushed herself away from the stream of fire as her strength began to dwindle away. The chronic dull aches and burning pain within her chest were almost impossible to ignore, but she wasn't going to give up. She had to find a way out.

As the flames and heat subsided, the earth suddenly began to shift once more. Dirt and rock began to fall from above, showering down upon Alyssa. Her heart persisted to race as she pushed herself to her feet and took a few steps back. Uktena was getting close. She could hear her body twisting through the tunnel, her loud breaths exhaling from her large lungs.

Alyssa took in a deep breath, preparing herself, fighting the tormenting fear. She turned around and made a run for it down the corridor. A few of the oil lamps in the area had fallen onto the damaged floor and shattered. Glass littered the area and small fires consumed the oil that leaked from the broken lamps. Their light shined brightly, illuminating parts of the area as Alyssa focused on another corridor that stretched to the left. The one she was in continued its path and made a bend towards the right. Steam was steadily pushing its way out of cracks and crevices within the walls, the humidity intensifying the further she traveled. The sweat was beginning to drip down her sides as it continued to push from her pores, attempting to cool her exhausted body.

Alyssa glanced behind her and saw the dragon turn its large head into the corridor she was in. It released another high pitch cry, piercing her ears as it echoed past her. Alyssa yelled in fright and tripped over a few pieces of broken brick and concrete. She fell to the jagged floor and into a puddle of warm water as it splashed on her arms and face. Alyssa gasped and wiped the water away with one clean sweep. She glanced behind her and watched Uktena pull her way towards her, its bright eyes glaring back at her. Alyssa pushed herself up and ran down the path, following it carefully to the right. Darkness began to fill the warm atmosphere of the wide tunnel. Most of the oil lamps had faded out in this area. A little light however, shone from above through the large cracks and tears, guiding Alyssa down the path. She scurried down it, scanning for a way out.

The earth's shifts carried on while Uktena twisted its body through the corridor. Alyssa couldn't help but glance behind her as she witnessed the dragon reaching the bend, slamming its bulky head into the side of the brick wall. Earth and brick collapsed from it, crumbling to the floor. Alyssa about lost her footing, stumbling forward as she continued to push further down the path. She could hear the splash of water from the dirt and rock that fell into the small pools behind her. The dragon was too close for comfort. She was gaining on her, gaining speed. Alyssa began to pant and wondered how much more of this she could possibly manage.

There's got to be a way out!

Uktena continued to trail behind her as she ran towards the end of the corridor, the dirt and rock shifting under her boots. A path was now visible as it stretched to the left and right. She stopped once she reached it and glanced down both of them. The path to the right stretched off into the darkness, but the path to the left had a little light from the oil lamps that still hung intact. Some of the wall had collapsed as brick and soil covered most of the floor. A little water covered parts of floor as well as it glistened from the small fires in the oil lamps. Alyssa saw the path she wanted to take and quickly started running down it, focusing her attention on the wall and ceiling that had collapsed.

That's my way out...I can climb out of here.

The adrenaline pushed into her veins continuously, giving her the extra strength she needed to pull herself out of the underworld. She focused on the debris pile and suddenly heard another harsh scream exit from Uktena's lungs. The dragon was getting close to the corridor she was in, the earth shifting with more force.

Alyssa stopped once she reached the collapsed brick wall and looked up at the pavement that had split open. The moon was now high in the sky, its light pushing through the clouds and shining down on the valley brightly. Its light touched Alyssa's face gently. She was finally beginning to feel a bit of hope.

Parts of the broken pavement from the street above lay around Alyssa as she carefully stepped onto the brick and climbed her way up to it. Water was dripping down her arms and into her shirt sleeve, sending a chill throughout her weary body. She ignored the shiver and took every step up the jagged mound quickly, but carefully, not to make a sudden mistake. Alyssa looked back at the corridor she had come from, seeing Uktena turn her head around the bend. The dragon screamed once more sending Alyssa into full gear. She quickly pushed herself to the pavement and reached the ledge, grabbing a tight hold of it. Her heart was pumping quickly as she pulled herself to the road and crawled away from the gap. She gasped for air and pulled herself onto the sidewalk, her muscles fatigued. They ached and throbbed extensively. Alyssa knew she had to find a place to recuperate. After the things she had seen, she had to clear her mind and focus on her next move.

The soft quakes that still shook the earth and rattled the leaves in the trees that remained standing after all the quakes as Alyssa pushed herself to her feet. She groaned at the muscle fatigue and aches as she started jogging down the sidewalk. It didn't take her long to realize where she had ended up. She examined the familiar area, surprised that it wasn't as badly damaged as the area she had come from. A few trees and lamp posts still stood and a few buildings that made up the probate office and jail house sat across both sides of the street. A couple of tears in the road stretched as far as the eye could see, and there were some pieces of concrete littering it. A light breeze gently pushed away fallen leaves across the street and eased some of Alyssa's tension. The quakes were slowly fading in the distance, and the atmosphere was growing calm, allowing her to relax. The dragon was gone, for now, remaining in her underworld that she had created under the town. Perhaps it would stay there, never allowing itself to come up from the pit of the earth.

The cool breeze that whistled through the air brushed against Alyssa's face, drying the dirt and sweat on her forehead. She was relieved. It washed over her body intensively, breaking it down piece by piece. Her body began to tremble and her breathing began to stabilize. Her heart rate began to slow to a normal pace and her fear began to subside. Alyssa knew how lucky she was to still be alive.

And then she saw it. Tears began to fill her eyes once she noticed the name carved into the large stone outside the building ahead. The Rockdale Valley Precinct, as calm as it appeared, stood in the distance. Alyssa took in a deep breath, sighing softly as she allowed the tears to fall onto her cheeks and trickle down to the ground. She carefully pushed herself forward, down the sidewalk and towards her second home she called it, the police department.

There's got to be someone here...Maybe more soldiers if not police officers...I can't be the only person to have seen what I have witnessed tonight.

Alyssa slowed to a walk and stopped once she reached the stairs to the small station. She took one last look behind her and sighed in relief once more. The dragon still remained under the ground, nothing was in sight. Maybe it didn't see her escape.

Alyssa looked back at the door to the precinct and took in another deep breath. She was anxious.

It's so quiet...Will did mention an evacuation...It doesn't seem like I'll have much luck here, but at least I can try.

She took in a breath and carefully jogged up the stairs to the door. She hoped that maybe someone would still be lingering around. Perhaps that person could be Kevin. He did call not too long ago as Alyssa still wondered about the odd voicemail. The pain and soreness continued to stretch across her body as she tried to clear her mind. She knew she had to focus. She couldn't allow her mind to play tricks on her now.

Alyssa grabbed the handle to the door and pulled it open. Her heart began to pump quickly once again, the anxiety overtaking her system as she began to pray, stepping inside the small, cool lobby of the precinct.

"Patrick...Hey, Patrick...Are you okay?" Will asked, kneeling over a large sinkhole. The pavement had collapsed from the sudden shift in the earth. Patrick was resting on his stomach below. He was breathing heavily as he carefully pushed his chest up off the ground, looking up at Will.

"Yea, I think so," he said and Will glanced at the creature that lay near him.

"Could you try climbing out? I'll give you a hand," Will said and walked to the other side where a few pieces of pavement had broken off in segments.

Patrick looked at the devilish creature as he gently pushed himself to his feet. Its eyes were closed and blood covered most of its tough hide as it oozed from the wounds and onto the ground.

"What the hell is that thing?" he whispered, carefully walking to the collapsed pavement where Will waited above.

"I don't know, but if we encounter any more we will surely run out of ammunition."

Patrick shook his head, lost for words, and gently stepped up onto a segment of pavement and grabbed the ledge from another above. He carefully pulled himself onto it. Will leaned down and extended his hand. Rock and dirt gently rolled down to the pit below as Patrick grabbed Will's hand tightly.

"That was a close one," Will said and pulled Patrick out into the alley he stood in.

"You got that right," Patrick replied and sighed in relief. He glanced back at the beast below as it remained still. "What do you think that was earlier?" he added and looked back at Will who was examining the deserted alley.

They had run a few blocks from the press until the pavement gave way, collapsing into pits below. Parts of the brick walls from the two buildings that stood beside the narrow alley had cracks running throughout them as concrete and dust lay around the ground. A few trash cans had fallen on their sides; their contents lay scattered near them.

"I'm not really sure. I'm afraid there could be more of these things," Will replied.

Patrick pulled a couple of antiseptic wipes from his rucksack and handed one to Will. He carefully opened the other and began wiping the few wounds on his face and arms.

"It just sounded a bit different," he replied.

Will placed his antiseptic wipe into his pocket, thinking about the strange distant screams as well as the frequent quakes that occurred just before the ground collapsed in the alley.

Alyssa could have run into more of these things...What if she is still trapped? Hopefully she got out safely...What exactly did we get ourselves into?

"I'm really not sure what exactly is going on in this town. I don't think anyone can explain this. The earthquakes and tremors are peculiar and not to mention that thing down there," Will said.

Patrick turned to look back at the creature below.

"My team was killed by that thing and if there are more of them, we don't stand much of a chance. Neither does this town," he added and Patrick looked back at him.

"Thankfully we didn't encounter anything like this, though we didn't get too far once we received the call from Specialist Morton," he said.

Will mumbled. "Did it take a while to get here? I don't know how long I was out back there. Where is the rest of your team, anyway?"

"We got separated after receiving the call. But just between us, I think the captain has been acting a bit strange. He was briefing us about the north side of the city which has been barricaded by another brigade. The only way to get through is to get into City Hall. It seems important to him. Our radios have been acting a bit odd though. It just seemed as if the captain had other things on his mind. His radio volume was also low. He finished this talk before responding to you, and I didn't believe he was going in the direction to your location once we started moving. When I was able to get away, I got turned around so it took me a bit. Something didn't seem right to me," Patrick replied.

Will slowly nodded, becoming confused and concerned.

No one really knew what to expect...It's definitely worse than we thought. The radios have been acting a bit faulty...

"Well, I'm sure there's an explanation. The captain wouldn't let us down. Even if you all had made it, I'm not sure if the incident earlier could have been prevented," he said as Patrick slowly nodded. "But we should go find Alyssa. She could be hurt," he added.

"Who was she anyway?" Patrick asked.

Will walked to the end of the alley and examined the area, looking for another way around. Patrick followed him, checking their six frequently.

"She was a former cop and was actually coming back to this city to find help. I don't think she was even aware of the evacuation orders that were given out and the severity of the destruction. But regardless, she's a survivor," Will said.

"I agree," Patrick replied and looked at the damaged street they stood by.

"Most of this side of town has been destroyed, but maybe we can try another route. Hopefully we can find her and get to the operation center so we can inform the others on what has happened."

"Alright, let's move," Patrick ordered as he and Will quickly made their way west that would take them back to the Rockdale Valley Progress.

CHAPTER SIX

A LYSSA WAS STANDING OVER THE sink in the bathroom, staring at herself in the dingy mirror. Water was dripping off her face and into the sink, washing the dirt and blood toward the drain. She was breathing deeply, thinking about the hellish creature, the dragon, and William Thompson. Blood and dirt stained most of her skin and clothing and her hair had frizzed from the humidity of the underworld the dragon had claimed.

Alyssa continued to stare into her own eyes in the mirror, ignoring her rough appearance.

Uktena...What could have possibly brought you here? Especially when you only existed in my nightmares...Why do I feel as if the events here have some sort of connection to my dreams? Those whispers...That growl back at home and near the ledge? I'm not sure if I want to find out the truth...What will everyone think when they realize what has been destroying this place? I need to find Will or perhaps his group...Maybe he's still alive. But I really need to find out what the hell happened to my parents and why...

Alyssa took in a deep breath and felt a little anxiety rush throughout her. She continued to stare into the mirror at her own eyes, the strange feeling beginning to creep within her once again. It crept slowly throughout her, igniting the nerve endings in her brain and speeding up her heart rate. Alyssa breathed heavily and continued to focus her attention into the mirror, drawn to it. She felt hypnotized, unable to shake out of the trance. And then, without warning, the image of devilish eyes, similar to those of a serpent, quickly flashed back at her. Her eyes widened as she pushed herself away from the sink. She took a couple of steps back, her body trembling. She breathed deeply and looked around the quiet bathroom. It appeared vacant. The light was shining dimly on the tile floor, its soft touch glistening in the puddles of water that accumulated near the drains. It was quiet, too quiet. Alyssa slowly looked back at the mirror, trying her best not to stare into it.

Why is this happening to me...?

She snatched a paper towel from the dispenser and wiped her face. It took all she had not to allow the fear to send her into panic. She took a deep breath, releasing it slowly.

The lobby was empty...Where is everyone? I should probably see if Heather left a change of clothes in her locker like she normally does and just get out of this god forsaken place. I was so stupid to come here! I should have checked in with the news...or just answered my damn phone!

Alyssa was still angry with herself. She could have driven miles away to the next town if she would have known the valley did in fact receive the mandatory evacuation order. She could practically hear herself groan in her thoughts as she tossed the paper towel into the trash receptacle and stepped up to the door.

I need to regroup with these soldiers.

She carefully pulled the door open and stepped back into the dim hallway near the locker room. A few lights were on as Alyssa walked down the hallway and passed a couple of windows. She glanced out the last one, wondering if there were more hellish creatures lurking about. She couldn't comprehend how an entire town simply vanished.

Alyssa approached a small flight of stairs in the hallway. She remembered how busy this hall got during shift changes. Everyone would do a quick catch up in the locker room or find something to make fun of the chief about. Alyssa didn't think Robert ever meant to be as funny as he was. But then again, he came back to laugh at himself at times. Alyssa truly missed being around it all.

She carefully stepped up the four stairs and looked behind her, sighing from the recent thought.

Farewell...

The hallway was empty and calm as she turned her attention back in front of her. The locker room was on the right. For the first time ever, it was silent. It was room that was always busy, full of conversation.

Alyssa pulled open the door and stepped into the room around the corner. A couple of bags were strewn on the floor, and a few personal hygiene products were lying near them. Some of the doors to the lockers were hanging open, exposing their contents. Alyssa walked past a bench, recalling the last time she was there. She was so eager to get her things and get out without being stopped by one of her colleagues. Now she wished she would have had that last conversation with her team.

Alyssa sighed and stepped up to Heather's locker, opening it carefully. The soft screech disrupted the calmness, sending a chill rattling down her spine. She blocked the negative thoughts that tried to creep into her mind and scare her senseless. If she allowed it, it would send her into a pure panic stricken phase, one that would almost be impossible for her to escape from. She took in a deep breath, relaxed, and smiled at the contents in her friend's locker.

Thank you Heather...

Alyssa quickly pulled her torn and battered shirt over her head and onto the floor and grabbed a navy blue Rockdale Valley Precinct t-shirt from the locker. She looked behind her, throwing the shirt over her head and onto her shoulders. She hurriedly pulled the shirt down once her arms were through the sleeves and glanced back towards the door. It was still quiet, she perceived. Alyssa turned and grabbed a white hair band from a small cosmetic bag and gently placed it around her wrist. She carefully closed the door to the locker and pulled her hair back into a ponytail. She was already feeling better after pulling her hair up and off her shoulders.

Okay...Now to get out of here and hopefully find some military personnel...

Alyssa quickly stepped back into the dim hallway and made her way back to the lobby. She stopped before reaching the doors and noticed a few blood splatters behind one of the secretaries' desks. She stared at them, her gaze following a small bloody trail that stretched down the hall to her right. It led to the dispatch and conference rooms.

Something did happen here...How did I miss this when I came in? Someone could still be around! Oh no...

Alyssa carefully pulled her M9 out of the holster and held it up towards her chest. She ignored her frequent fear and slowly followed the blood trail into the hallway. One light was on above as it illuminated the hall and parts of the rooms around it. Alyssa passed a couple of pictures that were taken around the town and stopped once she reached the door to the dispatch room. It hung slightly open, and a bloody hand print was smeared near the handle. The trail continued up the hall and towards the large conference room in the back. Alyssa ignored the trail and slowly pushed the door open, holding her pistol out. She scanned the dispatch room quickly and noticed a woman resting on the floor near a long desk. All the computer screens and keyboards were shattered and smashed, plastic lay strewn across the floor. Casings to nine millimeter rounds were lying on the floor near the desk, catching Alyssa's attention as she approached the woman and kneeled down beside her. She was already familiar with the woman's hair, but refused to believe that it was her. No one would ever have a reason to harm this lady...

Alyssa placed her M9 back into its holster and gently placed her hand on the woman's blue blouse.

"Ma'am?" she asked softly and slowly pulled her onto her back.

The woman's eyes were closed and blood was splattered on her face and bleach blonde hair. She had two bullet wounds in her chest. The blood was beginning to dry on her clothes and around the wounds.

Alyssa sighed sadly, looking at the woman. It was one of the secretaries, the one closest to her since the accident. A tear slowly crept into her eyes. Whenever trouble and despair would arise, Alyssa knew that this particular person was the one to come to for peace of mind.

Not you Kristin...Why would someone do this to you...?

Alyssa glanced over her shoulder, looking towards the door. She took in a deep breath and collected herself. She had to keep it together. If anyone was still in the building, she would have heard them by now.

I just don't understand...What the hell is happening in this town!

Alyssa slowly looked back at Kristin and noticed a piece of crinkled paper near the desk that was beside her. She stared at the black ink and carefully picked the note up. Whoever wrote it appeared to be nervous or afraid. It seemed to be done in haste as Alyssa carefully read the words ...

I'm not sure if anyone will get this. I've tried numerous times to contact help, but the satellites and phone lines must be down. If anyone gets this please do not trust anyone...not even the soldiers deployed here. This precinct was attacked by a man in military uniform. I believe he was Army. I wasn't able to get the rank or name. I don't believe he saw me. Please, if anyone gets this, find a way to get out and report it. I will try and make my way to Trinity Hospital. KH

Alyssa couldn't believe what she just read as she slowly lowered the piece of paper from her face. She thought about the phone call from Kevin earlier and the scratchy voicemail. She also thought about Will. He was Army...

KH...Kevin Headley...Oh no, my partner, my best friend...This had to have been him. I wonder if I could have prevented this...Damn it! I wonder if he even made it to the hospital. I don't think he would have misjudged the person behind this betrayal...

Alyssa released a heavy gust of air and slowly stood up, folding the note. She looked back at Kristen and placed the note in her pocket.

"I'm so sorry...I promise...I will find out who did this," she whispered as she turned to go back to the door. She glanced over at the switchboard and saw pieces of broken equipment around it.

Someone did not want them to get a hold of anyone...I wonder what happened to the officers that were here? And speaking of which...where's all of third shift?

Alyssa became confused as she stepped back into the hallway and checked both directions. The lobby remained clear and quiet. She turned her attention back at the blood trail. Alyssa carefully pulled her M9 back out of its holster. She quietly followed the trail, passing a couple of more pictures of officers and one of the police chief. Alyssa remained alert and stepped up to the conference room. She slowly walked inside, scanning it quickly, expecting the worst. Blood covered most of the floor and parts of the walls. Its stench suddenly filled her nostrils and sent the wave of nausea throughout her gut. Alyssa's heart dropped. She slowly lowered her pistol and stared at the few bodies on the floor. There was another secretary, Jennifer Richardson, who was lying on her stomach with a bullet wound in her upper back. Alyssa noticed her long brown hair that was resting across her right arm as well as the cute glasses she always wore. Only they were not on her perfect round face. They were tossed to the floor next to her, crushed.

There were three officers lying lifelessly near the large, round table in the middle of the room. Alyssa turned her attention to them, the adrenaline beginning to pump into her veins once more. Grief was filling her aching heart. This was her family, her team, and everyone was treated as such. It was something the precinct valued the most.

Alyssa struggled to remain calm as she carefully stepped around the table and stopped. She already knew the officers. She recognized their faces and features immediately. Two had been shot in the back, but the other one, the amusing sergeant with the bigger gun, appeared to have been executed. Blood covered the area near them as their lifeless bodies lie slumped on floor.

Why would someone do this! If only I could have been here...I'm sorry...I am so sorry...

Alyssa took deep breaths and continued to stare at her fellow officers. She was still in shock from the possibility of one of the soldiers actually being involved. She pondered a likely motive. None of it made any sense.

These people didn't deserve to die like this! My friends...What were these murders after!

She exhaled her breath heavily and took a few steps back until the door to the lobby suddenly opened. Alyssa gasped at the loud, harsh sound as it echoed throughout the west wing of the building. She turned to face the hallway and froze, holding her pistol tight. Her heart raced and pounded deep within her chest as the loud footsteps that soon followed were heard entering the building. The heavy door slammed shut and the footsteps returned, coming in her direction slowly. Alyssa took a few steps back, fear quickly rushing throughout her body. Her breaths became loud and heavy as she stepped back near the large window that overlooked the courtyard.

Oh God...They've come back!

Millions of thoughts were running throughout her mind until the sounds of glass bursting echoed behind her. Alyssa screamed in fright and tried to run to the hallway, but something heavy and large slammed into her back. It threw her foreword, forcefully slamming her into the floor near the door. Glass slung in all directions, raining down against her back. She heard a loud thud. Something had landed right behind her. Alyssa gasped for air and became a little disoriented as she slowly rolled onto her back and tried to focus on what appeared behind her. It slowly came into view, another one of the demonic creatures. Its features were slightly different from the one she had encountered earlier. Its color was a different shade, more crimson hues. Its claws were also longer and jagged. Alyssa groaned and pushed herself away from the vile beast.

No...not another one!

The large creature took a heavy step towards her, its teeth curled over its angry snout. Alyssa's vision became fuzzy as she rolled on to her stomach, about to push herself to her feet until her eyes met those of a young man who was clothed in a digital military uniform. He slowly stepped into her view, gripping onto an M4 assault rifle. His other hand was caressing the belly of the M203 attachment. Another soldier with only a pistol stepped up beside him and Alyssa froze, watching the young man with the rifle slide a grenade into the launcher. She suddenly became overwhelmed with vertigo and breathed deeply, trying to regain control. She could hear the ferocious scream of the reptilian creature behind her as she slowly turned back over and collapsed on the floor. Pain throbbed in her head and her eyes began to flicker. She didn't care about what was going to happen next. She felt as if she were in a dream.

"Get back!" the young man yelled and he began to fire a few rounds into the creature's chest. The burst of rounds echoed throughout the conference room until they suddenly ceased. Alyssa heard a few loud footsteps behind her and felt a soft, warm touch press against her shoulder. Her eyes slowly closed, but the image of the beast remained in her mind.

"Get her out of here!" a voice yelled as the devilish beast screamed back at them. Alyssa began to take slow breaths as the young man's voice as well as the creature's taunting scream became muffled and eventually faded away. She slowly drifted off to another world, the view of the conference room fading away to an image of darkness and a soft voice from her father, "It's going to be okay Alyssa...It will all be over soon..."

"Alyssa!" Will yelled. He and Patrick stood near the shopping center and newspaper press. The pavement around them was destroyed from the recent quake, torn and ripped open. Parts of it had also collapsed into the earth below leaving most of the area inaccessible. Heat was pushing its way up from the tears and large openings, its warm touch brushing against their faces. Patrick was kneeling down by a sinkhole while Will paced around the large openings where the road had collapsed.

"Will...I don't believe she is here. Maybe she was able to escape," Patrick said and stood up. He looked over at Will who was staring down towards the sewers below.

"This is the area where she fell. Maybe she did find a way out. I just didn't want to take the chance on leaving someone behind," Will said, thinking about his past. It always found a way to creep back into his mind.

Patrick approached him. "It's too dangerous around here. Who knows when the rest of the pavement will collapse? We need to find the captain," he said and Will took one last look around the area, letting his thoughts go. The gentle breeze pushed against him, sending the heat from below towards his face once more.

"Strange..." he said and paused for a second, allowing the warmth from below to touch his skin. "The air down there is...really warm."

Patrick looked into the opening and shook his head. "All of this is just strange. I can't comprehend it," he replied.

Will took a deep breath and checked his ammunition. "Let's load up. It's possible that we will run into more of these things along our way. The operations center isn't too far from here, right?" he asked. Patrick examined his pistol, checking his cartridge.

"It's not too far. We need to take Main up to Dorchester."

Will reloaded his rifle and nodded as Patrick placed his pistol into his hip holster.

"Hopefully we can find some survivors on our way," Patrick added and began walking toward a small road behind the shopping center. Will quickly followed, thinking about the nasty creature they encountered and Alyssa.

Hopefully we won't run into any more of those things. Maybe Kyle will have more answers for us...I sure hope Alyssa got out safely. I wish there was more that I could have done for her.

"Let me test this radio again. Perhaps you can check the GPS and see if there is any short cut," Patrick said, pulling out his radio.

Will gently retrieved his device as he checked their surroundings for anything suspicious. All he could hear was the soft breeze that continued to flow around them as it pushed paper and leaves across the ground. A few cracks and tears stretched across the pavement and throughout the brick walls of the buildings that stood in the area. Will glanced at a few cars that were left abandoned in the parking lot. Glass lay strewn around the pavement as he and Patrick stepped over a few shards. Will glanced back in the direction he last saw Alyssa, the atmosphere remaining calm until the sounds of static echoed from Patrick's radio. Will shook from the startle and looked at Patrick as he fumbled with the radio. He was turning a few dials, a sense of frustration appearing on his face. The static continued to sputter.

"I'm really not sure what's interfering with our LMRs, but it is becoming very frustrating," he stressed.

Will nodded. "I had the same problem," he responded.

Patrick sighed and placed the radio back in its case. He stepped up to the small road and examined the area. Will stopped once he reached him and examined his GPS device. The small road was cluttered with trash and debris as broken brick lay around parts of the building. A tall cement wall stood to their left. Patrick examined a few privacy fences that stood on the ground above the wall, noticing some of the wooden posts leaning in different directions.

"So if we go through here and make a left it will take us up to Edgemont Drive which will then take us to Main Street. That looks to be the quickest route," Will said and Patrick nodded, turning his attention to him.

"We weren't too far from that area when we got the call from you guys. I just hate that it took me so long to get to you," Patrick said as he and Will carefully made their way down the road.

"But you came. You tried your best. Like I said before, even if you had made it earlier, I don't think it would have changed the outcome of what happened. You very well could have been killed yourself. I was just lucky," Will replied, carefully placing his GPS back into his vest pocket.

Patrick thought for a moment as Will carefully scanned the area ahead.

"I can't help but wonder what happened to the Captain and Master Sergeants Kennedy and Stephenson. They never showed up," Patrick said and thought about his team.

"Something could have slowed them down. Let's not think negative. Once we get to the operation center, I'm sure we will get some answers," Will replied.

He and Patrick reached the street and cautiously walked across it. Patrick cleared his throat and took in a deep breath. Will examined the new surroundings as they stepped up to the sidewalk and began making their way left that would take them north to Main Street.

The area resembled a war zone. Smoke rose from a few abandoned cars that had collapsed with the pavement ahead and a few small trees had fallen to the ground. Most of the homes in the nearby neighborhood were destroyed. Wood and debris were lying around the grass and driveways, and glass was strewn about. The atmosphere remained calm and peaceful, however. It didn't match the mood of the valley.

Will and Patrick carefully made their way to the tactical operations center, feeling like a paranoiac. The frequent glances over their shoulders, the sudden noises in the distance, and the soft whistles in the wind were just enough to make them feel delusional. It was the strong sense of evil that had now struck them. It lingered in the atmosphere, silently torturing their restless minds as they attempted to push forward unscathed.

CHAPTER SEVEN

KYLE WAS STANDING OUTSIDE THE operation center, allowing the cool breeze to run through his hair as he inserted a clip into a Colt 1911. He stared at the pistol and a slight smile curled across his face.

Just look at you...

He admired the .45's appearance, looking it over as if it was the Venus De Milo.

You are definitely going to make this mission easier for me...and a lot more enjoyable...

Kyle's smirk froze on his face and he slowly lowered the pistol as he heard the door open from the trailer that was adjacent to the tent he was standing by. He turned around and walked into the tent, placing his pistol on the table, his devilish smile fading. The footsteps came quickly down the small deck stairs and into the tent as Master Sergeant Brad Kennedy came into his view. Kyle watched him approach, examining the look of frustration on the soldier's face.

"We should have taken them out long before making our way to that damn police station," Brad stated, his face remaining full of frustration.

Kyle thought for a moment as Brad continued, "Now we have some random civilian to worry about, let alone the police chief who has the keys to get us where we need to be."

Kyle slowly nodded. "Calm yourself...I didn't have a good shot. There will be plenty of time to be rid of them."

"Captain...We also need to think about the group."

"I don't think you should worry about the others, Master Sergeant. The radios are not working, and we won't be here for too much longer anyway," Kyle replied and turned his attention outside.

"But the barricades…How are we going to get by?" Brad asked as he remained standing in place, watching Kyle's body language from behind.

"The secretary said that Robert was on his way downtown before the destruction became serious. Go there and try and find him. I'll keep an eye on things here," Kyle said, turning his attention back to Brad. Brad's expression didn't change.

"I hope this doesn't take up too much of our time," he replied.

"It's the only option we have now," Kyle replied. He grabbed the Colt 1911 and began walking toward the stairs of the deck. Brad watched him carefully as he approached the door and placed his hand on the handle. Kyle looked back at him, his face firm.

"Be back here at 2200 hours," he ordered and disappeared behind the door.

Brad turned his attention to the three Polaris ATVs that sat near the entrance to the tent and felt a bit of anger wash over him.

Now I'm becoming his flunky…This all better be worth it in the end.

He stepped out of the tent and approached one of the four-wheelers. His mind was preoccupied with the perilous mission as he sat in the seat of the ATV, switching the engine on. He glanced back at the small trailer, taking a deep, steady breath.

I don't think he was aware of how serious this shit had gotten… but I intend to deliver…by any means necessary. I refuse to be walked on by this old man.

He carefully backed the ATV and turned the steering handle to the right. He looked into the distance, already having an idea of which way to go. Brad gripped the handle and gave it full throttle, speeding past the buildings in the cul-de-sac. He drove towards a dark alley that sat in between two of them as he focused on the deserted area, ignoring the bothersome anxiety that spilled into his gut. He contemplated the task, wondering how he and the person in whom everyone had trusted could get away with such a daunting mission. It was too late for him to turn back now, too late to even consider changing his mind. Their scheme had already started and nothing, not even he, could stop it.

"Dad? Dad where are you?" Alyssa called out as she looked around the haunting underworld she stood in. Darkness filled the atmosphere and fire and lava surrounded her sides. She heard his voice in the distance, but all she could hear now were the bubbles and crackles of the lava pits and the fire that were slowly consuming the area. The intense heat was pushing against her skin as Alyssa forced herself forward. But for some odd reason, walking was becoming a difficult task.

Why can't I move? Why am I back here!

Fear rushed throughout her, intensifying even more so as she heard the low growl, the familiar snarl, rumble behind her. Alyssa turned around and saw only darkness. Then, another growl followed with strange, distant screams echoed around her, pounding into her ears. Her heart raced away as she searched frantically.

"Dad!" Alyssa yelled and turned around, attempting to take a step forward. She felt as if she were wearing iron boots as she tried to take another forceful step. She wasn't going to be able to keep at it. It was near impossible! Alyssa gasped, her strength quickly vanishing as she fell onto the rough terrain. Death was knocking at her door. She could feel it, the dark, evil presence. It had sucked the life out of her, leaving her there to perish in agony.

"Dad...Please come back!" she could hear herself scream within her mind. She tried to open her mouth to speak once more, but no words were coming out. She had become mute.

Grief and anxiety washed over her as she tried to pull herself across the rough terrain. Her fingers gripped the rock tightly and she pulled with all of her might. The intense heat pushed relentlessly against her skin, burning her. She didn't believe that she was going to survive much more of the torture.

Alyssa's hands and arms shook from fatigue and pain as she persisted to drag herself with whatever strength she had left. But she suddenly froze. The dreadful, menacing growl spit out into her left ear. She closed her eyes tightly and watched as the image within her mind morphed to a familiar place. She was suddenly standing in the middle of town. People were rushing about, searching desperately for a way out, screaming for their lives. Fire consumed everything around her, eating away at the remains of the valley. Alyssa stared, breathing heavily, looking at the recognizable buildings and landmarks that burned to ashes...And then the rumbling growl was heard once again and Alyssa heaved a heavy sigh, closing her eyes, begging for the presence to go away...until a little light slowly began to fill her eyelids...

Alyssa's eyes suddenly opened into a small, wide room. A large light was shining above her. She gazed at it, wondering what had just happened. She was afraid to blink as she thought about the familiar underworld she was just in.

Just another nightmare...The same nightmare...

Alyssa slowly blinked and continued to stare at the bright light above.

That awful, guttural sound...Could I have just heard things earlier today? Or could it all be related?

Her thoughts paused as she heard someone place a pen or pencil down on a hard surface. She glanced to her left and saw a young man in a digital military uniform sitting at a small table, reviewing a file. Alyssa's heart began to race, suddenly recalling the incident that had occurred at the precinct and the letter she found from her former partner. Reality quickly set in as she let go of the nightmare she had just escaped from to focus on this soldier.

I almost forgot, but how did I end up here?

She continued to stare at the young man until his attention eventually met hers. Alyssa's heart dropped as the soldier sat up straight and stated, "Oh, you're awake."

She didn't know what to say. She stared blankly into his dark brown eyes and remained unresponsive. He waited patiently, listening to Alyssa's deep breaths.

"Don't be afraid...You are safe," the soldier assured.

"Where...am I?" Alyssa faltered and wondered if she sounded odd as she tried to ignore the negative thoughts that were running through her mind.

"You are in Rockdale Valley. This is the operations center for my group. I'm Christian Moseley. I'm a medic with the Army," he said, sitting the file down on the desk and turning all his attention to her.

He seemed nice, but she wasn't going to give in too easily. She remained silent as she began to remember everything that had happened before she woke up in the small room. Suddenly, all the images flashed into her mind. She thought about her parents and their house, the strange monster lurking about, and then the dragon...

"Can you give me your name?" Christian asked.

His expression didn't change. Maybe he was used to this. Alyssa was trying to read his body language as he remained patient. She carefully sat up and took in a deep breath.

"Alyssa Bennett," she responded and placed her feet on the floor, remaining seated on the large, black sofa.

"Can you recall anything?" Christian asked.

Alyssa thought about the Rockdale Valley Press and the precinct. *Uktena...Hmm...This guy will think I am insane if I mention what I have seen. I shouldn't say much, but where the hell do I start?*

Alyssa bit her lower lip and collected her thoughts. "I..." she started to say and paused.

Christian watched her carefully, examining her expression.

"I recall almost everything...Just not how I got here," Alyssa carefully said and looked into Christian's eyes.

He nodded. "Well Travis and I found you, but perhaps you can tell me what happened at the police station?" he asked.

Alyssa's expression turned to confusion as she shook her head.

"I don't know. I got there hoping to find help and...that's what I found," she replied, her eyebrows pulling down.

"Hmm…" Christian mumbled.

"I would have never come back to this place if I knew it had gotten this severe. I just thought…" Alyssa took another deep breath and continued, "I just thought I would be able to find help."

"There was a mandatory evacuation. We were sent here to find survivors and evacuate the ones who were not able to get out in time. There is a possibility of terrorist activity though I'm not sure if the public is aware. You actually traveled here?"

"I know it sounds odd. I stopped watching the news. I was unaware of the evacuation," Alyssa replied and looked at the ground.

"What happened? Why did you need to find help?" Christian asked, becoming a bit confused himself.

Alyssa looked back at him and thought about her parents once more.

"It's all right if you do not want to talk about it," Christian added.

"I really don't know where to begin with this."

"Take your time."

Alyssa nodded and organized her thoughts about the events that had led her there as she also thought about what information to give out. She had to be careful.

"Will, I don't believe anyone here is alive," Patrick said as he stood inside the entrance of a small law office.

"I thought I heard something," Will replied. He was standing near a large desk in the waiting area. Glass and debris littered the floor as a few blood stains covered the carpet. The office was quiet which seemed to rattle Patrick's nerves. Anxiety began to build within him as he carefully watched their surroundings.

"The TOC is right around the corner. I think our priority right now is to locate the Captain or next in command," he said, hoping Will would reconsider.

Will slowly nodded. "I understand. I just thought I heard something. I wanted to be certain. Let's go," Will replied and approached Patrick who took a few steps back from the broken glass door. Patrick examined his expression, seeing his disappointment.

They were becoming discouraged, their hope of finding anyone alive disappearing rapidly.

Patrick stepped back into the gloomy atmosphere and began making his way down the street. Will trailed behind, deep in thought. He didn't think they would find anyone and he wasn't sure what was left of their group. His biggest fear was reaching the operations center and it being vacant. There would be no way to get out, no way to get assistance.

We would be stranded here...

The uncertainty, the fear, flushed throughout his body. He took a deep breath and glanced at Patrick, following his gaze to a small road that they were approaching.

"Dorchester. The TOC is on the left in a small trailer," Patrick said, and looked over his shoulder at Will. Will looked at him, raising an eyebrow.

Patrick shrugged. "They have the tent beside it. The office that was using it is currently under construction," he added and Will nodded.

"I see," he said and they both stepped onto the road and walked toward the small trailer that stood in the distance.

Did someone know what was going on?

Will mumbled to himself and focused his attention on the tent that stood beside the trailer, noticing a couple of four-wheelers sitting near it.

"Someone has to be here," he said and Patrick noticed that the power in the area was still on. Lights were gleaming inside the trailer and on the wooden deck. Patrick sighed in relief and approached the small set of stairs that lead to the door. Will approached the tent and looked inside. A few tables, chairs, and ammunition cases sat neatly arranged, but no one was there. He shook his head and turned back to the set of stairs where Patrick waited.

"Maybe they are inside," Will said and approached the stairs, stepping up them carefully.

Patrick opened the door and he and Will stepped inside the small office. Kyle was sitting at a desk behind his laptop and quickly stood up, a look of shock appearing on his face. "Will…Patrick…What the hell happened?"

Patrick closed the door gently. Will approached the two sofas in the center of the room and stood near the tall bookshelf. "I guess I could ask you the same thing, Captain," he stated and folded his arms.

"I apologize, Sergeant First Class. The LMRs haven't been working properly. As soon as we began making our way to your position we encountered many inaccessible areas and not to mention a couple of quakes," Kyle replied without hesitation and looked at Patrick. "And you disappeared."

Patrick tried to read his expression. It was either full of irritation or suspicion. He couldn't put his finger on it.

"I'm sorry, Captain. We got separated after the earthquake. I decided to take an alternate route to Thompson's location," he responded and thought about Kyle's peculiar behavior from before as he decided not to express his feelings about it. Something was odd.

Kyle slowly nodded and turned his attention back to Will.

"Captain, I'm not sure if you know exactly what is going on around here, but there is a thing lurking around this place and it killed my team. Nothing seems to slow it down. We need more artillery. There could be more of these things, and we don't have the appropriate firepower to put a quick stop to them," Will stressed, his face becoming flushed.

"So all the stories we have been told are true after all. Specialist Tidwell and Moseley encountered something earlier as well," Kyle replied.

He slowly walked to a window behind him and folded his arms against his chest. Will and Patrick watched him as Kyle took in a deep breath.

"I've been given a code name for the creatures in case they turned out to be real. We didn't want to take the information the civilians had given us *too* lightly…"

"You already knew about these things?" Will interrupted, uncrossing his arms.

Kyle looked back at him quickly, his eyes filling with anger.

"Like I said, Sergeant First Class. We couldn't ignore everything the civilians were telling us. We came prepared, but it seems to be more serious than we thought. We were not expecting anything like this," he responded firmly. "Now that will be the last time you interrupt me, Sergeant First Class," he added and Will took in a deep breath.

"Yes, Captain."

Kyle slowly walked back to the desk and closed his laptop. "What did it look like?" he asked.

Patrick stepped up to one of the sofas and leaned his body against one. Will thought for a moment. He could practically hear the vicious scream from the beast in the back of his mind.

"It was large…and demonic looking. It had large claws and teeth, yellowish eyes…It looks as if it came straight out of the pits of hell."

A look of concern appeared on Kyle's face as he remembered the description given to him once before.

"The angra," he finally stated. "That's the code name."

Will shook his head in disbelief, looking away. He couldn't comprehend why the captain left that important detail out. Perhaps if they would have been made aware of their possible existence.

Could it have prevented the incident at the press?

Will gulped silently, absorbing the information.

"Where are Master Sergeants Stephenson and Kennedy?" Patrick suddenly asked, changing the topic.

Kyle carefully sat down behind the desk and looked at Patrick.

"Master Sergeant Kennedy went to the downtown area to locate the police chief. He was supposed to have met us here but something may have happened, slowing him down. He has access to City Hall which will lead us into the area that has been barricaded by the other platoon. Master Sergeant Stephenson…didn't make it," he stated and watched Patrick's expression. It quickly changed from concern to anger, his face and body tensing as he pushed himself away from the sofa.

"What happened?" Will asked.

"When we were headed to your location, the road collapsed," Kyle replied and Patrick threw his arms down.

"This is crazy, Captain! Everyone is dying! And we still have an immediate reason to stay here?" he shouted, his heart beating rapidly.

"Calm yourself, Sergeant First Class!" Kyle firmly exclaimed as he stood back up.

Patrick was breathing heavily. He thought about their group and why Kyle had no expression of remorse what so ever.

"I understand that we did not expect the severity of this mission. No one did. But we have strict orders. As soon as Master Sergeant Kennedy returns we will go to City Hall and meet the other platoon. Hopefully we can make contact with the others, but our top priority right now is to find and evacuate civilians. The evacuation location is Trinity Hospital. Is that clear?"

"Yes, sir," Will responded and turned away.

Patrick stood still. "Yes, sir," he finally said and turned to walk back to the door. He was still full of anger and frustration as he pulled the door open and disappeared outside. Will watched him close the door, taking a deep breath in. Kyle slowly sat back down behind the desk, taking another deep breath.

"Captain..." Will began and looked at Kyle, his face deeply concerned. "I don't believe we can accomplish this mission with just our rifles and pistols alone. Who knows what we will run into now?" He was extremely worried, not only about the civilians and the valley, but for their own lives at that.

"I've been trying to reach command, but with no success. As I stated, our LMRs aren't working. The cell phone service in the area is also down. I have no way of making any contact outside of Rockdale Valley," Kyle stated with frustration. "That is why it is important to complete our mission in this area and meet the platoon in the northern region of this town," he added and Will looked at the ground.

We were doomed when we landed in this valley...

"Oh and Will...I'm sorry about Alex. I know he was a good friend of yours. It's a shame how many men we've actually lost this evening. We will get to the bottom of this," Kyle said, interrupting Will's thoughts.

Will looked back at him. "Yes sir," he said and sighed softly, thinking about the incident at the Rockdale Valley Progress.

I can't believe I made it out of there alive. Maybe this other platoon will have what we need.

Will's thoughts were interrupted once more as the door that stood to his right suddenly opened. He watched Specialist Christian Moseley approach Kyle, but then a young woman slowly stepped up to the doorway. She was wearing a navy blue t shirt and blue jeans and was examining the fresh bandages wrapped on parts of her arms. Her hair was pulled back into a ponytail.

"The civilian will be fine, Captain. She has quite a story though," Christian said.

Kyle stood back up, pushing his chair under the desk. Will looked back at the young woman. She eventually met his gaze after lowering her arms.

"Alyssa?" Will asked, surprised.

"Will…" Alyssa uttered. She was surprised to see him as well. She didn't expect him or his friend to survive that thing that had attacked them in the street.

"I didn't think you made it out," Will added.

Kyle and Christian looked back at them, confused. Alyssa became nervous. She couldn't keep the dark images from the precinct let alone the letter from Kevin out of her mind. She remained quiet as Kyle spoke up, "So you two have already met?"

"She found me at the press after the incident occurred. We got separated," Will responded, watching Alyssa's expression carefully. She seemed off or afraid. Will couldn't tell which one, but he was curious.

"I see," Kyle said, turning his attention back to Christian after noticing the t-shirt she was wearing. "What's the back story?" he asked calmly as Will approached Alyssa. She was watching Kyle and Christian have the conversation that they had earlier as she slowly looked at the floor.

"Are you alright?" Will asked.

Alyssa looked into his eyes and hesitated. She glanced at the others as they carried on. They were uninterested, not paying any mind. Alyssa gulped and turned her attention back to Will. She couldn't hide her fear, and she knew Will was catching on to it.

"Why don't you take a seat," he suggested.

Alyssa nodded and followed Will to one of the sofas. They both sat down, and he watched her concernedly, wondering what could have her so tense. Alyssa kept her gaze at the floor, full of thought.

I should tell them...We are all in danger now.

She sighed and broke her silence.

"I know what has been causing the destruction in this town," she said calmly.

Kyle paused and looked away from Christian, focusing on Alyssa. Christian looked at Alyssa as well and then back at Kyle. Kyle held his finger, motioning for him to wait a moment as he carefully listened to Alyssa's calm voice.

"Do you remember when we left the press? I heard these...strange sounds. I became overwhelmed. Do you remember that?" she asked and looked back at Will, forgetting about the other two soldiers standing in the room with them.

"Yes, I do," he said.

"I continued to hear them especially when the earth began to tremble," she added and took in a deep breath. "When I fell below, the whispers stopped..." Alyssa paused and thought about the mythical beast. It's large, fiery eyes, the fire that danced around its pupils, and the fearsome scream that bellowed from its lungs haunted her mind as she looked back at the floor. "There is a dragon under this valley," she said and closed her eyes. She could practically hear the jaws dropping to the floor. Will looked at Kyle who was staring at them in dismay.

"Alyssa...You were passed out for quite some time. You must have dreamt this," Christian said.

Alyssa opened her eyes and took a deep breath.

"You've got to be mistaken," Kyle responded, looking back at Christian. He shook his head in disbelief.

81

"I know what I saw, and it was before I went to the station. Besides, haven't we seen something else lurking about that's a bit bizarre as well?" Alyssa asked and Will stood up, walking around the couch. He had placed his hand over his face and closed his eyes. Alyssa ignored him and kept her attention toward the captain. His expression was plastered with confusion. He didn't seem like he knew how to respond.

"I've seen this before. You were disoriented. All of your thoughts and dreams are probably still in a jumble. I wouldn't come to any conclusions just yet," Christian responded and Alyssa shook her head.

"No. We are in more danger now than we thought. You must believe me," she begged.

Christian sighed and quietly walked to the room he had come from. He quickly opened the door and disappeared behind it, closing it calmly. Alyssa could tell he left before he could become too angry and impatient with her. Kyle watched the door and then turned his attention to Will who had walked to the other side of the room across from Alyssa. He sighed and stepped out from behind his desk. "I'm going to get some water," he stated casually and approached the door that Christian had gone into. Will watched him disappear behind it before turning his focus back to Alyssa. She was already looking at him, her bright blue eyes catching his attention.

"Are you troubled, Alyssa?" he asked calmly, hoping not to offend her. He wanted any information that she could give them.

"I don't want to talk about that, Will," she blurted and quickly looked away. She didn't mean to express that thought.

I need to find a way out of this area and away from these men. How can I trust them? Maybe this information will keep them busy. I really need to be careful about what I say though...Damn it!

"Is that what you indeed saw?" Will asked.

He remained standing near the wall across from Alyssa and he seemed concerned. She looked at him and Will knew that she didn't have to respond. He could read it in her telling expression.

"You know, you are right. After what we have seen today, we shouldn't be surprised about what else we could possibly run into.

I'm sure Christian is just in denial," he said and walked to the back of the sofa that sat across from Alyssa. He placed his hands on it and carefully leaned against it, thinking about his mission.

How can we accomplish this task if there are more of these so called angras lurking about...and now the possibly of some kind of dragon? We do not stand a chance! Patrick was right...

A half smile rose across his face as he thought about Alex's statement while they were at the press.

I guess you were right too buddy...Satan is under this town.

Alyssa watched him carefully and thought about how she could possibly get away without being too suspicious. She wanted to find Kevin, but most of all she wanted to find her father.

I heard your voice dad...Somehow you are with me. I know you are still alive. I've got to find you. I don't think I can do this by myself.

Their thoughts were interrupted as the door to the entrance of the trailer suddenly opened. Patrick quickly stepped in and carefully closed the door behind him.

"This is bullshit, Will," he stressed and paused, noticing Alyssa sitting on the couch. "Oh, pardon me."

Alyssa nodded, remaining silent.

"Patrick, this is Alyssa. She made it after all," Will said, ignoring Patrick's remark as he pushed away from the couch.

"Well let me introduce myself properly," Patrick said and approached her, extending his right hand to her. "I'm Patrick McCallion."

Alyssa shook his hand firmly. "Alyssa Bennett."

"So how did you manage to get out?" Patrick asked as he sat across from her.

Alyssa straightened herself up and Will joined them, sitting beside Patrick.

"I was able to find an area where I could climb out," she responded.

"How did you find us?" Will asked.

"Christian and Travis found me at the station. I had an encounter with another one of those creatures. There are more," Alyssa replied.

Will shook his head, becoming frustrated himself.

"Well thankfully you are safe," Patrick said and stood up. He walked to the window in the back and looked out it as Will carefully moved over to where Patrick was sitting.

"Did you explain to Christian about your situation?" he asked and Alyssa nodded.

"Maybe my parents are at the hospital..."

"Well that is our evacuation point. We should be moving to that location soon," Will replied and looked behind him as a door opened.

"Sergeant First Class Thompson, glad to see that you are okay."

Will nodded to the soldier that walked into the room.

Patrick turned to look back at him as well. "Specialist Tidwell... You look rough," he said, looking at Travis's battered uniform and face.

"It's been hectic out there," Travis replied and Will stood up. Alyssa remained sitting. She watched the soldiers carefully.

"Tell me about it. This place is going to bury us alive if we don't get out of here soon," Patrick said and Travis quickly nodded.

"I don't believe anyone is still alive in this town. Did Moseley tell you about the bloodbath in the police station? It reeked of death," Travis stated and Will quickly looked at Alyssa. Grief struck her once again as she thought about her friends and coworkers.

"No, we arrived not too long ago," Patrick replied and Travis approached him. Will was still looking at Alyssa, watching her look away as she sighed sadly.

"What happened?" he asked her concernedly, remembering the first conversation they had in the press.

"Everyone was dead when I got there," she replied and bit her bottom lip.

If only they would stop asking all these damn questions...

"We weren't able to take a good look around. The moment we got there, we found a survivor and we were also attacked by some kind of monster," Travis said, completely oblivious to Alyssa sitting nearby.

Patrick quickly replied, "So were Thompson and his team. The captain said they were given a code name, the angra. What frustrates me is that this land is unstable and the group is dropping like flies.

84

It's not safe to stay here. They should destroy this place before these things escape."

"Damn…What the hell is going on in this valley?" Travis asked, looking back at Will and Alyssa. "Oh…I didn't even realize you were awake. How do you feel, ma'am?"

"I'm fine," Alyssa replied and looked away again as the door behind her opened. Kyle hurriedly walked into the room and approached the desk where his laptop sat.

"Sergeants First Class Thompson and McCallion, you have a new objective," he stated.

He sat down behind the desk and looked at the soldiers firmly. "I need you two to meet up with Master Sergeant Kennedy downtown. He may need some assistance with locating the police chief," he added.

Alyssa quickly looked at him. A little hope mixed with anxiety began to wash over her as she watched him carefully. She didn't want to seem too enthusiastic.

"Yes sir," Will said.

Patrick became confused. "Captain, I still don't understand why we can't move to City Hall right away," he said.

"We need to locate and secure Mr. Armstrong. He has access to City Hall. That building is a historical landmark, and we need to respect his wishes of not destroying it just to get around the barricades. If you find any survivors, escort them with you and rendezvous back here immediately. I know you are concerned and upset Sergeant First Class, but do not question your objective," Kyle responded.

Alyssa pushed herself to her feet. "Captain, perhaps I can be some assistance," she said and hoped she knew what she was getting herself into.

I know exactly where Robert will be if he is in the downtown area and as soon as I find him, I will tell him everything. He'll know what to do.

"You are a civilian. I can't put you in harm's way when it is my responsibility to keep you safe until evacuation."

"I understand, but as a police officer and close friend of Mr. Armstrong, I could be helpful with the objective. Besides, if Robert is downtown, I know where he'll be. I do not consider myself just a civilian, Captain," Alyssa said and Kyle thought for a moment.

Perhaps I could use her after all. Someone who knows the city very well and has police training? She has everything I need...This could be easier than I thought!

"Well, if you insist. Perhaps you could be some assistance to us. You already have the basic skills we could use," he said and Alyssa nodded.

"Are you sure about this, Alyssa?" Will asked. He remained standing across from her, surprised at her sudden change. She nodded and looked back at Kyle.

"Well if you stand by us we will do the same for you. Specialist Moseley had mentioned a situation regarding your folks earlier. We will do whatever it takes to determine their whereabouts and what may have happened," Kyle said and Alyssa nodded once more.

"Thank you," she said sincerely.

"Your holster and pistol were placed in the room you were examined in. You will need those, I'm sure," Kyle added and pointed to the door that Christian had entered.

Alyssa nodded and walked to the door, disappearing behind it. Will waited for her to close the door before looking back at Kyle.

"Make sure you load up. There's plenty of ammunition in the tent. I'm not sure what you all could possibly run into," Kyle said and Patrick walked to the front door of the trailer.

"Yes sir," Will stated and followed Patrick outside.

"Specialist Tidwell, I need you outside on the lookout until they come back. Specialist Moseley will assist you."

"Yes sir," Travis said and made his way out the front door as well. It shut quietly and silence filled the room. Kyle stared towards the door, a sense of uneasiness spilling into his gut. It was making him extremely uncomfortable. He carefully leaned back in the desk chair and folded his arms, pondering the possible outcomes of his mission. He knew what he got himself into was going to be extremely challenging and difficult, but it was a risk he was willing to take. Times were getting harder and people now-a-days were desperate and easier to bribe. He was one of them, but he knew he could use this to his advantage as well as he also thought about his soldiers or as he called them, minions.

I will definitely keep Alyssa around for a while. What a shame though when the time comes to it. She's such a rare woman...and beautiful at that. And Thompson. How the hell did he make it out earlier? I can't be caught off guard again, but perhaps I can use the both of them along side Kennedy for just a while. Let's just hope what Alyssa has seen is not accurate...

Kyle took in a deep breath and looked at his watch. He was becoming nervous. Time was slipping away from him and he lacked the patience needed for this task. He was determined to be successful. He had no choice now.

Chapter Eight

ALYSSA WAS STANDING NEAR THE desk where Christian had sat earlier, attaching her holster to her hip. She remained quiet as she kept a close eye on Christian. He was standing near the back door, examining his radio. It didn't seem to bother him that she was there.

"Are you leaving?" he calmly asked and lowered the radio, glancing at her.

"I'm going to tag along with you all for a bit. I offered my assistance," Alyssa replied and carefully placed the M9 into the holster.

Christian stared at her for a moment and noticed a difference in her.

"You must have had a change of heart. What about your folks?"

"Captain Smitherman stated that he'd do what he could to help me. Besides, I can't sit back and watch this place be consumed by all this destruction. If there's something that I can do to help, I'm in."

Christian narrowed his eyes as if in thought, but then he took in a deep breath and tilted his head back, examining Alyssa's expression.

"Well if you say so Officer Bennett. I guess I should apologize about earlier. It's really hard to believe what's going on in this valley. We can't make any contact with command. We can't get assistance. It seems like the Captain has become more eager to get to the hospital..." he said and paused, sitting his radio on a bookshelf that was standing against the wall next to him. He felt as if he was rambling to the wrong person about the issues they were facing.

Alyssa slowly nodded and stepped back to the door. She didn't feel comfortable being in the same room with him alone. Something about him was different. It made her anxious.

"Well if you are planning on going with Thompson and McCallion, good luck," Christian added and felt the floor gently rock beneath his feet.

Alyssa looked back at him as she placed her hand on the door knob. She felt it too. Christian was looking around him as they felt the trailer rock some more.

"Another quake," he said and Alyssa slowly shook her head. She had a strange sensation within her as she responded, "Something is outside."

She lowered her hand from the door knob and carefully pulled her M9 out from her holster. Christian looked toward the window as a loud screech began to pierce their ears. It sounded as if there were sharp knives dragging across the vinyl siding, tearing and ripping through it with ease.

"It knows we are here. That thing actually followed us?" he asked softly, carefully pulling his M9 from his holster and holding it close.

"There could be a lot of these things around here. It may not be the same one," Alyssa replied, her anxiety level intensifying.

She suddenly gasped, and looked towards the back of the room. The back door near Christian quickly swung open, startling the two of them. Christian looked over his shoulder, his heart suddenly racing. Will, Patrick, and Travis rushed into the room with their guns tightly in hand. Alyssa examined their firm expressions and stood still while Travis closed the door quietly.

"It's here," Will said and checked his magazine. He stepped around Christian and carefully approached Alyssa.

"We should get out of this trailer," she suggested and noticed Christian approaching the window from the corner of her eye. Travis was locking the dead bolt to the back door as Patrick turned his attention towards Will.

"No, Christian! Get back!" Alyssa shouted and Will quickly looked back at Christian who was leaning toward the glass.

"I don't see anything…" he said and suddenly, the glass shattered in his face as large claws tore through his torso, snatching him out of the trailer. Glass slung onto the floor and towards Patrick, bouncing off the walls and furniture. It all happened too fast for him. He blinked and froze. Christian was gone.

Travis loaded the M203 on the belly of his rifle. "Go!" he ordered and ran toward Will and Alyssa.

Will turned to reach for the handle of the door while Alyssa stared at the shattered window, completely immobilized with fear as she watched the monster from the police station pull itself into the room. It was the same one. Its large claws dug into the walls of the trailer, and it opened its large mouth, screaming viciously at them. Blood covered most of its thick hide. The wounds it received earlier were still visible. The monstrosity was an established killing machine, stalking its prey until its very last breath.

Will quickly opened the door to the lobby and grabbed Alyssa's arm, pulling and pushing her into the room with no hesitation. She stumbled and lost her balance, falling below Kyle's feet. Her body hit the floor and she yelped, pain striking her within her chest. She coughed and glanced up at Kyle in surprise. He was standing near her, aiming a 1911 into the room. A look of fear covered his face as he stared at the creature in pure shock. He had only received information regarding them and was made aware of their frequent sightings, but never had he seen one for himself. He didn't think that they would be this broad and atrocious. It was a sight straight out of a horror flick.

Patrick had pushed himself up against the wall. He was breathing heavily and was completely stunned. Travis was standing near Will, pressing his finger against the trigger of the grenade launcher. He steadily aimed and pulled back the trigger, firing a grenade at the angra. The explosion pushed the beast onto its side as its shrieking cry echoed throughout the trailer. Patrick looked away and closed his eyes, the heat brushing harshly against his skin, pushing him against the wall even more. He groaned through clenched teeth and clutched his M9 tightly.

"Get over here, McCallion!" Travis yelled, hoping Patrick would take the opportunity to get to them before the creature could get back on its hind legs.

Patrick was still breathing heavily, looking back at the others who stood near the doorway. He was afraid to move, but he knew he was allowing too much time to slip by before making a decision. He watched the beast carefully.

Kyle was helping Alyssa to her feet, and Will was aiming his rifle at the beast, waiting for a response from Travis and Patrick. Suddenly, the angra leaped back onto its feet and released a piercing cry that stung their eardrums. Alyssa screamed in fright and took a few steps back. Patrick hesitated, but decided to make a run for it. Travis stepped to the side, allowing an easy exit for him. The angra released another scream and jumped towards him.

"Fire!" Will yelled and Travis shook his head, his finger resting against the trigger of his rifle.

"I don't have a clear shot!" he shouted back and Patrick yelled in anguish. The angra snatched him with its large jaws, sinking its teeth into his back and shoulder as it threw him towards the broken window.

"Get out of the way!" Kyle yelled and pushed Will to the side.

Travis began firing his M4 at the beast's flesh and Kyle aimed his 1911 at its head. The angra screamed once more and turned its attention to Kyle, staring at him with its large, yellow eyes. Travis ceased fire and took a few steps back. The fear shot through him. The look of the beast's wicked eyes and evil stare was enough to make him retreat. The power behind the creature was too great. Even after the impact of the grenade and the 5.56mm rounds, it still stood, weakly, breathing heavily. Its inhale and exhale of breath was raspy and loud, sending chills down all of their spines. It remained standing and glaring at Kyle as if it were taunting him.

"You picked the *wrong* place to raid..." Kyle muttered and fired two rounds into the beast's skull, sending it back to the floor.

The angra screamed and struggled before resting its body on the carpet. Kyle kept the 1911 aimed at the beast, afraid it would miraculously get back up. Travis released a gust of air from his lungs and lowered his rifle. Patrick was gasping in pain as he remained lying on the floor surrounded by broken glass and blood. Will stepped into the room and approached the angra quickly and cautiously. He wasn't sure if the thing was dead or alive as he carefully stepped around it and towards Patrick. Alyssa stood in place and watched Kyle lower the large pistol in his grasp. The pistol looked familiar to her. She stared at it and thought about the officer that carried one similar to it. It was a prize of his, something he normally showed off to the ones who only had nine millimeters or forty caliber pistols. Sergeant Wesley was his name.

The officer that was obviously executed at the precinct. He was such an asset to the station, to this community...

Alyssa glanced at Will, watching him kneel down beside Patrick. "You are going to be alright," Will stated. Wounds surrounded Patrick's shoulder and blood continued to ooze onto the floor.

"Moseley's...rucksack is near the shelf," Patrick choked and his body began to tremble.

His skin was beginning to lose its tone, and his breathing was becoming difficult.

"I'll take care of him, Thompson," Kyle said and jogged around them and to the rucksack sitting on the floor. He picked it up carefully and opened it, retrieving gauze and bandages. Will stood up and allowed Kyle to kneel next to Patrick.

"I need you and Alyssa to head to the downtown area immediately. We can't waste any time now," Kyle stressed and held the gauze onto the wounds and began wrapping the bandages on top of them and around his shoulder. He then grabbed clips to secure the bandage, morphine, and a syringe. Will watched him clip the bandages and draw out the morphine. Kyle quickly injected the painkiller into Patrick's arm and placed the syringe next to him on the floor.

Will continued to watch for a moment. They had just lost two of their best medics. He couldn't help but wonder about the fates of the few medics that were still out there.

"Tidwell, you stay here with me. I'll need your help around here," Kyle added and Will took a few steps back.

"Hang in there, McCallion. We're going to get you out of here soon," he said and Kyle began to search through the rucksack. Travis tossed his M4 over his shoulder and onto his back, quickly making his way to Kyle and Patrick. He kept his composure rather well, a trait that took some time to strengthen.

Will turned around and looked back at the monster that lay lifelessly on the floor. Alyssa had already approached it. She was staring at it, thinking about her nightmares and the creatures that dwelled within them. Now that she had the chance to examine the angra and its details closely, she realized how similar they were. Alyssa slowly shook her head in disbelief.

I must be losing my mind...

Alyssa closed her eyes and rubbed her head gently. She thought about the hellish underworld and how it had become a part of her (and the residents') reality. She didn't know what was real and what wasn't anymore.

"Alyssa..." Will said and Alyssa lowered her hand and opened her eyes. "We need to go."

Alyssa took one last look at the angra and nodded. Will was concerned, but decided to ignore his thoughts as he turned around and approached the back door. Alyssa carefully followed and glanced at Kyle. He was cleaning and wrapping the rest of Patrick's wounds. Patrick's face was so different. Its once peachy color had faded and his eyes were closed, his body drunk with morphine. Alyssa sighed softly and followed Will onto the deck and into the tent.

"Know how to use one of these?" Will asked and held up an M4 carbine. Alyssa secured her M9 into the holster and carefully took the rifle from Will's grasp. She nodded and pursed her lips. She knew that their night was going to get even more interesting, and they weren't even sure of what else lurked about in the wilderness of Rockdale Valley.

"Thankfully we won't be traveling by foot. There are two ATVs outside. Since you know the area, I'll follow you," Will said and made his way out of the tent and to the four- wheelers that sat in front of it.

Alyssa gently secured the M4's sling over her shoulder and placed the weapon onto her back. She watched Will examine one of the Polaris ATVs and hoped that she was making the right decision by assisting his group. She could get herself in some serious shit if she weren't careful. She had to find Robert fast.

Alyssa approached the other ATV. Will was sitting down in the seat, watching Alyssa examine the Polaris next to him. He was still curious to why she had been so short with them earlier.

"Are you sure you want to do this?" he asked again, switching the engine on.

"Yes," she replied and sat down in the seat, switching the engine on as well. "Follow me," she added and carefully turned the four-wheeler away from the tent and began driving it towards an alley at the end of the cul-de-sac.

Will followed closely and kept a watchful eye on their surroundings as the roar of their engines echoed throughout the region and awakened the silent night.

As they carefully drove through the wreckage and debris, Alyssa's heart began to ache. She truly loved this town and driving through the familiar areas that were now trashed and destroyed deeply saddened her. She looked around and thought of these places as she and Will carefully drove through the deserted road.

They passed the post office where she would always run into Mrs. Betty, the kind, old lady with curly gray hair and a funny laugh. They passed the small grocery store that was owned by the cutest old couple who had just celebrated forty years of marriage. You could always find the best deals there, and the atmosphere was always pleasant. They also drove by a few small neighborhoods that were once the only houses in the valley. As night fell on the town, it seemed to Alyssa that everyone had simply perished. No one was in sight. The roads had cracks and tears throughout them, some completely gone due to a collapse in the earth. Trees and power lines had fallen. Cars and trucks were left abandoned with most of their windshields shattered onto the pavement. A few of the houses and buildings received extensive damage as well. Parts of them had collapsed from the quakes. Glass and wood particles littered the area and trash and leaves rolled gently with the breeze across the grass and pavement.

Alyssa felt torn. Tears began to fill her eyes, but she refused to let them spill onto her cheeks. She preferred to hide when in pain, but now it was too difficult for her to keep these kinds of emotions from showing. This made her feel extremely weak.

Alyssa's thoughts suddenly faded and she regained her composure. She noticed the small gas station in the distance. Soon they would be overlooking downtown. Once she saw the rows of businesses that made up the downtown area, her anxiety level grew. All she had to do now was find Robert. She hadn't looked behind her to check on Will, but she could still hear the engine to his Polaris roaring behind her. She would have preferred to do this mission alone.

Alyssa's heart began to race as she noticed a couple of police cars and fire trucks left in the middle of the road ahead, abandoned. A few of their lights were still flashing brightly, but still no one was in sight. Alyssa slowed down and they passed all the emergency vehicles cautiously. She scanned through the cars and the area around them but still had no luck with spotting life. Once they passed an overturned bus, she came to a stop in the middle of the road that split through downtown. Rows of businesses were connected to one another on each side of the street and continued around the bend to the right. Will came to a stop beside her and looked around, his face in awe. Alyssa noticed a familiar ATV in the distance. It sat near the valley's elegant and prominent fountain. A large factory stood behind it and appeared vacant. She scanned the historical area carefully. Like the rest of the southern valley, it seemed dead and wasted.

"Isn't that one of yours?" Alyssa asked and looked at Will.

He was examining the Polaris in the distance and nodded.

"I believe so," he replied.

Alyssa moved her four-wheeler to the side before switching the engine off. Will followed and parked his next to hers. He eased himself off carefully, staring towards the other ATV.

"Let's split up. I'm going to check this area," Alyssa said without any hesitation, hoping Will would accept and venture off on his own. She slid off the four-wheeler, trying to read Will's expression.

Will glanced at the bookstore they stood near and thought for a moment. Alyssa grew apprehensive.

"Alright, I'll try and find Brad. Hopefully we can locate this police chief," Will replied and Alyssa took in a deep breath through her nostrils and released it slowly.

"Okay. Be careful," she said and turned to approach the bookstore that sat next to the café.

Will nodded and replied, "You too."

He turned away and made his way down the deserted street to the other Polaris. He left with no questions and without looking back. Alyssa was relieved. Maybe she had fooled him after all.

Silence soon filled the atmosphere as Alyssa watched Will cross the street and disappear into an antique store. Once he was out of sight, she turned around and looked at the small bookstore. She loved this one better than any large bookstore chain miles away in the city. There was something about mom and pop stores she was fond of.

Alyssa approached the large glass window and peeked through it. A few shelves had fallen over and books and cards littered the floor. It looked empty, just like everything else. She sighed and glanced at the entrance to the café. Her first priority was to find Robert, regardless of who or what else she may run into.

She carefully approached the entrance and stepped over the restaurant's sign that usually stood on the sidewalk near the glass door. She realized that the glass itself had been broken. A few shards were still left intact. Alyssa gently pulled the door open and locked it in place. She glanced in the small restaurant, a familiar stench rushing through her nostrils as a look of disgust formed on her face. She carefully stepped inside and her mouth dropped. She slowly looked at all the debris in front of her. Tables and chairs had been thrown over and dishware and more glass were shattered on the carpet. Blood covered parts of the floors and walls, and Alyssa noticed a few tablecloths on the floor, spotted with dirt and blood. Her heart sank. She realized that the cloths were covering up the bodies of the deceased. How long they had been there was a mystery. Blood seeped through the white linen and the carpet, its strong scent congesting the dining area. Alyssa didn't know where to start. She stared at the scene and glanced toward the back near the bar. It was quiet. There were no signs of life. Everything was still, too still. It rattled Alyssa's nerves. She decided to shake the nightmarish images from her mind and approach the kitchen in the back. She took steady breaths, keeping an eye behind her. She didn't want any unexpected surprises.

My God...This is just terrible. What if we were too late?

Alyssa cautiously stepped up to the double doors that lead to the kitchen and peeked inside the small, oval window. Food and cookware covered the tile floor and flour and breadcrumbs dusted the countertops. No one was in sight. Alyssa slowly opened the right door and looked inside. Silence filled the area and it smelled of cooking oil. She took a deep breath through her nostrils. Maybe if she didn't find Robert she could still get away from Will and his group of Green Berets so she could find Kevin. He was one person she could still trust.

Alyssa realized that idea was probably the only option she had left and slowly closed the door. As it shut softly, her heart suddenly sank deep within her chest. A soft click was heard directly behind her, sending the adrenaline throughout her body. She knew what it was immediately and slowly raised her hands, staring in front of her.

"Who are you?" a man's voice asked behind her. He seemed confused in his tone. Alyssa thought about the pistol on her hip and the M4 resting against her back as she carefully spoke up. "Officer Bennett. I'm here to help."

"Turn around slowly," the man demanded and Alyssa slowly turned to face the stranger. She was breathing heavily, staring at the .38 Special that was aimed directly at her. She then turned her attention to the man who was holding it and examined his clothing and facial features. He didn't look hostile. Maybe he was scared. His thick, dark brown hair was ruffled, and his brown eyes focused on her with fear and suspicion. He wore civilian clothes that were torn and battered. He appeared nervous, his breaths inhaling and exhaling rapidly.

"You don't look like a cop," the man said and continued to point the revolver at her.

Alyssa slowly pulled the sling down on her shirt. "Look," she stated. She flashed the logo on her shirt, and the man shook his head in denial.

"It's just a shirt. I can't trust anyone in this town anymore. The residents have gone crazy, and then monsters began to show up. People started to loot and some vanished."

"I know...I've seen the things. I understand your fear, but you must believe me. I'm assisting a group with the Army Special Forces, and there's a soldier here with me on the other side of the street checking out those areas," Alyssa replied. The man slowly lowered his pistol halfway.

"Josh...Josh!" a scratchy voice called out. It came from the left side of the building as Alyssa and the man quickly looked towards the shaky voice.

"I'm out here! One second!" he called back and Alyssa took in a deep breath, realizing the man in front of her was this Josh character.

"Josh...who is back there?" she asked.

Josh was still gripping onto his .38 Special, staring at her. "How do I know I can trust you?" he asked, ignoring her question.

"Because I may be the only one who can help you," Alyssa replied.

"Alyssa?" the shaky voice faintly called out.

Alyssa looked back towards an open door near the dining area, and Josh lowered his pistol to his side. He took a few steps back, taking a deep, steady breath. Alyssa was finally able to lower her hands. She dropped them to her side and walked toward the open door.

"Thank you," she stated sincerely once she stepped passed Josh and approached the door that lead to a hallway. It stretched to the left and right of her as she looked to the left, noticing the office. She could see a pair of legs and a chair, but the rest of the body was hidden by the wall. Alyssa slowly approached the man.

"It's Alyssa," she said and stepped to the left before getting too close so she could see the rest of the man that was sitting in the chair. Her heart dropped once her eyes met his face. She quickly approached the man, kneeling down beside the chair he sat in. She didn't want to believe that the raspy voice was his. She denied the possibility.

"Oh my God...Chief..." she said and examined Robert's wrapped up wounds. Blood had seeped through the cloth and onto the chair. Alyssa noticed a few drops that had trickled onto the floor as well.

"I thought that was you...Why did you come back here? I thought you were leaving for a while," Robert forced out. His voice was shaky and his skin was pale.

Alyssa became overwhelmed as she thought of everything that had happened since her arrival into town.

"I didn't know it was like this..." she said and broke down. Tears began to fill her eyes and her voice became weak. "I don't know why all of this is happening. I'm so afraid," she blubbered.

Robert took a few deep breaths. "Alyssa...you need to get out while you still can. There are things out there that are very deadly. People have been disappearing not to mention the Mayor who is amongst the deceased, and we've also been hearing some strange noises deep underground. It's probably going to get a lot worse. You must leave now," Robert choked and began to breathe heavily.

Alyssa wiped the tears away and looked at the man who had become family to her.

"My parents are missing, Chief. Their house was obliterated. Someone or *something* was there. I came to find them. I had no choice," she said and noticed Robert's concerned expression.

"Oh no…Alyssa, I am so sorry that you have been pulled into the middle of all this. I am so sorry…" Robert said and closed his eyes, his body weakening. A few tears were rolling down his cheeks.

"Chief, what are you talking about?" Alyssa asked, confused from the statement. She wiped a few more tears that dripped down her cheeks and sniffled. Robert slowly opened his eyes and looked at her.

"You…just need…to get out," he said weakly.

Alyssa became nervous and afraid as she looked behind her, noticing Josh standing in the hallway.

"I think we're in a lot of danger, Chief, not only because of the strange things happening here," she said, turning her attention back to him. He was still looking at her, but decided not to respond. His body was weakening as the minutes went by.

"I went to the station and there was a massacre. Everyone was dead, *murdered.* They weren't killed by the monsters stalking this valley. They were actually killed from gunshot wounds. I found a letter from Kevin. He stated that the person behind the murders was a man in military uniform. Probably someone deployed here right now," Alyssa stressed.

Robert became alarmed as he thought of the soldiers he was going to meet earlier.

I was going to meet a Captain Smitherman…I wasn't expecting this to become a death trap. Oh God, why did this have to happen? It wasn't supposed to get like this. They all must be after the same thing. If only I had a choice before. This may have been prevented…

Robert's thoughts were interrupted as Alyssa urgently stated, "We need to get you out of here."

Robert slowly shook his head. "Alyssa…look at me. I'm not going anywhere," he replied.

Alyssa's heart ached. She tried to think of something to say, but nothing was coming to mind. There was no hope left for him so she refused to mention Uktena. She sighed softly and closed her eyes, fighting back the tears that were trying to push their way out.

"Please...could you get me a wet dish towel from the back?" Robert asked. Alyssa nodded and slowly stood up. She looked down the hallway and noticed that Josh was gone.

"I'll be right back," she said and made her way back down the hallway and into the restaurant.

Josh was standing near the entrance, looking out it as Alyssa made her way back to the kitchen. She took in a deep breath and cleared her mind as she pushed open one of the large doors and looked around. Working in the restaurant industry back in her teens, she knew exactly where to look. In the back the chefs usually kept their clean towels on racks or shelves. Alyssa quickly stepped around the dish pit and to the prep area in the back. After she passed two large sinks and stainless steel countertops, she noticed a shelf towards the right. Some towels and sanitizing buckets were left unused as she examined the contents of the shelf. Alyssa sighed heavily and looked down at the tile floor, her heart continuing to ache. She wasn't ready to return to Robert, not yet anyway. She couldn't help but ponder. Deep down she knew she was going to be on her own. It was too risky to stand alongside the soldiers, and it seemed that the civilians were a bit paranoid as well.

More tears finally made their way down her cheeks as she broke down once again and collapsed on the cold, hard floor. Alyssa buried her face into the palm of her hands and continued to cry. She didn't know what to do. She didn't know who to trust. She became more afraid and alone than she could possibly imagine. But she knew she had to get herself together somehow. If she was going to survive this, she had no other options.

CHAPTER NINE

DEATH WAS ALL THAT MADE up Rockdale Valley. Will was beginning to lose hope. He didn't think he'd find any survivors or Master Sergeant Brad Kennedy for that matter. All he saw in each of the stores he had stepped foot into was death. The area even smelled of the deceased. Will had seen casualties before, but this was different. The valley resembled the after effects of an apocalyptic war.

"Brad!" Will called out as he stepped out of a barber shop and back onto the sidewalk near the large fountain. The last two stores were trashed and had no signs of life. Brad wasn't among the dead either, and Will had no idea what the Chief looked like so he decided to keep looking. He carefully approached the large fountain and examined the factory that stood behind it. It looked old and abandoned, but the landscaping around it was kept up rather nicely. A few trees and rosebushes stood near the large building and green Bermuda grass sat on both sides of the concrete walkway. The path stretched from the sidewalk and to the double doors of the factory. Will approached it, keeping a close eye around him. The atmosphere remained quiet and calm.

Will stopped once he reached the doors and examined the sign that stood near it in the grass. He was about to enter a feed, farm, and tractor supply company as he carefully grabbed one of the doors and pulled it open. The strong scent of grain and oat quickly filled his nostrils. It was a smell he wasn't used to. He stepped inside the large, old building. It was dark. The little light from outside came through the stained windows but shone dimly onto the wooden floor as Will scanned the area. There were a few rows of shelves situated in the middle of the room and they contained all sorts of farming products necessary to clean and care for gardens and animals. Towards the back were tables that contained animal feed and hay bales. Will examined an office across from him and walked toward it. There was a large window by the door which was hanging open. He noticed a row of light switches on the wall near a first aid kit once he stepped inside the office and flipped a few on. The lights remained off, and Will glanced at a desk that sat against the wall. Paper and files were stacked on top of it, and a computer monitor sat off centered.

It's too quiet...there's no one here.

Will carefully stepped out of the office and looked at a flight of stairs.

"Is anyone here!" he yelled.

Silence quickly filled the area. He continued to look around as he walked to another set of double doors beside the office. The windows were too stained to look out so he carefully pushed the door open and stepped outside behind the building. A few outdoor equipment and tractors sat in the lawn to the right and a large creek split through the earth, traveling around the back side of downtown. It was flowing fast but gentle as Will slowly stepped off the concrete slab and approached the water's edge. He took in a deep breath and stood near the creek once he reached it. The sound of the water streaming away and the gentle touch of the wind on his face relaxed his mind and body as he examined the surrounding areas. A small field was located behind the creek and far in the distance, the mountainous terrain made up the rest. They stretched as far as the eye could see, wrapping snuggly around the valley. A part of the terrain eventually caught Will's attention as he realized some of the earth in the distance had been pushed upward into jagged ledges. They looked steep.

How much longer can we afford to stay here? No one is left... and hopefully the ones who were able to get out did so safely. We are wasting our time here...

Will took in another deep breath and looked toward the tractors. He noticed a large patch of dirt and sand beside the gates of the tractor yard and a smaller field with trees and benches beside the parking area. He admired the valley's beauty and in some ways its serenity. He was able to look past the devastation and see the placidity the way it once was. Will breathed in the fresh air. He felt comfortable at the moment.

It's a shame that a place like this would experience something so drastic...so bizarre...

His thoughts were quickly interrupted as he heard a couple of voices in the distance. Will became alert and approached a large, blue tractor, hiding himself behind it. He was staring into the distance where the voices were coming from. They became louder. He knew they were heading in his direction. He breathed slowly, quietly, waiting for them to come into view. The footsteps were soon heard, and Will looked around the tractor, catching a glimpse of two soldiers walking around a wooden shed that was located near the small park area. He could hear the gravel underneath their feet, the stressed tones in their panting breaths. After a moment, Will finally realized who the two men were. He sighed in relief and carefully came out from behind the tractor, making his way towards them. The two soldiers stopped, looking at him in surprise.

One raised his hand. "Thompson!" he called out.

Will waved in return. He was thrilled to see someone remaining from their group. He carefully opened the gate to the tractor yard and jogged to the two soldiers.

"Privates Watkins and Wainwright. I can't tell you how happy I am to see you both," Will said and shook their hands once he reached them.

"We could say the same. Our radios haven't been working. We, ah...lost Specialist Perez and Private Harper. We were trying to make our way to the TOC, but some of the roads are heavily damaged. So we took this route," Evan Watkins replied, breathing heavily.

Both of the soldiers' uniforms were battered and covered in dirt and dust. A few scrapes and bruises were on their arms and faces, blood drying on them.

"What happened?" Will asked and Evan looked at Carlton Wainwright.

"The building we were in collapsed. We were lucky to have made it out," Carlton replied and looked towards the creek near them. He was winded and upset. There was frustration in his tone and his eye brows were pulled together, tensed. Will felt sorry for the kid. Even for his youthful age, he had a good sense of right and wrong, and he also had a really big heart.

"We lost a few others today as well," Will replied. "Everything that the residents have stated has been true. Right now we are trying to find Master Sergeant Kennedy and locate the police chief. I can fill you in on details later. I have a former cop assisting me at the moment. She's searching the other side."

"So has the mission changed?" Evan asked.

"No, but our top priority is to locate and secure the police chief. If we find survivors on our way then we will escort them to safety which is still Trinity Hospital. But the chief hadn't met up with Captain Smitherman yet, so this is why we are here. We need to get into City Hall. It'll get us through the barricades. The chief has what we need," Will replied. Evan and Carlton nodded.

Will turned and looked back at the factory. "I haven't found anyone left alive in this area. I think we should go and check on Alyssa. Maybe she's had more luck," he added.

"Where did you find this lady?" Evan asked as they began walking towards the street by the factory.

"She actually found me. My team and I encountered this large creature. Captain says they've given it a code name, the angra. They are very powerful," Will replied and took in a deep breath, exhaling roughly. "It killed my team. I on the other hand was just lucky. Alyssa happened to find me in the press after trying to hide from the thing," he added and Carlton shook his head in astonishment.

"What the hell?" Evan whispered, awestruck.

"Well we haven't come across anything but death and destruction. We were trying to get a couple of survivors out of the office we were in, but it didn't hold up long enough for us all to get out," Carlton said, completely oblivious to what Will had just stated about the angra. He felt terrible about the people they had tried to save.

"Don't beat yourself up about it, okay?" Will said and looked at Carlton as they stepped into the street and made their way across it. He slowly nodded. Will knew he had a lot to learn from this job. He was in his place once before.

Alyssa was still sitting on the cold, tile floor. Her tears had finally ceased. She knew she couldn't sit there all day and wonder what her next move was going to be. She carefully pushed herself off the ground and grabbed a dish towel. After rinsing it with cool water, she squeezed out the excess and slowly made her way out of the kitchen. Alyssa was hoping that the chief hadn't become worried about her as she pushed open the double doors and stepped back into the restaurant. Josh was behind the small bar getting a glass of ice water. He glanced at her, noticing her flushed face.

"Are you alright?" he asked.

Alyssa nodded and carefully made her way back to the office where Robert waited. He was still sitting in the chair and his eyes were closed. She held the towel and placed her hand gently on his arm. He moved slightly and slowly opened his eyes. His skin had become paler and his breathing had become irregular. Alyssa knew he didn't have much longer, but she hoped she was going to be able to stay with him for as long as she could.

"I brought you a towel," she said and handed it to him.

"Thank you," he replied slowly.

Alyssa carefully sat on the desk near him and sighed.

"Here…" Robert said and slowly opened his hand that was resting in his lap. Most of his strength was gone. Alyssa reached down and carefully picked up a set of keys.

"I was...going to meet a Captain Smitherman...and give these to him. The large key will get you into City Hall. Please...get yourself to the hospital. Get out of here," he added slowly.

Alyssa nodded, remembering what the captain had stated at the tactical operations center.

"I know who the captain is..." she said and paused.

Should I even go back and give these to him? Why does this have to be so difficult...Some of the soldiers seem sincere, but I've been fooled before.

"Alyssa..." Josh called from the hallway, interrupting her thoughts. Alyssa looked up at him.

"There are a few soldiers coming this way," he said and disappeared back into the restaurant.

Alyssa slowly looked back at Robert. He was looking at her, but he wore no expression. She knew he didn't have much time remaining. Her anxiety grew.

"Chief...I don't know what to do," she whispered.

Robert took in a deep breath. "You must...listen to your heart. If...you feel you can't trust any of these men...Go. But I don't think... you can do this alone. There's...something...I need to tell you," he said forcefully. Alyssa became more afraid as the adrenaline began to rush into her veins once again. She was terrified.

"What is it, Chief?" she asked and focused all of her attention on him.

He was breathing heavily, slowly wiping his face with the wet towel. A tear had dripped down his cheek as he took a deep breath in.

"Your father...was..." he whispered and began coughing. He had to take a few more deep breaths before spitting anything else out.

"Alyssa...Please...Just...get out..." he added softly and his breathing began to slow and his eyes began to close.

Alyssa pushed herself off the desk and stared at his body as it slowly slumped over in the chair. Her heart pounded and the tears began to fill her eyes.

"Robert..?" she asked and remained staring at his lifeless body.

Oh no...what was he about to tell me? Oh why did I have to break down earlier! I should have just got the damn towel and came straight back. I could have had more time. Maybe he could have given me the answers I needed...Damn it! Why is this happening to me! Why!

Sadness and anger overwhelmed her as she clenched her teeth and balled her hands into fists. She quickly stepped out of the office and into the hallway, making her way back to the dining area. Once she stepped back into the restaurant, she noticed Josh and Will as well as two other soldiers talking outside. She stopped and stared at them, ignoring the awful stench and hidden bodies. She wasn't sure what they were talking about. Their voices seemed eager, but low. Alyssa relaxed herself and looked back at the keys in her hand. Perhaps she could sneak away and get into City Hall herself. She carefully stuffed the keys into her pocket and looked back at the others outside. She was becoming more afraid. She wanted to get out of the area. She wanted to get away from everyone and just be alone...Or did she? She kept questioning herself. She was confused and desperate, her body panic stricken.

"Well Josh, thanks for the information. I'm sure we would have run into Kennedy if he were still in the area," Will said. They remained standing outside near the entrance to the café.

Josh nodded. "You all were just too late. The damage has been done. I don't think Robert will be able to come back with us either. He was losing too much blood, and there was really nothing that I could do," he said and Will looked into the café. He noticed Alyssa standing in the middle of it, staring back at them with an expression he couldn't quite read. He slowly stepped up to the door.

"Alyssa?" he asked concernedly.

She took in a deep breath, collected her thoughts, and carefully approached them outside. Will stepped out of her way as she walked out of the restaurant and onto the sidewalk. She didn't look at the other soldiers or Will for that matter. She focused her attention onto the pavement in front of her.

"The chief is dead. His wounds were just too severe," she said and wiped under her eyes.

Will could see her pain and slowly nodded. "Were you able to speak with him?" he asked.

"Yes..." Alyssa said and looked at him. She refused to say more as Will quickly replied, "Were you able to get what we needed?"

Alyssa waited to respond and took in a deep breath. She knew she couldn't lie to him. She was never a good liar anyway, and now it was too late for her to run.

Damn it...

"He did give me the keys to City Hall. I'm sure that's all the captain needed, right?"

Will nodded, respecting her tense, strained tone and looked at the other two soldiers. "Privates Watkins and Wainwright, this is Officer Bennett. She will be assisting us," he said and Evan and Carlton nodded.

"We could definitely use more like you, ma'am," Evan said, admiring her.

Carlton wasn't sure what to think as he continued to study Alyssa's features. He could tell she was young with a pretty face, but he wasn't sure if she would be able to keep up with them after being placed in the midst of a new war, one that only existed in horror stories.

Alyssa nodded at the soldiers and looked back toward the road as she carefully stepped up to it. She closed her eyes and took in a breath, trying to calm herself so she could focus on what her next move was possibly going to be. She ignored the conversation that Will and the others started to have as an image started to creep into her mind. It looked to be the underworld she was so familiar with, but she wasn't sure why at this very moment. There were crystals hanging inside the cave, and there were a few pits of bright, hot lava. There were no volcanoes in the area which confused her as to why they were there in the first place. Then the peculiar growl echoed in her mind, and the image of the familiar devilish eyes flashed back at her. Alyssa quickly opened her eyes and stared ahead, her heart beating rapidly. The strange sensation began to erupt inside her and the adrenaline began to flush into her veins, warming her body quickly.

She looked back at the others. They were still talking about the events occurring in town until Josh noticed her worried expression.

"What is it?" he asked and the others looked at her.

They all became alarmed as Alyssa urgently stated, "We got to get out of here."

Will looked around, remembering this look in front of the press.

"We need to get out of here now," she added, the odd whispers beginning to flow with the breeze around her. She wasn't sure if the others heard them, but she decided to keep quiet about it especially after she noticed Evan looking at her peculiarly.

"Uh, are you okay?" Evan asked.

"You don't understand…" Alyssa said and frantically scanned the area. "She's here," she added.

Will glared at her. "She?" he asked and watched Alyssa approach her ATV.

As soon as she sat down, she looked up at him and realized that she may have said a bit too much. No one else had seen the thing yet. Before she was able to respond, something moved in the distance, catching her attention from the corner of her eye. Alyssa looked toward the fountain and noticed five large dogs walking in the middle of the street. Will and the others looked as well until Josh gasped and slowly stepped toward Alyssa. That's when she realized that they were not dogs, but large, silver wolves. There thick, gray fur laid back, their noses sniffing the wind.

The two wolves in the front suddenly stopped and looked at them.

"Alright…let's go. Watkins, Wainwright, you two take that four-wheeler. Josh, you can ride with us," Will said and carefully walked toward Alyssa. She quickly pushed herself back and allowed him to take control as he sat in front of her, switching the engine on. Josh sat behind Alyssa and looked back at the wolves as they began prowling toward them, their heads lowered.

"Come on!" Will exclaimed.

Evan and Carlton jumped on the other Polaris and fired the engine up. The loud roar of the engine sent the wolves into frenzy as they howled and began running toward them. Will stomped on the gas and drove up onto the side walk, turning the Polaris back towards the way they had come from. Carlton and Evan quickly followed.

The wolves were getting closer, their drool spilling onto the pavement around them after every vicious growl. More howls were heard in the distance, awakening the area and echoing in the distance. Alyssa was completely shocked that the wolves were actually in the valley. She thought it was only a rumor that they had traveled to this area. She turned and buried her face into Will's vest, becoming more frightened.

Both four-wheelers drove through the deserted street and towards the emergency crew that still sat abandoned in the middle of it as Evan looked back at the pack of wolves that continued to chase them. He quickly aimed his M9 at one and began firing, missing with every shot. The cracked, jagged street threw off his aim as they drove over large tears in the pavement.

"Shit!" Evan exclaimed and looked at Will, feeling an awkward sensation. The ground had begun to shake.

Alyssa pulled her face away from Will's vest and looked behind her, seeing the silver wolves stumble as large cracks began to rip through the pavement. Josh looked behind him as well and began to feel the instability of the Polaris.

"What the hell?" Will asked and looked at Carlton who was having trouble controlling his ATV.

"Uktena," Alyssa said softly and realized that the whispers that had once surrounded her ceased.

"Can't this thing go any faster!?" Evan exclaimed.

Will was able to drive ahead and past the abandoned emergency vehicles, getting a further lead.

"I think something is wrong!" Carlton yelled and began to panic as he heard the wolves yelp.

Evan looked behind him and witnessed the earth push upward and suddenly fall. The road quickly collapsed, sending the pavement and parts of the earth deep into pits below. The wolves fell into them and disappeared as the earth continued to collapse behind them, trailing them as if it was trying to consume them. The emergency vehicles began to slide and fall into the large pit as the back end of the fire truck and its ladder were sucked into the ground.

"Go!" Evan yelled and Alyssa and Josh watched in horror as the ground beneath Carlton and Evan quickly came up, sending their Polaris into the air.

"What the…!" Carlton exclaimed and Evan jumped off to the side as the large snout and head of Uktena came up from beneath them. The earth stopped shaking and the pavement suddenly stopped collapsing into the deep pit. Smoke and dust floated above the long trench as the ground settled in place.

Josh and Alyssa watched Carlton's Polaris erupt into flames once it crashed onto the pavement near a building, its fire brightening up the area. Alyssa gripped tighter onto Will's vest, overwhelmed with fear. The sudden explosion caused Will to skid to a halt as he looked behind him, his mouth quickly dropping. Carlton and Evan were gone, and a small fire blazed towards the sky. The dragon was briskly pulling herself out of the earth, her long snaky body pushing off slabs of pavement along the way.

"My God…" Will whispered, frozen by what he was witnessing.

Uktena pulled half of her body out from the underworld and slammed her palms and claws into the pavement around her, opening her large mouth and releasing a piercing cry at them. Alyssa gasped and covered her ears, the cry pushing past them. Uktena pulled the rest of her body out of the crumbled earth and floated towards the sky.

"What are you doing!" Josh exclaimed. He was full of fear and his heart was racing away. He continued to hold onto his .38 Special, knowing it was useless at this point.

Will glanced toward the fire and realized that the others were nowhere to be seen. He was breathing heavily, wondering what to do next as Alyssa gasped, "Will! Go!"

He quickly sped down the deserted street as Uktena lowered herself to the pavement, slowly closing in on them. Alyssa looked back at the dragon and gazed into her fiery eyes. Uktena stared back into hers, the fire dancing around her pupils. Her gaze began to mesmerize Alyssa. She had suddenly forgotten about clinging onto

Will's vest and Josh's tightening grip from his legs against her thighs as she began to feel calm. The world around her slowly began to fade and Uktena and downtown Rockdale Valley disappeared. Another image began to project into her mind as she carefully turned and buried her face gently into Will's vest once again.

"Why is the area taped off, Dad?" Alyssa asked her father. They were standing in the woods of the mountains near Rockdale Valley. They had reached a small meadow surrounded by mountainous rock. Yellow caution tape was secured around trees near a tight entrance to a cave and large boulders and rock sat near the small entrance. They had just passed a sign stating Government Property which already made Alyssa nervous.

"I'm sure there is an explanation. Just wait one second," James said and went under the tape and approached an older man who had a concerned expression on his face.

"James...I thought it was just going to be you and Robert," the man said softly.

"Come on, Brian, you know how Alyssa and I enjoy a journey through the trails. What's this about?"

Brian took in a deep breath and the image slowly faded to the back porch of the Bennett residence. Alyssa was sitting down in a chair, watching the sun fade behind the acres of trees. Her father had just stepped out onto the porch and closed the glass door near her. Alyssa turned her attention to him and sighed softly.

"They are getting worse," she said and her father sat in the patio chair next to her.

"The doctor did say it may take some time before they go away. But look at it this way, these dreams could be a way of trying to help you release all of your fears," he replied. Alyssa looked at his hand. He appeared to be holding some kind of chain.

"I don't understand why you won't just tell me what happened," she said with a bit of frustration.

"Because I'm not ready to, Alyssa. I don't think it will help you get better. My main concern is your health right now."

Alyssa sighed heavily and looked back at the fading sunlight.

"There is something I would like to give you though," James added and held up a necklace.

Alyssa looked back at him, noticing the polished red rock. The pendant was white gold and it gently caressed the stone. The sunlight touched it and Alyssa was mesmerized by its luster.

"It looks like a gemstone. Where did you get this?" Alyssa asked and gently grabbed the necklace, pulling it to her.

"I had it made by Mrs. Rose from downtown. The stone came from our hike in the mountains," James replied and slowly stood up.

Alyssa admired the necklace, but no memory was coming to her. She couldn't remember the evening in the mountains, and it didn't matter what surprises her father gave her. It wasn't going to help her recall anything, and it wasn't going to make her feel better. She knew if she asked about the accident again, her father would walk away... like he always did...

And as quickly as it began, the image faded to a blur. Her vision remained fuzzy, and she could hear herself screaming into the palms of her hands as blood dripped steadily from her nose onto her shirt.

"Alyssa!" Will yelled and tried to check on her as he looked behind him quickly. He noticed the blood dripping from the palms of her hands onto her blue jeans and gasped. Josh yelled in fright and began firing his .38 at the dragon's face, knowing it was useless.

"Oh shit! Hang on!" Will yelled once he turned his attention back in front of him. He had no time to turn the Polaris safely to get out of the way of the tall, jagged ledge in the pavement. Will clenched his teeth as they jumped over it. He could feel Alyssa's grasp getting tighter on his vest until the Polaris slammed into the pavement below, blowing out a front tire. Josh and Alyssa were thrown off to the side and Will suddenly lost control of the four-wheeler as it swerved around violently. He gasped and pushed himself off, rolling onto the pavement near a car. Josh had sat himself up and pushed himself toward an abandoned truck, fear overwhelming him. He hoped the beast hadn't spotted him.

The dragon came over the ledge and slowly stopped, floating its long, snaky body above the ground. Josh pushed himself behind the tail end of the truck and watched as Alyssa crawled across the pavement, gasping for air. Her necklace was hanging over her shirt, dangling in front of her. She noticed the red stone gleaming brightly and stopped, gently placing the pendant into her hand. She carefully wiped the blood away from her face and stared at the mysterious necklace, ignoring what waited behind her. The stone glistened in the moonlight brightly, as Alyssa stared at it, mesmerized. Gunfire suddenly erupted in the distance, startling her as another loud scream exited the lungs of Uktena, piercing through the atmosphere. Alyssa felt weak, but she carefully rolled onto her back and sat herself up slowly. She noticed Will running across the street toward her from her peripheral vision, firing his M4 at Uktena's snout. Alyssa couldn't help but gaze into the eyes of the dragon. It glared back at her and the necklace that was lying in the palm of her hand, not shaken by the bullets that struck it repeatedly. The red hues of the rock began to illuminate and the atmosphere around them grew calm and silent. The gunfire suddenly ceased, and Will fell to his knees beside Alyssa, grabbing her arms as he looked at the blood that was on her clothes. He was frightened and full of adrenaline. All he wanted to do was get Alyssa away from the beast.

"Come on!" he yelled and realized that the dragon was glaring into Alyssa's blue eyes. It hadn't moved yet, but Will didn't want to sit there any longer.

"Are you alright?" he whispered, but Alyssa remained unresponsive. It looked as if she were in a trance. Will noticed her unique necklace and turned his attention back to Uktena.

The dragon's loud exhale of breath sent a chill down Josh's spine as he watched the scene in horror. He was afraid to move. The fear and anxiety froze him as he took steady breaths, trying to remain calm.

The wind began to pick up and Alyssa began to breathe heavily. The strange sensation continued to consume her, crippling her stamina and reflexes. Her thoughts were frozen. Her mind was blank. But all of this was quickly shaken as a grenade suddenly exploded against the side of Uktena's snout, erupting into hot, bright flames. The dragon screamed ferociously and lifted toward the sky as another grenade exploded near its neck. Will pulled Alyssa up and noticed Josh stepping around the truck.

"We got to move!" Josh exclaimed and Will nodded.

"Come on, Alyssa. Snap out of it," Will said firmly and Alyssa looked into his bright green eyes. She quickly nodded in agreement and Will began pulling her towards an alley as gunfire began to echo in the distance.

"Let's move," he said and they began running towards the dark alley.

Alyssa took a glance behind her and watched the dragon swiftly disappear back into the earth from the large pit it had created. The ground around them began to shake as they carefully ran through the rugged street. After passing a few abandoned cars and jumping over large tears, they carefully ran past a few other offices and into the trashed alley.

"Wait up!" a familiar voice called out behind them.

Will stopped and looked back towards the street. Alyssa was panting. She quickly approached the brick wall they stood near and slid her body down against it, sitting down on the cool concrete that made up the alley. Evan was jogging toward them, covered in dirt. Blood was dripping down his arms and the side of his face. Scrapes and cuts were visible on parts of his skin. Josh slowed to a walk and stopped near the end of the alley, glancing back at Evan. He was still in shock and was becoming impatient.

"I thought that was one of you," Will said and Evan approached him, catching his breath.

"Carlton didn't make it," Evan stated and looked back toward the deserted street, his face distraught.

"Can we just get the hell out of here, please?" Josh immediately asked. Will and Evan turned their attention to him.

"That thing is gone...It went back underground," Evan replied.

Josh shook his head. "And it can come back. I seriously don't want to be here when it does." He was quite surprised at their odd tones. They seemed to be at ease which made no sense to him at all.

Will nodded in agreement and looked at Alyssa as she continued to breathe heavily. She didn't know what to say and she didn't know how she felt. She couldn't help but think about what had just occurred as she tried to put it together.

"Evan, why don't you take Josh to the TOC. It isn't too far. We'll be right behind you," Will replied and glanced at Alyssa. Her heart quickly dropped.

Oh God...this is it...

Alyssa's heart began to race as Evan approached Josh and escorted him out of the alley. Neither one of them looked back. They disappeared around the corner quietly and silence fell around the area.

Will took in a deep breath before turning his attention back to Alyssa. She was still sitting on the ground, her body resting against the brick. She was looking at him, fearful.

"You need to start talking," Will said firmly as he pointed his finger at her. He was frustrated and angry. Alyssa could hear it in his tone and see it in his face. All he had to do now was grab his gun. There was nothing she could do to prevent what was about to happen. Her anxiety began to rise and millions of thoughts began to race through her mind. She looked away, trying to ease the tension. She was beginning to accept her fate.

"Too many of my men have died today, and I think you know *more* than you have told us," Will added, folding his arms.

Alyssa remained unresponsive but a sudden intuition erupted inside her. She let the seconds pass and began to feel calm as she watched Will change his appearance. He released his breath softly and uncrossed his arms but remained standing in place. The creased lines in his forehead relaxed, and he took a deep breath through his nostrils. He seemed concerned and sincere. She suddenly felt as if she could truly trust him. He did save her life and put himself in harm's way just to get her away from Uktena.

How could someone like that be a murderer too?

And Robert was right. There was no way she could go through this alone. She had to open up to someone…Someone who was willing to listen.

"Alyssa, you've been acting odd ever since they brought you to the operations center…"

"I found a letter…" she interrupted as she thought about the horrific scene at the precinct. Will focused all his attention on her as she continued, "And it was from my former partner." Alyssa paused and took a deep breath, refusing to allow any more tears to fall.

"Those people at the precinct, my friends, were murdered…by someone in *your* uniform," she added and looked into Will's eyes.

"You think it was one of us?" he asked.

"I don't know," Alyssa replied and looked at the ground. "But I don't believe my partner would have made a story up like that."

"I know my group very well, Alyssa," Will said and paused as she turned her attention to him. "They are all good men. And what exactly would tempt one of them to commit such a crime here?"

"That's something I hope to find out very soon, Will."

"Well, I believe your former partner was mistaken," Will replied and Alyssa could only stare into his eyes. He still seemed sincere, but she didn't have any more words for him.

"Look…I want to help you, but there is still more I need to know," Will added and took a few steps closer to her. Alyssa was watching him carefully as he continued, "What is going on in this town?"

Alyssa looked away. She knew she was connected, but she wasn't sure how or why.

"I don't know, Will…"

"Yes you do. Did you see the way that thing was looking at you? And then these sounds you heard back at the press. Don't tell me you don't know anything," Will quickly interrupted. He was determined for some answers. He knew Alyssa was leaving something out.

Alyssa became a bit overwhelmed as she began to breathe heavily. She didn't respond, but Will decided to wait patiently. All grew quiet. The atmosphere around them became calm, tranquil, and the wind slowed to a comfortable breeze. Alyssa knew she was safe, however. She could feel it within her.

"There was an accident..." Alyssa finally stated and more tears filled her eyes. "I suffered some amnesia. I can't recall anything that happened, and my father has refused to talk to me about it. But soon after, I started to have these nightmares..." she paused and closed her eyes as the tears began to roll down her cheeks. It was becoming difficult to speak, but she decided to continue regardless.

"I rarely got sleep...and when I did, I suffered from night terrors. I would wake up with these bruises on my body, and I'm always fatigued and in pain," she added.

Will slowly knelt down beside her. "Is this the reason why you are no longer a cop?" he asked.

Alyssa looked into his eyes and nodded. "I believe these nightmares are connected to that part of my past. And...the past two times I've come face to face with Uktena as she is called, I've gotten these visions. I think they are the reason for the nose bleeds. But I believe these visions are of my forgotten past as well. I know I'm connected to the incidents here somehow, but that is all I know," she said and sighed softly.

Will didn't know what to say. He thought it was all too surreal.

"You probably think I am insane," Alyssa added and personally felt that she was.

"No," Will replied calmly.

"Maybe I'll get some answers...Maybe I won't. I do fear about the fate of this town though as well as our own lives. That's all I can honestly tell you, Will," Alyssa stated.

Silence filled the area as they both remained quiet. Will was still a bit shocked, but after all of Alyssa's confessions, he truly felt that he needed to help her now. Even though she didn't have all the answers, a part of him felt that she may be the only one who could possibly put an end to the nightmare.

"Some way or another...We will get to the bottom of this," Will said and extended his hand.

Alyssa looked down at his palm and then back into his eyes.

"You can trust me," Will added.

Alyssa bit her bottom lip and slowly placed her hand in his as he carefully gripped it and helped her to her feet. She dusted her pants off and gently wiped under her eyes with the back of her hands, distracting herself from the uneasy feeling she now had.

"Thank you," she replied.

Will nodded and looked at Alyssa's necklace that rested against her blue shirt.

"Where did you get that?" he asked.

"My father gave it to me."

Will nodded, thinking about its unique luster.

"And it also has something to do with the accident," Alyssa added and carefully placed the pendant back under her shirt.

"It seems to have significance," Will said and they began making their way out of the alley.

"I felt that it did too. I believe my father was hoping that it would help me recall some things, but it didn't. I guess in time it will," Alyssa replied. All she could do was think about her parents and Robert. She still wanted to find Kevin and the one who committed the murders at the Precinct, but she was becoming more afraid of what else lied in their paths and what truths awaited them. She knew the walk back to the operations center was going to be long and quiet. Too much had happened and all she wanted to do was ponder her thoughts and pray.

Chapter Ten

"**D**AMN IT, BRAD YOU SHOULD have been back by now," Kyle mumbled and opened the bottom drawer to the desk he was sitting behind. He quickly retrieved a satellite phone and closed the drawer silently. He held the phone carefully and watched the front door of the trailer for a moment. A little anxiety began to build within him as he approached the window near the door and looked out it. The street was empty and clouds hovered over the mountains in the distance. The wind was brushing through the small trees outside the offices in the cul-de-sac and against the window he stood by.

Kyle took in a deep breath and began pressing buttons on the satellite phone. He was losing his patience, and the stress was beginning to make him unsteady.

If they don't show up with that son of a bitch I will blow that building into bits! Brian better have another plan if all else fails...

Kyle quickly placed the phone to his ear and waited. As the rings went by, his blood began to boil.

"Captain…" a voice finally stated from the receiver.

Kyle sighed heavily with frustration and quickly responded, "Brian…I'm still waiting on Master Sergeant Kennedy and the other two to return from downtown. I sure hope you have another plan if this objective fails."

"Give them a little more time and relax. You are beginning to worry for no reason. Now…who else did you get involved? I told you that I will give you assistance if you need it. We have to be careful of whom we trust," Brian replied. He seemed calm but firm.

"One of my Sergeants and a former cop," Kyle responded and paced around the room.

"A former cop? You let a former cop for this town get involved? What were you thinking?"

"She knows the area...And she has the skills we could use. Besides, when the time comes I will get rid of her personally and anyone else I use. They are not even aware of what's going on. You should trust my judgment."

A heavy sigh was heard in the receiver as Kyle realized that Brian was now angry.

"Who is this former cop?" Brian asked firmly.

"Her name is Alyssa. I highly doubt she will catch on to anything."

"Alyssa...Alyssa Bennett?"

"Yes."

"Damn it, Kyle! She wasn't supposed to get involved here! She wasn't even supposed to be here in town!" Brian shouted and Kyle could hear the uneasiness in his tone. He wondered how he knew this woman as Brian sighed once more and continued, "I'll explain later. Give Brad thirty minutes to return. If he does not, then breach the damn door to City Hall and move to the hospital. We need to find James...Alyssa's father."

Kyle's eyes widened. "James is Alyssa's father? He is apparently missing, Brian," he replied, becoming agitated as he sat down behind the desk.

"He isn't missing...He's here."

"Then why don't I just interrogate Alyssa when she returns? Perhaps she's hiding something."

"No!" Brian exclaimed and continued, "She was not supposed to get involved here. Leave her out of this, Captain. That is an order."

Kyle's patience grew thin as he tried to stay calm. "Is there something you need to tell me, sir?" he asked.

"I've known the Bennetts for a very long time. I'll leave it at that until you arrive at the hospital. I'll see you soon," Brian said and hung up.

Kyle began to clench the phone tight. He wanted to crush it in the palm of his hand and throw it out the window as far as he could.

Then I will let Ms. Bennett live until I find her father...Or better yet, I could have her stand alongside me. I will no longer have to take orders from this hoity toity government official especially when we meet with James...

Kyle placed the phone in a large vest pocket and secured it as he opened the front door and stepped out onto the small deck. He took in a deep breath of air and closed his eyes as he cleared his thoughts.

Alyssa apparently has no idea...

Kyle opened his eyes and looked toward the cul-de-sac. Something had caught his attention. Two men were walking toward him, staggering with fatigue. He recognized one but not the other as he examined the stranger's appearance. Both appeared to be hurt and exhausted. Kyle noticed their stressed expressions and battered clothing. He slowly stepped down the stairs and onto the pavement, watching them carefully.

"Private Watkins," he stated firmly once the two men were in range.

Evan looked away from Josh. "Captain," he replied and approached him. Josh followed and glanced behind him, wondering about Will and Alyssa.

"Where is the rest of your team?" Kyle asked and folded his arms. He wanted to pull out his pistol and get rid of them now as he thought about the 1911 secured in his holster.

"They didn't make it, sir. Private Wainwright and I did run into Sergeant First Class Thompson downtown though. He and Alyssa should be here in a moment."

Kyle cleared his thoughts. "Did they find Chief Armstrong?" he asked.

"I was made aware that he didn't make it," Evan replied.

Kyle sighed and fought back the urge to retrieve his gun as he looked at the civilian standing next to him.

"And what is your name?" he asked firmly.

"Josh Walker."

Kyle slowly nodded and examined the .38 Special he was carrying.

"You from these parts, Mr. Walker?" he asked.

"Yes, sir," Josh replied.

"Okay. Evan, why don't you take Mr. Walker inside and assist him with his wounds until Thompson and Ms. Bennett return?"

"Yes, sir, but before I do, you need to be made aware of what lies below this town," Evan said and took in a deep breath.

Kyle could sense the urgency in Evan's tone so he paused and allowed him to continue.

"It's massive, sir. I believe you would classify it as a...*dragon*. Isn't that what it looked like, Josh?"

Josh nodded and watched Kyle's expression as it remained surprisingly the same.

"Ms. Bennett did mention something about a large beast being under the valley," Kyle replied and Evan became confused. He couldn't believe Kyle's calm state after what he had just witnessed downtown.

"Captain...The situation just got worse. What are we going to do?"

"I'm thinking, Private," Kyle quickly stated as he stepped around Josh and paced in front of the tent. He didn't know what to do. He was becoming extremely anxious and he was trying not to allow his anger to get the best of him. He began to feel that his mission was going to be impossible to complete now with a true confirmation of the large beast. He was still unable to paint a picture of it in his mind.

Evan watched him for a moment and looked at Josh.

"Let's just wait for the other two to arrive before I make any decisions," Kyle finally said and stepped inside the tent. Josh felt a bit uneasy. Kyle had intimidated him. He looked at Evan concernedly.

"Come on. I'm sure he's just in shock like we all were," Evan said and they stepped up the stairs of the deck and went inside the trailer.

Kyle heard the door close and he clenched his teeth. He had reached his limit as he closed his eyes and wondered how he was going to get rid of these men without anyone becoming suspicious now. Things were not going as well as he thought.

Brian better not be wrong about this...

Kyle opened his eyes and quickly picked up a chair, glancing at a table with a few files on it.

You had no idea it was going to get this bad!

His rage was released as he threw the chair at the table, knocking off a bottle of water and a few files. The paper floated to the floor and the bottle rolled across the pavement before coming to a stop near ammunition cases. Kyle sighed heavily until he heard a familiar voice outside.

"Everything alright, Captain?"

It was Will. He was standing near the entrance to the tent with Alyssa standing by his side. Kyle looked back at them and noticed their concerned expressions until he caught a glimpse of the blood on Alyssa's clothing.

"Yes, I apologize...What happened?" he asked, looking at Alyssa.

"Uh, I'll be fine, Captain. Just a nose bleed," she responded.

"Well, why don't you get cleaned up and have Private Watkins take a look at you before we make our way to City Hall," Kyle said and Alyssa nodded.

"Yes, sir," she said and slowly made her way to the stairs.

Will and Kyle watched as she went up the steps and disappeared behind the door.

"Private Watkins told me about the encounter you all had," Kyle said and Will turned his attention back to him. He was still thinking about the talk he and Alyssa had as he responded, "It appears Alyssa was right after all, Captain. And unfortunately our four-wheelers were destroyed."

Kyle shook his head in disbelief. "Did you happen to find Master Sergeant Kennedy?" he asked.

"No sir. He was in the area though. We did find his four-wheeler," Will replied.

"Something may have happened..." Kyle said and paused as he thought for a moment.

"We did find the police chief. He, however, didn't make it. Alyssa has the keys to City Hall."

Kyle slowly nodded. "Alright. Well, how about you get the resources we need before we go. It's going to be a long walk without the ATVs," he added.

Will nodded, examining Kyle's odd behavior. "Yes, sir," he carefully stated.

Kyle quickly approached the stairs and jogged up them. Will slowly stepped inside the tent.

"Captain?" Will asked.

Kyle took in a deep breath and looked back at him, fearing more questions.

"How is Patrick?"

The adrenaline was now pumping into Kyle's veins. He remained calm as he placed his hand on the door knob. "He didn't make it."

Alyssa was experiencing a bit of déjà vu. She was standing once again at a sink in a small bathroom in the office. She was staring at the red water that was dripping into it, sore and exhausted. Water trickled from her face and hands, separating the dirt and blood from her skin. Alyssa slowly looked into the small mirror that hung over the sink and thought about the image she saw in the mirror at the station, a little fear beginning to build within her.

How much time do we have before Uktena reappears? Will I survive long enough to learn the truth to this nightmare? This stone... What could be the significance? What happened that night with my father...?

Alyssa sighed heavily and grabbed a small towel that was hanging on the wall near the door beside her. She gently patted her hands and face dry and continued to look in the mirror.

Will seems so sincere...I can trust him, can't I? He doesn't seem like someone who would commit such a heinous crime. But looks, however, can be so deceiving.

Alyssa slowly placed the towel back on the hanger and stepped out of the bathroom. She looked around the small room and examined a few shirts that were piled on a chair near a tall bookshelf. They were folded neatly, and Alyssa noticed the company's logo on the front left pocket as she approached them. She knew she could use another shirt as she examined the blood and dirt on the one she was wearing. Alyssa picked up one of the shirts and unfolded it, looking at the size that was labeled on the tag. She smiled and placed the shirt down, glancing back at the door that led into the lobby. She quickly grabbed the bottom of her shirt and pulled it over her head. The faint smell of blood entered her nostrils as she tossed the shirt to the ground.

Goodness...

Alyssa noticed the fresh wounds on her body. She still wore the bandages that were wrapped around areas of her arms and ribcage, but there were fresh contusions, scrapes, and cuts across her entire body. Blood was beginning to dry on her chest and back, tightening the skin in the affected areas. She could feel the pain all over.

She groaned, realizing that she was going to have to get them cleaned up before going anywhere. She couldn't risk infection. Alyssa sighed heavily and suddenly the door opened from the lobby. She glanced up and noticed Evan stepping into the room, but quickly turning around once he noticed her half dressed.

"I'm so sorry ma'am..." he said and stared into the lobby.

"It's alright. I was just changing my shirt," Alyssa replied and quickly pulled the grey shirt over her head.

"I was coming to ask if you'd like for me to examine and dress any wounds you may have," Evan said and slowly peeked over his shoulder as he watched Alyssa pull her arms through the sleeves of the shirt.

"There is one on my back that I need help with. I can manage the rest I'm sure," she replied and looked back at him.

He was young and handsome especially after cleaning his face off. She could also tell he was curious. It was obvious when he looked at her with his southern charm at times, but she wasn't interested in a young soldier or any man for that matter. After having been fooled in the past, she decided to give it a rest for a while.

"I have my things in there," Evan said and Alyssa nodded as she followed him into the lobby. Josh was standing in the back behind the desk, looking out the window. Kyle was placing his laptop into a bag, appearing deep in thought. Alyssa approached the couch and sat down, sighing softly. Evan carefully grabbed a few items from his rucksack and sat next to her.

"Here are a few antiseptic wipes," he said.

Alyssa took them and placed them in her lap. "Just pull my shirt up to my shoulder and I will hold it for you," she stated.

Evan carefully did so and allowed Alyssa to hold it up while he opened an antiseptic wipe. There was a short tear along her right shoulder blade and blood was slowly oozing out it. A few scrapes covered that side of her back as well. Evan gently began patting them with the antiseptic wipe.

"This cut on your back will need butterfly stitches," he said and Alyssa nodded. After a few minutes of cleaning the cuts and scrapes, Evan turned his attention to the nasty tear along her shoulder blade.

"This may hurt a bit," he warned and the door across from them opened as Will stepped into the room, carrying a heavy rucksack. He glanced at Alyssa as she gasped from the pain in her shoulder. Evan was cleaning it carefully, holding onto a few butterfly stitches. Will approached the desk and placed the bag on top of it.

Kyle quickly zipped up his laptop case and looked at him.

"All set," Will said and looked at Alyssa.

Evan was attaching the butterfly stitches on the wound and closing it up. He secured the stitches tightly, but gently, using a soft and steady hand. Alyssa was staring at the ground, ignoring everything around her. Will looked back at Kyle, sensing his eagerness.

"Alright. It's time to move," Kyle finally responded.

Josh slowly stepped away from the window and looked back at the others. He was becoming more nervous, keeping a close look out. Evan gently placed a bandage over the stitches and pulled Alyssa's shirt back down.

"Thank you," Alyssa said and stood up.

Evan nodded and grabbed his bag, standing up as well. Will looked around concernedly and asked, "Aren't we missing someone?"

Kyle became impatient, but kept his cool as he looked at Will. "Such as?" he asked firmly.

"Specialist Tidwell."

Kyle hesitated and held his breath as the earth around them began to shake, rocking the trailer gently. He looked behind him and held onto the desk as Will and the others kept their footing.

"What did I tell you...That damn thing is back!" Josh exclaimed.

Will glanced at Alyssa as the earth began to intensify. The trailer rocked and pictures fell from the walls. The glass windows began to rattle and books fell from the shelves.

Alyssa dropped to her knees and covered her head, fearing a collapse. Evan quickly kneeled and held onto the end of the couch, keeping an eye on her and the others. Josh suddenly lost his footing and fell to his side, gasping. The earth began to shake more violently until the sounds of pavement and brick collapsing echoed around them.

And then the harsh scream. The dragon was just outside as the thunder from the collapsing brick and pavement continued. Alyssa released a cry and fell to her knees. She closed her eyes tightly and covered her ears with the palms of her hands. The ear-piercing shriek from Uktena was about to make her heard rupture.

Just go away...Please! Go away!

The earth shook for a few more seconds before it slowed to a quiver, eventually stopping. The ground settled and everything became still and quiet. Josh was breathing heavily and remained on the floor, looking at the back window. A few cracks had spread throughout it. Kyle was still gripping onto the desk as Will tossed the straps to the rucksack onto his shoulders, allowing the bag to rest against his back. He glanced at Alyssa who was looking toward the back of the office.

"We need to go," he said firmly and took one step toward the door as Uktena's claws tore through the roof, ripping pieces of it clean off.

Wood and debris rained down on them, stirring up dust as it floated around the room. Will jumped to the floor near the couch, dropping the rucksack. He quickly covered his head and clenched his teeth. Josh yelled and pushed himself off the floor, covering his head the best he could. Kyle shielded his body under the desk and stared at the large beast. It released another piercing cry and gazed down upon them. Her teeth were large and her eyes were bright, the fire continuing to dance around her pupils.

Adrenaline and fear erupted within Kyle as he watched the dragon glare down at them. He realized that her gaze was focused on someone else, and he took in a deep breath, trying to figure out his next move.

Alyssa was pulling herself toward the door until she fell onto her belly and rolled over. Evan had already reached her side, placing his hand on her shoulder. Alyssa sat up and quickly met the beast's gaze.

"Why are you doing this me!" she yelled and tears began to fill her eyes.

Evan stared in shock. Josh had stumbled near the couch, pushing off a piece of wood that had fallen on him. He grabbed onto the fabric, watching in horror.

Uktena lowered her snout and narrowed her eyes as the mesmerizing glare made Alyssa's vision fuzzy once again.

"No...Stop..." she whispered and covered her eyes, quickly entering yet another dark place...

"Wow..." Alyssa whispered, carrying her maglite in the middle of a large crystal cavern. The luminous crystals shone brightly as Alyssa slowly turned her flashlight off. She couldn't believe what she was seeing. There were many crystals of all shapes and sizes illuminating the area, but only one caught her attention. It was centered in the middle of the area and was extremely large. Other smaller crystals of different shades surrounded its base, embedded into a large rock. Alyssa slowly approached it as a smile rose upon her face. She had never seen anything like this...

Once she reached the large crystal, she carefully touched it. It was absolutely beautiful she could hear herself thinking and lowered her hand. The image slowly faded to another area of the cavern. She was suddenly standing in front of a large, rectangular rock that protruded out of the ground. The front was smooth and had a piece that jutted out from the middle of it. It contained a bundle of small crystals, carefully snug in the base. In the center was a small bed where one red gem sat. There were carvings etched into the large rock above the crystals, and it appeared to be of an ancient language. Alyssa turned her attention to them. She carefully touched the etchings, sliding her finger across them. She didn't know what they symbolized and looked below them at another carving that was in the shape of a small, snake-like beast. She carefully ran her finger across the carving and began to wonder how old they were. Her hand then moved to caress the base of the crystals. Alyssa stared at them in awe and glanced at the red rock that rested in the small bed between them. The beautiful stone began to mesmerize her, putting her in some sort of trance. She gazed at it and smiled. Alyssa proceeded to touch it before carefully picking it up out of its resting place. She grinned brightly, admiring the beauty of the stone, but gasped, suddenly glancing behind her. A loud gust of wind was heard in the distance and she could feel the breeze brush against her, wherever it came from. It sounded similar to an exhale of breath, but only from something much larger. Alyssa could feel the adrenaline burning in her veins. She stared into the darkness until unusual whispers slowly surrounded her. They got louder and louder when a pair of dragon-like eyes suddenly flashed before her. The image quickly faded to one of her brother. He was standing in the hallway near the door to his bedroom, a look of pure exhaustion on his face. The skin under his eyes was dark, his body pale and fatigued. His words were forced out as he slowly stated, "Please...whatever you do...don't go down there..." and the image became a blur...

Alyssa's vision was fuzzy as she realized that she was back in the office. A little blood was making its way down her nose, and she noticed Will and Evan trying to help her to her feet. She breathed heavily, shocked from the last part of her vision as she looked back at the dragon. It slowly raised its body and opened its mouth, releasing another loud and ferocious cry. Alyssa cried and heard Kyle yell from behind the desk as he quickly stood and aimed his M4 at the beast's face. He pulled the trigger to the M203 and fired a grenade as Josh stared in fright. The explosion lit up the night and sent Uktena into a fury. The dragon quickly slammed her snout into the side of the trailer, knocking it off its cinder blocks. Alyssa screamed as they all fell to the carpet. The couches and desk slid across the floor and glass shattered. Wood particles and insulation fell from the collapsed ceiling, and the wooden deck snapped lose and split in several places as soon as it hit the pavement. Once the trailer suddenly settled, Will pulled Alyssa to her feet and yelled at the others, "Let's go!"

Evan scrambled to his feet and pushed the door open with all his might. Josh quickly stood and ran to the door as Kyle fired another grenade at Uktena's snout. Alyssa clenched her teeth as the grenade exploded and sent a wave of heat against their backs. Will grabbed her once more and pulled her out the door, Josh and Kyle quickly following. A loud inhale of breath was heard behind them as Uktena sucked in a deep gust of air. Alyssa realized what was about to happen and gasped.

"Get down!" she yelled.

Will held his breath as he and Alyssa climbed through the broken deck and jumped to the pavement. The others quickly followed and rolled across the pavement as Uktena released a powerful stream of fire that engulfed the trailer and tent. Evan took in a deep breath and pushed himself to his feet, turning to face the dragon as he raised his M9. The intense heat brushed against them, burning their skin through their clothing. Evan took a few steps back and Kyle rolled onto his back near Alyssa, panting. Will sighed heavily and stood up, watching the fire consume the operations center. It's crackling wails and its radiant blaze awoke the night and warmed the atmosphere as it climbed high in the sky.

Uktena slowly and swiftly appeared above the blaze and released another dreadful scream toward them. Alyssa carefully rolled onto her back and pushed herself away from the hot flames. Will took a few steps back, firing his M4 at the beast. Beads of sweat pushed their way out onto his forehead as a few began to trickle down the side of his face. They were running out of options. He didn't know what would help them now.

Evan began to fire his M9 at Uktena's snout. He knew he was only angering the beast and took a few more steps back, wondering if they should all try and run for it. The dragon snarled and raised its large palm above the blaze, claws stretched apart. Will gasped and froze. Kyle stiffened and looked at Alyssa. He couldn't understand why this beast was interested in her and only her. His reflexes quickly took over as he rolled on top of her, using his body as a shield. Uktena's palm slammed on top of them and her talons dug deep into the pavement as her hand roughly embraced them. Alyssa screamed loudly and Will continued to fire bursts of rounds at Uktena's snout. The dragon turned her head and lifted her palm up, locking Kyle into her grasp. Alyssa was still screaming and lying on the pavement, struggling as Will and Evan ceased fire.

"Kyle!" Will yelled and the dragon screamed once more, floating toward the sky.

Evan fired a couple of more rounds until Will yelled, "Cease fire!"

Evan lowered his M9 and stared at the dragon as it slowly turned her snaky body and began making her way north toward City Hall. Alyssa slowly sat up, completely shaken and in shock. Kyle had just saved her life. She sighed heavily and watched Uktena slowly disappear.

"Fuck!" Evan shouted, gripping onto his pistol.

Will took in a deep breath and looked at Alyssa. She carefully pushed herself to her feet, wrapping her arms around herself. Will approached her. "Are you alright?" he asked.

She nodded and looked back at the fire that was continuing to consume the remains of the operations center, trying to fight the numbness she now felt. She couldn't comprehend it anymore.

Will looked back at Evan. He was placing his M9 back into its holster, his face flushed.

"You okay, Private?" Will asked.

"Yes, sir."

"Captain must've known what he was doing..." Will sighed and continued, "We just need to find this other unit...if we can make it there in time and in one piece." He noticed someone from the corner of his eye and quickly looked toward the other side of the street.

"Josh..." he stated, confused.

Josh approached them from across the street. "I'm sorry, but... there was no way I could just stand there and wait for that thing to kill us all," he said.

Will turned to look back at the fire. Evan ignored Josh's comment as well. He was full of anger. He had no hope left in him. They had already lost many and were sure the others still out there had perished as well. The mission was on the way to a total failure.

Alyssa took a deep breath and looked back at Will. "He saved my life..." she said calmly.

Will slowly nodded and looked down at the ground.

"I don't care how long it takes...but I will stand by this group until this is over. We will figure out a way to put an end to this," she said and looked away, thinking about how she may be able to help.

Will looked up at her and remained quiet.

"There is no way we can do this without the Air Force," Evan stated and reached into his rucksack, grabbing another wipe for Alyssa's face. He approached her and handed it to her carefully. Will thought for a moment while Alyssa cleaned the blood away from her face and hands.

"Alyssa, are you sure that is what you want to do? Because you can leave as soon as we get to the hospital," Will finally said, ignoring Evan's remark.

Alyssa nodded. She knew she was going to find the murderer behind the incident at the Rockdale Valley Precinct regardless of what man in uniform she stands by. She was determined, but she knew she also had to stay focused on the most important situation which was now Uktena.

"Alright. Since you know this valley, you lead us to City Hall," Will said and looked at Evan. "She's one of us now. So we need to listen to any information or advice she gives us."

"Yes sir," Evan said and Josh remained quiet.

Will looked back at Alyssa. He didn't mind her standing by their side, but he wanted her to escape when she had the opportunity to. It would probably be the only chance she had if it became available.

Alyssa took in a deep breath. "Okay," she said and looked back at the fire and continued, "Let's go." She wasn't sure if she was ready though. She felt a bit of queasiness and fatigue as she began walking toward Main Street, thinking about her brother. Will and Evan followed with Josh trailing behind. Josh knew he didn't quite fit in, but he wanted to be in the safety of the group. He had been stuck in the hell downtown, witnessing many gruesome deaths and cataclysmic events. Fear wasn't a term he could use to classify the way he felt. He was absolutely petrified.

As they all pushed forward, Alyssa thought hard of her visions and their significance to the events in the valley. She also thought of their possible connections to the accident in the forest, but the vision of her brother however, had suddenly brought back other unpleasant memories...

CHAPTER ELEVEN

A LYSSA'S FACE HAD GROWN CLAMMY and pale after the long, debilitating hike to the historic marble building of City Hall. Trailing through the collapsed streets and buildings of the southern valley intensified her queasiness, weakening her stomach to certain smells that lingered in the air. Evan was there every step of the way, acting as a caregiver. It bothered Alyssa in some ways. He was acting more like a sick puppy than an Army Green Beret.

"This is it," Alyssa said and took in a deep breath, wrapping an arm around her sensitive stomach.

"Are you going to make it?" Evan asked.

Will was examining the barricades attached to both sides of the marble building. They extended around a few other offices before turning towards the back and wrapping around parts of the northern valley. He began to ponder exactly why they were placed by the other units in the first place. It could definitely detour an *animal*, but would it stop a monstrous *beast* from tearing through it if that is where it intended to go? Will shook his head in disbelief.

"Yeah," Alyssa replied and pulled the set of keys the chief had given her out of her pocket.

Evan quickly examined the white marble and the metal bars that covered the windows beside the wooden double doors. The building stood out amongst the rest. It was the only one like it in the valley. It was definitely the most alluring and probably the safest due to its solid structure. The quakes hadn't caused any damage from what they could see.

Josh noticed Alyssa struggling with the keys and approached her, watching her hands and fingers tremble through the set.

"Here," he said, taking them from her carefully. "Which one is it?"

"The...larger one," Alyssa replied. She took long, steady breaths, trying to calm her nerves. She felt like she wasn't going to make too much longer.

Josh quickly unlocked the doors and pulled one open, glancing at Will. He had approached a set of the barricades, examining them more closely.

"Here, let me help you," Evan said, placing a hand on Alyssa's back and helping her walk into the large lobby.

"I got it," she replied and Will glanced at Evan, quickly following them inside the building. He noticed Alyssa's tone and was becoming a bit annoyed with Evan's behavior let alone the situation at hand.

The area they stepped into was silent, and the cool temperature made the hair on their arms stand straight up. The room was well decorated with antique pictures of the valley and historic landmarks. There were a few decorative plants and two large wooden benches that sat against both marble walls. A long, dark rug stretched in front of them to another set of double doors and stopped before two other rugs stretched off in opposite directions and down two hallways. A few lamps that hung on the walls shone dimly, illuminating the area lightly. The cooler temperature was very soothing to their weary bodies, but it wasn't enough to stop Alyssa from regurgitating. She immediately ran for the bathroom around the east corner, disappearing into the ladies room.

Josh sighed heavily. "I'm going to take a look around. We might be here a while," he said, looking back at Will and handing him the set of keys. He trusted Will's opinion. He fit the role of acting commander now that the captain was gone, and he didn't make him feel uncomfortable like the captain had done.

Will took the keys and stared in the direction Alyssa ran to, hearing the commotion in the bathroom.

"Alright. Hurry back," he replied.

Josh nodded and walked away. Evan watched him caress his .38 Special before turning left down a hall. Will took in a deep breath and folded his arms across his chest. He couldn't stop thinking about Uktena and the devilish monsters. He couldn't comprehend the reason for such hellish existence, the peculiar story to Alyssa and her nightmares. He never believed the paranormal shows on TV, let alone the exorcisms of the possessed that supposedly occurred in real life. He didn't think Alyssa was one of these victims, but something obviously wasn't normal with her.

"So...Can you tell me a little bit more about Alyssa?" Evan asked, interrupting Will's thoughts.

Like what?" Will asked, glancing at him.

Evan could see the confusion in his expression, the frustration in his tone. He wasn't sure why exactly. "Well, her odd behavior for one," he said in a low voice, hoping Alyssa wasn't able to hear or come around the corner. "We weren't briefed about what was truly going on. But you remember how she was acting downtown, I'm sure. And then the incident at the trailer..." he added and Will cut him off.

"Don't fret over it. I hope to talk her in to leaving when we get to the hospital. She's got a lot going on," he replied.

"What about this dragon? Is the other unit even going to believe us?" Evan asked.

Will thought to himself.

How can anyone believe what's going on in this valley?

"Just leave it to me to talk to their commander about this," he finally said and Evan nodded, wishing that Will would say more and stop being so short with him.

After a few seconds passed, Evan decided to change the subject. "Well, she's a pretty girl. Something about those blue eyes..." he said.

Will nodded, and looked back at the artwork, organizing his thoughts and plans. He really didn't feel like talking, especially about women anyway. Evan mumbled to himself and glanced back at the hall towards the bathrooms. No sounds were to be heard, alarming him.

"Well, I'm going to go check on her," he said and before he could take a step forward, Will quickly grabbed his arm and pulled him around, holding him firmly. Evan stared at him in shock, his eyes wide with concern.

"I know what you are doing…And I don't like it," Will said firmly, glaring into Evan's dark brown eyes.

"What is this, Sergeant First Class?" Evan asked, jerking his arm away from the tight grip.

"She's a cop. I'm sure she can handle it."

Evan's eyes narrowed a bit.

"Don't get your head all up in the clouds and lose focus on *your* mission," Will added, hoping that it would sink in Evan's youthful mind.

"Hmm…It seems as if *someone* already has," Evan murmured, raising an eyebrow and stepping away from Will as he approached the hall Josh had gone down. Will watched him disappear and sighed heavily.

I need to get myself together. I'm taking my frustration out on the wrong people. Evan is still young…Why do I care?

Will slowly walked to a bench and sat down, placing his face in the palms of his hands. He was stressed out. His only hope was to find the other unit and get them to contact the appropriate authorities regarding the severity of the events occurring in Rockdale Valley. The Army had plenty of firepower, but perhaps if the Air Force got involved…

A door around the corner suddenly opened and closed softly, startling Will. He quickly stood up and watched Alyssa turn the corner sluggishly. She was holding a paper towel, looking at him remorsefully. Will was speechless. He wasn't sure if she was okay or not and for some reason he couldn't find the right words to say to her.

"I'm sorry…" Alyssa finally said and took in a deep breath. "I'm really not sure what came over me. I feel a bit relieved. Better," she added.

"Good. We can't really drag you around like this. You wouldn't make it," Will responded, standing in place.

A slight smile curled upon Alyssa's face. The dark circles under eyes were already fading.

"I think I need to lie down for a moment though," she said faintly.

Will could tell she was still weak and nodded, forgetting about his top priority which was to position themselves at Trinity Hospital.

"I don't believe you will be comfortable on these benches..." he stated, looking back at the wooden bench against the wall.

"I know. There's an office over here. Could you help me?" Alyssa asked, taking a few steps towards the hall that Josh had went down.

"Alright," Will replied and approached her, carefully removing the M4 from her shoulder and gently wrapping an arm around her back. He assisted her to the small office down the hall, holding a bit of her weight due to the weakness and fatigue in her muscles. The office had a long counter on one side with a few computers sitting behind it. It belonged to the secretaries. The room was comfortable, relaxing. It had very little artwork or displays.

"Thank you," Alyssa said when she was finally on a soft couch against the back wall.

Will nodded and took a few steps back, placing her M4 on the end table and looking towards the hallway. Soft footsteps were heard coming around the corner. Alyssa ignored them and carefully laid down on the comfortable cushion, closing her eyes and thinking about her brother.

"The place is empty," Josh said, approaching Will.

Evan was right behind him, a bit annoyed.

"Maybe the barricades came to good use after all," Will replied and glanced at Alyssa. She was still lying on the couch, her eyes closed and her hands placed on her belly.

"Private Watkins, I have a proposition for you," he added, looking back at Evan. Evan looked him in the eyes and waited.

"How about you take Josh and get a head start to the hospital," Will said. It was more of an order than a question. "I'm going to stay behind," he added, speaking in a low voice and stepping out into the hall.

Josh nodded.

Is she going to be okay?" Evan asked.

"Yes, she just needs a breather I think. We can catch up with you both soon," Will responded and said no more.

"Yes sir," Evan replied and nodded towards Josh. Josh turned around and led them to an exit on the west wing near a set of stairs. He didn't want to wait any longer than he had to.

Will slowly walked back into the small office and sat down in a soft chair near the door. He watched Alyssa carefully. She appeared to be deep in thought, tuning everything out around her. Will sighed heavily as he watched her. He knew their relationship had changed ever since the talk they had in the alley. Perhaps that was the reason why he felt so protective of her now.

Alyssa took in a deep breath and opened her eyes. She stared at the ceiling above her, refusing to look anywhere else. After a few moments passed, Will broke the silence.

"What did you see?" he asked calmly, remembering the pain staking expression on her face at the trailer.

Alyssa kept her eyes on the ceiling, thinking about the vision. "My brother," she murmured and thought some more.

Will didn't respond. He continued to watch her carefully.

"I didn't think all of this would bring those memories back up…" Alyssa said and paused. She slowly looked at Will and took in another deep breath. He could see the sadness in her eyes, the worry. And for some reason, he cared.

"They said he was sick, though I didn't believe that at first. I know he and a friend went out to the trails. I was young so I don't remember everything that happened, but I know he kept to himself a lot. He stayed in his room most of the day. And then after a rough night, he came to me," Alyssa said and looked back at the ceiling.

"He looked pale, fatigued. The skin under his eyes was dark, creepy looking. I don't think he had slept in days, weeks maybe," she added and paused for a moment. "He told me…whatever you do, don't go down there."

Will looked at her for a long moment, confused.

"I believe he was telling me about the cavern I visit in my nightmares," Alyssa stated and closed her eyes, thinking about the sudden visions that would rush through her mind. "And I believe that is what I did when my father and I went to the trail in the mountains a few weeks ago…before any of *this*."

"What happened to your brother?" Will asked.

Alyssa looked back at him and slowly sat herself up, sighing softly. Will stiffened, hoping he hadn't offended her by asking.

"We don't have to talk about it…"

"No, it's okay. It's actually nice having someone to talk to about all of this. It was hard to talk to my father. About the night terrors and my sleep deprivation that is. It bothered him really bad for some reason. He would always walk away," Alyssa replied.

Will nodded and waited.

"My brother took his own life…"

Silence filled the room for a few moments. Will suddenly thought about a friend in the Army that had committed suicide years back. Nothing would help save the young soldier, and his family didn't speak to him much so there was no assistance there. His steady girlfriend had left him also and he was days away from deployment. It was such a sad time for the group.

"I'm really sorry," Will replied.

"It was a long time ago. I was only thirteen. But it just confuses me more."

Will could see the frustration in Alyssa's face as she continued, "What does his death have to do with the incidents occurring now?" Alyssa paused and sighed. She had ideas, but that was it, just ideas. She went into this cavern and had done something to release hell on earth. That was one idea.

Alyssa grabbed her necklace, pulling it out from behind her shirt.

"And I was the one that actually found this…not my father," she said, examining the stone her pendant cradled.

Will couldn't stop thinking about the cavern she had mentioned as he quickly asked, "This cavern you speak of. Is it nearby?"

Alyssa nodded, placing the necklace behind her shirt. "I believe so…" she said and sighed. "This has really been difficult. I want to remember, but now I'm afraid to."

"I couldn't imagine, Alyssa," Will replied and looked down at the ground. He didn't have any suggestions. Nothing was coming to mind that may help them or her for that matter.

"Well, I'm not sure how you feel at this moment, but we won't be able to accomplish anything unless we try and get moving," Will said, turning his attention to her calm face.

"I know. I'll be alright," Alyssa replied. She took in a deep breath and looked into his eyes.

"Thank you," she added.

Will nodded. He didn't have to say a thing. He could see the sincerity in her eyes and what she was referring to. She had confided in him and only him. She would probably say more as the night went on and just maybe Will and the other soldiers would be able to figure out what steps to take to end the nightmare they were all facing. He never prayed so hard.

Evan was still a bit irritated as he and Josh attempted to find a door that wasn't locked. He was completely caught off guard from Will's tone, and he still wasn't sure why Will said the things he did in the first place. He was completely out of line. Evan tried to shake the image from his thoughts. Perhaps he was getting a bit overboard with the kindness, but he didn't deserve a reaction like that. He took a deep breath and looked around the small oval lobby in the north sector of City Hall. The cooler temperature was still sending chills throughout his body as he ignored the quivers that shook down his spine.

"Is something bothering you?" Josh asked, looking back at him. He was curious about the heavy sigh and the sudden change in his attitude.

Evan quickly snapped out of it. "No. I just want to get to this hospital," he said.

Josh nodded and approached a hallway with a set of stairs in the back. He didn't care about anything other than evacuation. Evan followed and glanced at the double doors behind the small stairwell.

"These better not be locked," he murmured.

Before Josh could push open the door, a faint crash was heard upstairs. Evan quickly pulled his M9 from its holster, aiming it towards the second floor. Josh about jumped out of his skin as he stumbled back against the cool, double doors.

"The place is empty my ass…Did you forget to check upstairs?" Evan asked.

Josh pursed his lips in a hard line and carefully drew his .38 Special, ignoring the statement. Evan stared towards the second floor for a few seconds before taking a couple of steps forward.

"Can we just leave, please?" Josh asked, impatiently.

"Look, since all you care about is yourself then by all means, go. But I have orders," Evan said and glanced at Josh. "You can stay down here and wait if you'd like," he added.

Josh fought the urge to respond. He was getting tired of the kid's attitude.

Evan cautiously stepped up the stairs, one step at a time. He aimed steadily towards the hall, his finger touching the trigger gently. Josh watched from below and took in a deep breath. He decided to wait a few moments as Evan stepped into the hall and made his way down it slowly.

The hall was dark. There was a small opening up ahead that appeared to be a balcony overlooking a section of the oval lobby they were in earlier. A little light shone from that area, but Evan was focused on a door to his right. It was hanging open inside a dark room. He became a bit nervous, but carefully made his way down the hall towards it. He took in a deep breath once he reached it and swiftly stepped inside the large room, scanning his pistol across it quickly. The thick blinds against the barred windows were left open and a dim light from the moon touched the large rug in the middle of the floor softly.

Evan's eyes soon adjusted and he examined the room carefully. There were a few desks and chairs neatly arranged near the wall on the right and there were a few couches against the wall next to him. Nothing seemed out of place. A few pictures hung slightly off center but that was it. Evan decided to step back into the hallway and make his way past the balcony and into another large room with two hallways. One stretched towards the left and the other stretched off in front of him. Evan sighed and lowered his pistol.

This place is bigger than I thought it was...

Another crash was heard towards the left followed with a faint gasp as Evan glanced towards the long hallway.

"Hello!" he called out and began walking towards it quickly. "I'm here to help!"

Silence filled the area and Evan raised his pistol. He wanted to be prepared just in case. After stepping past two restrooms, he noticed a few flower arrangements on the floor. A vase had shattered, glass littering the long rug that stretched down the hall. The bright flowers that once occupied it were scattered on the floor, unbundled. Evan stepped around the mess and glanced down the hall. He heard a few faint pants coming from a room to the left as he slowed his walk.

"I'm not here to hurt you..." Evan said calmly and approached the room cautiously.

"Who...who are you?" a female voice asked. It sounded strained.

Evan lowered his M9 halfway and cautiously stepped inside the room. He noticed a row of desks, computers, and printers but what caught his eye was a young lady sitting near the wall beside a desk chair. Her long, brown hair was lying across one shoulder and her chocolate brown eyes were focusing on him with fear. She wore a nice, pink blouse with charcoal tinted leggings that were torn in some spots. A pen and pencil holder was lying next to her, a few pens scattered across the floor. Evan noticed the tears on her cheeks and the blood on her arm and leg. He carefully placed his pistol in his holster and approached her slowly.

"My name is Evan Watkins. I'm a medic with the Army," he said calmly and kneeled down next to her, removing the rucksack that rested against his back. He placed it on the floor gently.

"What is your name?" he asked her, opening his bag and grabbing a few items.

"Jessie," she responded and wiped the tears away. "Are you really here to help?"

Evan opened an antiseptic wipe. "Yes ma'am," he replied.

Jessie cleared her throat and nodded. "Of course," she stated and looked at the few cuts on her leg, sighing softly.

"May I?" Evan asked and Jessie nodded. She knew she was gullible, but she felt that he meant no harm.

"So…could you tell me why you are up here?" Evan asked and gently pulled one side of her legging up and past the few cuts on her lower leg.

Jessie cleared her throat and watched him carefully as he cleaned the wounds. A few more tears were filling her eyes.

"My family and I became trapped after the frequent quakes earlier today. Thankfully they slowed down, but since then, everyone had left…or…been killed," she said. She was having trouble talking about the difficult topic as she sighed once more.

"We should have left when we had the chance, but we didn't think it was going to get this serious," she said and paused, taking a deep breath before continuing. "I witnessed my family *die*…My fiancé and I were able to get out, but he…" she sniffed and fought back the tears as she continued, "disappeared when this…thing showed up. It looked like a monster. He told me to come here and that he would meet me. He didn't want me to go with anyone else but him so that's why I became frightened when I heard you downstairs."

Evan nodded and carefully bandaged her leg. "I understand. I'm sorry about your family, Jessie, truly I am," he responded.

Jessie nodded and wiped the remaining tears away. She was trying to compose herself as she took a deep breath in, exhaling it softly. Evan clipped the bandages in place and gently pulled her legging down.

"Thank you, Evan," Jessie said and slowly pushed herself to her feet.

Evan zipped his rucksack and tossed the straps over his arms, allowing the bag to rest against his back again. He stood up and watched Jessie dust her arms off.

"So do you know what these things are?" Jessie asked, unsure if he knew what she was referring to.

"Just that they were given a code name, the angra. We aren't sure where they came from," Evan replied and heard footsteps in the hall behind him. He quickly drew his M9 and turned around, staring at the open doorway. Jessie gasped and took a few steps back, brushing against the cold bars against the window.

"Evan?" a familiar voice called.

Evan sighed in relief and placed his pistol back into his holster. "In here, Josh," he said.

Josh slowly appeared in the doorway and took a deep breath. "Everything okay?" he asked.

"Yes. Did you have a change of heart?" Evan asked.

"Enough. I thought I heard something outside. I didn't want to check it out alone," Josh replied.

"Of course you wouldn't. Jessie, this is Josh. He'll be coming with us to the hospital," Evan stated, looking at Jessie. She didn't seem happy about the statement.

"Why the hospital?" she asked.

"There is another unit there assisting with evacuations. They can get you to safety," Evan replied, now confused by her tone.

"I'm not leaving until I find my fiancé."

"If you saw this monster going after him chances are slim that he is still alive, ma'am," Evan replied.

Jessie's mouth dropped and she suddenly slapped him across the cheek. Josh's eyes widened and he slowly turned around, glancing out in the hallway. Finally someone put the kid in his place.

Evan cleared his throat and stared at Jessie for a moment.

"Don't you dare say that..." she said and more tears began to fill her eyes.

"I'm sorry, ma'am. That was a bit out of line," he said and rubbed his cheek, taking a few steps back.

"Yes, it was. Nathan will come. I know he will."

"You don't want to stay here and wait alone, do you? I have orders to report to the hospital. You'll be safer with us."

More tears fell onto Jessie's cheek. She didn't want to stay here alone anymore, but she didn't want to take the chance of leaving Nathan behind either. She placed her face in the palms of her hands.

Evan sighed. "Look, we can try and find him on the way," he replied and Jessie slowly lowered her hands.

"I'm sorry. I know you are right. I just don't want to leave him behind. I don't want to lose him."

Evan patted her shoulder. "I understand," he replied and looked at Josh. He had disappeared into the hallway, pacing back and forth near the doorway.

"Let's get out of here, shall we?" Evan stated and he and Jessie stepped into the hall.

"Are we ready?" Josh asked.

Jessie nodded and Evan started walking back to the stairwell, ignoring the question. Jessie followed and Josh took in another deep breath. He knew he wasn't wanted around, but as long as he got to the hospital in one piece he didn't care. He was ready to leave and meet up with his family in Ohio.

There was a difference in the atmosphere once they stepped out of the back doors of City Hall. The wind had picked up and dark, puffy clouds were now rolling in from the mountains. An abandoned news crew van as well as other vehicles sat near them in the vacant parking lot. A large walkway stretched out in front of them and towards the lot as it split in both directions once it reached the pavement. To the left, a small road stretched alongside the building before curving off around a bend. Rows of small businesses sat across the street and one large Annabelle home. It was a visitor's center. A small welcome sign sat beside the sidewalk that led to the set of the stairs to the two story white house.

Josh was scanning the area nervously. The sound he heard was loud and all he noticed was a trash can on its side, its contents scattered around the tin barrel. Evan was already gripping on his M9 as he examined their surroundings.

"Maybe it was just the wind..." Josh stated and glanced at Evan.

"Let us hope so," he replied and gazed at the news crew van. Its side door was left open and camera equipment sat abandoned on the pavement beside it. Evan carefully approached it, one hand resting on his pistol. Jessie watched Josh follow him before turning her attention to the road and the visitor's center. Her heart ached for her family and for her fiancé. She wanted to find him and nothing more.

Jessie shot a quick glance back at Evan and Josh as they approached the van and examined it. She rubbed her lips together and quickly began making her way to the small road. She just wanted to take one quick look down it. It was the reassurance she needed to tell her that he probably wasn't coming. Jessie fought back the negative thoughts and slowly walked across the street, checking both sides. The area was vacant, but not still. The wind was brushing through the small trees in the area and pushing light debris across the ground. Its whispers whistled through the air and through her long hair as it brushed it off her shoulders. Jessie sighed and stopped once she reached the sidewalk, stepping onto it carefully. A few more tears were filling her eyes as she looked down the road towards the barricade that went across it and in between the buildings. She looked in the other direction as the road stretched off towards a small field with one gas station standing at the corner before it turned left around a descending bend. Larger trees stood by the bend and a few boulders sat across the street from them. Green moss covered parts of the rock and bases of the trees around the boulders. Jessie stared through the thickness of the greenery and looked at the small spring that flowed gently down its path, descending with the road before disappearing around a corner. This part of the valley was extremely beautiful with its abundance of green plants and trees, its crystal clear springs and rivers, and its rolling terrain. It made the area one of the most sought after peace and relaxation spots after a long week on the job.

Jessie took in a deep breath before sighing calmly. She continued to stare down the road until her attention was taken by a dirt road that split through the small field of trees. Something was lying at the foot of the path as she focused on the dull metal. It looked similar to a dog tag chain. Her heart suddenly sank and her mouth slowly dropped. She was afraid to move, her body frozen. She didn't think it was possible. The sounds of footsteps coming across the pavement suddenly interrupted the thoughts rushing through her mind as she shook from the startle. Evan had already reached her before she turned her attention to him.

"What is it?" Evan asked.

"Uh, nothing…I was just checking the road for any…possible signs," Jessie said and looked down at the sidewalk.

Evan already had a feeling to what she was referring to as he nodded. Jessie quickly wiped away the tears that snuck down her cheek and looked back at the dirt road.

"Well let's get moving if you don't mind. It will be a bit of a hike," Evan said and began walking down the sidewalk towards the dirt road. Josh quickly followed as Jessie slowly trailed behind. She kept a close eye on the dog tag and watched as Evan walked past the path, oblivious to the metal. Josh didn't seem to notice either. He kept a watchful eye on their surroundings. Jessie took in a deep breath once she reached the dirt road and quietly knelt down by the broken necklace. She gently picked it up and dusted off the dirt that coated the inscription. She carefully stood up and read the tag. As she read the words slowly, the worst of her fears rushed throughout her mind. The adrenaline began to erupt within her, burning her veins. She let out a low gasp and her heart raced. Josh and Evan glanced back at her and stopped as they watched her look down the dirt road. Her expression was distraught.

"Did you find something?" Evan asked and remained standing in place.

Josh took a few steps towards her and stopped. Jessie looked at them. The pain was unmistakably on her face. She looked back at the dirt road and then back at them.

"It's Nathan's…" she said.

Evan stared at her as she looked back down the path.

"He was here…" she added. "We were so close to this area when that thing attacked us…"

"Alright, stay calm," Evan replied and began walking towards her.

Jessie glanced at him quickly. "Please…go on without me!" she shouted and began running down the path towards the field of trees, kicking up dust along the way.

"Damn it," Evan gasped and looked back at Josh. "I'm going after her," he stated and quickly began running down the dirt road as well.

Josh looked around the calm atmosphere that surrounded him. He didn't want to be alone. He had no choice but to follow them. He sighed heavily with frustration as he ran after them.

"Nathan!" Jessie yelled. She gripped tightly on the dog tag and ran as fast as her legs could move her.

"Jessie! Stop!" Evan yelled, catching up to her quickly.

Jessie gasped and pushed harder. Dirt and dust continued to kick up from behind her as she pushed past the rows of trees. Evan gritted his teeth and pushed harder as well.

"You're wasting your time!" he shouted and reached out, grabbing her arm firmly. Jessie gasped and tripped, stumbling over her feet and falling towards the rough terrain. Evan stumbled as well, catching his fall with his arms. Jessie slid across the dirt and yelped. She coughed and took in a deep breath before pushing up on her arms slowly.

"Ugh, are you crazy!" she yelled, tears filling her eyes once again and spilling onto her cheeks.

Evan pushed himself to his feet and dusted himself off. "I'm sorry…" he stated.

Josh slowed to a walk once he reached them and examined the thickness of the trees, ignoring the situation that was unfolding between the two. The set of woods the road split in between was a bit nerve-wracking for him. Anything could be hiding in the brush.

Evan carefully knelt down beside Jessie and extended his hand.

"Let me help you," he said and Jessie ignored him, pushing herself to her feet and gently dusting the dirt off her arms and clothes. Evan sighed and stood back up.

"He's probably around here somewhere! I don't want to take the chance on leaving him behind, can't you understand that?" Jessie gasped and wiped the tears away from her face. She was breathing heavily as Evan tried to calm her down.

"I'm really sorry, Jessie…"

"You said we could try and look for him along the way, Evan."

"Yes, but in the direction to the hospital. I can't waste any time looking for one guy in this town."

Jessie shook her head. "Well, I'm not asking you to help me," she stated and began walking down the path slowly.

Evan followed, keeping his distance. "I really don't want to leave you in this wilderness…What did you find anyway?" he asked and watched Jessie as she looked at the ground.

"It was Nathan's dog tag."

"He's military?"

"No. His father made it for him when he was a child. His father was a Marine…" Jessie said and paused, slowing her walk. Something had caught her attention in the dirt.

"Now what is it?" Evan asked.

"I…I don't know," Jessie hesitated and kneeled down by the strange tracks imprinted in the soil. Her gaze followed the tracks to the trees. A few had fallen over as a couple of branches lay near the edge of the path. Evan looked at them as well and shook his head.

"You see, Jessie…I don't think you want to be out here alone. You could get yourself killed."

Jessie rolled her eyes and stood back up. "What do you think they belong to?" she asked, and placed the dog tag in her pocket.

"Could be the things lurking around this place."

"I don't believe so…" Josh quickly stated, stepping up beside them. Evan and Jessie looked at him.

"Those beasts haunting this valley are large…This looks to be from something a bit slimmer," Josh added.

Evan looked back at the tracks and thought about the angras. "How do you know?" he asked, examining the details in the soil.

"Well, these don't look as wide," Josh replied and looked towards the forest.

Jessie slowly approached the edge of the path and stared past the large fallen trees. It was quiet, except for the breeze whistling around them. Evan stepped up beside her as Josh continued to examine the tracks.

"Do you feel that?" Jessie asked as the wind began to pick up, pushing past them and through the leaves in the trees. Evan closed his eyes, feeling the warm air brush against his face.

"Yes."

He opened his eyes and stared toward a meadow.

"Wait here...I'm going to take a closer look," Evan said and carefully stepped over the trunk of a fallen tree and made his way through the brush.

Josh stepped up beside Jessie and checked their surroundings, fearing a possible encounter. Jessie watched as the overwhelming adrenaline flowed through her veins. Her heart was beating at a faster pace, her eyes focused on Evan's every move.

Evan pushed through the brush and detached his small flashlight, holding it tightly after turning it on. He carefully climbed over another tree and stepped down a trail before entering the small meadow. There were a few patches of grass near the trees, but the terrain had been disrupted in the middle. The soil had been pushed back and a large, round hole stretched down steadily into the earth. Evan released his breath quickly, shocked at what he was seeing. It was a large hole, a tunnel, carving down into the dark earth. Only one thing could have created it. Evan took a step forward and halted. The large, fearsome beast appeared in his mind. He could feel the heat pushing out of the tunnel and around him as its warm touch brushed against his skin. He glanced back at the others.

"I found something!" he shouted.

Jessie looked at Josh. He sighed heavily, wishing they could continue to their destination.

"I guess we should take a quick look, but we need to get out of this area incase this thing comes back," Josh stated and climbed over the large tree trunk that was lying in front of them. Jessie slowly nodded, afraid. She carefully followed him until they reached Evan. He was staring into the dark tunnel, his flashlight beaming into it.

"I believe this is where the dragon came to..." Evan said and looked at Josh.

He was anxious as he stared into the darkness. "We shouldn't be here," he whispered.

Jessie's eyes widened. She became speechless as Evan glanced back into the tunnel.

"A...dragon? Did I hear you correctly, Evan?" she finally asked.

Evan looked back at her. "Yes. Would you like to lead the way so we can check this out?"

Jessie stared at him in horror.

"I didn't think so, ma'am. You see...You can't go running off by yourself. It's too dangerous. Are you with me?" Evan asked.

Jessie stared at him for a moment and slowly nodded.

"If Nathan is still alive...I am sure he will know where to go. The hospital is a safe haven, evacuating the residents and any other survivors. A unit is assisting them as well as the northern valley. You need to trust me," Evan added.

Jessie sighed. "Alright. I'm sorry," she said and looked away.

Evan glanced back towards the large hole and took a few steps towards it. Josh's bottom jaw slowly lowered as his heart raced.

"You are seriously not considering going down there...Are you?" he asked.

"Yeah...I think I am," Evan replied, shining his flashlight into the darkness.

Jessie gasped. "No...Please don't..." she whispered.

Evan glanced at her as he stepped up to the entrance of the tunnel.

"We should just keep moving...We don't have anything to stop this thing, Evan," Josh stressed.

"Just stay put. I want to take a peek to see what this thing could possibly be up to under here. It could help us when we group with the other unit," Evan replied and carefully started to descend down the dark, hot tunnel.

"You are absolutely insane," Josh said and folded his arms as he examined their surroundings once more. The fear was beginning to make him extremely uncomfortable.

Jessie was breathing heavily as she watched Evan's light disappearing around a bend in the deep tunnel. The atmosphere grew quiet once again, and the feeling in their guts became more uncomfortable as the time slowly inched by.

Chapter Twelve

LYSSA WAS STANDING NEAR THE restrooms getting some water from the fountain. Will waited in the hall. He was examining some of the artwork, trying to free his restless mind. The paintings of the valley in its earlier years were beautiful. There was much more greenery back in those days.

Alyssa took in a deep breath after the last sip of water she took and exhaled it softly.

"Alright. Let's get going," she said and approached Will. "I really appreciate you staying with me. The little bit of rest I was able to get did help some," Alyssa added and Will nodded, holding out her M4.

"Thank you," Alyssa stated and carefully placed the strap over her head and onto her shoulder, allowing the rifle to rest against her back.

"You're welcome. I'll let you lead the way," Will said and allowed Alyssa to step around him.

He followed her down the hall and around a corner before stopping in front of a side door. Alyssa gently pushed against it, but the door didn't budge.

"Here. I got it," Will said and Alyssa stepped out of the way.

Will retrieved the keys from his vest pocket and flipped through them, thinking about the one she had mentioned earlier. Alyssa watched him grab the large key and unlock the door. He gently pushed it open and held it as Alyssa stepped out onto the sidewalk that faced the street. She checked their surroundings as Will locked and closed the door behind her. The northern valley had more patches of green forests and fields. The hills and mountainous terrain were more visible as they rolled in the distance behind the offices. Alyssa loved this part of the valley. The state park and campgrounds were not too far from where they were as well as the valley's main river. It was a crystal clear, winding river that split through the northern valley and towards the mountains. It was a river free of dams, always clean and cool.

Alyssa glanced at the large hill towards the west, staring at the cathedral that sat on it. It overlooked the valley, and its large clock on the front tower shined very brightly at night. Alyssa sighed and looked towards the east.

"This place is very beautiful," Will said, stepping up beside her.

Alyssa continued to look down the street, listening to the creek that flowed through the rocks and pebbles in the distance. She slowly nodded.

"It is indeed," she said faintly. Her stomach was still bothering her, but she refused to allow it to slow her down. She had already allowed too much time to slip by.

"Well, the hospital is this way. It'll be a rough hike. There are a lot of hills," Alyssa said and started walking towards the east where the road curved off to the left around a steep bend.

Will followed, staying beside her and watching her body language. As they passed the parking lot, he glanced towards the back of City Hall, noticing an abandoned news van with its side door open. His heart fluttered as he thought about the broadcast before he and his group were deployed there. It was from the same news station. Will looked away and took in a deep breath.

"You okay?" Alyssa asked, noticing the tension in the exhale of his breath.

"Yes, just trying to keep it together. There is much to discuss with the commander of the unit we are going to meet soon," Will replied.

Alyssa nodded as they continued down the street and around the bend. As they descended, she glanced through the trees, spotting the creek. It flowed at a fast pace, splashing over large rocks that sat in the way. The noise rattled her nerves and the sudden change in the weather didn't help either. The last thing they needed was an unexpected storm.

"So…Where are you from?" Alyssa asked and turned her attention to Will, hoping a little conversation would ease her nerves. He kept a steady pace beside her as they continued their trek.

"Trying to get to know me, Ms. Bennett?" Will asked and glanced at her, half smiling.

Alyssa's cheeks flushed as she turned to focus her attention back on the vacant road. It was curving through a thick patch of woods and brush. There were no buildings or houses, just the nature of the valley.

"Well, just trying to make conversation. With everything that has happened…I'm trying my best not to dwell on it and lose my train of thought. I'd hate to make a wrong turn now," Alyssa replied sincerely, returning the half smile.

"I understand. Well, I'm from Pennsylvania. I've been currently living near Fairfax for the past four years now. I joined the Army when I was nineteen. What about you? Lived here all your life?"

"Yes. I grew up here," Alyssa replied and thought of her childhood.

"What made you want to become a cop?" Will asked.

"My father was a cop, and my brother was…in the process of joining the academy at the time. I guess you could say it's in our blood. My father taught me how to use firearms at an early age and to abide by the law. The Air Force was second on my list. I've heard stories about being a military cop," Alyssa replied and glanced at Will.

He snickered. "They get deployed a lot and the hours can be rough," he stated.

"So what made you want to be a Green Beret?" Alyssa asked, intrigued.

Will took in a deep breath and looked ahead at the road they descended down.

"I wanted to make a difference in my life. My mother raised us kids. I have a younger brother, probably around your age, and an older sister. My father abandoned us when we were young and it left a huge scar. I wanted to be better than him. I wanted to be able to help others no matter the situation..." he replied and paused.

Alyssa glanced at him, examining his expression.

"I guess you could say I needed the structure. It's made me a better person."

Alyssa looked down the road as well. They were approaching another street to the right as she glanced at it.

"You seem to have your head on straight," she said and smiled.

Will smiled as well and took another glance at her. "The Army is disciplined. It has taught me a lot. I'm sure you have a bit of the same structure from going through the academy, though I'm sure it wasn't as rough..."

Alyssa bit her bottom lip. She liked the statement, but the past few weeks had been difficult. She wasn't the same person anymore, and the structure she once had had been taken away from her. She wanted it back. It made her ache for the life she had before the accident.

"Did I say something wrong?" Will asked and followed Alyssa to the street on the right. It ascended through the wilderness and stretched towards a small bridge that went over the rapid creek bed. Alyssa shook her head and stared towards the bridge.

"No, not at all," she replied and paused, sighing softly. "I was just thinking about how my life was before...Before the accident that is," she added and looked at Will. He was watching her concernedly.

"I see," he stated.

"You know...This isn't me, actually," Alyssa said and tried to find the right words to what she was describing as she noticed Will's confused expression.

"I was much more...*alive*, happy...It's crazy what these nightmares and lack of sleep have done to me."

"It can definitely take a toll on someone's mind and body. I understand, Alyssa. I don't judge you at all," Will replied.

Alyssa could sense his sincerity and felt a bit relieved. She hated to bring back up the negativity, but a little bit of weight off her shoulders eased some of her pain.

"What will you do if…you are unable to find your parents?" Will asked, breaking the short silence.

Alyssa hesitated. "I haven't actually thought about that. But now that you mention it…I'm really not sure. I only had my brother, and I have only one grandfather still alive and he's in a senior home," she replied and thought for a moment.

Will was beginning to feel a bit sorry for her. His parents were still alive and he had a grandmother still living. He had a big family and they all lived in Pennsylvania, keeping contact with one another quite regularly.

"I have a few friends I can stay with. I'm sure I will figure it out. I'm not in the least bit concerned," Alyssa said and looked towards the creek they neared. She didn't want Will to see the lie behind that. She was terrified.

Will remained silent and took the opportunity to finally examine the beauty of their surroundings. As they approached the bridge, Alyssa took in a deep breath. The fresh air was soothing. The wind continued to blow around them, warning them of a possible storm approaching over the mountains. The darks clouds were rolling slowly in the distance, hovering over the mountaintops. Alyssa hoped it would pass without a single drop. They were not close enough to the north side of town to feel comfortable with getting just a little wet before finding shelter.

"Wow…" Will stated as they stepped over the bridge. He stopped once he reached the middle and approached the side, looking down at the winding creek that began to descend and stretch off to the east. Will noticed a few houses in the distance. They all sat on individual properties that were securely wrapped with wooden fences.

"This place is very scenic. I love it," Will added, resting his body against the side of the bridge as he stared into the distance.

"You must not get out much," Alyssa said, stepping up beside him.

"Very rare do I nowadays. I used to go camping though when I was younger. That was as close to nature as I would get. I bet it was amazing to grow up here," Will replied. He watched the creek race down the hill, splashing over anything that got in its path.

"I have many wonderful memories..." Alyssa stated and looked down as the vision of the bridge suddenly changed into a scene from what appeared to be a dark cave with a shallow creek running through it. It flowed peacefully and around all the large rocks and jagged edges that jutted out from it. Large and small illuminating crystals hung from the ceiling and the walls, creating a soft glow that lit up the area gently. In the middle of the image, she stood, standing at the edge of the creek. She held onto a maglite, staring at a large, rectangular rock that sat on the other side of the creek. She stood in awed silence, her expression frozen with wonder. And then the sudden image of the familiar devilish eyes flashed into her mind quickly, the vision slowly fading back to the bridge.

Alyssa quickly closed her eyes and cleared her throat. The nausea was coming back, intensifying by the second. Will glanced at her, watching her cover her mouth to cough. Alyssa opened her eyes and looked at the pavement. Another vision crept into her mind, flashing an image from the cavern once more. She was standing in the middle of it, walking slowly around, gazing at every crystal in amazement. Her view was fixated on her as if she were watching herself through someone else's eyes. Then she heard the familiar growl. It was coming from deep within a set of lungs. She could almost feel it deep within her own chest as she watched herself quickly walk to another area of the cavern. She passed two rocky pillars, glancing at the markings etched into the walls. Her flashlight lit up the area around her brightly, but the light slowly faded as she watched herself disappear around a corner...

The vision became black before it slowly faded away. Alyssa was now staring back at the bridge, gripping the side of it. Her eyes closed tightly and she was breathing heavily. She continued to cough and fight back the nausea with all her might. Will had placed his hand on her back and held her free arm with the other.

"We need to get you to the hospital. There will be medics there to help," he said and Alyssa slowly leaned back and stood up straighter, breathing deeply.

"What is happening to me?" she whispered.

Will remained silent and looked up the street as it continued to ascend through the wilderness and curve off to the left.

"Come on. I got you," Will stated and helped her across the bridge.

Alyssa cleared her throat once more. The nausea was slowly subsiding and she felt as if she was getting a bit of her strength back.

"I'll be alright until we get there," she said and Will lowered his hands and kept a close eye on her as she paced herself up the hill.

"A cold glass of water would be nice," Alyssa added, continuing to breathe deeply.

"Yes it would," Will replied.

They remained silent as they continued the trek up the hill. The land was finally flattening out as it curved off to the left, stretching north. There was a small sign by the road stating the location of the valley's state park and campground. Will took in a deep breath as the wind pushed against them gently, whistling around. He continued to keep a close eye on Alyssa as she remained quiet, carefully walking down the empty street. They remained silent for a while until the forest began to dissipate into a green field. The street they were on began to curve around a bend, wrapping close to a river bed that was now coming in view. It flowed slowly, its trickles softly heard in the area. The chirps from crickets became clamorous and persistent and the constant hoot from an owl echoed in the distance across the river in another set of trees. The air was much cooler, relaxing their fatigued muscles. It relieved a bit of Alyssa's pain and nausea. She breathed the fresh air deeply and stopped, staring towards the river bed. It slowly curved with the road before stretching east. The road they stood on eventually went north. Alyssa sighed softly and slowly began to approach the river's edge. Will watched her for a moment and soon followed, stepping into the grass and keeping some distance behind her. Alyssa stepped around a small tree and past a few large boulders before coming to the water's edge. She carefully kneeled down by it and gazed into the crystal clear water, seeing the sandy bottom. A few large rocks sat below and she could see some small fish still swimming about.

Alyssa was still staring into the water once Will reached her side. He knelt down beside her and watched her place her hand into the cold water. She carefully pulled her hand out and gently wiped her face and neck. The cold touch was soothing and it gave her a bit of an energy boost, something she needed. The fatigue was taking a toll on her.

"Sometimes..." Alyssa began to say and paused as the water dripped down from her face and neck. "I feel as if something else has control over me."

"Did you see something again?" Will asked, curious.

"Yes. It was out of nowhere too. I felt as if I was in another body... staring at myself from the distance. I was actually watching...*me,*" Alyssa replied and slowly stood up.

Will did the same and leaned against his left leg, allowing the right side of his body to relax.

"I'd be lying if I said I wasn't concerned," he said and Alyssa looked into his eyes, trying to read him. She saw the change in him at City Hall, but she wasn't sure why.

"This is so surreal...No one should ever endure something like this. What you and the rest us have endured," Will added and looked towards the bend in the river. He could see the tips of buildings in the distance and this made him feel a bit relieved. The weather hadn't changed yet. The wind still blew around them and through the branches of the trees, and the dark clouds continued to roll through the valley.

Alyssa looked towards the buildings as well. She finally felt a little bit of hope inside her as she thought of her parents. This was the motivation she needed.

"My parents could be there right now..." Alyssa said, continuing to stare towards the buildings.

Will glanced at her. "You're right," he replied, hoping for her sake.

"I've got to keep pushing myself. I can do this," Alyssa said and began walking towards the street near the bend. Will followed, keeping up beside her.

"I assume the hospital is in that direction?" he asked, pointing towards the buildings in the distance.

"It is," Alyssa replied, breathing heavily. She was feeling weak and her muscles were tired. Her mind was becoming fuzzy, and she wasn't able to think clearly at the moment, but she knew where they were going and that was all she cared about. Will was becoming nervous as the minutes slowly passed. Alyssa's health appeared to be dwindling away. Her face looked more pale and drained, her body was dragging with fatigue, and her breaths came out fast and heavy.

As they turned the bend and made it down the road, Will became anxious. They had passed a small gas station and express shop before reaching rows of offices and small clinics. The hospital wasn't too far away now.

Alyssa slowed herself and eventually stopped, placing her hands on her knees. Will stopped and stepped in front of her.

"It's not much further..." he said.

Alyssa panted as she nodded. "I know...I'm not sure if I can make it though," she gasped and slowly pushed her hands away from her knees, straightening up.

"Yes you can. I know you can," Will urged and looked behind him.

Alyssa continued to breathe heavily as she nodded. "Alright, I'm right behind you..." she said and Will glanced back before continuing forward. As he turned his back to her and pushed ahead, Alyssa followed. She could sense the anxiety in him and the urgency in his tone. He wanted to get them to the hospital. He wanted to get them to the safest location. Alyssa could see that he was worried. He was scared for her. She had to be as strong as he was no matter the challenge.

I can do this...I got to keep fighting...

But Alyssa's thoughts were abruptly interrupted as the familiar growl that haunted her, pierced through the silence behind her. She quickly stopped in her tracks, her heart sinking deep within her chest. She could see that Will was completely unaware. He continued forward, examining the area carefully. Alyssa exhaled her breath in a low gasp and looked behind her. The parking lot to the offices and clinic was small. There were a few short trees on small patches of grass near the road and parts of the parking lot. The area was vacant and the lights were off from what she could see through some of the windows. The tallest of the trees stood behind the building and continued to sway with the wind as it pushed through them. Alyssa continued to scan through the area until her vision became fuzzy once again. She gasped once more and looked back in front of her.

"Alyssa?" Will asked, walking back to her quickly.

She remained silent as she stared into his eyes. Will became nervous and carefully placed a hand on the side of her arm.

"Talk to me..." he stated.

Alyssa's eyes began to tear up. "Will...Please...If something happens to me, please find my parents...James is my father..." she choked.

Will quickly nodded. "Yes, but you are going to be fine..."

Alyssa froze as her eyes became more of a blur. She slowly placed her hand on Will's arm as he continued to hold onto hers.

"Alyssa?" Will asked, and the image in front of her suddenly changed...

She was now standing back in the small opening with her father in the woods. The entrance to the cavern was on her left. Her father had approached Brian, a look of confusion on his face. Alyssa slowly went under the yellow Government Property tape and watched her father and their close family friend speak.

"...What's this about?" James asked and folded his arms.

Brian sighed and cleared his throat. "This...is the cavern that Richard came to," he hesitated and watched James's expression change from confusion to shock.

"What did you say?" he whispered and lowered his arms.

"James, it's been twelve years..."

"How could you bring me here...Why would you bring me here? You know what that did to us," James replied angrily.

Brian looked at the ground, nodding. "We've finally come to realization that the tale truly existed once upon a time. You've got to stop denying it...You could finally be at peace with Richard's..."

"Don't say it!" *James shouted and looked back at Alyssa. She was still standing near the trail, looking at them with a bit of fear in her eyes, hearing every word.*

"I'm sorry, James..." *Brian said and waited for James to turn his attention back to him.* "But this cavern...James, you know it's not so ordinary..." *he continued.*

James's forehead pulled down, confusion appearing in his eyes again.

"We believe it contains the riches of the valley...The truth to its secret...The legend behind the tale..." *Brian said and Alyssa could feel her heart beating faster. She turned her attention away from her father and Brian and stared at the entrance to the cavern. But before she could take a step forward, the pair of bright yellow, dragonish eyes flashed in front of her, a loud shriek following after it...*

Alyssa screamed in fright as the image quickly faded to darkness. Her lifeless body fell towards Will as he grabbed onto her arms and pulled her up to him.

"Alyssa!" he yelled and slowly knelt down with her. He quickly examined her, feeling for a pulse and checking for breathing.

What the hell happened? What is going on with her!

Alyssa's eyes were closed and she remained unresponsive. Will quickly leaned in and pulled her onto his back, allowing her to rest on his shoulders as he pushed himself to his feet, looking back towards the hospital's direction.

"I got you...You are going to be okay," he said and walked as fast as he could down the street, ignoring everything beside him. His focus was straight ahead and to a street on the left. It was going to be a tough walk, but nothing was going to slow him down now.

Chapter Thirteen

THE HEAT IN THE TUNNEL began to intensify as Evan carefully stepped down the rugged path that led deep into the earth. His light shined brightly against the walls, and he kept his eyes focused at the darkness ahead. A strange noise was also heard, making Evan a bit nervous. He was beginning to doubt his decision as he stopped in his tracks and listened carefully. He kept his pistol aimed directly in front of him, his light resting against the top of it as he held it carefully with his other hand. He focused on the faint noise, unaware of where or what it was coming from. It sounded as if something was bubbling, popping from a thick liquid. Evan remained calm and wondered if he should continue any further. His fear was slowly elevating.

I can't stand here and wonder why I did this now...I got to keep going.

Evan released his breath slowly and walked down the path. It continued to descend deep into the earth, the heat intensifying with each step he took. As he got deeper and deeper into the tunnel, the path began to turn slightly to the right. A soft glow was seen against the wall, illuminating the area. Evan lowered his flashlight and recognized the new sound that crackled in the distance. He took a deep breath in and held it once he reached the bend, carefully stepping around the corner. It took him a moment to examine the area and gather all the information. He released his breath in a low gasp, awestruck. There was a large opening with a few more corridors carved into the earth. Parts of the sewer were visible across the river of lava. Fires engulfed the oil that spilled from the broken oil lamps that once hung on the brick walls of the sewers. The river of magma flowed slowly, and air bubbles pushed their way to the surface, popping and spewing.

Sweat began to drip down Evan's forehead as he stared at the hellish underworld.

It's the worst of our fears...All of this could erupt and destroy the valley...or worse...

Evan's jaw slowly lowered. He began to think about the dragon and the possibility of it leaving the valley once it burned to dust. If the world became aware of its existence, there would be widespread fear and chaos. Life could cease to exist.

Evan shook his head and froze in place as the earth slowly shook. The lava spewed about and continued on its course, pushing past soil and rock. Dirt and pebbles fell from above, falling around and against Evan. He quickly wiped his face and turned around. The earth slowly stopped trembling and the ground settled, but the fear was building within him at a fast pace. He didn't want to be down there much longer and risk being trapped if the ground above suddenly gave way. Evan pointed his flashlight back down the tunnel and began jogging down it. The darkness ahead soon gave way to a dim light and the cool breeze was pushing into the tunnel, brushing past him, relieving his anxiety. Evan took a deep breath in and reached the bend, seeing the leaves in the trees ahead.

"Hey guys!" he called, jogging out of the tunnel and back into the small meadow.

Evan stopped in his tracks and looked around. The area was vacant and the only whispers he could hear were coming from the breeze that continued to whistle through the brush.

"Josh? Jessica?" Evan asked and took a few steps forward, looking in every direction.

"Over here," Josh said, climbing over the trunk of a fallen tree that was lying near the foot of the trail.

Evan became a bit alarmed as he watched Josh approach him alone.

"I'm sorry. I tried to stop her..." Josh began to say as Evan interrupted, "Where did she go?"

Josh took in a deep breath. "She walked back to the dirt road and said she wanted to wait there. It wasn't long when she said she saw someone," he replied.

Evan sighed heavily. "She doesn't understand," he said softly.

"We can't keep chasing her around..."

"I know," Evan snapped back and walked back to the path, climbing over any debris that was lying in his way.

Josh followed, becoming more impatient as the minutes passed. Evan looked down both directions of the dirt road once he reached it, ignoring Josh as he came up beside him.

"She went that way. It leads to a couple of neighborhoods, a park, and a church," Josh said, pointing in the opposite direction of City Hall.

"And you couldn't stop her?" Evan asked, glancing at him.

"Unless you would have wanted me to use excessive force. She said she saw a few people. I think she recognized them."

"Well if you don't want to travel to the hospital alone, then you're going to have to come with me a little while longer. If there are more people around this hell, I need to find them."

Josh took in a deep breath and looked down the dirt road. He didn't feel guilty that he wanted out of the valley as bad as he did, but as he thought of civilians or tourists being left behind to die made him feel a bit uneasy.

"I understand. I'll come with you, but I don't feel we should keep giving this lady second chances when all she has done is run off," Josh replied.

Evan nodded. "You're right. This is it...If no one comes with us they'll be on their own," he replied.

"Good. Follow me," Josh said and began jogging down the path.

Evan carefully followed, keeping a watchful eye on their surroundings. They passed one Estate, an Annabelle home from the early 1800's with a small historic sign near its gates. It was a home passed on from generation to generation from one of the early known settlers. It rested on a large lot of thick Bermuda grass and surrounded by acres of trees that hid it from the rest of the community. Evan admired the beauty of the area and wondered what was to become of it after what he had seen below its foundation. Everything could collapse, but when was an uncertainty.

After jogging down the hill and up the next, Josh and Evan had reached a road. Across from it was a neighborhood made up of small townhomes, but what caught Josh's attention was the church that sat on the hill towards the west. Evan glanced at it as well, looking at the large clock on its tower. It shined brightly, illuminating the old stone it was built from. There were soft yellow glows coming from the stained glass windows on both floors making the church appear alive and homelike. This confused Evan. He wasn't sure why anyone would seek refuge there when there were evacuations taking place at the hospital. Then he thought about faith and how he had forgotten his own. Perhaps faith was all that was left to aid them.

"Wait...Isn't that her?" Josh asked, pointing towards the church.

Evan refocused and looked at the young lady that was standing near the large, wooden door out front of the building. Three other people were standing near her.

"That's definitely her," Evan replied, watching Jessie and the man in front of her.

It seemed as if they were arguing. Jessie had her arms crossed and the man's body language didn't seem too relaxed either.

"Well hopefully she found this Nathan character," Josh stated and began walking across the street towards the church. Evan followed and thought of the possible reasons of this assumed argument.

Josh was only happy to see the northern valley not as badly damaged as the southern portion. There were a few cracks and tears, but that was all he noticed. As they crossed the street, they continued to watch their surroundings through the little light that shone from the few street lamps and the clock on the church's tower.

The large, stone building didn't seem to welcome only the people who searched for shelter or a safe haven. A few large crows sat on the tall, black gates that wrapped around the yard and towards the stairway to the door. There frequent caws sent chills throughout their bodies as the fear that once lay dormant awoke once more to rattle their nerves...

Will could see the bright lights of Trinity Hospital shining behind the trees as he continued to run towards the street that led to it. He was anxious to get there after having to pause a couple of times to readjust Alyssa's weight. The hilly terrain didn't aid in the trek either, causing the fatigue in his muscles to intensify.

Will fought back the urge to stop as he approached the street, ignoring the other small buildings that stood near the two story hospital in the distance. There was an evac helicopter sitting silently on the helipad near the emergency room entrance, and there were a few humvees sitting in the street near the hospital's main entrance. There were mobile hospital units situated in the lawn, and there were soldiers and medics rushing about. A few military cops stood out front of the double doors and in the street near the humvees. There looked to be a lot of chaos. Some of the medics were rushing about, and there was a lot of commotion at the mobile command unit.

Will felt relieved as he noticed two soldiers jogging towards him, rifles in hand. They were two of the military cops that stood and kept a look out. They seemed concerned and a bit surprised to see a lone soldier about, but they could also see the alarm in Will's face, the lifeless body resting against his shoulders.

"She needs a medic immediately," Will panted once the two cops reached him.

"Yes, sir. I believe our mobile units are at capacity, but there are still doctors in the hospital. This way, sir," the young soldier replied and began jogging to the entrance.

"Thank you, Private," Will said and followed him, glancing at the young military cops that stood out front. They each had a pistol strapped to their thighs, and they carefully held M4 assault rifles. They were definitely prepared for something. Will was curious to know if they had seen the beasts lurking around the valley or if they were even aware of the much larger one that was lying below it.

Will followed the soldier into the hospital and tried to examine the faces of the soldiers that walked about, hoping to see any familiar faces from his group. He was breathing heavily as he carried Alyssa around a corner passed the registry desks and to the emergency department. Nurses and doctors continued to work with patients and behind their stations, no worry or strain on their faces. It made Will feel good about the people here. They were full of determination no matter the risks or circumstances.

"Miss!" the young soldier called and a young lady in red scrubs carrying a clip board quickly approached him.

"We need another room," he added.

The young lady glanced at Will and then at Alyssa. "Yes, please follow me," she said and led them to a small room on the right. Will followed, trying to ignore all the medical equipment that buzzed and beeped around him. He absolutely hated hospitals. He didn't like the aroma, all the loud noise, and the depressing atmosphere. Only a life or death situation would drag him to one.

"Beth!" the young lady called and stopped once she reached the small room. She looked back at Will and gestured to the bed. Will quickly looked at the young soldier.

"Thank you, Private," he said and walked to the bed, lying Alyssa down gently. The young soldier nodded and disappeared down the hall.

"Okay, I'm going to try and be quick about this. I'm Laura. I'm with patient registry. Your nurse is Beth. She should be here in just a second," the young lady said and held up her clip board. Will was still breathing heavily, focusing most of his attention on Alyssa.

"I need the patient's name and date of birth," Laura stated and looked at Will, pen in hand. Will was distracted as a nurse quickly walked in and examined Alyssa.

"Hi, I'm Beth. Was she knocked out from a collapse?"

"Um, no…We were on our way here and she was feeling sick. She passed out," Will replied.

"Hmm…" Beth mumbled and checked Alyssa, feeling for a pulse and checking her breathing.

After a minute of silence, Beth carefully placed Alyssa's arm next to her after feeling her pulse in her wrist. She placed her fingertips gently on her neck and throat before moving along to examine her body. She carefully pulled her shirt up, examining the bandages.

"Goodness. She looks like she crawled out from all the debris in the southern valley..."

"She's definitely been through a lot. Will she be alright?" Will asked.

"I'm sure she will. We'll get an IV started for her. I'm going to find the doctor so I can speak with him. He should be by soon. Please let me know if her condition worsens before I return," Beth said and Will nodded.

Laura smiled at Beth as she stepped out of the room and down the hall. Laura turned her attention back to Will and cleared her throat.

"Okay, let's try this again..." she said and Will took in a deep breath. He wasn't going to be able to answer all these questions. He was sure of it.

"Her name is Alyssa Bennett. I do not have a birth date," he responded.

"Do you know if she lives around here?"

"She does. She was a cop for this town."

Beth glanced back Alyssa. "Okay," she replied and walked to a small laptop on a tall stand. She sat her clip board on the counter and began typing. Will ignored her, turning his attention back to Alyssa. It bothered him to see her in this condition. After looking her over he could finally see how exhausted she truly looked. She still had a lot of dirt on her arms and parts of her clothing were spotted with dried blood. Her hair was falling out of the tie she had used to pull it up with as the shorter pieces in the front hung beside her face.

Will looked back at Laura.

"Okay, I have one Alyssa Bennett. Occupation Rockdale Valley Police Department...birth date...hmm..." she paused and glanced at Alyssa. "It fits...I know I have seen her around."

Laura picked up her clip board and began writing.

"Would you know an emergency contact?" she asked.

"No..." Will replied and thought for a moment. He didn't know of another contact, and he couldn't leave her here alone. He wanted to make sure she was evacuated safely.

"Just put myself," he added.

Laura looked at him for a moment. "Um, okay. I'm sorry that I have to do this, but I need to make sure it's up to date and that we have it on hand in case we lose access to the computer. May I have your name please?"

"William Thompson."

"And a contact number?"

"It's..." Will paused and looked into the hallway. A couple of soldiers had passed the door and he felt as if he recognized one. He quickly stood up.

"Um, here's my card, ma'am. All the information is there. Excuse me one moment..." Will said and quickly retrieved a business card, handing it to her.

"Oh, alright..." Laura hesitated, taking his card.

Will stepped out into the hall and looked down it. There were quite a few soldiers walking about and a few men and women in scrubs and white coats. Will mumbled to himself.

"Is everything okay?" Beth asked, startling him.

Will turned around. "Uh, yes."

"Alright. I'm going to get the IV started now, and we will keep a check on her vitals," Beth said and stepped into the room.

Will slowly stepped back inside, giving her space. Laura had finished her business on the computer and quickly picked her clip board up and walked out of the room. Will slowly approached Alyssa and watched Beth get an IV set up for her. He began to think about her parents and the possibility of them being there. Alyssa had begged him to try and find out. They could possibly be in the area if not.

"Beth...I was hoping you could help me," Will said and looked at her as she hung the bag above Alyssa's bed.

"Okay," Beth replied and opened a pouch with tubing and a needle.

"I need to find out if her parents are here. I believe they were in some sort of accident. Is this the only hospital in town?"

Beth nodded. "It is...The next town is miles away. You could ask Laura. If her parents allow that information to be disclosed then we would be able to share that with you," she replied and began searching for a good vein on Alyssa's arm. Alyssa remained unresponsive, her body still and calm.

"Alright. Thank you. I've got something to take care of. Could you please page me if something comes up?" Will asked.

"Of course," Beth replied.

"Thank you," Will responded and took one last look at Alyssa. Another thought hit him as he began to search through his pocket. He gently caressed a coin and placed it carefully into Alyssa's hand. Beth glanced at him and slowly smiled. Will carefully stepped away. He was afraid to leave her alone, but he had to find the commander and see if any of his group was in the building. He knew he recognized one.

"Don't worry, sir. We will take good care of her," Beth said after placing the IV in and starting the machine up. Will nodded and stepped out into the hall before he could change his mind.

The atmosphere was noisy and hectic. Will fought to ignore it, quickly scanning the hall as he approached the lobby and patient registry. The soldiers that were walking about and the few that stood by the doors didn't seem familiar, but he noticed the one that helped him earlier. He was talking to another military cop. Will stepped up to him and cleared his throat.

"Is the young lady alright, Sergeant First Class?" the young soldier asked, turning his attention to him.

"I believe so. Again, thank you. I was hoping you could tell me who is in command here," Will stated.

"Yes, sir. That would be Major Eric O'Connell. He should be outside."

"Thank you, Private," Will said and stepped past the soldiers and through the glass doors. As he stepped outside, he stopped and took a deep breath, releasing it slowly. He observed the area carefully and collected his thoughts. He wasn't sure how this commander was going to react with such news, but he was hoping for the assistance they desperately needed or at least a possible plan of action.

Will carefully stepped down the few stairs and scanned through the insignias of the soldiers around him until he saw one that met the description. He was a much older gentleman with short, silver hair and was walking towards him with a young medic at his side, discussing something. Will watched them for a moment until they got closer so he could read the name. He cleared his throat and stepped up to them, saluting the major.

"Excuse me, Major, I need to talk with you about a very important matter, please," Will stated and the major looked at him for a brief moment before turning his attention back to the young medic at his side.

"Just do what you can until the other helicopter returns," he ordered.

The medic gave a nod. "Yes, sir," he replied and walked away.

The major turned his attention back to Will and returned the salute. His expression was serious. "Hmm…Sergeant First Class Thompson. I know I have seen another green beret around here, but I don't believe it was you…"

"Hopefully there are a few left from my group, sir."

"You were the group deployed in the southern valley," the major stated, crossing his arms.

"We were, and we've encountered many…things. We lost our commander. I believe myself and maybe just a handful of others survived," Will said and watched the major's face become a bit alarmed.

"What happened?"

"Major O'Connell…Have you or your men seen any strange things here?" Will asked.

"No reports of anything…*suspicious* actually being seen have been brought to my attention, but a few of our men haven't returned from their search and rescue mission. I had a few go out to try and locate them. Our main focus has been the injured and the evacuations."

Will sighed. "Were you given any reports of things they've classified as angras?" he asked.

"Angras?" The major became confused, raising an eyebrow.

"They are large beasts...demonic-like beasts. They are almost indestructible, and they have killed many, sir. I know all of this is going to sound absurd."

"You've got that right."

Will took in a deep breath and remained calm. "We need your help, Major. There's more going on, and if the rest of the world finds out what is occurring here, there'll be mass panic."

"What else are you trying to tell me, Sergeant First Class?"

"There is a dragon below this town. It's huge, snake-like. We believe it's the reason for the earthquakes..."

"Thompson, did you hit your head? How in the world do you expect me to believe any of this?" the major asked, uncrossing his arms.

"I have a young lady with me. She will be able to verify everything. My commander was only briefed about these angras. He wasn't even aware of the dragon. But now it is just myself and Private Evan Watkins. We need to destroy these things before they attempt to escape," Will replied and the major stared at him for a long moment before sighing softly. He could tell Will had been through quite a bit, but this wasn't what he was expecting or even prepared to hear.

"I wasn't made aware about anything..." the major began and shook his head, continuing, "anything *monstrous* or...possibly out of the ordinary actually being spotted." He paused once more and Will slowly nodded.

"So the residents weren't making any of those ridiculous stories up, I see..." the major added and looked Will in the eyes. "And you are not making any of this shit up, right Sergeant First Class?" he asked firmly.

"No sir. We've been up close and personal with all of them. We don't have the right firepower. It takes too much to slow them down, and they don't drop without a fight," Will replied, thinking about Alex and the rest of his team. The major looked at him for a brief moment and turned away, examining the area. Everyone around the vicinity was busy and completely oblivious to their conversation. The major cleared his throat and turned his attention back to Will.

"Alright, Thompson. I will see what I can do. Unfortunately our radios haven't been working properly so we lost contact with command…"

"Your radios are out too?" Will asked. He still couldn't comprehend what was interfering with them in the first place.

"Yes. It's odd. They were working fine when we first arrived yesterday. It was just a few hours ago when they became faulty."

Will thought to himself as the Major continued, "Well I'll go talk to my pilots before they take this next round. You…hang around. Take it easy for a moment."

"Yes, Major," Will replied and glanced over the major's shoulder, seeing a man in a black business suit and tie step up the first set of stairs. All of a sudden, it felt as if time slowed for him. Everyone was walking at a slow pace, stress appearing on their faces, but the only thing Will was able to focus on was the man in the business suit. He was walking up the stairs casually as if he had no idea on what was going on in the valley. There was a calm look on his face and his dark brown and grayish hair was clean cut and combed to the side. He appeared relaxed. A bit too relaxed for the situation that was taking place there.

The major glanced over his shoulder and realized who Will was staring at.

"Ah, don't mind him. He seems out of place, but he's secret service. He's been keeping an eye on things. The way I see it, my men and I do our jobs and he does his," he said, looking back at Will.

Will nodded and watched the agent casually walk by. He glanced at Will, looking at his uniform before making eye contact with him. Will slowly nodded his head once towards him. A slight smirk curled across the agent's face as he turned his attention to the entrance of the hospital, stepping up the next flight of stairs behind Will.

"Excuse me, Major O'Connell, we have a problem," a soldier said, coming up from behind the major.

"Okay. Private. Thompson, we'll be in touch," the major stated.

Will saluted him and the major quickly returned it before turning away. Will watched as he followed the young soldier to a mobile unit. He watched for a moment and took in a deep breath, looking around the area one last time. It seemed safe, but an unsettling feeling was lingering in his gut. He looked back towards the entrance to the hospital. He hoped the major was going to take this seriously.

Chapter Fourteen

"JESSIE!" EVAN YELLED, WATCHING HER follow the others into the large church on the hill. "She had to have heard me," he added and sighed heavily.

Josh ignored the statement. He was just trying to keep an eye around them until they were in the building. He was still thinking about the tracks and if the thing that created them was in the area. He feared another encounter with a monstrous beast that they have yet to see.

Evan picked up his pace and began jogging towards the stone stairs that sat between the large, black gate. Josh followed, ignoring the large crows that continued to caw on the fence. As soon as Evan reached the stairs, he carefully jogged up them, examining the front yard of the church. Small stone statues of angels were placed in the grass near the small, short trees that stood around the yard. Stone benches were placed by the path that led to the church. It was a beautiful place, even though church was something Evan wasn't too fond of. Being forced into it at a child eventually drove him to disappear at eighteen and join the military, knowing that would separate him from the pressure of his parents.

Josh carefully followed Evan up the stairs and towards the wooden double doors. He glanced up at the top of the church, where the large clock shined even more brightly. Evan gently grabbed the cold, metal handle and pulled the large door open. As he stepped inside the dim foyer, Jessie and three others looked at him. Evan took in a deep breath, frustration appearing on his face.

"I hope you are done running now," he said sarcastically and glanced at the three civilians standing in the room with her. The male standing in front of Jessie had his arms crossed, his eyebrows pulled down. His battered black t-shirt was a tight fit, his muscles broad and self-evident. The female standing close to his side, her long, sleek black hair resting against her back, appeared nervous and afraid. Her dark brown eyes were shooting back and forth between him and Jessie. She wore a long, thin strapped dress that was ripped in some areas. The male that stood further behind them appeared calm. He seemed to be hiding his true fear. His short, thick brown hair was unkempt, strands stuck to his forehead from the perspiration. His shirt and jeans were also battered.

Josh closed the door quietly and looked around the dark foyer. Sconces hung around the room, their candles burning dimly. The stone walls were almost bare with just a couple of pictures and tapestries hanging on them. A large area rug was in the middle of the floor, and a few old fashioned couches sat against the walls with a few end tables beside them. The area was dark, and there was something odd lingering in the atmosphere. Josh could sense it.

Jessie sighed heavily and rolled her eyes after Evan's remark, looking back at the man in front of her. "You could have gone back after him," she stated angrily.

"Are you serious? With what? My bare hands? Aren't you forgetting that I have Ariana with me?" the man firmly asked.

Josh stood and watched, feeling a bit awkward. Jessie let a few tears roll down her cheeks before taking a deep breath in.

"We understand how you feel, but you are being a bit selfish," the man added.

"He would've done it for you, Ray!" Jessie yelled and a door suddenly opened behind her.

"What's this ruckus?" a shaky voice asked.

Jessie looked behind her as the others stared into a dark hallway. An old, petite woman with white hair pulled back into a long ponytail slowly stepped into the lobby. She had dark eyes and chestnut skin and wore a few pieces of jewelry related to her Native American heritage.

"And you are?" the man in front of Jessie asked.

"I'm Dena. This is my church," the old woman said.

We're sorry to intrude. We thought that this place would be safe," Ariana stated softly.

Evan glanced at her, examining her chocolate skin and long black hair. The old lady snickered and slowly walked around them.

"Well you are welcome to stay...but it is no safer in here than it is out there," she stated and opened one of the double doors across from the entrance.

"Um, a little hope would be nice," Ariana whispered as Dena disappeared into the other room.

The man in front of Jessie shook his head and glanced at Evan and Josh. "Creepy...So are you here to do evacuations?" he asked Evan.

"Uh, yes, but the actual evacuations are not taking place at this location."

The man took in a deep breath as Jessie quickly stepped around him and into the room Dena had went into. Evan watched her disappear before continuing with his response. "What was that all about earlier?" he asked, concerned.

"She doesn't understand why we weren't able to help her fiancé'. There was some kind of thing chasing him. There was nothing we could do. We lost sight of him in the woods," the man replied remorsefully and Evan nodded. He knew that if it was the angra that was chasing Nathan, they would have all been killed if they had attempted to help him.

"By the way, I'm Ray. This is Ariana and my friend Jeffrey."

"I'm Evan and this is Josh."

"How come you are alone?" Ray asked as he examined Evan's military uniform.

"My group and I were deployed in the southern valley. We lost most of our men," Evan replied and carefully removed his helmet and rucksack. A little weight off his back was quite a relief as he took in a deep breath. Josh slowly stepped around him and looked around the room.

"I'm sorry to hear that," Ray replied.

Evan nodded as he sat his bag down on the desk. "We are going to make our way to the hospital soon. That is where the evacuations are currently taking place. I have two others that will be trekking that way soon. You all can come with us. I can get every one of you to safety," he said.

"But what about those monsters out there?" Jeffrey asked.

Evan had almost forgotten that he had been standing near them this whole time. "It's a risk, but it's the only option we have," he replied.

"You don't think help will come?" Ray asked.

"I'm sure the other unit at the hospital has been coming around searching this side of the valley. But after all I have encountered tonight, I'm not sure how much longer they will keep any of us here."

Ray looked confused and glanced at Ariana. She seemed fearful as she carefully grabbed Ray's hand.

"I would suggest that you all get a bit of rest. I don't plan on staying here too long," Evan added and stepped into the hallway on the left, disappearing down it quickly.

"Well, we should take his advice. I'll try and find some food in the kitchen for us. Why don't you find a place to relax?" Ray asked, looking at Ariana.

She nodded. "I'll be in the library."

"Alright. Jeffrey, how about you give me a hand?" Ray asked as Ariana went into the hallway Evan had went down.

"Sure," Jeffrey stated and they walked towards a hallway on the right that led to early childhood education classes and the kitchen.

Jessie glanced around the small lobby she had stepped into. There was a spiral, metal staircase to her right and a few chairs and couches to her left that sat around a small coffee table. A few orchids sat on small end tables and there were more sconces burning on the walls. Jessie glanced at the wooden, double doors across the room from her, looking at the one that hung open. She quickly approached it and stepped into the cathedral's worship hall. She watched as Dena lit a few candles on an elegant alter that stood on the stage. Jessie slowly walked down the rug that stretched between all the neatly rowed pews and towards the stage.

"Excuse me…Mrs?" Jessie asked once she had gotten close enough for the old woman to hear her.

Dena slowly looked back at her. "Yes, my dear?" she asked.

"How come you haven't tried to leave?"

Dena smiled. "There are forces in nature that we cannot control. If it is my time, I will go no matter where I am at. Besides, this is practically my home," she stated and turned around to face her. "This church was the first ever built when this valley was founded. It has been passed down from my family for generations. Since my husband passed, I began to come here every day and take care of it," she added.

Jessie slowly smiled. "I admire that," she whispered and sighed.

"What troubles you, my dear?" Dena asked and carefully stepped down from the short stage.

Jessie looked at her for a moment. "I lost everyone…including my fiancé," she said and began to tear up once more.

"Oh my dear…" Dena began to say and sighed softly. "Please, sit down."

Jessie carefully sat down at the first pew and Dena followed, sitting down next to her.

"I was lucky to have met Evan, the soldier that is here. He will probably be the only one to get me out of this place, but my heart tells me not to lose hope…that my fiancé could still be out there," Jessie said, thinking about Ray's remarks.

"Well if that is how you feel, I would keep holding onto that," Dena replied and Jessie looked at her.

"I'm…still a bit surprised at your comment earlier. Do you know how serious the devastation is here?" Jessie asked.

Dena looked away.

"I'm pretty sure it is serious. I've heard the strange noises…the screams…I've felt the quakes too. Thankfully the damage here hasn't been catastrophic," she said and slowly stood up, her expression a bit wary.

"You really don't mind us staying here for a bit?" Jessie asked, remaining seated.

"No, my dear. This home is welcome to anyone, but if it's a safe haven you seek then I would suggest that you leave the valley as soon as you can. You won't find one here now," Dena responded and turned away, walking down the aisle between the pews and back towards the foyer. Jessie watched her for a moment. She felt sorry for the old woman, but there was something about her that was beginning to make her feel nervous. Jessie took in a deep breath and looked at all the candles burning near the cross. It was very inviting, relaxing. It made the atmosphere feel warm, easing any pain and trouble. They didn't exist here. This made her feel safe for the moment. The peace and quiet was soothing. She was able to dwell on her thoughts and what she needed to do to be at peace with herself and the situation she had to endure.

After spending what felt like precious hours looking and speaking with other soldiers, Will carefully scanned the area out front of the hospital one last time before going back inside to continue his search. He didn't want to miss the opportunity of finding someone from his group. Perhaps they could have more information for him. It was a chance he didn't want to miss. What concerned him the most was the absence of Private Watkins and Josh Walker. He could have sworn they would have beaten him to the hospital.

Will turned and stepped up the last few steps to the entrance, walking past the few military cops and back into the persevering lobby. He walked carefully around the other soldiers and looked down the hallway on the left once he approached the registry desk. There were a few waiting areas and a cardiovascular unit before the hall turned around another corner.

"Can I help you?" a young man asked from behind the desk.

Will looked at him and thought for a moment. "Oh, right. I'm sorry. I was hoping you could help me locate...relatives," he stated, glancing at the clerk's name tag as he crossed his arms, covering his nametape.

"I'll see what I can do. What is the last name?" the young man asked.

"Bennett."

"Alright."

He began typing away on a computer as Will read his name tag. "Thank you, Ian," he responded.

"No problem."

Will glanced back towards the entrance, watching the soldiers and medics work as Ian continued to type away. It wasn't long though as he responded, "There is one Bennett in my system."

Will sighed. "I brought Alyssa here, sir. If there are no others, well, I appreciate you taking the time to check," he replied.

"Uh, no problem. I'm sorry," Ian replied.

Will nodded and carefully made his way down the hall on the left, scanning through the waiting area as he uncrossed his arms. The cardiovascular unit was dark and vacant. Will took in a deep breath and watched as the unfamiliar faces went around him. A few glanced at him while the others didn't pay him any attention. He began to wonder if he was mistaken earlier. Perhaps he didn't see anyone, but the major had mentioned another green beret. Will turned around and looked back towards the emergency department. He wanted to check on Alyssa before making one last attempt. He carefully walked back down the hall and past the registry desk, stepping around every busy nurse or doctor that rushed around the area. He hoped to be out of this madhouse soon.

As Will approached the room, he slowly stepped inside and leaned his body against the frame of the door, crossing his arms casually. Alyssa was still lying in the same position, but it looked as if the nurse had cleaned her up a bit. Most of the dirt and blood had been wiped off and she was covered with a thin, white blanket. She looked comfortable. Will listened to the IV machine as it continued to pump fluids into her body. He hated the sound of it. This was the last place he wanted Alyssa to be and as soon as she awoke he was going to make sure she was the next one on the evac helicopter. He didn't care if she could assist them anymore. He wanted her out of the valley.

Will continued to stare at Alyssa until someone had caught his attention from the corner of his eye. He glanced towards the person, pushing himself off the frame of the door. The soldier looked injured as he turned up a flight of stairs, caressing the side of his body. Will noticed the insignia on the soldier's sleeve and quickly walked towards the stairwell. He stopped once he reached it and glanced up the stairs. The soldier was already around the corner and up the next flight of stairs. Will could hear him and trailed behind, glancing at the small spots of blood on the tile as he made his way up the steps carefully. Something didn't seem right. He paused and looked behind him. Nothing seemed out of the ordinary. Everyone continued to stay busy, paying him no mind. He wondered how this soldier slipped by without anyone noticing his wounds.

Will looked back at the stairs and slowly made his way up them, stepping around the blood on the floor. He carefully turned the corner and made his way up the last flight of stairs slowly, staring into the hall up ahead. His mind was racing with thoughts as he was completely unaware of the soft footsteps coming down the hall on the second floor towards him. Will's heart was already racing, thumping loudly in his ears as he stepped into the hallway, almost running into the man with the nice business suit. The man stumbled back and cleared his throat, a bit agitated.

"Excuse me," Will stated and stepped around him.

"Are you lost?" the man asked, turning around to look back at Will.

Will stopped and turned to face him. "No, sir, just hoping to find anyone left from my group. That is all," he replied.

"I see...You were with the green berets deployed in the heart of the destruction?" the man asked.

"Yes, sir," Will replied, becoming anxious. He didn't like this man, and he didn't care about his government status. The man stared at him for a moment, his eyes slightly narrowing.

"Well, Sergeant First Class…good luck," he simply stated and stepped down the stairs.

Will stared at him, watching him disappear around the corner below.

What was that all about?

Will looked back down the hall the man had come from and shook his head. He didn't have time for distractions. He had to find this soldier. Will glanced at the floor and noticed the few spots of blood continuing down the hall. This was going to be an easy task.

Will quietly followed the trail, hearing voices coming from a room up ahead. His heart continued to thump loudly as he took steady breaths and walked quietly, hoping not to alarm anyone. As he came close to the room, he stopped, hearing shuffling and footsteps. Will quickly stepped into a dark office and pressed his body against the wall near the door, hoping whoever it was would step in the other direction. He took in a deep breath and held it as the steps came into the hall and slowly disappeared down the opposite end of it. Will released his breath slowly and began to wonder if he should be hiding in the first place. He didn't like the unsure feeling he had in his gut, but he wondered if he was being a bit overboard. Besides, it was definitely someone from his group. There was no reason to be nervous about that.

Will quickly looked towards the back of the room as a loud double-click was suddenly heard. He was aware of the sound, but refused to put his hands up as he stared at a young man with thick, dark brown hair and a battered blue uniform. Will was in a bit of a shock as he stared at the Glock nine millimeter that was aimed directly at him. He breathed slowly through his nostrils, releasing it silently, trying to remain calm.

"Are you sure you want to be pointing that at a green beret?" he asked carefully, watching the young man breathe heavily. He looked alarmed, anxious.

"What are you guys doing in there? I know you all are planning something," he said, shaken.

Will raised an eyebrow. "Look, I just got here. I don't know what you are talking about," he replied.

"You are lying."

Will examined his uniform, noticing the badge on his shirt. "Wait...You're a cop for this town?" he asked.

The young man didn't respond. He continued to aim his nine at him, breathing steadily.

"I have a young lady here with me...You should know her. Alyssa Bennett," Will stated and watched the young man's eyes widen as he continued to point the pistol directly at him.

"What did you do to her...Why is she here?"

"I didn't do anything, you can trust me..." Will replied and suddenly remembered the conversation he and Alyssa had in the alley. This man was probably aware of the bloodbath.

"I cannot trust any of you," the young man stated angrily.

Will took in a deep breath as the young man continued, "How do you even know Alyssa? She was supposed to have left earlier this evening."

"She found me at the press after my group was deployed in the southern valley. I brought her here. She's not well."

The young man looked pained, but he continued to hold his pistol steadily at Will.

"She is in room six in the emergency ward," Will stated and paused a moment before continuing, looking into the young man's eyes. He was hoping to make him realize that he was no threat. "And I believe I know why you are having a problem trusting me. Alyssa was a bit wary at first too...once members from my group found her at the station. They saw the aftermath of a massacre."

The young man was having difficulty keeping his composure, but he refused to lower his pistol. "I was there...if Alyssa hadn't put in her leave she would have been there too. She was my partner, and a very close friend, so if you..."

"She found your letter," Will firmly interrupted, and the young man gasped.

"You say it was a man in my uniform," Will added.

"It was! I know what I saw. That bastard thought he had me before joining his accomplice."

Will took in a deep breath. He didn't have time for this. "Look, I'm here to help. I'm not sure why anyone deployed here would commit such a crime. It doesn't make any sense. But I will stand beside you as I have with Alyssa. I only came up here because I thought I saw someone from my group. I assumed that they all have been killed," he stated and the young man slowly lowered his pistol, staring at him for a moment before saying another word.

"You cannot expect me to trust you right away..." he finally stated.

"I know," Will said and felt a bit relieved.

"I'm Kevin Headley. If you don't mind, I want to see Alyssa now."

"I'm sure she would be happy to see you. She is unresponsive at the moment..." Will replied and Kevin sighed and nodded, looking Will over as he approached him.

"By the way, the name is Will Thompson," Will added and Kevin stepped towards the door, ignoring his response as he glanced over his shoulder at him.

"You know...whether you see it or not, your men in their have been scheming. They are after something, and I intend to find out before they cost us any more innocent lives in this hell. And I won't hesitate to shoot even if it means *you* or one of your boys."

Will stared at him for a moment. He had every right to feel the way he did, so he refused to show any animosity. Kevin turned around and glanced out in the hallway, making sure it was clear. Will watched him step into the hallway and walk quietly towards the stairwell. He took in a deep breath and waited for Kevin to turn the corner before turning his attention back towards the room with the commotion. But he wasn't ready to continue yet.

If the allegations are true, what on earth would these men want? What the hell could they be after? And why would they have needed to kill all those innocent people?

Will rested his body against the door. He refused to believe that someone from his very own group would possibly commit the crime.

He knew all of them very well, and they were all good men, even the young recruits who enjoyed to joke at times or get carried away during a mission. None of them had the hearts to carry on such a horrifying task, one that would include the murders of innocent civilians. Will sighed softly and closed his eyes. He wanted to clear his thoughts before going into this room. He wasn't sure what he was about to step into or if he'd be stepping back out alive.

CHAPTER FIFTEEN

LYSSA WAS RUNNING AS FAST *as she could down a dark, rugged corridor. The spine chilling screams continued to echo behind her as she fought back the heavy weight that she felt upon her shoulders. She wasn't carrying anything. It felt as if there was pressure pushing down against her, making her work much harder for the exit. Alyssa pushed through the corridor and reached a ledge on a high cliff.*

"Oh God..." she whispered and heard the beast coming down the corridor quickly. She glanced behind her and saw the bright eyes of the monster and slowly allowed herself to fall back. The beast and the corridor quickly disappeared as she fell down from the mountainous wall and into a warm, deep river far below. There was more intense pressure on her back as she pushed to the surface, breaking through it and taking a deep breath of air. Alyssa coughed and quickly swam to shore. She didn't look back as she kicked her feet as hard as she could. Eventually, her feet touched ground and she crawled out of the water, gasping for air. She couldn't allow herself to give up. She had to keep pushing forward. She carefully pushed herself to her feet and stared at the ancient cathedral that now sat in front of her.

"Dad?" Alyssa asked and glanced behind her towards the cliff above.

The dark sky was all that shone down on her as she looked back at the church. It looked like the old cathedral of Rockdale Valley, but Alyssa wasn't sure why it was sitting here near the mountains and the river bed. She slowly walked towards it until the ground began to quiver under her feet.

"Alyssa..." A voice called from the church. Alyssa gasped and tried to run towards it, but had trouble as the ground began to quake even more.

"Dad!" Alyssa yelled back as the earth around her began to split and crack.

Intense heat pushed their way through the crevices, burning her skin. Alyssa clenched her teeth and jumped over a large tear in the ground, seeing the bright lava below. The adrenaline and fear rushed throughout her as she raced for the stairs, stumbling as she did.

"Dad!" she yelled once more.

"You can make it, Alyssa..." a familiar voice called and Alyssa leaped to the stone stairs as the earth behind her collapsed and fell. She quickly grabbed the second step, the rest of her body dangling behind her. The heat was more intense as it pushed upward out of the pit, burning her skin once more.

"Richard...is that you! Please, help me!" Alyssa yelled and the familiar screams and cries echoed obtrusively around her as she tried to pull herself up with all of her might. The earth continued to quiver, loosening her grip on the stone stairwell.

"No!" Alyssa shouted and closed her eyes as a bright light began to shine all around her...

"No!" Alyssa yelled. She was thrashing her body around on the small, hospital bed as Kevin held onto her arms.

"Alyssa, you're okay," he said calmly.

Alyssa opened her eyes, choking for air. She looked around the small room and at herself. "Will?" she asked and finally her eyes met Kevin's. Alyssa stared at him for a moment, and a smile quickly rose upon her face.

"Kevin? You're alive!" she gasped and pulled him to her, hugging him tightly. "I thought I'd never see you again..."

"I'm alright..." Kevin replied and patted her back before pulling away. He placed his hands on her bed, leaning against it. "I thought you were going to high tail it out of this place," he stated, returning the smile.

Alyssa took in a deep breath, regaining her composure. "So did I…" Her excitement had suddenly faded. "Unfortunately my plans have changed," she replied.

Kevin could see the frown behind that statement. Alyssa leaned herself back against the pillow and felt something beside her. She carefully patted the cold object and gently caressed it, bringing it to her.

"Did it have something to do with the message I left you?" Kevin asked, watching Alyssa examine the challenge coin. A slight smile curled upon her face as she lowered her hand and looked at Kevin. She lost her train of thought as she remained silent. She couldn't help but think of the reasons why Will would leave his coin with her.

"Alyssa?" Kevin asked.

Alyssa snapped out of it as she shook her head. "I'm sorry…"

"It's alright."

"So much has happened, Kevin," Alyssa stated, pushing the coin into her pocket. "I went to my parents to drop my bags off and something had broken into their home. It was trashed…and there was blood…I don't even know if they are alive," she added and remained strong as she fought back the urge to show any kind of emotion.

Kevin's heart sank. He looked up to her father very much. "Oh no…I'm so sorry, Alyssa…" he replied.

"I didn't get much of your message. It was very scratchy."

"I wanted to let you know that the situation took a turn for the worse. The valley started to crumble apart. I wanted to make sure you were on your way out of this area," Kevin said and sighed, thinking about the events before the massacre.

"…Things had gone from bad to much worse in a matter of minutes today. It all started late yesterday evening, and it came without warning. The constant quakes and tears throughout the town…Then the screams…Some were from people, and others were from something else. There was a lot of gunfire. Thankfully some of the residents had left in time, but there were still many that hadn't yet, not to mention the first responders and hospital staff. The situation wasn't taken as seriously as it should have been. And as we waited for the Chief to return, these two soldiers came out of nowhere..."

"I don't want to know," Alyssa interrupted and looked away. She didn't want to try and paint such awful pictures in her mind when she had already seen enough of her own.

"I went there looking for help. I saw the bodies..." Alyssa said. "And the Chief is also dead, Kevin," she added, her heart heavy with sorrow.

Kevin pushed himself away from her bed. "What?" he asked, astonished.

Alyssa looked at him and sighed. "He was injured badly. There was nothing we could do," she replied and Kevin approached the counter, resting his body against it. He took in a deep breath and shook his head. A few moments passed before he finally broke the silence.

"I ran into your friend upstairs," he stated and Alyssa remained quiet.

"He...seems decent. But we really need to be careful of who we trust, Alyssa."

"I know," Alyssa replied softly and thought about all she had told Will. There was no time to second guess herself now.

"Will has been very...kind. I don't know where I would be if it wasn't for him and his group. They saved my life more than once," Alyssa added.

Kevin slowly nodded. "We just need to watch our backs. It's been very difficult for me to be around all these soldiers here, not knowing which one could have pulled the trigger. And there are a few of them upstairs speaking in private. They are looking for someone... Someone very important. I don't know what they are after," he stated and Alyssa became nervous.

Kevin sighed. "We don't need to be here especially me being in uniform. They are going to kill us all, and if they find out your one of us, they'll kill you too. We need to catch this next helicopter out of here, Alyssa. I'm serious," he added.

Alyssa could see the severity in his eyes and thought about her nightmare.

The ancient cathedral...and Brian's peculiar remark...I know I heard my brother's voice.

Alyssa released a low gasp.

The ancient legend? Oh God, it's all connected. My brother wasn't just sick! I was right. What if the tale is true? This is a sign... It's got to be a sign...

"I can't leave," she said.

Kevin's eyebrows pulled down. "Why not, Alyssa?"

"You wouldn't understand. Like I said before, you'd think I was going insane."

"Try me."

Alyssa looked at him for a long moment. She didn't know where to begin as she thought about the haunting weeks after the accident that eventually led her there. She took in a deep breath and collected her thoughts. This was going to take a while even with the idea of leaving some of the major details out.

Will's heart rate had finally slowed after taking a few deep breaths and clearing his restless mind. The room close to him was suddenly silent which made him a bit uneasy. They probably heard the commotion between him and Kevin. Will couldn't worry anymore. He needed to get in there before things got too suspicious. He slowly stepped out into the hall and made his way down it, staring at the room on the left. The lights were bright, but no sounds were coming from it. He carefully slid his hand down to his sidearm as he approached the room and peered inside. It was a large conference room with an oval table and fancy chairs. Will slowly stepped into the room and watched as the two soldiers sitting at the table glanced back at him. He examined their faces, not recognizing the two and looked at the one soldier standing near the window with his back facing him. He was looking out the window, supporting his weight against the a/c unit attached to the wall. He looked pained.

Will cleared his throat. "I'm sorry to interrupt. I was just hoping to find someone from my group," he stated.

The two young soldiers at the table looked at the one standing by the window. He slowly looked back at Will. He was taking steady breaths with one arm wrapped around his lower torso. His hand was pressed firmly against his side, blood appearing through his uniform. His face was stained with dirt and dried blood. Even with all the injuries, Will recognized the soldier immediately.

"Master Sergeant Kennedy..." he said, shocked.

Brad's eyes widened a bit. "Well if it isn't Sergeant First Class Thompson. I'm a bit surprised, forgive me."

"What happened downtown?" Will asked, stepping toward the table.

Brad took in a deep breath and gasped lightly. Will could see his pain and almost hurt for him.

"I got...caught in the rubble," Brad replied shortly and looked back out the window.

"Why don't you see a medic?" Will asked.

Brad snickered. "It doesn't matter, Thompson. No one is getting out of this town alive."

Will couldn't believe his tone. He knew Brad very well. He was a brave and strong-willed soldier, one with dedication.

"What has gotten into you, Brad?" Will asked informally.

Brad quickly looked at him, his eyes full of irritation. "You know, you are very lucky to have made it this far. Everyone else is dead," he responded coldly.

"Just about. Private Watkins and I are still in one piece. I have a former cop with me as well."

Brad looked back out the window, his heart sinking within his chest as the adrenaline rushed in. "A former cop?" he asked.

"Yes. She came back to this town to try and locate her parents. She wasn't aware of the evacuation order," Will replied, feeling unsure of what all to share with him. He was acting strange.

"I see," Brad stated, feeling relieved.

"Master Sergeant, Captain Smitherman didn't make it."

Brad stared into Will's eyes for a moment, trying to read him. "Did you...witness this?" he asked slowly.

"Yes." Will replied.

Brad looked back out the window. Will could sense his uncertainty, his fear. He wasn't sure what had him so off.

"We need a direction, Master Sergeant," he stated.

Brad remained silent for a long moment. Something seemed to be building up within him. It was a slow progress, but Will could see his body language changing from casual to tense.

"Do I look capable of being active commander?" Brad finally asked and looked at him. His expression had also changed.

Will took in a long breath and exhaled it slowly, sensing his defeat. "Then let me take you downstairs so someone can have a look at you," he said firmly.

"No."

"Then as acting commander I order you to come with me," Will said and took a step around the table until Brad pulled his M9 from its holster and aimed it directly at Will's face. Will froze in place. The other two soldiers remained as still as they could as they tried not to stare at Brad. They were becoming extremely anxious.

"I'm not going anywhere," Brad stated and took in a deep breath.

"What are you doing up here, Master Sergeant?" Will asked calmly. "Who is that secret service agent that was just up here?"

A smirk rose upon Brad's face. "Just as you said Sergeant First Class, a secret service agent."

"Cut the shit, Brad, what's going on?" Will asked firmly, trying to hide his fear as he stared at the barrel of the nine millimeter aimed directly at him.

"How dare you, Will..." Brad stated softly.

Will's eyes widened, but he held his ground.

"You know, I always liked you, Thompson. I truly hate what had to happen to the group...and it's such a shame what will become of *you*." Brad added, holding his pistol as steady as he could, his body weakening quickly.

Will stared at him in shock. The other two soldiers remained silent as Will breathed deeply.

"What the hell are you talking about?" Will asked carefully and the ground slowly started to shake beneath their feet. The floor quivered and the pictures rattled against the walls. Will released a low gasp and kept his footing as the two soldiers held onto the table. Brad kept his balance against the window seal, staring at Will with no alarm in his eyes. He slowly lowered his pistol, a smirk rising upon his face once again.

"You see…Nothing is going to stop this. You might as well stay and enjoy the finale that has yet to come…"

"You've gone mad…You've forgotten our mission."

"This mission…is an abject failure," Brad replied and held the smirk on his face as Will stumbled back to the door, the earth continuing to quake beneath their feet. Will grabbed the door frame and took another look back at Brad. He was collapsing to the floor, his face becoming pale. The two soldiers stood, preparing to evacuate.

"You may want to get out of here while you still have the chance, Thompson. This valley…is known for its *deadly* secret…"

Will didn't respond. He watched Brad's body slump to the floor before stumbling out into the hall, balancing himself against the wall as he pushed forward. All he could think about now was Alyssa.

"Oh no…not now…" Alyssa whispered, sitting up in the bed. Kevin glanced out in the hall, hearing a few screams as he held onto the counter. The jars that sat on it rattled and moved out of place as the IV machine tried to roll around the floor. Alyssa carefully grabbed it and held onto it as tight as she could until the earth slowly stopped shaking. Her eyes were wide and she began to breathe heavily as she looked around. Everything suddenly grew still and calm. Kevin glanced back at Alyssa, still hanging onto the counter.

"That's probably our cue to go, don't you think?" he asked.

"Yes. Could you get this needle out?" Alyssa asked and carefully started pulling the tape off the IV tubing.

Kevin took in a deep breath and grabbed a few pieces of gauze from a drawer. "I'll try," he said and approached her. "Alright... careful now." He paused and glanced over his shoulder, hearing footsteps outside the room. Will had just reached the door, his face full of concern.

"Did something happen?" Kevin asked, turning around.

Alyssa glanced at Will and held the needle in her arm steady. "Will. Are you okay?" she asked.

Will felt relieved to see Alyssa awake, but he noticed a little discoloration in the skin under her eyes again. He decided to ignore Kevin's question for now. He wanted to check on Alyssa first.

"Yes, I'm fine. You look exhausted though," he said and approached her.

Kevin stepped out of his way and watched him carefully. Will glanced at the tape that was pulled off the IV in Alyssa's arm and then to her eyes.

"Will...What happened?" Alyssa asked, concerned.

"I ran into someone from my group. He was injured and... completely delusional. I couldn't believe some of the things that came out of his mouth, but besides that, we need to go," Will stated and picked up the few pieces of gauze on the side of her bed.

"I tried to tell you," Kevin stated.

Will could hear the frustration in his tone and remained calm. "He lost a lot of blood. So much has happened. I'm sure it's..."

"Oh please. You're either in denial or you're trying to cover it up," Kevin interrupted, crossing his arms.

Will looked at him, but before he could respond Alyssa cleared her throat. "Enough. This is not the time," she said as calm as she could.

Will relaxed and turned his attention back to her, placing the few gauze strips on her arm where the needle lay embedded. "And I sincerely apologize, Alyssa, but I don't believe your parents are here," he stated.

Alyssa felt saddened. She remained quiet as Will pressed onto the gauze strips. She had already prepared herself for that information.

"Alright, hold still," he stated and quickly pulled the needle out, pressing firmly on the strips before any blood could escape.

Alyssa held her breath. The worst part about the IV was taking it out. She dreaded it the most.

"Okay. I'm going to get you on that helicopter. The other one should be back any minute," Will stated and looked at Kevin. "Could you find me a band-aid and bandage please?" he asked.

"Will...I'm not leaving. Not yet," Alyssa said and felt her heart race.

Kevin quickly searched for the items as Will looked back at her. Alyssa could see the alarm in his eyes. Something was really bothering him.

"Look, I know you feel somehow connected to this, but I fear the worst has yet to come. And I feel it is coming very soon. I spoke with the other commander. You should let my men and I handle this," Will replied.

"You won't be able to stop it. I must go to the ancient cathedral. I believe some answers await me there. Please..." Alyssa begged, thinking about her last vision near the cave entrance as well as the recent nightmare.

"Alyssa..." Will stated and shook his head. "You are getting on that helicopter...if it means I have to escort you to it," he added and looked at Kevin as he handed him a band-aid and red bandage to wrap around it.

Alyssa sighed and looked away as Will placed the band-aid on her arm, securely wrapping it with the red bandage.

What happened while I was out? Something has thrown him off. But I cannot argue with him...There's no way I would win that battle.

"Now, please, just wait here until I return," Will stated and glanced at Kevin. Kevin gave a slight nod and looked at Alyssa as Will stepped out into the hall, disappearing into the crowd that now rushed about. Alyssa sighed heavily and refused to make eye contact with Kevin. She could see him from her peripheral vision, sensing his odd expression.

"Well as much as I don't want to agree with the soldier, but he is right. There is no reason for us to stay here. And you know we need to go and we need to do so now," Kevin stressed.

"Kevin…" Alyssa said and finally looked at him. "I am going to that cathedral with or without you two. My father has to be around here somewhere, and I intend to find him. I don't care what registrar told Will. I must stop this chaos before anyone else dies because of me."

Alyssa's heart began to race some more as Kevin raised an eyebrow. "So you really think you are the reason for this plague?" he asked and leaned against the counter, crossing his arms.

Alyssa took a moment as she thought really hard. She was finally coming to the conclusion that she was indeed the reason for all the destruction and death that made up Rockdale Valley and it was painstaking.

I am responsible…There isn't much of a doubt about that. I'm the one with the signs…the visions…the nightmares…I…did this.

Alyssa slowly sat up and swung her legs over the bed, remaining seated on the soft cushion. "Yes," she replied.

"And you're the reason for the monsters? The so called dragon you've seen?" Kevin asked, remembering the absurd details he thought regarding her story.

"Once again, I told you that you would think I was going insane."

"Well, you were right about that," Kevin replied.

Alyssa looked at him, her face pained. "I refused to talk to anyone but my therapist because of that. You're supposed to be my friend. I really need your support, okay?" she said and closed her eyes, fighting hard not to express the pain and despair that built within her.

"Don't you understand? I have *no one* now," she added and looked at him sadly.

"I'm sorry, Alyssa," he said and pushed himself off the counter, approaching her. "You've got to understand how hard this is for me to believe, but…you know I will always have your back. And you know I've always been upfront with you also," he added, patting her back.

Alyssa sighed heavily. "There's been too much death...This town was our home. These people were our family and friends," she said and tried to think of all the times the valley shined. There was no reason to fear the place back then.

"I know. You are right. We've lost many today, and I want the one responsible for those murders found. I want that traitor to pay," Kevin replied and felt his blood beginning to boil.

"We'll find him. He's amongst us somewhere. It's only a matter of time," Alyssa said and looked at him. "You are one hundred percent sure that they were soldiers, not civilians?" she asked, praying it wasn't someone close to Will.

"I am. I should be able to point them out if they were here in this hospital," Kevin replied and Alyssa took in a deep breath, releasing it slowly. She glanced back out in the hall, watching people scurry about.

"Alright. You were really lucky, Kevin," she replied.

"It was more than luck...Someone was definitely looking out," Kevin said and thought about how he was able to hide from the two soldiers that began to open fire at them. A storage room with a broken light bulb helped conceal him. But his heart ached. He was unable to save his co-workers...his friends.

Alyssa sighed softly and thought about Will and who he had spoken to from his group. She wanted to know what this person said that had his nerves so rattled. She also wondered if this person was the one who pulled the trigger at the station. Alyssa became a bit frustrated as she assumed that it probably wasn't. That person was probably elsewhere, searching for whatever or whomever he or she wanted so badly.

The silence in the room was pleasing, but the noise in the hall continued as Alyssa watched soldiers, nurses, and doctors rush by the door. Kevin had approached the counter and leaned against it once more, his mind full of thought. Alyssa glanced at him and began to feel odd as whispers slowly entered her mind. She took in a deep breath through her nostrils and held it until the earth began to quiver beneath them once again. Kevin shook from his thoughts and held onto the counter, watching Alyssa slide herself off the bed and hold onto the cushion. The seconds that passed felt more like minutes. The whispers continued to flow around Alyssa and she remained as calm as she could. She noticed Kevin watching her closely. He was becoming more fearful and was beginning to wonder if Uktena truly existed. He couldn't think of any other possibilities that would cause the valley to quake so much.

The lights began to flicker around them, sending everyone in the halls into panic. More screams echoed down the halls, and Alyssa could hear others yelling to get under cover in case of a possible collapse of the floor above.

"She's not going to stop..." Alyssa whispered and Kevin glanced at her, not quite catching all of her statement. Alyssa closed her eyes and prayed. As soon as she silenced her mind, the earth stopped shaking and everything quickly settled. Kevin sighed heavily in relief and heard the few in the hall gasping, questioning the situation and if they needed to move everyone outdoors. Alyssa opened her eyes and took a few deep breaths. People began to move about once more and she listened carefully to the heavy footsteps that got close to her room.

"Come on, Alyssa. Let's go," Kevin said and looked at her. She appeared to be in a daze, her mind elsewhere. He approached her and placed his hand on her shoulder. Will quickly jogged into the room, seeing the strange expression on Alyssa's face. Alyssa watched as the room became fuzzy, slowly changing into the darkness of the familiar cavern...

She could see herself running down a tight corridor, a soft touch of a light not too far ahead of her. She was holding a couple of items, but she wasn't able to make them out from the view she was looking from. But then a deep rumble was felt within her chest, and the earth began to quake. Rock and dust fell from the cavern's ceiling and walls, spilling onto the path. All of a sudden, she watched as she slowed her pace and collapsed on the cavern's floor. She rested her head against it and released the two items that were in her hand as the view she saw from inched closer and closer to herself. Alyssa was able to see the two items, a circular rock perfectly carved in the shape of a small gear and an oddly shaped red stone.

"Alyssa!" she heard from the distance. The view from which she was watching from quickly pulled back and the vision slowly faded away...

Will was holding Alyssa up and Kevin was at her side, calling her name. Worry was spread on both their faces as they tried to get her attention. Alyssa looked around, breathing heavily. She felt fatigued, but the whispers returned, sending the adrenaline back into her body and building the strength back into her muscles. Will held her steady and looked around. Kevin watched, confused. He was completely frozen, not sure what to do. Alyssa refocused her attention on Will, noticing his odd expression as he turned his attention back to her.

"I hear them..." he said and Alyssa's eyes slowly widened. But before she could respond, the lights began to flicker once more before going out completely. All grew silent until glass shattered in the distance, raining towards the tile floors and bouncing off of them. Loud thuds quickly followed and Alyssa gasped. Will looked back into the hall, hearing the screams and the sudden burst of rifles.

"What the hell?" Kevin gasped and Alyssa knelt down, retrieving her rifle and pistol. It wasn't long until the familiar screams from the angras echoed in the hospital. Their screeching cries pierced through the halls and covered the sounds of the constant gunfire.

"It's a pack," Will stated and turned the light on the top of his rifle on. Alyssa stood back up, placing the M9 in its holster. She held onto her M4 carefully, turning the small light on as well.

Kevin retrieved his pistol and looked at them. "What are these things?" he asked, frightened.

"Code name, angra. They are very large, hard to kill demonic-like beasts," Will said and glanced at Alyssa. "Are you going to be alright?" he asked.

Alyssa cleared her throat, trying to put aside the vision she saw and nodded. "For now," she replied.

"Okay. We are going to stay low and get out through the lobby. It's the closest exit," Will stated and Kevin stared out into the hall, hearing the screams and gunfire continue. Everyone that ran by the door was soldiers he noticed. Alyssa nodded and listened as the sounds of helicopter blades were suddenly heard.

"Shit, we got to hurry. Let's go," Will said and quickly approached the door, glancing down the hall in both directions. His eyes were wide, focusing on every angle of the hall. There were soldiers firing at two of the large angras, and he could already see the wounded and the dead on the cold floor. He took in a deep breath and looked at Alyssa and Kevin.

"Stay low, stay close," he stated.

Alyssa and Kevin nodded and Will stepped out into the hall, rifle aimed directly in front of him, locked and loaded. Alyssa followed close behind, scanning the hall and the nurses' station. She could see the panic stricken faces of the soldiers as a few were pulling the remaining patients out through the lobby doors. Kevin's eyes widened as he finally spotted one of the angras down the hall. A few soldiers were stepping back, firing at it as it tried to dodge the stream of bullets. The other was on top of one soldier, screaming ferociously, taunting the soldiers in front of it. It wasn't long before the stench of blood filled the area. Alyssa tried not to breathe and clenched her teeth when another piercing cry echoed once more throughout the hospital. It sounded as if there were more than just the two down the other end of the hall.

"We can make it!" Will yelled and stepped into the lobby, making a run for the double doors. Alyssa and Kevin followed, trying not to look behind them. Will quickly pushed one of the doors open and held it, allowing Alyssa and Kevin to step out onto the walkway. Alyssa and Kevin paused, watching as soldiers closed the doors to the mobile hospitals. A few soldiers were hidden behind the humvees while others kneeled onto the lawn, their rifles aimed towards the hospital. Other soldiers escorted patients and civilians to safety. Many were yelling in all directions, barking orders, trying to remain calm. It was all overwhelming as Alyssa stared, awestruck. She was having trouble catching her breath, her heart racing away.

Will stepped up beside her and glanced towards the helipad. The helicopter was flying away in the distance, blades whipping loudly, its light shining brightly through the trees.

"No…" he whispered and glanced towards the humvees on the road, ignoring the chaos that continued inside the hospital.

What do we do now…?

Alyssa glanced at Will, watching as he scanned the lawn. "Will… You need to trust me. It could be our last chance," she said and Will looked at her, unable to respond as the earth began to quiver once more.

"Shit!" Kevin shouted and held his ground as Alyssa gasped, stumbling around on the concrete. Will grabbed her arm and stared in front of him as the concrete began to split.

"We got to move!" he yelled and they stumbled to the side and onto the lawn. Kevin followed, collapsing to his hands and knees. He began to crawl forward, trying to get away from the hospital's entrance as the haunting screams continued.

"Everybody out!" A soldier yelled from the lobby and a few began to stumble out the doors. Will and Alyssa pushed forward and fell to the soft grass, crawling quickly away as the sounds of brick crashed behind them, shaking the earth even more. Glass began to shatter and sling in all directions, striking a few soldiers and tearing through their uniforms. A few soldiers had leaped out to safety, but some quickly disappeared beneath the rubble.

Kevin covered his head and continued to push himself forward, away from the unstable building. Concrete and brick continued to crash, pounding the earth, its loud boom awakening the night. Alyssa and Will pushed forward until they reached a safer location near the street and rolled over onto their backs, leaning up to stare at the side of the building that had caved in on itself. Dust and smoke rose above the debris, filling the night sky with its fog. Will was breathing heavily, watching the soldiers that had leaped from the building crawl slowly away from it. The earth began to slow to a quiver, allowing more stability for the soldiers to move away. Alyssa looked back at Will as Kevin finally reached them. He collapsed on the ground beside Will, overwhelmed with adrenaline. His breaths were coming and going rapidly.

"Will…you heard them too. It's a sign. Please…" Alyssa begged.

Will stared at her for a long moment, taking a deep breath in. "Alright," he said softly, remaining seated as the earth stopped shaking. He didn't believe they had any other options.

"What are we going to do?" Kevin asked.

"We are going to this cathedral. I think I need to see for myself," Will said and watched as the soldiers in the lawn ran to help the wounded.

Kevin groaned and pushed himself to his feet. Alyssa sighed in relief, but was still fearful. Uktena could appear at any moment.

Will carefully stood up and helped Alyssa to her feet. She glanced back at the hospital as soldiers were now trying to find another way in so they could help the ones that were trapped. She was deeply saddened and afraid. Hell had erupted and the only thing the soldiers wanted to do was to save the innocent lives that were stranded in the middle of it. Little did they know that this was a battle that wasn't going to end without the right kind of power, a power that didn't come from the barrels of their assault rifles. Alyssa couldn't comprehend why a man wearing that uniform could burst into a police department and kill everyone. She was beginning to doubt Kevin's claims.

Will approached one of the humvees, greeting the soldier that was manipulating with the radio. Alyssa followed but stayed near the side of the vehicle as Kevin trailed behind; keeping an eye out around them for any more of the monsters he had just seen inside the hospital. He was still in shock from the image.

Will cleared his throat. "We need to use this humvee right away," he said firmly. The young soldier stared at him for a moment and then glanced at his sleeve, seeing the crossed arrow dagger emblem. He could sense Will's urgency and felt a bit overwhelmed by it.

"Uh, yes Sergeant First Class," he stated and quickly stepped out of the vehicle. "The radio isn't working. We've been having trouble with all of them lately," the young soldier added.

"Thank you, Private. I'm sure we won't need them," Will stated and Alyssa grabbed the sleeve of his uniform before he could sit down in the driver's seat. Will looked back at her concernedly.

"Shouldn't we tell everyone to leave before...?" she paused and bit the side of her lip.

"There is nowhere for these people to hide, and I don't want to be responsible for widespread panic here," Will stated before she could mention the beast's name and glanced back at the young soldier, nodding in appreciation as he opened the back door. Alyssa carefully sat down in the seat, hoping that nothing would happen once they left. Kevin quickly went back around the vehicle and to the passenger side, opening the door. He sat down in the seat, admiring the interior. After Will carefully closed Alyssa's door, he approached the driver's seat, sitting down and pulling the door shut.

"Just get around these guys, and go straight for a bit. You'll make the second right," Kevin stated and Will started the engine, slowly pulling out and around the other vehicles. Alyssa looked towards the hospital and watched the chaos continue to unfold. She didn't want to talk. She was trying to figure out what could possibly await them at the church, if there was anything at all. She never truly believed in the actual story of Wahkan, but it was the only thing that was beginning to connect with Brian's statement regarding the legend. Suffering from amnesia after the accident had become very stressful, and she knew she couldn't leave the cathedral with nothing to show for. Something had to be there.

Chapter Sixteen

J OSH REMAINED STANDING OUTSIDE THE cathedral after the others decided that it was safe to go back inside. The recent quake wasn't the worst that they had experienced that day, but it left him in doubt. The ancient building seemed safe, however. It was just the dust that he could feel raining down on them from the ceiling. He wasn't sure how stable the building was anymore.

He turned away and stepped onto the lawn, examining the old stone. Nothing looked alarming. There was no damage to its structure. Josh took in a deep breath and rubbed the back of his neck. Perhaps he could convince the others that it was time to get moving. There was no sense in hanging out in the church any longer.

Josh approached the door and opened it. Before he could take a step inside, he heard a familiar sound in the distance. He stopped and glanced towards the street. He could hear a faint roar of an engine, and he could see the headlights behind the bend. It was coming in their direction, the one chance for a possible ride. Josh's heart began to race, filling with excitement. This could be their only ticket out of the valley.

He watched the oncoming vehicle carefully as it turned around the bend and made its way towards them. He examined it carefully and stuck his head inside the lobby, keeping the door open. "Hey! There's a vehicle coming! It looks military!" he yelled.

Evan stepped into the room and quickly jogged to the half opened door. "Don't get too excited yet," he stated and stepped out onto the walkway.

He could see the headlights in the distance and eventually made out the rest of the vehicle.

"You're right," Evan said and quickly ran down the walkway towards the stairs, waving his arms.

Josh stepped out onto the lawn as Ray, Ariana, and Jeffrey rushed out the door behind him.

Ray smiled. "I knew they would send help," he said and Ariana hugged him. Josh glanced back at them, feeling a bit of hope as well. Their hellish night could possibly come to an end after all.

"Over here!" Evan yelled, continuing to wave his arms towards the oncoming humvee. Josh walked down the path as the vehicle slowed and stopped at the curb near the stairs. The others trailed behind, smiles on their faces.

The vehicle doors opened and a familiar face stepped out and stood by the driver's door, staring back at Evan. "Private Watkins?"

Evan could sense the confusion, but smiled. "Sergeant First Class. Good to see you," he replied and Will nodded, glancing behind him. Alyssa was slowly stepping out of the vehicle, looking at the others that waited on the walkway. Kevin stepped out of vehicle as well, closing the door carefully.

"I was beginning to wonder why I couldn't find you at the hospital," Will stated, turning his attention back to Evan.

"Well we got off course once we left City Hall and..." Evan paused, looking back towards the others. Jessie was now standing at the door, watching.

"Found a survivor who refused to cooperate and we ended up here," he added.

Will glanced at the others who waited patiently. "At least you found survivors. That's good news," he said.

Evan nodded. "And how are you feeling?" he asked Alyssa as she stepped up to the sidewalk he stood on.

"I'm alright," she stated and Evan studied her face, realizing how exhausted she looked.

"Are you sure? You look rough," he said and Alyssa sighed softly. Her patience was running out and she was still fearful. She had many questions running throughout her mind and she only hoped she could find what she was looking for.

"Yes," she replied and Kevin stepped up beside her, glaring at Evan.

"Another cop. Nice to meet you, sir. I'm Private Watkins, but you can call me Evan."

Kevin nodded, extending his hand. "Kevin Headley," he said, shaking Evan's hand. Even though he couldn't recognize him, he was still uncertain about being around a bunch of soldiers. He refused to trust any of them.

"So…Are you here to get us out?" Ray asked, approaching them. Ariana, Jeffrey, and Josh followed behind him, but Jessie remained standing by the door, watching carefully. She wasn't sure if she was ready to leave. She sighed softly. It was nice to see the humvee. She knew she could be on her way to safety, away from this dreadful place. But the thought of possibly leaving Nathan behind continued to interrupt with what she knew was right.

Will glanced at Ray and cleared his throat. "Not exactly," he said. Ray's hopeful expression quickly vanished as he looked at Ariana. "An incident occurred at the hospital. I'm sure they may continue to do evacuations, but we're here for a different reason."

Evan's eyes narrowed a bit. He remembered Will being short with him earlier and he was getting tired of it. "Sergeant First Class, you need to fill me in on what exactly is going on here. I need to know," he stated.

"I briefed you on the topic…"

"That's just it. Briefed," Evan snapped.

Will cleared his throat and felt his blood beginning to boil until Alyssa released a heavy sigh. "Please…Let's just go inside where it is safer and I will tell you," she said.

"I really don't see how much longer we'll be safe in this ancient place especially if another quake comes. The building could collapse on us," Evan responded.

"It's been able to withstand it for this long, hadn't it? I won't be long, Evan," Alyssa said.

"And we'll take everyone to the hospital as soon as we are done here," Will said, looking at Ray and the others behind him.

Ray shook his head and turned his attention to Ariana, wrapping his arm around her shoulders as they walked back to the cathedral. Jeffrey trailed behind, thinking to himself. Their expressions bothered Alyssa. She could sense how they felt. She was the one hindering their way to safety, but if she didn't go through with this, she would risk losing a lot more than just the valley.

"It sure has been a while," Alyssa said, looking at the large clock tower on the front of the church. She could recall some moments going when she was a kid, but the death of her brother changed everything. Her father decided not to go to church anymore, and her mother kept to herself more as time went on. Her mother tried to hide her true feelings now that she thought about it. Perhaps that was one reason Alyssa got so close to her dad. He became more protective of her, and he did have an influence on any of the choices or decisions she was going to make. Her mother wasn't so outgoing like they were. Alyssa and her dad would go fishing, hiking, trail riding, camping, and anything else that involved the outdoors while her mother stayed home, keeping herself busy. And then Alyssa followed her father's footsteps into law enforcement, becoming a police officer. All of the extracurricular activities eventually slowed down. It was always a special treat to get out before the accident in July.

Alyssa and Kevin carefully went up the steps and towards the entrance to the cathedral as Evan stood still, staring at Will. "So what happened at the hospital?" he asked.

Will glanced at Alyssa and watched as she and Kevin disappeared behind the large wooden doors before turning his attention back to Evan. "Alyssa passed out and thankfully woke up before it got serious, but I found Master Sergeant Kennedy."

"That's good. Where is he?" Evan asked.

"He didn't make it. He was injured badly and he…wasn't acting himself," Will stated and shook his head, recalling the scenario. "Kennedy was gone before it got bad. We soon had to get out of the building. The angras are in the area and possibly the dragon," he added, looking back towards the entrance to the church.

Evan examined his expression and his body language. He could see something was truly bothering him. "There's something else isn't there?" he asked.

Will glanced back at him and began to think about Patrick, Tidwell, and Moseley. Something didn't seem right.

Patrick was suspicious at first...and now he is gone. Christian was a great soldier and focused all of his attention on the mission and now he is gone, but could he have survived those wounds? We were quick to respond...And Travis...where did he disappear to?

Will sighed and shook his head.

And now I'm hearing things too...

"It's nothing," he said softly, rubbing his forehead, hoping the tension headache that was starting to brew would go away before he stepped inside the cathedral. Evan watched him for a moment and decided to let it go for now. There was much to discuss, and he wanted to hear Alyssa out.

The atmosphere inside the cathedral grew tense in a matter of seconds as Ray paced around the lobby, his frustration slowly elevating. "I really don't care why you came here. I just want to know if you will be able to help us," he stated. His arms were folded and he was growing angry. Ariana was standing by his side trying to calm him down with a reassuring pat. Alyssa didn't blame them for being upset. They had gotten their hopes up.

"You heard Will outside. You just have to be patient with us. I promise we'll leave soon," Alyssa stated and Ray shook his head.

"Let's just sit tight for a little bit longer, okay?" Ariana whispered. "There's a nice banquet hall upstairs with a small patio outside. It will be safe, and we can get some air."

Ray glared at Alyssa. Kevin cleared his throat and took a step towards Ray, wearing no expression on his face. Ray half smiled and slowly turned away, making his way towards the lobby with the spiral staircase. Ariana had her arm wrapped around him as she led him away. Deep down she was scared, but she knew Ray's temper would get out of hand if she didn't intervene. Jeffrey decided to follow them, keeping quiet. Alyssa felt she needed to keep a close eye on him. He looked unsure outside and now he seemed to be contemplating something. This made her nervous. She didn't want to take too much time searching the place before something drastic happened. Kevin sighed and stood back next to Alyssa, not sure what they were going to find there exactly and was a bit confused by it all to begin with.

"So what's going on? Are they no longer doing evacuations?" Josh asked. Jessie stood close to him, trying to be a part of the conversation but with a distance.

"They were while we were there, but I'm not sure what's going to happen now," Alyssa said and glanced at the door as Will and Evan stepped inside.

Josh felt his stomach drop. He wanted to be sick, but somehow he was able to keep it together. There was no use in getting worked up now.

"Okay, please fill me in Alyssa. I've been confused by all of this. I've kept quiet, and I've abided by my orders, but I believe I am owed some sort of an explanation especially if I'm going to stand by your sides in this," Evan said, looking at Alyssa as he closed the door behind him.

Will crossed his arms casually and stood near Evan as he waited. Alyssa nodded and Kevin became a bit anxious. It was hard enough to be in a room with one soldier, but now there were two and he didn't like the young soldier's tone.

Alyssa took in a deep breath. She was hoping to sum this up for him.

"Alright, I understand. To make a long story short, I was in an accident with my father and a close family friend. I've been struggling for some time, trying to recall what happened. I suffered amnesia, but lately the memories have been coming back to me. I believe the truth to what happened eventually led to the events here. I, ah…" Alyssa said and looked at Kevin. He was trying to read her unsure expression, but wasn't able to understand it. She feared this part of the story.

"I...also feel that the old tale about the lost cavern here wasn't just a tale at all."

"What?" Kevin asked, completely shocked from the statement.

"That silly tale about the Indians?" Jessie asked.

Alyssa glanced at her. She had forgotten she was in the room with them. "Yes," she replied and Will looked at her, not sure what to say.

"Uh, okay...not sure if I know that one," Evan said becoming even more confused and irritated.

"Alyssa, it's just a scary story to tell kids at a campfire," Kevin said, remembering the old story when he was a child. Everyone in Rockdale Valley was familiar with it.

"I thought the same thing at one time," Alyssa stated. She was nervous from everyone's disturbed expressions.

"Why now, all of a sudden?" Kevin asked, stepping back to get a good look at Alyssa's face.

"I can recall a scene outside this cavern I went to, the night of my accident. My father's friend made an interesting comment, and it got me thinking," Alyssa said.

"Alright..." Kevin said, waiting for her to continue.

"He said the truth to its secret, the legend behind the tale. This cavern, it was the one Richard went to before falling ill. It's starting to make some sense now," Alyssa said, thinking about the vision of her brother.

"I thought Richard killed himself," Kevin quickly responded and Alyssa cringed. She closed her eyes and took in a deep breath. Will became anxious. Evan was speechless.

Alyssa slowly opened her eyes and stared at Kevin. "He did," she replied.

"I didn't mean..." Kevin began to say and Alyssa interrupted, "Yes, you did. You've always had a problem with opening your mouth before thinking about the consequences."

She stared at him for a moment and regained her composure. She looked back at Evan and sighed. "I remember my brother always talking about an old book written about this tale. He became obsessed with it. I remember him and his friends talking about the story and how the book was kept hidden here in this cathedral. No one believed him. I didn't believe him...or that stupid tale..." Alyssa said.

Will now realized why she had brought them there. "Do you think it will give you some answers?" he asked.

Alyssa nodded.

"What is it about?" he added.

"Well, the tale was told a bit differently to us when we were kids. It was like a good ghost story. It spoke of Native Americans that had lived in the valley and how they happened to find a hidden cavern in the mountains that contained rare treasure. One night when the tribe went into this cavern to hold a spiritual ritual by its leader, Wahkan, they kept hearing these sounds...like breathing..." she said and stopped, thinking about the vision when she had found her red stone. She took in a deep breath and shook the thought away.

"They said a dark spirit dwelled there, and they felt as if it protected them and the valley. So they cursed the cavern to protect it and its riches that way no one would be able to get their hands on the precious gems they grew to love. And then the tale went on about kids stumbling upon this cavern years and years back, how most didn't return home and the few that did had suffered greatly," Alyssa said and Evan quickly shook his head.

"Do you actually believe this story?" he asked, looking at Will.

"This is the first I've actually heard about it," Will responded.

"I'm sorry...My memory has been coming back to me slowly. This just came to me not long ago. Earlier I wouldn't have expected it at all. I had let that go so many years ago," Alyssa said, sighing sadly. She had thought something odd had happened to her brother, but her father denied it. She grew up letting go of the tale and believing that her brother was truly sick.

Evan shook his head. "This is just ridiculous..." he stressed and paused, looking away. "All of it is."

Will remained quiet as he watched Evan look back at Alyssa. "None of it makes sense, but I do believe time is running out for this place. We are wasting our time here, Will," Evan added and Will uncrossed his arms.

"What are you trying to tell us?" he asked.

Evan glanced at him. "I found a large hole in the ground back near City Hall. The tunnel stretched down into the earth and brought me to a section that was open. There was...lava. It was flowing everywhere and down other corridors, some that made up a part of the sewer system. This place could erupt at any time, who knows? I think our only option is to leave this place," Evan said and Alyssa gasped, placing her hand on her chest as she could feel her heart sinking, her knees weakening.

Kevin grabbed her arm, steadying her. "Whoa...Are you alright?" he asked.

Josh and Jessie stared at Alyssa, alarmed. Will watched her carefully as she breathed deeply.

"It's actually happening..." she stated almost in a pant.

"What exactly?" Kevin asked.

"My nightmares...It's what I saw. It's what I've been struggling with these past few weeks. Those images of the cavern...the monsters...the valley collapsing and erupting into flames..." Alyssa gasped and paused to catch her breath.

"Okay, I thought the tale was one thing but now you are scaring me. Who are you?" Jessie asked, her face full of fright.

"Rockdale Valley *is* running out of time," Alyssa said, ignoring Jessie's comment as tears began to fill her eyes. She was full of fright and despair. She wasn't ready to accept the valley's fate or accept the fact that she may never see her parents again. She didn't know where to turn now, and she wasn't sure if there was much hope left that she could hang on to.

Alyssa closed her eyes and let the tears fall. Kevin continued to hold her arm, still surprised from it all.

"You aren't screwing with our heads, are you?" Evan asked.

Will shot him a look. "Private Watkins, please..." he stressed firmly.

"How can you believe this nonsense? She's bullshitting us! After the behavior I witnessed downtown, I knew she was crazy!" Evan shouted and Kevin released Alyssa's arm, his body trembling with anger. He quickly approached Evan, pulling his arm back and punching him as hard as he could across the jaw. Evan stumbled back a few feet, placing his hand on the side of his face. Jessie gasped and Josh stared in shock, trying to keep his distance. Alyssa's mouth dropped as Kevin stood still, waiting for Evan to respond. He wanted a fight. He wanted to take all his anger out on anyone wearing that uniform.

Will quickly grabbed Evan's arms before he could lunge at Kevin. He struggled, attempting to break free. Kevin folded his arms and stared at him, his eyes narrowed.

"Let it go, Private!" Will shouted.

"He punched me, damn it! Let me go!" Evan yelled, continuing to struggle in Will's strong grasp.

"I SAID STOP, *PRIVATE!*"

Evan stopped struggling and took a deep breath in, staring at Kevin as he did so. Will slowly released his arms, watching him closely.

"It's your lucky night, Mr. Headley," Evan stated and looked at Will, his eyes full of anger. Kevin took a few steps back, claiming his spot by Alyssa as she stared at him, speechless.

"Private, I think you need to find a place to cool down and get it together. If time isn't on our side right now, then we shouldn't be wasting it arguing about this," Will stated.

Evan walked around them and towards the lobby.

"I'll join you, if you don't mind," Jessie said, quickly catching up to Evan. He didn't respond as they disappeared behind the door quietly. Josh watched them close the door before turning his attention back to Will and Alyssa. He gave up on the possibility of escaping now. He felt it was time to accept his fate and fight as long as he could. Rockdale Valley was now a ticking time bomb.

Will took a few steps closer to Alyssa and sighed. Kevin watched him carefully. He was beginning to hate Evan, and he wasn't sure how to feel about Will yet, but there was something different about him. He wasn't able to pin point it yet.

Alyssa looked into Will's eyes, and Will could see the hurt and the pain within hers.

"I told you…that you could trust me," he said.

Alyssa thought about the conversation she had in the alley, the moment she thought her life was going to end. He had been so sincere, so concerned after she realized that he wasn't going to cause her any harm.

"I need to know if all of this is indeed true," Will added.

"Yes," Alyssa responded shortly and waited as Will slowly nodded.

"I never believed in the supernatural…But I will help you for as long as I possibly can…only if there is a chance to end this," he said.

Kevin could sense the honesty, but refused to accept it right away. He couldn't understand why this soldier was willing to stand by his partner's side even after the statements she had made. He didn't believe in the legend. It was just a tale to him.

"Thank you, Will. If there is a possibility of putting an end to this, I want to try. I owe it to everyone," Alyssa said.

"Alright. Where should we start looking?" Will asked.

"The library," Alyssa replied.

"Where would you like me to search?" Josh asked, taking a few steps closer to them.

"Um, how about upstairs?" Alyssa said, surprised that Josh was offering his assistance. He seemed to be focused on one thing before and that was evacuation.

Josh nodded and looked around.

"The stairs are in there," Alyssa said, pointing to the door Jessie and Evan had gone to.

"Okay. Is there a particular name I should find?" Josh asked.

"Anything about Wahkan and the legend of Rockdale Valley," Alyssa replied and Josh nodded, approaching the door to the foyer.

"Thank you, Josh. Really," Alyssa added and smiled.

Josh nodded and opened the door, disappearing behind it.

"Well, I'm coming with you," Kevin stated, looking at Alyssa as she nodded.

"I will help you two out as well. How big is this library?" Will asked as Alyssa began to approach the door on the left.

"It's not that large, shouldn't take us too long," she replied.

Kevin followed Alyssa closely as Will trailed behind, trying to examine the cathedral's ancient appearance.

As Alyssa made her way down the hall, she continued to pray for some answers. There were still many gaps left to her past, many questions left unanswered. But most importantly, the people of Rockdale Valley deserved to know the truth to the devastation, the tragedy of so many lives lost. Alyssa refused to leave the cathedral empty handed. She had to find this ancient story.

Chapter Seventeen

RAY PACED AROUND THE PATIO on the second floor balcony, his mind racing with ideas of how to escape. Jeffrey was resting against the railing, his arms crossed. Ariana watched Ray carefully as she sat on a bench. The fresh air was able to calm her nerves, but she could see that it had no affect on Ray. His face was distraught, and he couldn't keep still.

"We could take their vehicle," he stated, finally pausing to look at Ariana.

She slowly shook her head, afraid. "That's Government property. Imagine what they would do to us," she said calmly.

"I was actually thinking the same thing, Ray. I believe we could get away with it," Jeffrey stated.

Ariana glanced at him. "You both are insane! What makes you think you could get away with this?" she asked.

"They don't know who we are. We leave, abandon the vehicle, and we are home free," Jeffrey said and pushed himself off the railing.

"I think it could work. There's too much going on around here for them to stop and try and find one vehicle," Ray said.

Ariana gasped and looked away. "I can't believe you two. We should just sit tight for a moment and really think this through," she said.

"Baby, we shouldn't sit tight and wait until this place finally comes toppling down," Ray replied.

"Or for one of those things to show up again," Jeffrey added.

Ariana sighed softly. "Believe me, I want to get out of here just as bad as you two do, but there are two soldiers here. I'm sure they can protect us. Let's just wait a little while and see what they do. Please?" she asked, hoping Ray would reconsider. Jeffrey turned away, shaking his head as he looked towards the mountains. Ray stared at Ariana for a moment and could see the begging in her eyes.

"Alright, but just for a little while. That will give us time to think about this and for them to finish whatever it is they are doing, okay?" he stated and Ariana nodded.

"Alright," she said and sighed in relief. She didn't want to commit a felony crime just to get out of the valley. She had a clean record, and she didn't have the heart to even pull it off. She hoped that the girl downstairs with the handsome soldier and the ignorant cop would hurry up before they could attempt this risky operation.

"I still don't know what I'm looking for exactly," Kevin stated as he scanned through books on a tall, long bookshelf. There were a few rows of shelves in the middle of the small library and some standing against the walls. There were three small tables with two chairs each that sat on the right side of the room. A large grandfather clock sat behind them against the wall, its pendulum swaying softly. The room was very dim with a dark, relaxed appearance. The church was beginning to confuse Will. He assumed that they were all bright and lively. This one was a bit depressing to him.

"I'm not a hundred percent sure myself. I've never seen the thing. Just look for anything about Wahkan," Alyssa said, scanning through books on another shelf.

"We don't even know if it exists. This is hopeless," Kevin stressed.

Alyssa sighed and ignored his statement. Will mumbled to himself as he scanned the shelves against the wall. Most of the books were pertaining to Christianity, but he had ran across a few Native American Heritage stories, nothing that seemed to catch his attention regarding a cavern or a possible legend, and nothing regarding Rockdale Valley. He was beginning to wonder if searching for this book that may or may not exist was becoming a waste of precious time.

After countless minutes of eye-straining and silence, Will quietly sat at one of the tables and tried to conjure up any ideas. Kevin sighed and shook his head once he reached the final shelf of books. He approached Will and carefully sat across from him.

"This isn't going to work," he said softly.

Alyssa continued to scan through a few remaining books frantically. She knew they were running out of patience, but she wasn't ready to give up yet.

"You would think there would be something written about this story now that I think about it. It's very well known throughout this valley. Every child should have grown up hearing about it at least once," she stated and began to pace around the room.

It's got to be related...What else would Brian's statement mean?

Alyssa groaned and slowly approached the table where Will and Kevin sat.

"I must be missing something...I could have sworn it was related," she said softly, leaning against the table.

"That's because it's just a tale, Alyssa. I'm sorry, but it's *just* a story," Kevin said as politely as he could. He didn't want to upset her again.

"Kevin, look at what's going on around us. Are you sure you want to say that the legend is just an interesting story?"

Kevin took in a deep breath. "I do believe something extremely odd is going on here, but I don't believe it has anything to do with that tale," he replied.

"If you were told differently as a child then how is the legend truly written or told?" Will asked as he wondered if Kevin was right. This was beginning to sound crazy.

"I...I don't know...It was such a long time ago when I wanted to seek the truth after my brother passed..." Alyssa stuttered.

Kevin sighed heavily. "And you never did because it's just a *damn* tale..." he stressed and Alyssa gritted her teeth, pushing herself away from the table. The anger and anxiety began to build up within her as she failed to keep herself together.

"I didn't have the chance to seek the truth back then! My father put a quick stop to that, and I finally had to let it go! Before…" Alyssa paused and sighed heavily. "Before forgetting about it all together…I was just a kid," she said sadly. She wanted them to understand everything she had been through. She wanted them to believe her.

Kevin slowly shook his head and Alyssa stared at him, her eyes beginning to narrow. "My brother is *dead* because of that legend… That's why he fell ill. And you want to say that the cavern doesn't exist? I've been in it, Kevin," Alyssa stated and pulled her pendant out from behind her shirt, holding it up so Kevin could get a good look at the stone.

Will took in a deep breath, hoping Kevin would just shut up so they could figure out what to do next. He knew Alyssa was in a fragile state.

"I found this in the cavern between a bed of crystals. Above that bed were engravings of another language, inscriptions. I've been having these hallucinations and visions. I'm not going crazy. They mean something. It's *not* just a coincidence," Alyssa said and quickly placed the pendant back under her shirt.

"When it came to my brother, we didn't speak of it. My father was in denial, it's obvious now. He didn't want to talk about it. And after my accident, I'm sure he was thankful that I was unable to remember. Maybe that's why he has refused to talk to me about it for this long," she added.

Will remained quiet. He was trying to absorb all the information and think about everything else that she had shared with him.

"Alyssa, I don't want to upset you. I know you've been through a lot since the accident. We could see it at the station before you left. But don't you think you are chasing a lost cause now? If only you could hear yourself," Kevin said.

Alyssa stared at him, still surprised that he refused to believe any of it. Her eyes began to tear up as she took a few steps back.

"You know…I would expect that from everyone else here, Kevin, but not from you…" she said softly and quickly turned away, exiting the room before they could see the tears spill down her cheeks.

Kevin sighed and watched Alyssa close the door before looking at Will. He was still staring at the table, unsure of what to say. Kevin cleared his throat and looked away.

"I didn't know Alyssa's brother well," he stated and paused, trying to recall memories of him. "I saw him from time to time back when Alyssa and I were kids, just hanging out. I remember the day she told me what he'd done. It was a total shock. No one can ever comprehend why anyone would do such a thing. But if what she is saying is true, how could something like that be kept quiet for this long? It doesn't make any sense," Kevin added and Will shook his head, still unsure, but something deep down continued to tell him not to look the other way just yet. There was still that possibility of some truth behind it all.

"Have you stopped to think that there could've been a good reason to keep quiet about it? Imagine the possibilities," Will said.

Kevin glared at him. "What is it with you, Will?" he asked.

Will became confused, refusing to respond at the moment.

"Your *boys* were deployed here for a whole 'nother reason but you are intent on aiding her," Kevin added.

Will took in a deep breath and thought for a moment. He couldn't help but think about his past. "I've lost my group, my soldiers…my friends…" he finally stated and took in another deep breath, releasing it slowly. "Alyssa soon confided in me after we were acquainted. Since then I've felt that she truly needed me. I've failed people before, not that I wanted to. I'm a green beret, I've seen a lot. I don't want to fail her. If there's the slightest possibility of correcting this situation, I want to be there to help. Perhaps then my group wouldn't have died for nothing," he replied.

Kevin slowly nodded and looked away. Will was beginning to sound like an honest soldier to him, one with a good heart.

"Well, I guess everything should be considered. I'm just really worried about her. I want her to get out of here and stop chasing this dream. She's not the same person anymore," he said.

"You should go check on her. We're wasting time here now," Will suggested.

"I'm sure I'm the last person she wants to see right now. This isn't the first time I've voiced my opinion and upset her. Maybe you should try. You seem to have a way of speaking to her," Kevin replied, suddenly regretting that last comment.

"I'll let her have her moment," Will said.

"Ha, women. They sure do need it at times," Kevin replied and smirked, a bit relieved.

Will half smiled and thought about what he would possibly say to her. He had to be quick about it as he glanced at the pendulum in the old grandfather clock. It ticked slowly, breaking the silence, time steadily slipping by.

Alyssa had stepped down the other end of the dim hall and had approached a closed door. She knew it led into the cathedral's worship hall, and she still wasn't sure why she wanted to go into this area after not having set foot in this church since she was a kid. But she was running out of options. Everyone but Will thought she was losing it. Maybe she needed to seek a little help elsewhere.

Alyssa placed her hand on the cold knob and turned it gently, pushing the door open slowly. She could already see the light from the candles that sat on the alter, burning brightly. The pews, were neatly rowed, and the area was empty and quiet. Alyssa stepped into the chapel and looked at the second floor balcony that overlooked the worship hall. She sighed softly, thanking the area to herself for being vacant. She needed to be alone.

Alyssa slowly stepped around the wooden pews and approached the stage, staring at the candles and the large cross. She took in a deep breath, her body beginning to tremble. She wasn't sure if it were nerves or if the room was just chilly. She fought through it and stopped once she reached the stage. She gazed at the large cross and slowly looked down at the floor, feeling ashamed of herself to even look at it.

I'm in desperate need of guidance...I don't know what to do...or where to turn...But whichever it is, I cannot do it alone. I have lost my family...I've lost the chief and my fellow officers...and now it seems as if I've lost my best friend...

Tears began to flood Alyssa's eyes and spill onto her cheeks as she allowed herself to fall to her knees, her face burying into the palms of her hands.

I know I haven't set foot in a church for so long, and I hope that I could be forgiven...This has been so hard...Ever since my brother passed, my life has not been the same. I need to know the truth...

Alyssa took in a deep breath and released it heavily.

No wonder my father wanted to keep quiet about everything. He was not fond of humiliation or embarrassment. He was probably trying to protect me and his reputation this entire time.

She slowly wiped the tears away and glanced back at the candles.

Please let there be hope for my parents...please let them be out there somewhere...I need them...

"I can't do this alone..." Alyssa whispered and paused, listening to soft footsteps coming up from behind her. She tried to wipe away the remaining tears that dripped down her cheeks as her heart began to beat faster. The footsteps stopped not too far from behind her and Alyssa sighed, looking at her lap. She allowed her nerves to relax before speaking. She already had a feeling of who it was.

"Come to lecture me some more?" she asked.

"No..."

Alyssa froze, feeling a bit nervous as she realized that she had mistaken Will for Kevin. His calm voice made her relax some more. It was somewhat relieving. She didn't need to hear anything else from Kevin.

"I wanted to see if you were okay," Will said as he remained standing behind her. Alyssa continued to look at the candles, their flames mesmerizing her.

"I'm sure I don't have to answer that one for you," she said softly.

"Your friend is really worried about you, Alyssa..." Will said and paused as he watched her carefully push herself to her feet. She continued to stare ahead, wiping away the last few tears. She didn't want Will to see her so torn. She didn't want him or anyone else to feel bad for her.

"My friend...doesn't even know what all I've truly been through. No one does..." Alyssa replied and finally looked at him. "Until you..." she added.

Will remained silent as he couldn't help but stare at her flushed face. She was suffering.

"How could I tell anyone before any of this? I only had my nightmares and my forgotten past to haunt me then. And now the flashbacks started to come as soon as I met Uktena, and I've had no choice but to confide in you all and look what that has done," Alyssa said and took in a deep breath.

"Why did you choose me, Alyssa?" Will asked.

Alyssa stared at him for a moment, remembering the way she felt before. "Because I trust you," she said softly, almost in a whisper. She had to open up to someone. Robert had stressed it, but she truly felt that she could put her trust in this soldier.

Will took a few steps closer to her, and Alyssa's heart began to beat faster once again. The anxiety was bothersome, the warmth rushing throughout her even more so. She didn't like this new feeling. She didn't want to attach herself to anyone during this chaotic time.

"Then please, listen to me. I don't feel that we should stay too much longer, and we aren't left with any other options it seems," Will said.

"Just give me a little bit more time. It's got to be here somewhere..."

"We may not have enough of it, Alyssa. We should see if Josh was able to find anything. If not, we should get the others and return to the hospital. That may be the only option we have left unless you may know where else this book could possibly be here," Will said and could see a bit of resentment in her eyes before it faded to uncertainty.

Alyssa kept her mouth closed, her lips in a frown. There was no use in trying to beg, and she wasn't sure of where else to look in the church. Will sighed and Alyssa stared into his eyes, not sure of how to respond as Will returned the gaze, only his was slightly different. She could see something behind it, and it began to make her feel extremely uncomfortable. This was the change she was beginning to see in him before except it had suddenly elevated. She slowly looked away, breaking the gaze as she sighed softly.

Will took a step back. "I'll give you a moment. And we may consider other options, but that all depends upon you, Alyssa," he said and turned away, walking down the aisle towards the foyer.

Alyssa watched him, the overwhelming burden weighing down her shoulders and back as the sadness filled her aching heart. She wanted to forget about it all. She wanted to leave Rockdale Valley. But how could she? She would let everyone down. She would be responsible for each and every death. How could anyone live with that over their heads?

Alyssa allowed a couple of more tears to fall from her cheeks before turning her attention away. She was not going to allow herself to give up now, and she refused to allow Kevin or Will to try and make her think otherwise.

CHAPTER EIGHTEEN

EVAN WAS STANDING IN THE clock tower feeling calm, but a bit annoyed as he watched the clock's gears turn. Jessie was standing nearby, watching him.

"Well, where did you find Alyssa?" she asked.

"I didn't. Will did," Evan responded.

"Oh," Jessie replied and looked away. Evan glanced at her, crossing his arms.

"She definitely caught me by surprise with the way she was acting when I met her though. It was a bit suspicious, yet alarming to me. I tried to help her and get to know her so I could fully understand, but Will put a quick end to that," he said with a bit of frustration.

Jessie raised an eyebrow. "Is that jealousy I'm catching?" she asked, half smiling.

"Not at all," Evan replied and looked away, thinking about the moment he caught her changing in the office. She was definitely attractive, but after everything that came out of her mouth earlier he was beginning to think that something was odd with her. He wasn't sure if she was disturbed, but he felt that she needed some kind of help.

"I still think what all we heard downstairs was crazy, but with Thompson being active commander now, I don't have much of a choice but to abide by his orders."

"Well, I'm starting to think that anything is possible here. You say there is a dragon…I've seen those monsters. Everyone will think we are crazy if we tell them what we've witnessed," Jessie said.

Evan slowly nodded.

"You know, I remember hearing this tale she speaks of over and over as a kid. Everyone knows the story here. I used to wonder if it really happened. It used to scare me...*a lot.* Some of my friends sworn that the kids were never found and that an ancient, evil spirit haunts that cavern. I don't know Alyssa, so I don't want to ignore everything she is saying. We should probably give her the benefit of a doubt," Jessie added.

"Yeah. Well, have you made up your mind yet?" Evan asked.

Jessie looked down at the ground.

"You know you have someone here that can get you out. As soon as they finish up, we are on our way to that hospital."

"I know. It's just really difficult for me to accept, but I'll go," Jessie said and looked at him.

"Thompson won't be able to refuse getting everyone to safety. It's our top priority. And again, I'm sorry for your loss," Evan said and Jessie nodded, looking the other way. She still wouldn't believe that Nathan was truly dead. He could still be out there...

Alyssa took in a long, deep breath, preparing herself for the trip back to the hospital. She didn't know where else to search, and she knew they couldn't spend too much time in the cathedral. It would take all night looking for one book. She took one last look at the candles and the cross before turning around and walking down the aisle between the pews. Her mind was rushing with ideas of what to do next, her anxiety rising. She wasn't ready to leave yet and before she could get near the double doors to the lobby, the side door she had come from earlier suddenly opened. Alyssa glanced at an old, petite woman that slowly stepped inside the chapel, feeling a bit nervous as she tried to scurry to the door.

"Oh...I didn't know we had more company," the old woman said.

Alyssa stopped and turned to look at her. "Uh, we were just leaving. I'm sorry to intrude."

"No intrusion. This cathedral welcomes everyone."

Alyssa watched as the old woman walked between the pews to the aisle, smiling.

"Um, thanks," she replied and turned to walk away until the old woman spoke up. "Wait...I recognize you..." she said and Alyssa stopped again, turning to face her. Her heart was pumping quickly, the adrenaline rushing throughout her. She didn't know this woman or at least she didn't think she did.

"You do?" Alyssa asked.

The old woman approached her and her eyes slowly raised.

"Yes...Little Alyssa, but not so little anymore. My, have you grown."

"Do I know you?"

"You probably don't remember, child. I'm Dena. This is my church. It has been a part of my family for many generations."

Alyssa tried to recall memories here, but there weren't many of them coming to her.

"Why have you come here?" Dena asked.

"Uh..." Alyssa stuttered and paused, staring into Dena's dark eyes.

Dena narrowed them slowly, sensing her worst fears.

"What have you done?" she whispered.

Alyssa became frightened as she froze. She didn't know what to tell this woman. "I...I don't know..." she said, shaken.

"I can see it in your eyes...Tell me, child," Dena said gently.

Alyssa breathed heavily and took a step back as the ground began to quiver beneath their feet. Dena looked around her before looking back into Alyssa's eyes, her face full of shock.

"I was trying to deny the possibility of this..." she whispered, astonished.

Alyssa continued to breathe heavily as she responded, "You know the legend?"

"Yes, it exists, but I am sure you already knew that," Dena replied and the earth became still, the dust quickly settling.

Will and Kevin stepped into the chapel, startling Alyssa as she glanced behind her, ignoring Dena's statement. Dena stared at the two men and became agitated. Alyssa turned her attention back to her, taking a deep breath, trying to calm her nerves.

"What is it that you want so badly?" Dena asked.

"Nothing...Just the truth..."

"For many *years* we have protected it...And for many years people avoided the area, fearing evil in its purest form," Dena said and paused as Will and Kevin stepped up beside Alyssa. Alyssa didn't pay them any mind. She was completely focused on Dena, trying to recall anything.

Dena ignored the men, looking directly into Alyssa's eyes.

"Only one incident occurred in our time where people became missing, one suffering for many years before finally being placed into an institution. People eventually left it alone and it became a forgotten tale. But these past few generations, people became thrill seekers, looking for a new adventure. And then the secret got out... and your brother snooped into a restricted area, almost dooming us all," she said angrily.

Will and Kevin remained speechless, awestruck and confused.

"Please...I do not know what all happened. I was too young," Alyssa said, hoping for more information.

"He found the key to get into the cavern, the same one you obviously used. Thankfully my grandson didn't go in with him, and thankfully your brother didn't take anything, but he was cursed for stepping foot behind those walls. He was lucky to have gotten out of the cavern altogether." Alyssa's mouth slowly dropped as the image of her brother flashed into her mind once again.

"Now you have followed in his steps, haven't you?" Dena asked.

"I don't remember, Dena," Alyssa whispered, trying not to become upset.

"Then why have you come here? After your brother's death, your father never came back to this church, and he was determined to make sure you wouldn't make your way back here to go digging in attempt to research what may have been the cause."

"Why would he do that?" Alyssa asked. "Why would he try and hide the truth?"

"To protect you, I'm sure...The truth would've led to risks that were too great to chance. Imagine if the world caught wind of the truth behind the legend. Imagine the attraction it would've gotten. Imagine the consequences," Dena stated and took in a deep breath, exhaling it softly. "Now we have failed to protect it and everyone else," she added and Alyssa carefully pulled her pendant out from behind her shirt.

Dena looked at it and her eyes slowly widened.

"I cannot recall everything that I did the evening my father and I went to that area in the mountains, and I don't know the true story. By the way my father acted, he had no idea that his friend had brought us to the cavern my brother went to, obviously the cavern you speak of, the one I never believed to have truly existed until recently."

Dena sighed heavily. "Then you two...were *betrayed*," she stated.

Alyssa frowned. "No...Brian has been a family friend way before I was even born. What would have been the reason behind that?"

"Do you know what you have right there?" Dena asked, glaring at her pendant.

"A rock? I'm not sure why I held onto it, but my father had it placed in the necklace and gave it to me after the accident," Alyssa replied hesitantly, holding the pendant carefully.

Dena snickered, shaking her head. "One thing I learned from my elders...Never doubt a spirit," she stated and took in a deep breath.

Alyssa stared at her as she continued, "Your father refuses to believe the legend. He denied it...He *feared* it. He thought your brother was brainwashed into believing and that perhaps he was suffering from post traumatic stress after the night he explored the cavern. And now you...Alyssa, what you have is a very rare, uncut *gem*, the red diamond, carved from the rock by the legendary Wahkan himself. It was the gift given to the beast they believed dwelled in the cavern. He felt it to be sacred, and that all the rare stones that were etched into those walls belonged there. No one else had a right to touch them. Someone close to you wanted those riches...which led you to awaken it..." Dena said and Alyssa's eyes widened.

"Awaken what?" Kevin interrupted, becoming a bit concerned himself.

Alyssa remained quiet, overwhelmed with fear.

"The legendary beast, Uktena...The guardian of the sacred cavern, the beast he worshipped," Dena replied and took another step closer to Alyssa, her hand slowly extending towards her face.

Alyssa became frightened and took a step back as Kevin put his arm in front of her.

"Don't worry...I'm not going to hurt you..." Dena said and carefully touched the side of Alyssa's head, closing her eyes. Alyssa's heart began to race, and Will was beginning to feel a bit uneasy. Kevin lowered his arm, watching carefully.

After a moment, Dena quickly pulled her arm back, her eyes widening. "He possesses you..." she whispered.

"Who, Dena?" Alyssa asked.

"Wahkan," Dena gasped and took a few steps back. "Get out of this cathedral...You have doomed us all!" she shouted, full of fear.

Alyssa gasped and about fell to her knees as Kevin and Will grabbed her.

"Come on, Alyssa. We need to get out of here," Will stated firmly and paused as a few haunting screams were heard in the distance, coming from outside. Dena gasped and looked behind her. She stared at the stained glass windows near the stage, her mouth slowly dropping.

"The demonic beasts..." Dena whispered.

"The angras," Will stated and Dena looked at him.

"You've seen the journal?" she asked and the sounds of glass shattering echoed throughout the chapel.

Alyssa gasped as Will pulled his rifle over his head, aiming it towards the stage, ignoring Dena's question. Kevin quickly drew his Glock nine, one hand still wrapped around Alyssa's arm. Dena looked behind her once again and watched as the two large beasts slowly stepped around the corner by the stage. Their lips were curled up over their sharp teeth, heads lowered, stalking them like prey. Their long claws stretched out, ready to dig into their next victim.

Dena gasped and her heart felt as if it was going to beat out of her chest as Will stepped around her.

"Get out of here..." he ordered.

Alyssa quickly got herself together and pulled her assault rifle over her head. Kevin released her arm and aimed at the first angra as it released a loud screech. The second bolted towards them, leaping over the first row of pews. Dena turned around and Kevin pushed her out of the way as the gunfire erupted from Will and Alyssa's assault rifles. Kevin took a few steps back and fired a few rounds at the one that jumped towards them. It had split one of the pews in two as splinters and wood particles scattered across the floor. Dena tried to pull herself back to the aisle as the angra stood near her, releasing another cry towards Kevin.

Will released the trigger to his assault rifle and snatched a grenade from his belt, loading it into the grenade launcher attached to the bottom of his rifle. Alyssa continued to fire at the angra near them and held onto the trigger until her gun clicked. The angra fell back and jumped to the side as blood spilled onto the floor. Alyssa gasped and fell to the long, running carpet that stretched down the aisle, crawling towards Dena, holding her rifle carefully. Will glanced at her before aiming the grenade launcher towards the angra near the stage. It slowly crept around it and the pews before stopping at the aisle they stood in.

"Get up!" Alyssa yelled as she tried to pull Dena to her feet.

Dena gasped, struggling to breathe as she carefully pushed herself to her feet. Alyssa held onto her arm as Will fired the grenade. Alyssa clenched her teeth and Dena shook as the grenade exploded and knocked the angra to the floor. The loud scream echoed throughout the chapel as the angra squirmed about, thrashing its bulky body.

As the gunfire and screams continued, Ray, Ariana, and Jeffrey bolted through the door to the balcony that overlooked the chapel, gasping in fright at the scene below. Evan, Jessie, and Josh came through the door near the spiral staircase and Evan jogged to the railing.

"Oh my God..." he whispered.

Jessie's eyes widened as she stared at the monsters below.

"Now are you guys ready!" Ray yelled.

"I've got to help them," Evan stated and Ray grabbed Ariana's hand and pulled her to the staircase.

"Then we will wait for you in the humvee," he stated and Jeffrey followed them as Josh retrieved his .38 special.

"You're not going with them?" Evan asked and Josh shook his head.

"I'm done running," he said and Evan smiled, appreciating the new Josh.

"Look out!" Kevin yelled and reloaded his nine millimeter as the angra nearest to them dashed through the row of pews towards Alyssa and Dena. Will gasped and dropped his rifle, jumping towards them. Dena quickly stepped back as Will grabbed Alyssa, knocking her out of the beast's way. Alyssa yelped as she hit the floor and heard the painful cry from Dena as the angra's claws ripped through her chest and pulled her down, slinging her to the floor. Will carefully grabbed Alyssa's rifle from her grasp, reloading it with one of his clips and aiming it towards the beast's face. Kevin kept his composure and glanced up at the balcony as gunfire from two different weapons fired down towards them, tearing through the angra's side. More blood spilled onto the floor around it as Will pulled the trigger and fired a few rounds at the beast before it suddenly fell back towards the pews, collapsing onto the floor. It squirmed for a moment before releasing its final cry.

"The other one isn't finished yet!" Evan yelled from above as Will glanced at him.

Kevin stepped down the aisle and around Will, aiming his pistol at the struggling angra near the stage. Alyssa quickly pushed herself to her knees, crawling towards Dena's still body. Will carefully stood up, rifle aimed and ready as he kept an eye on the angra Kevin approached.

Alyssa carefully grabbed Dena and pulled her up some, allowing her body to rest against her lap. Blood was dripping from her mouth and from the wounds in her chest as her eyes struggled to stay open.

"Dena!" Alyssa yelled, patting her arm. "Please...stay with me..."

Dena's eyes opened halfway and Alyssa became saddened.

"I didn't mean for any of this. It wasn't my intentions..." Alyssa said and paused as a few rounds from Kevin's pistol broke the silence. Will kept a close eye as Alyssa continued.

"Please Dena...if there is a way I can end this..." she stated and the earth slowly began to quiver once more.

Dena's eyes opened a bit more as dust and pebbles fell from above. Alyssa didn't care. She continued to hold onto her lifeless body, not willing to move.

Dena slowly met Alyssa's gaze. "Sacrifice yourself," she whispered and opened her hand.

Alyssa's heart dropped from the statement as she glanced at the large key she held and back towards her eyes, not sure if she should take it or leave it.

"In my office...near the library. There is a door...Below, you will find...what I'm sure you seek," Dena whispered.

Alyssa gently took the large key and looked back into her eyes.

"Please forgive me..." she whispered back.

Dena's eyes slowly closed and her body fell limp. Alyssa bit her lower lip as her body trembled with anger and sadness. She gently laid Dena's body on the cold floor, ignoring the few gunshots that continued to bounce against the walls.

"Alright let's go!" Evan yelled from above and he and Josh disappeared behind the railing while Kevin glanced at Will.

"You guys get out of here! I'm right behind you!" he shouted and turned his attention back to the last angra as it screamed and struggled against the floor, blood and tissue surrounding its body.

Will picked his rifle up and handed Alyssa's back to her. Alyssa grabbed it and glanced at the side door that led to the library. She was breathing heavily and refused to look at Will as she took one last look at Dena's body.

"Alyssa…" Will stated and she ignored him, looking back at the side door. The earth continued to quiver, the dust gently raining down from the ceiling.

"Alyssa, we need to go *now*…" Will stated urgently and Alyssa gasped.

"I've got to get this book! There's got to be another way to stop this!" she said and pushed her way to the side door, struggling to keep her balance.

"Alyssa!" Will yelled and a few more shots erupted from Kevin's pistol, putting an end to the remaining angra.

Will chased after her as she pulled the door open and ran down the hallway. He pushed past the pews and grabbed a hold of the door frame, catching his balance as the quake began to intensify.

"Alyssa! We don't know how much longer this building is going to hold!" Will yelled and pushed himself into the hallway and around the corner, watching as Alyssa entered the door at the end of the hall. He glanced at the stone walls, witnessing the cracks forming through them. His eyes widened as he pushed down the hall and into the small office Alyssa had ran into. She was already at the door in the back, unlocking it with the large key and pushing it open with all of her might.

"Alyssa, wait!" Will shouted once more and pushed himself into the room, struggling to keep up with her. Alyssa stepped down the small, stone steps as they spiraled down into a dim lit basement. She held onto the walls and guided herself down quickly and carefully, determined to get her hands on the legend.

Alyssa stopped once she reached the room below and kept her balance as she continued to push her hands against the walls, keeping herself steady. Will came up from behind her quickly and stopped, looking up at the ceiling as cracks tore through it. Pebbles and dust fell around them as he gasped. Alyssa quickly looked up as the ceiling split. Her heart sank and her body froze in place until she was suddenly pushed forward, thrown to the ground quickly. A loud crash was heard behind her as she covered her head. Large pieces of stone and brick continued to cave in and crash behind her, their loud booms stinging her ears. Alyssa clenched her teeth and closed her eyes tightly until the earth stopped shaking and silence filled the area. The smell of dust and stone flushed the room as a cloud of smoke rose towards the damaged ceiling. Cracks and large tears had torn through it and parts of the walls as they held unsteadily.

Alyssa slowly pushed herself slightly up, coughing as she looked behind her, fearing the worst. Will?" she asked hesitantly.

As the fog cleared, she could see his body lying near the foot of the stairs, debris surrounding him. Large stone piled behind him in the stairwell, blocking their only exit.

Alyssa gasped and crawled to where Will was lying still. "Will..." she said once again and didn't get a response.

Tears began to fill her eyes as she removed his rifle and pushed him onto his back, resting his head in her lap. She felt a little bit of hope as she realized he was still breathing, and his heart rate felt normal. As she carefully pulled her hands away from the back of his head, blood smeared across her palm, alarming her. Alyssa looked around the room, hoping to find any items that could help her stop the bleeding. The small room was dark with only a little light from the few candles that still burned. There was a large, wooden desk, a small bed, and one large picture that hung on the wall, nothing more. Alyssa became nervous as she looked at a small hole in her shirt. She put her finger through it and ripped a piece of the shirt off. She carefully wrapped it around Will's head, securing it in place before allowing his head and upper back to rest against her lap. Alyssa sighed helplessly, and the tears began to fall. She gently rested her arms and hands on his chest, rubbing it softly.

"I'm so sorry..." she whispered and her head hung down in defeat, her eyes closing.

CHAPTER NINETEEN

"NO! STOP!" EVAN YELLED AND glanced at Josh as he was helping Jessie up from her fall to the sidewalk. The earth had split in places and trees were brought to the ground from the quake. The dust from a part of the cathedral that had collapsed raised high in the sky before eventually clearing up around the area. Jessie was gasping for air as she pushed herself to her feet, looking at the rubble behind her.

"You two stay here! Find the others! I'll...I'll be back with help!" Evan yelled and ran after the humvee, jumping over large tears in the pavement.

Josh was breathing heavily as he looked back at the remains of the cathedral.

"Oh no..." Jessie whispered and Josh stepped back up the stairs and approached the rubble carefully. It looked as if a section of the cathedral collapsed, destroying the western side of it. Part of the building still remained intact. Josh took in a deep breath, releasing it slowly as he scanned the area, hearing a soft groan. He glanced towards the yard near the front of the building and saw the man in the police uniform pulling himself away from part of the rubble.

"Officer Headley!" Josh gasped and jogged to him.

Kevin was coughing, covered in dust as Josh knelt down beside him. He placed his arm around his, offering support.

"Are you alright?" Josh asked.

Kevin pushed himself to his knees and looked around. "Yea... Did the others make it out?" he asked.

"I haven't seen Alyssa or Will yet. The survivors took off with the humvee and Evan is trying to go after them."

Kevin's eyes widened. He quickly pushed himself to his feet, dusting his uniform off. "They left the room before I did. They had to have made it out," he added.

"Officer Headley, they are probably around here somewhere…" Josh mentioned and Kevin interrupted, "I appreciate the respect, but please, call me Kevin."

Josh nodded. Kevin looked towards the sidewalk, seeing Jessie approach them slowly. He glanced back towards the rubble.

"I'm going to try and look," Kevin stated, fearing for Alyssa and Will. He carefully began climbing over the remains of the foyer as Josh watched. Jessie came up next to him, biting her bottom lip. "I'm afraid to help," she said, feeling a bit saddened from the possibility of the two lost having been killed.

"It's okay. Just hang tight. I'll help him," Josh said and approached the rubble as well, climbing over it carefully. Jessie took in a deep breath and looked behind her. Evan was no longer in sight and the atmosphere had grown quiet. She was now ready to accept the fate of her fiancé and the valley she grew up in. Time was no longer on their side.

The cool, dark room began to ease some of Alyssa's tension as she remained seated with Will against her lap, time inching by. The seconds were beginning to feel like minutes, minutes feeling like hours. She was beginning to wonder if the others would find them in time or if they were even okay.

Alyssa took in a deep breath and sighed heavily, examining her surroundings more closely, her arms still caressing Will's chest. She was afraid, but she did her best to remain calm as she surveyed the room. The walls shown signs of minor damage but the ceiling had many cracks throughout its stone. One area looked as if it could give way at any moment. If another quake occurred, she was sure it would collapse.

Alyssa exhaled her breath slowly and glanced at the few items that were in the room. The small bed had caught her attention earlier as she thought about Dena and the possibility of her living below the church. She shuttered a bit from the image and glanced at the large picture that hung off centered on the wall. In the painting was a tribe of Native Americans around a big fire. They were all sitting around it except for one. He was standing near the fire, arms raised high towards the flames, and his mouth was open, his hair brushed back from the apparent wind. The other Native Americans were leaning in different directions, perhaps from the moving or dancing of their bodies. The sky was painted dark with a few clouds and stars. The moon was large, its phase a waning crescent. They were located in what appeared to be a meadow near the mountains. A cave entrance was to their left.

Alyssa focused on the top of the blaze, noticing the figure the fire was morphing into, the legendary beast they claimed to worship. Her mouth slowly dropped as she stared at the painting, the awkward sensation erupting inside her body. Her eyes remained open, mesmerized from the picture as the image within it began to move. The tall blaze began to dance about and the tribe began to sway back and forth, speaking in an unknown tongue, the whispers that would sneak into her mind. The Native American standing up kept his arms raised, his long hair being pushed back from the wind, shouting a message as the inscriptions she had seen etched into the large rock in the cavern began to flash in her mind. And then the fire blazed high, erupting into a quick image of the dragon before settling back down. Alyssa's eyes finally blinked, the sound of Uktena's deep rumble of breath disappearing within the back of her mind. She blinked again, realizing the picture was now still.

Alyssa released a heavy sigh and turned her attention back to Will, trying to fight the sudden fear that was now building within her. Her heart was pumping fast, the adrenaline flushing through her system. She wanted to hide and never look back.

"Please, Will...wake up..." she whispered, wiping away the old tears that were beginning to dry on her face. She sighed once more and suddenly heard shuffling noises above her, getting closer by each second. Alyssa could hear the cracks forming within the ceiling as the shuffling stopped. She felt a bit of relief as she carefully laid Will onto the cool floor and pushed herself to her feet.

"Hello!" she yelled, looking above her. She could hear the faint, muffled voices above her in the distance.

"Down here!" Alyssa yelled and looked towards the collapsed stairwell, quickly approaching it. She noticed a small opening and could smell the air from outside. The collapsed stone surrounded the stairwell and poured at the foot of the room. Alyssa looked at it, realizing how lucky she and Will were.

"Alyssa! Will!"

She heard Kevin's voice in the distance and smiled once more, the fear and pain diminishing. "We are down here!" Alyssa yelled back and heard more shuffling until she saw Kevin lean down towards the opening, peering into it.

"Oh, thank God. I was so afraid that you got buried alive," he said, relieved.

"We almost did. Will got hurt. He knocked me out of the way right when the stairwell collapsed. He's unconscious. We need to get him out of here," Alyssa replied, glancing back at Will's still body.

Kevin looked away, listening to Josh. Alyssa was unable to make out what he was saying so she waited patiently. Kevin nodded and looked back at Alyssa.

"Evan said he was going to bring help back. Right now we will try and see what we can find to get your guys out," he said.

Alyssa nodded. "Okay. Did everyone else get out?" she asked.

Kevin returned the nod.

"And are you alright?" Alyssa asked, looking at all the dust that covered his uniform. He had a few abrasions and some bleeding that was beginning to dry on parts of his arms.

"Yes," Kevin said and looked away. He knew he barely made it out in time and was thankful that his life was once again spared.

"Just hang tight. We are going to see if we can find anything. There's a neighborhood close by, I'm sure I can find something in a tool shed," he said and stood up, quickly disappearing.

Alyssa noticed his odd expression, the strange tone in his voice and stepped back, feeling guilty once more.

I have gotten everyone involved in this. It's all my fault. I should have just taken Will's advice and got out while I had the chance. What was I thinking running off like that?

She sighed heavily, and refused to allow anymore tears to fall as she looked back at Will. She felt terrible for him. He had saved her life again.

Alyssa slowly approached him and knelt down, placing her hand on his face. He still felt warm and his breathing was steady. She stared at him for a moment before turning her attention to the wooden desk. An elegant candle stick sat on it, its flame burning brightly. There was something else that sat in the middle of the desk, wrapped in a small Aztec design blanket. Alyssa began to feel a bit anxious as she pushed herself to her feet. She glanced at the bed and decided to grab the comforter. She didn't want Will to lie on the hard, cold floor. She folded it up and was able to push it under Will's head and upper back. That way he could at least be comfortable. Alyssa glanced back at the desk and took in a deep breath, preparing herself. This could be the final key to helping her regain everything she had forgotten.

She slowly approached the desk, eyeing the blanket and nothing else. Her heart began to beat faster and faster the closer she got to it, her breathing becoming heavier. All she wanted was the truth and a possible way to end the nightmare.

Alyssa stopped once she reached the desk and slowly pulled the blanket away from the item it was concealing. She handled it with care, hoping not to tear anything. As she sat the blanket in the chair by the desk, she stared at the thick hide that bound the small, old journal together. Nothing was inscribed on it. Alyssa wasn't too surprised as she continued to look at it, hearing a whisper in the distance. She looked behind her, her heart thumping wildly. Everything still seemed the same, nothing out of place. Alyssa slowly looked back at the journal and picked it up carefully, the whispering wind fading in the distance. She closed her eyes and took in a deep breath, relaxing her nerves.

Please let this be it...

She turned back around and made her way back to Will, holding the journal with gentle hands, fearing its condition. The short walk was a bit difficult, the anxiety overwhelming. Even though she couldn't remember the reason why she went inside the cavern, she truly believed that she had no intentions of awakening a plague to descend upon the valley.

And there is no way anyone would betray my family...especially Brian...

Alyssa carefully sat beside Will and placed the journal in her lap. She glanced at him and sighed softly. His eyes began to pull together, a low groan exiting his lungs. Alyssa quickly sat the journal to the side and sat up on her knees, touching Will's cheek gently.

"Will?" she asked.

Another groan was heard as his eyes began to flicker. Alyssa could feel the relief wash all over her, but she was also beginning to feel something different, something she hadn't felt in a long time. She was beginning to realize that she couldn't deny the feelings she was beginning to grow for him. He had been there for her since she arrived in the valley, and he was the one person to stand by her side regardless of the circumstances.

Will groaned once more and slowly placed his hand on the back of his head.

"What...What the hell happened?" he whispered.

Alyssa pulled her hand away and placed it on his shoulder. "You got hurt..." she replied softly and waited for Will to open his eyes. He slowly looked at her, rubbing the homemade bandage that was wrapped around his head. He proceeded to look around the room, trying to recall the last few moments before blacking out. Alyssa patted his shoulder, relieved that he was okay, but guilty at the same time. She gave him some time to recuperate and become comfortable enough to sit up before saying anything else. She wasn't ready to add any more stress for him. He had already been through enough.

Will took in a deep breath before finally sitting himself up. He continued to rub his head as he glanced at the comforter behind him, confusion appearing in his expression. Alyssa half smiled, turning her attention to the bed near them.

"I took it from the bed. I'm sorry. I didn't want you lying on the bare floor," she stated.

Will nodded and lowered his hand, looking back at Alyssa as she looked into his eyes.

"Strange...I felt as if I were in a dream," Will stated.

Alyssa watched him as he continued, "I...remember hearing your voice, but I couldn't see you."

"That's odd..." Alyssa replied and Will slowly nodded, looking back into her eyes. They were full of sorrow. Her lips pulled together before releasing a heavy sigh, shaking her head in anguish. She couldn't hold it in any longer.

"I'm so...so sorry Will," she said, keeping herself together, but her body wanted to fall apart. She was torn.

Will remained calm and looked at her casually.

"I got you into this..." Alyssa tried to say before Will finally shushed her. He took in a deep breath, exhaling it softly.

"Alyssa, I got involved when my group and I arrived here," he stated, recalling everything. Alyssa remained silent, allowing him to finish. "You did nothing. If it weren't for you, I would probably be dead by now," Will added.

"Why do you say that?"

"You allowed me to see what was *truly* going on...Something that my men and I wouldn't be able to stand up against alone. For that, I am thankful," Will replied and began rubbing his head some more, the pain throbbing throughout it.

Alyssa didn't know how to respond. She appreciated how Will was able to see the brighter side of the situation.

"Are you going to be okay?" she finally asked.

"Yea. My head just feels like it could explode," Will replied and glanced at the journal beside her.

Alyssa had almost forgotten about it as she quickly glanced at it. "Oh…" she said and picked it up gently.

"Is that it?" Will asked.

"I think so. It's a journal," Alyssa replied and took in a deep breath. "I'm afraid to open it."

"Why?"

"Do you remember what all Dena said?"

Will thought for a moment, thinking about the events in the chapel.

"Sacrifice yourself…That's what she told me," Alyssa said.

"It's not going to come down to that…"

"But what if it's the only way?"

"What if it's not?" Will asked and stared into her eyes.

Alyssa breathed deeply and slowly nodded.

"This is the reason why we are stuck down here. Open it," Will stated and Alyssa took a moment before turning her attention back to the journal.

"I want to know the truth, believe me…I just fear it," she whispered.

"I understand," Will said and Alyssa glanced back at him as she placed her hand on the cover, preparing herself to open it.

"It's going to be okay," he added.

Alyssa nodded and carefully pulled back the cover, taking in another deep breath, hoping for the answers she yearned for. The anxiety continued to build up within her as she breathed steadily; looking at the old, handwritten ink imprinted on the paper as she and Will read the carefully written words…

The evil spirit left behind in the forbidden cavern still lingers… Wahkan and his loyal tribe, lost to the darkness, waiting to be resurrected by the greed and the taking of an ancient treasure. The curse cast upon this cavern, deep within its walls, ensures the protection of these spiritual rocks, the sacred treasure to Wahkan. This is how his story is told.

In the beginning, long before the white man would claim the land, Wahkan and his tribe had stumbled across a hole carved into the mountain. Within that mouth, was a cavern full of bright and illuminating crystals. Further back were full of colorful stones, all etched into the walls. Wahkan believed the cavern to be sacred and that the stones were spiritual, magical. After celebrating their find, the tribe began to hear a wind, one that was never heard of before. It was frightful, which lead to many of the tribesmen running out of the cavern. Wahkan and only a few others remained inside. The few that stayed recalled Wahkan closing his eyes, listening to the wind, as if it were trying to tell him something. It wasn't long before Wahkan opened his eyes and looked at the other men that stayed to protect him. One could sense the uncertainty, one could sense the evil. A spirit had claimed Wahkan, taking over his very own soul.

That night, Wahkan made a large fire out front of the mouth in the mountains, telling the tribesmen of their sacred find and the secret he was told from the beast he claimed to live in the mountain. If any one man were to take the sacred treasure from the mouth in the mountains, a darkness will come after many days and nights of terror, until the waning crescent rises high into the sky...The land will be taken by the beast...Taken by the pits of the earth. Wahkan was told to protect the cavern...to protect the stones...to protect the beast...to destroy any one man that was tempted by greed...For that, he was given an everlasting life, even after death. His dreams and nightmares portrayed this message, giving him a glimpse of the images that could destroy the land.

So after etching a dark curse within the walls of the cavern, Wahkan held up the one that he believed to be the most spiritual, the red rock. It was the most sacred to him, and the tribesmen believed in their leader, and were taken by the spirit that lurked within the cavern to be given the everlasting life as they swore to protect it alongside Wahkan.

As the days and nights went by, many tribes that lived near the mountain were destroyed and soon time had caught up to Wahkan and his tribe. After his and the tribesmen's death, the remaining few *men and women claimed a new land to live out their days, speaking of the story told to them and soon the tale of the forbidden cavern was lost to the wind.*

I have heard many stories of the first settlers of the white man, claiming of children missing from explorations, many being tormented until their death, and many telling of a monster that lived in the mountain near their valley.

After cities were born, a man had been institutionalized from his exploration with friends and how his friends were never found. And soon more children were claimed missing, and the people of the valley became outraged. That was when my father and I swore to oath to hide the entrance to this mouth in the mountains...We would then build the door to hide the entrance within it that led to the sacred chamber, one that can only be opened from a native with a special key that we have made...

Alyssa stopped reading and glanced at the picture drawn on the page, her mouth slowly dropping. Will glanced up her, catching her expression.

"What is it?" he asked, and Alyssa's vision blurred as she thought deeply about an odd evening when her brother had returned home and was in a panic. She could remember him panting as he quickly handed her a rock carved into a shape of a gear. He refused to tell her exactly where he had went, but Alyssa assumed it had something to do with their obsession with the legend. He had told her to get rid of it, but she could recall giving it to her father after her brother passed, and he still denied her claims, refusing to believe any of it.

Alyssa closed her eyes and began rubbing her head. She had forgotten so much...

"I had this," she said and looked at Will.

He pointed at the picture. "This?"

"Yes, the night my father and I went to the cavern. My brother had given it to me, but I gave it to my father after he passed, hoping that he would realize that my brother wasn't just ill, that there was more going on," Alyssa replied and became frustrated. "I just can't remember how I got it back. I had to have opened this door. I don't think anyone else went in with me," she stressed.

"It's okay. Let's just keep reading. It will all come back to you," Will said and Alyssa sighed and continued where she had left off.

If anyone were to get inside these sacred walls, the curse will take hold and consume them until their death. If anyone were to take the spiritual stones from these sacred walls will not only be cursed, but will awaken the darkness to slowly blanket the valley and destroy it to the very core. The guardian will be awakened, the beast Wahkan spoke as Uktena, to fulfill this doom, and the devilish creatures called the Angras to destroy existence in the valley. A possession will take hold of the host and deteriorate its soul, until the waning crescent rises, and the valley burns...

No one must learn about the Legend of Wahkan. No one must know that this cavern exists. The stones etched within its walls are the most valuable. It will test a man...It can tempt a man. We must protect it, and we must protect the people of the valley. If the beast is known throughout the world, life will cease to exist, the world a burning wasteland. The forbidden cavern must remain hidden. No one will ever truly understand its power. Tales have been told about this story...as long as we can keep it a tale, the valley will be safe.

Dena Jacobs

Alyssa flipped the page and glanced at the picture hand drawn, representing the angra as they were told from the images in Wahkan's dreams. A few other pictures were hand drawn of the meadow and the cave entrance they called the mouth in the mountain. The rest of the pages were stories written of the incidents that occurred in the valley. There were many as Alyssa turned the pages, scanning through them. She was amazed at how much life was lost because of the legend, but was anxious to find something regarding a solution to stop it. Her anxiety grew with every page she turned, and Will could sense it. He could feel it. The beads of sweat were beginning to accumulate on Alyssa's forehead as she began shaking her head in denial. She was unsuccessful as she had reached the last page. She allowed her head to hang down heavily, her eyes closing.

Will carefully took the journal and glanced through it one more time.

"It's useless..." Alyssa whispered.

Will closed it and felt the anxiety burning within him as well. He was now afraid, but was able to remain calm for her sake.

"There's no hope left for Rockdale Valley. I have doomed us all," Alyssa added.

"We're not going to give up like that. There may not be anything written about a way to end it because this has never happened before. They probably don't know how to...They took an oath and... unfortunately they failed. My men and I will handle this," Will said and pushed himself to his feet. His head continued to ache, but the adrenaline was all he needed to give him the extra push.

Alyssa looked up at him, remaining seated on the hard floor. "I can end this," she said softly.

Will shook his head. "It will *not* come to that. We don't even know if it will work," he stated and extended his hand. "I'm going to get you back to the hospital, and you are going to leave this place," he said.

Alyssa took his hand, pushing herself to her feet. She didn't know what to say, and she didn't want to leave either. She felt that she deserved to burn with the valley. Will glanced around the room before eyeing the collapsed stairwell. "Now how the hell are we going to get out?" he asked as he stuffed the journal into his cargo pocket.

"Oh, Kevin found us. He should be back soon," Alyssa replied, watching him.

Will sighed and nodded. He placed his hand on the back of his head once again, rubbing it gently. Alyssa slowly paced around the room; trying not to overload herself with all the information she had been given. It frustrated her the more she thought about it. Even with all the new information she had just learned, she still had one unanswered question that bothered her the most: Why had she chosen to go into this cavern?

"Where did you get the cloth for my head?" Will asked and glanced at Alyssa's torn shirt. He hadn't noticed it when they were sitting down.

Alyssa looked at the bottom of her shirt as well. Some of her skin was now visible as she glanced back at Will.

"Thank you," he stated and lowered his arm.

Alyssa nodded and looked away. Will could see her uneasiness and fear. He knew there wouldn't be any words to change the way she was feeling. Therefore, he remained quiet, allowing her time to ponder. He also needed the time to think. He wasn't sure what he and the other unit would be able to do to change anything. They didn't have the right power to correct it.

Alyssa breathed deeply, thinking only about her possible sacrifice. It was too difficult to accept especially when she didn't even know the reason why she ventured inside the night she and her father went to the cavern. It was hard to accept in general. Deep down Alyssa knew that she would be able to do it if she were a hundred percent sure that it would stop it all and bring peace back to the valley. But the fear of pursuing it was hard to shake. It was hard to think about. It was too difficult for her to even imagine how her brother was able to go through with it...

Alyssa sighed and closed her eyes. She was ready to end this... one way or another.

Chapter Twenty

LYSSA WAS SITTING DOWN ON the end of the bed trying not to dwell on the legend anymore. She had already caused a headache to stir in the middle of her forehead, and she was just anxious to get out from beneath the rubble. They had been sitting and standing for what felt like hours waiting for Kevin to return. Alyssa was becoming worried. She had already lost track of the hour. They had been waiting for what felt like ages.

Will was still standing, his arms crossed. He was a bit concerned too, but he had already accepted his decision of returning to the hospital regardless. There was nothing else to reconsider. He gave Alyssa all the time to herself until she finally broke the silence.

"Will?" Alyssa asked.

"Hmm?" he mumbled in response.

"I couldn't help but wonder…Dena asked you if you had seen the journal, after you stated what the beasts were. And she is right…How did you know what they were called?"

"My commander told me that was the code name they were given," Will replied and looked away, wondering how the captain would have known.

"This is so confusing," Alyssa said softly.

Will slowly nodded.

"What if Kevin was right?" Alyssa added, refusing to look into his eyes.

"I can't see my men betraying us. The government may have already known about the legend," Will said. This assumption made him feel a lot better.

Alyssa carefully nodded and left it alone. She knew that the military was more like a brotherhood. Everyone looked out for each other and had each other's backs, but the uncomfortable feeling she had at the operations center was coming back to torture her a little more. She took in a slow, deep breath and held it as soon as she heard the familiar whispers surround her. Her body froze and Will glanced at her.

"Is that..." he asked and paused.

Alyssa slowly stood up. "Uktena," she replied.

"Why am I hearing this now but not before?" Will asked.

"I don't know, Will," Alyssa said, becoming fearful.

Will approached her and looked around. He was becoming a bit anxious himself. It didn't take long for the hard floor beneath their feet to quiver, sending dust and stone particles plummeting from the ceiling.

"Oh God..." Alyssa whispered, keeping her balance as Will reached out and took her arm. He was trying to steady the both of them. The earth continued to quiver and soon the whispers stopped and part of the wall in the stairwell collapsed. The stone crumbled down the rubble that was a part of the spiral stairwell and Alyssa hesitated.

"It's our only chance!" Will gasped and pulled her to the opening.

Alyssa struggled to keep her balance. Will was practically pulling her behind him as he grabbed a hold of the cracked wall, climbing over the rubble on the stairs. Alyssa pushed forward and climbed over the debris as well until Will yanked her out of the opening. A loud crash was heard behind them as the ceiling of the basement suddenly collapsed. More smoke and dust filled the atmosphere, blanketing it with its fog. The earth continued to quiver, intensifying by the minute. Alyssa struggled to remain on her feet and fell to her knees, catching her fall with her hands. Will's grip was lost and he allowed himself to fall to his knees as he grabbed Alyssa's arm again and began pulling her away from the remains of the cathedral.

As soon as Will pushed past the gate and reached a safer location, he dropped Alyssa arm. She collapsed to the ground, panting. Will rolled onto his back, and the earth slowly stopped shaking. Everything quickly settled. The dust and smoke continued to raise high into the sky, creating a hazy appearance in the dark atmosphere.

Will was breathing heavily, looking at the remains of the cathedral. Alyssa continued to lie on the cool bed of grass. She had already caught her breath, but the grass was comforting. She could lie there for the rest of the night if it was safe.

Will sat himself up and patted Alyssa shoulder. "Are you alright?" he asked, gasping for air.

Alyssa remained still as she responded, "Yes." She closed her eyes and took a moment. She was still in shock from the close call.

Will turned his attention back to the cathedral and scanned the area. He could see a neighborhood nearby but no signs of the others. His anxiety was growing with each and every second that passed. He didn't want to be in the area any longer.

Alyssa shook from a startle as a few pieces of stone began to crumble down from parts of the weak walls that still stood intact. They rolled and slammed into the rubble below, sending smaller particles bouncing towards the grass. Alyssa slowly pushed herself over and sat up, glaring at the pile of debris as silence began to linger in the area.

"We shouldn't wait here too much longer," Will stated.

"But what about Kevin and the others?" Alyssa asked, concerned. "We can't leave them behind."

"I'm sure they will know where to go if they cannot find us," Will replied and took one last look towards the neighborhood until a deep, muffled growl was heard near them. Alyssa's eyes widened as she looked at the remains of the cathedral. The deep rumble was coming from under the pile as another one was heard, lasting a bit longer than the first.

Will's heart began to pound even faster as he grabbed Alyssa's arm once again and pulled her up to her feet. She didn't think she was going to be able to use it anymore if Will continued to pull her around.

"We got to go," he said.

"Oh no, Kevin..." she whispered and Uktena's head suddenly burst from under the remains of the cathedral, pushing debris in every direction. Will didn't hesitate as he quickly pulled Alyssa with him and ran towards the street.

"We need cover!" he shouted and glanced towards the area they had come from earlier, seeing the thick forest.

"Come on!" Will gasped and they began running down the street, jumping over any cracks or crevices in the pavement. Uktena swiftly pulled herself out from beneath the rubble and floated towards the sky before swirling towards them. Alyssa refused to look back as they ran as quickly as they could towards the bend in the road. She trusted Will's decision and hoped Uktena wasn't about to attack her with any sudden visions. It would set them up for disaster.

Alyssa began to pant as she and Will reached the bend in the road. The forest stretched off to their right through hills, but the bright lights of vehicles caught Will's attention as they shone from the street around the next bend. Uktena trailed behind, lowering herself to the pavement as she released a loud cry behind them. Alyssa gasped and Will glanced behind them.

"Keep going!" he yelled, the adrenaline pouring into his veins. He decided to skip traveling through the forest. The headlights were a sure sign of a decent and quick getaway.

Alyssa noticed the headlights and the boost of energy raged inside her as she pushed forward, making it around the tight curve...

And then her body skidded to a halt as Will's arm slammed across her chest. Alyssa's heart skipped a beat as she stared at the few humvees and the massive tank that sat in the middle of the road. Infantrymen stood ready with their eyes looking down the sights of their rifles and rocket launchers. The gunners that stood in the back of the humvees held onto their machine guns, aimed directly towards them. Dozens of soldiers stood in front of and behind the military vehicles, all carrying heavy machine guns; waiting; anticipating. But the large cannon of the M1 tank staring back at them was the only thing Alyssa could focus her attention on. She suddenly forgot about Uktena.

"Will! Get out of the way!" Evan yelled from the crowd.

Will glanced towards him, recognizing the voice. "Shit! Let's go!" he yelled and grabbed Alyssa's hand as they began running towards the soldiers.

Uktena quickly halted once she turned the tight corner and slowly raised the front of her body, staring down at the men on the street below. A low rumble echoed deep within her chest and the gunfire suddenly erupted once Will and Alyssa were out of the line of fire. Alyssa clenched her teeth as they ran towards the left and around the military personnel, passing a few soldiers firing grenade launchers and machine guns. The loud explosions, the deafening sound of the heavy artillery rang in Alyssa's ears and then the sharp cry of Uktena pushed past her, sending her to the pavement near one of the humvees. Will lost his grip and fell back, catching himself with the palms of his hands.

"Alyssa!" he yelled, crawling back to her quickly. The gunfire continued to echo around them as he grabbed her and pulled her into his lap. Alyssa's eyes were open, but Will could sense that she wasn't there. She was back in the other world...

Alyssa's vision morphed to one of her bedroom. She was standing in the middle of it, looking over what she had packed for the hike with her father in the mountains. She was extremely nervous about this one. She could feel it deep within her. Alyssa took a deep breath, telling herself that the truth was waiting just up the trails...and she brought her hands to her. They were stained from dirt and soil. She could see the dirt under her finger nails and cuticles and could smell its earthy scent. In the palms of her hands she cradled a rock carved into the shape of a gear.

"Sergeant First Class!" a man yelled over the persistent gunfire. Will held Alyssa closely and looked at the officer, hoping it was Major O'Connell, but quickly realized that it was not.

"What the hell is going on here!" the major shouted.

Evan ran to his side and kneeled on one knee. Uktena's screams continued as her body swung to the side, missing the rockets that propelled past her.

"I can't explain now! I need to get her away from here! Destroy that thing!" Will yelled and looked at Alyssa. Her eyes were flickering and beads of sweat were pushing out from the pores of her forehead. Will glanced back at the major, reading his name.

"Where is Major O'Connell?" he asked firmly.

"Dead. We got his urgent message as well as some information from Private Watkins, but we couldn't believe half the shit that was told to us until we actually got here. I'm Major Lyle. Here, take this radio. There is a large plant near the lake not far from here. It's remote. Go through these woods and through the park. That's our extraction point. Go now!"

Will nodded and looked at Alyssa, noticing the blood trickling down from her nose.

"Not again..." he whispered and wiped it away.

"Sergeant First Class, I got the others to safety. Go...I'm going to stay and help these guys," Evan said and quickly reclaimed his place amongst the crowd. He didn't look back.

Will watched him until Alyssa began coughing profusely, her eyes suddenly widening. Will patted her back and gently grabbed her hand.

"Alyssa?" he asked calmly.

Alyssa clenched her teeth, the gunfire still ringing in her ears. She was breathing heavily, trying to regain her focus. Will placed his hand gently around her arm. "I'm going to get you out of here. Don't look back," he said and Alyssa nodded. Will quickly helped her to her feet, carefully watching the tank in the street. It was preparing to fire its primary weapon, and Will didn't want Alyssa to witness what it was about to do as he quickly led her through the forest.

"Fire the damn thing!" someone yelled in the distance and the anxiety began to flood in Alyssa's veins as she heard the cannon erupt. They had only gotten a few yards past the rows of trees once the loud explosion lit up the night sky. Uktena's loud cry pierced through the atmosphere as more gunfire erupted from all the heavy artillery. Will continued to push past the brush and Alyssa remained close behind him, following him around large boulders and oak trees. She refused to look back as she heard the faint shout, "Again!" from behind her. She held her breath and the cannon erupted once more, quickly exploding once it reached its target. The loud cry from Uktena was like no other. Alyssa could hear the pain, the torment. She stopped herself, and turned to face the direction they had come from. Her eyes widened and her mouth slowly dropped from the anticipation. Will gasped and stopped himself, quickly making his way back to Alyssa's side. He wanted to keep moving.

"Let's go..." he urged and stared above the trees as they could hear a few branches snapping, a few trees falling, and a massive thud hitting the earth, shaking it beneath their feet. The last remaining painful cry from Uktena slowly vanished and silence filled the area.

"What...What happened?" Alyssa whispered.

Will remained unresponsive. His body was frozen until the cheerful cries and the gunfire sounding off an apparent victory were suddenly heard. Will gasped in surprise, realizing what they had heard fall in the forest.

"They did it," he said and he could feel the sudden relief rush all over him. "They actually did it...Just like that."

Alyssa slowly looked at him. Her face hadn't changed. There was no surprise or sense of relief at all. She still felt the same and Will realized it. His expression slowly faded.

"Alyssa...It's over," he said.

"No, it's not, Will," Alyssa replied and looked away, slowly trailing down the path that eventually led to Lake Trinity.

Will followed, taking one last look where the other unit celebrated. Soon the gunfire ceased and the calmness blanketed the forest once again. Finally, Rockdale Valley felt as if it had a little bit of peace left. It surrounded them through the trees and the brush. The gentle wind had returned and carefully brushed past them, flowing softly through the leaves. It was a tranquil feeling, but something else was lingering in Alyssa's gut that wasn't so peaceful. She couldn't ignore the uneasiness.

Alyssa carefully walked through the forest, getting some distance from the soldiers who were carrying on with their mission. She could hear the engines rolling, the tank and humvees making their way down the road. She wanted away from all the chaos. She approached a small stream that flowed slowly through its tiny bed and stopped, closing her eyes. She took in a deep breath of the cool air and finally allowed her mind and body to relax. Will approached her and kept a short distance, examining their surroundings carefully.

"Alyssa, all we have to do is meet this unit at the extraction point. It's near the park. We are home free," Will said, hoping to persuade her into leaving once and for all.

"Even if Uktena is destroyed...How is that going to stop the rest of this plague?" Alyssa asked, turning her attention to him. She couldn't help but dwell on this self sacrifice that lingered in the back of her mind.

Will wasn't sure how to respond as he remained silent.

"Something possesses me. I can feel it. Dena was right," she added.

"Don't you think with Uktena being killed, it would put an end to all of this?" Will asked, recalling the words written in the journal. "She was the reason for the destruction anyway."

Alyssa thought for a moment. She didn't think it would change anything, and there were still questions that remained unanswered. There were now more confusing visions that added to the rest, but perhaps getting out of the valley would give her the time to figure out what she needed to do to help her end the curse and salvage what was left of the valley.

"Maybe you are right," Alyssa finally replied and sighed softly. "But what about the others? We need to find them before we try and leave," she added, thinking about Kevin.

"We shouldn't back track right now. We need to meet the other unit so we can explain to them what has happened here. Then the unit and I can finish up the search and rescue before we leave," Will stated.

Alyssa nodded, but she feared for the others safety. She also feared for Will's safety. If he were to return to the destruction once she evacuated, she wouldn't have any idea if he would ever return. She would probably never see him again. And Kevin...She had just reunited with her best friend, and their last talk wasn't so friendly. She was worried sick that she would never see him again. She wanted to tell him that she was truly sorry.

"Alright," Alyssa finally said and Will approached her, placing his hand on her shoulder. He knew how she felt.

Alyssa watched him carefully, still feeling a bit uneasy. She was afraid that there was some truth behind Kevin's accusations, but she had already forged feelings for him.

"I promise...I will do everything I can to find Kevin," he said sincerely and patted her shoulder.

Alyssa nodded and looked through the wilderness. "Thank you. I'm sure I can get us to the park from here," she said, clearing her mind so she could focus.

"Alright," Will responded and Alyssa lost her breath. A sudden gasp released from her lungs as she felt her heart sink. She placed her hand against her chest gently, feeling an awkward sensation wash over her body and exit it as if a strong force was removed from her shoulders; the heavy burden as she called it.

Will became alarmed and placed his hand back onto her stiff shoulder. "What is it?" he asked.

Alyssa's eyes were wide, her hand still placed against her chest. "I don't know..." she whispered. Her heart was beating rapidly but suddenly felt as if it froze once she heard the familiar growl exit from a set of lungs in the distance. It was the same haunting growl that had been stalking her, torturing her since the beginning.

Will's eyes slowly widened and he turned around, glaring past the trees. Alyssa lowered her hand away from her chest and stepped around him, staring past the trees as well. She scanned through the brush, and her eyes stopped on a dark shadowy figure standing near a large tree. Thick brush surrounded it, hiding all of its features. Alyssa squinted her eyes and tried to focus on the shadow, her heart racing away.

This is the thing that has been torturing me all this time...It has been following me, haunting me for a reason...

"Who are you?" Alyssa asked softly.

Will continued to stare at the shadow as another growl exited its lungs. Words couldn't describe the fear he was feeling. There was no power on earth that could hurt a spirit or a ghost. Their guns were useless.

Alyssa breathed deeply and listened closely as the wind brushed past her. Its whispers spoke softly into her ears and pushed strands of hair away from her shoulder. It was the Native tongue, and she suddenly realized who they were now up against...

"I really need your help down here, Kevin!" Jessie shouted from below the smoldering pit that she and Josh had fallen into. The damaged street in the neighborhood had suddenly given way, sending them into the winding corridors under the valley. She had her hand placed tightly against Josh's thigh as he sat gripping the wound on the side of his head. Dirt covered them from head to toe, and the smell of blood was beginning to fill the air.

Kevin was looking into the pit from above, examining the situation as he held onto a sledgehammer that he found in a storage shed.

"Damn it..." he whispered, trying to figure how he could help them. "Could you try climbing out? There's an area over here that has a slab of pavement leaning against the side," Kevin added.

Jessie looked at Josh and then at the wound in his leg. "I...I can't. I'm afraid he will bleed to death," she said. She was becoming queasy from the blood surrounding her palm and fingers. Its rusty smell was hard not to breathe in as she took steady breaths.

Kevin sighed and pushed himself to his feet. "Alright. I'm coming down," he said and approached the slab of pavement that was lying in the pit. He carefully climbed over it and slid his way into the hot and humid corridor. He could feel the heat pushing against his skin and the sweat accumulating on his face.

"Wow, Evan must have been right," Kevin said and jogged to where Josh and Jessie sat. Josh was breathing heavily, but there was still color in his skin. Kevin kneeled down next to him and sat the sledgehammer on the ground. He quickly began unbuttoning his blue uniform shirt.

"I'm going to have to use my undershirt. It's all I have," Kevin said and tossed the blue shirt on the ground next to him. He quickly pulled the white t-shirt over his head. Jessie looked away, keeping a firm hold on Josh's thigh until Kevin placed his shirt on top and began wrapping it tightly around his leg. Jessie moved her hands away and looked at all the blood drenching them. Josh groaned and removed his hand away from his head.

"Use the dirt to rub it off," he whispered, looking at Jessie's grotesque expression.

Jessie glanced at him, her body shaking.

"It's okay. We can wash them when we find a water source," Josh added.

Jessie held her breath and began rubbing her hands into the soil next to her. Kevin knotted his shirt securely and looked at the wound on the side of Josh's head.

"Damn...We need to get you to a medic," he said and put his uniform shirt back on.

"I'll be alright. Let's just get out of this hole," Josh replied and Kevin looked down the dark tunnel.

"I don't believe it's just a hole. There's no telling how far this thing stretches," Kevin said and Josh gasped as he tried to move his body.

"What do you think caused this?" Jessie asked, hesitantly.

"We all heard it," Josh stated, thinking about the distant, horrific screams from the beast. They were similar to the ones he had witnessed downtown.

"The dragon Alyssa mentioned?" Kevin asked.

Josh nodded.

Jessie's eyes widened as she shook her head in disbelief.

"I've seen it. Evan already explored a part of the underworld this thing has created," Josh added and looked down the corridor, the sweat dripping down the side of his face.

"The legend exists," Kevin said and thought about Alyssa and Will. They could still be trapped under the cathedral or worse from what they heard and felt.

"And you are...*certain*?" Jessie asked.

"You weren't in the chapel when Dena was speaking with Alyssa. She confirmed it. Not only was Alyssa right, but her late brother was too," Kevin replied, closing his eyes, sighing heavily. He felt a bit of shame within him. He wasn't there for Alyssa when she truly needed him. He had allowed Will to claim that spot. This angered him.

"We need to get to Alyssa and Will," he stated.

Jessie gulped, feeling Kevin's frustration as she carefully stood up. "How are we going to get out of this?" she carefully asked. Kevin stood up and grabbed the sledgehammer. Josh remained seated, breathing heavily.

"I don't know," Kevin said and approached the slab of pavement. He sighed, realizing that attempting to climb out was going to be a waste of time. He slowly shook his head.

"We got to find another way out. I could probably get you to the surface, Jessie, but that means Josh and I will be stuck down here. If you don't want to travel alone, we will need to explore this tunnel and find another way," Kevin said, looking back at Jessie.

"I will stay with you two. You will need help with Josh," she said.

Kevin nodded and approached Josh, extending his hand. Jessie knelt down beside him and wrapped her arm around his. Josh accepted Kevin's hand, and they carefully helped him to his feet. Josh gasped at the pain that stretched throughout his body and clenched his teeth until he found his footing. Jessie felt terrible for him and continued to keep her arm around his as her heart thumped rapidly. Kevin wrapped his arm around Josh's back and offered his support as well. They slowly began walking down the rugged tunnel, watching each and every step they took. The trek was going to be a long and miserable one. The heat and humidity continued to intensify the deeper they got down the corridor. There was no wind to soothe them and no light to guide them as they entered the dark underworld.

Kevin carefully paused and retrieved his maglite. He switched it on and shined it down the dark path with his free hand, slowly continuing their trek. Josh's arm lay heavily against their shoulders and they pushed forward, attempting to ignore the torturing fear that continued to dwell within them.

CHAPTER TWENTY-ONE

LYSSA AND WILL WERE STARING at the dark figure, their breaths exhaling loudly. The shadow remained still, hidden within the brush, not making a sound.

"Wahkan…" Alyssa whispered and suddenly felt immense pain erupting within her head. It felt as if her skull was trying to crack as she quickly dropped to her knees and grabbed her head, screaming in agony.

Will gasped and knelt down beside her, wrapping his arm around her as he watched her eyes close tightly. Blood began to pour from her nostrils, and she continued to scream as she collapsed to the ground.

"Alyssa!" Will shouted and looked back at the dark shadow in the distance. It remained in place, still and calm.

Alyssa could feel Will at her side, but another image was creeping into her mind as she slowly focused onto her parents' house in the far outskirts of the valley. The sun was starting to fade behind the acres of trees. Its gentle light touched the area softly creating a peaceful setting. Alyssa watched as the image moved passed the two cars in the driveway and to the front door. She could suddenly sense the fear as she witnessed the massive claws tear through the door, ripping it open. Her mother quickly walked into the living room from the kitchen, her face full of fright. Alyssa could feel the fear within her as she watched from the eyes of the shadow tear through the house, knocking over furniture as it chased her mother down the hall. Her father stepped out from their bedroom, pulling her mother back into the room with him. The image moved in quickly and tore through the room, slicing through furniture and the wall. Gunfire echoed throughout the bedroom, and Alyssa could feel the impact within her body as she gasped. She could see the shadow lunge for her mother, tearing its claws through her side. Her scream was blood curdling, making the hair on the back of Alyssa's neck rise. Her father continued to fire until the beast lunged at him and the image suddenly vanished, a new one quickly emerging. She was outside near her mobile home. She now saw herself locking the front door and turning to walk down the stairs of the deck. She was approaching her truck until the image slowly morphed into the view of the steep ledge where Alyssa stood, overlooking the valley. And then the image morphed once more to the street where Alyssa trailed behind Will as they made their way to the hospital. Alyssa sensed the déjà vu, recalling every image as they faded and her mind became blank...

"No!!!" Alyssa heard herself yelling as her body struggled against the cool earth. She realized she was back in the forest. She could feel the wind touching her face and the soft dirt cushioning her cheek. She didn't want to be there. She wanted to die and get away from it all. Will was at her side, trying to comfort her as best as he could.

"Mom!" she cried tearfully. "Dad!" Alyssa sobbed some more, the tears cascading down her face.

Will was feeling her pain and was fighting with all of his might to remain calm. He felt the awful emotions running throughout her as if they were pouring into his own body.

"Why did you do that to them! Why!" Alyssa shouted, mourning her parents' fates. Her eyes remained tightly closed and her hands still gripped the sides of her head. The pain began to subside slightly while another low growl exited the dark figure's lungs, a new image slowly creeping into her mind...

"Alyssa!" James yelled and ran into the corridor of the cavern. Alyssa could see herself lying on the cold rock and the two familiar items lying in front of her. She watched as her father picked up the two items and examined them quickly. His expression turned from fear to confusion as he picked up the red stone and the awkward rock

before proceeding to lift her into his arms. "I am not going to allow you to become a part of this, I swear..." he choked out painfully.

Alyssa began coughing and forced her eyes open. Her vision was hazy and the tears were still falling onto her cheeks as she glared at the dark figure in the distance.

"It was not my father's fault..." she forced out. She could feel Will next to her once again. He still had his arms around her, gripping tighter from the anxiety. She had almost forgotten about him as she focused all of her attention on the shadow.

"It was mine," Alyssa added and paused, allowing herself to sit up in Will's arms. Will was breathing heavily, watching the figure carefully. He was tempting to grab his rifle, but he wasn't sure what good it would do so he waited and prayed.

"Wait..." Alyssa said softly, staring at the shadow, a sudden intuition erupting inside her. "You wanted me to come here...You know who did this to me."

The wind began to pick up as it pushed past them and through the leaves of the trees, knocking over any weak limbs and twigs that barely hung onto the branches. Will's anxiety level was elevating, and the sweat was beginning to drip down his forehead. He wasn't going to be able to take much more as he continued to hold Alyssa steady. She watched as the shadow changed and slowly crept forward, allowing a little bit of moonlight to touch its features dimly. They were able to make out just enough to see the image of a Native American glaring back at them. His long, jet black hair laid flat against his shoulders. His broad facial features and muscles were noticeable and his skin was a deep chestnut. He remained calm and still, the wind not affecting him at all.

Alyssa breathed heavily and managed to push herself to her feet. Will slowly stood and lowered his arms away from her. He stared back at the apparition, his heart still thumping wildly. Alyssa carefully wiped the blood away from her face, ignoring the stench and took a deep breath in, releasing it slowly. "I'm not dead yet for a reason," she said softly.

"You...will finish this deed..." Wahkan said in a low, deep voice. His accent was strong but clear.

Alyssa's eyes raised and Will lowered his hand to his sidearm, preparing himself. He couldn't believe what he was witnessing.

"That is your fate," Wahkan added.

Alyssa became confused, but remained as calm as she possibly could regardless of how much her body trembled. "I...don't understand," she replied. "What deed?"

The wind began to pick up speed, pushing around them abrasively.

"You will find the one with the pure greed in his heart, the one who *truly* wants what you protect," Wahkan stated and paused as Alyssa stared in awe. "You will destroy him."

Alyssa's eyes widened. "I do not know who this person is...How will I even know?" she asked almost in a whisper even though she already knew she wasn't capable of fulfilling such a task.

"I...will guide you."

Will looked at Alyssa and she slowly turned to him, her expression full of dismay. Will's eyes were filled with worry, and Alyssa could see the fear deep within them. She didn't like it. The anger quickly poured into her system, washing away all of her fears.

"I'm not a murderer..." she whispered and slowly looked back at the spirit. "I don't even know why I did this! I am not going to become you. If anyone was so full of evil and greed then it was you," Alyssa said angrily, her eyes narrowing. "I am not afraid of you...I will end this!" she yelled and Wahkan suddenly lunged forward, his image quickly morphing into a creature similar to the angra. Its body was slimmer and more agile as it pushed through the brush swiftly. Will gasped and retrieved his pistol, unable to aim it fast enough as the beast leaped over them. Alyssa quickly turned around and watched as the creature knocked Will onto his back and placed its heavy foot roughly onto his chest. It released a shrieking wail and stretched out its dagger like talons, preparing to annihilate Will's existence.

"Will!" Alyssa cried out, her body frozen with fear.

Wahkan shot her a glare, his dragon-like eyes flashing brightly at her. Alyssa's eyes widened and stared into the eyes that had flashed within her mind multiple times since the accident, the pair of eyes that haunted her restless mind. The low growl rumbled within the creature's chest and Alyssa slowly dropped to her knees, her body weakening and her vision blurring once more...

An image of Will slowly came into view. It was when she had met him at the Rockdale Valley Press. They were standing on the sidewalk out front, and Alyssa was becoming anxious after hearing the strange whispers, but Will was completely oblivious. He was unable to hear them at the time she thought to herself as she watched the image fade to multiple scenes of Will's expressions. At times he was angry, fearful, calm, and persistent. Alyssa could feel her heart beating quickly, her body rushing with warmth as the image from the chapel flashed into her mind. Will's eyes were soft and sincere as he looked into hers, yearning to get closer to her... And then the image quickly faded to Will standing in the hospital room, looking at Alyssa in astonishment. He was able to hear the whispers that had suddenly surrounded them, but she couldn't comprehend why he was able to now and not before. She could feel the sudden frustration until the image suddenly changed to one she had never seen before. There was a new feeling, one she had never truly felt. Will was lying gently on top of her, his body caressing hers in the most intimate of ways. She could feel the heat rushing throughout his bare skin, and she could feel his face next to hers. His lips snug closely to hers, their bodies trembling, and as quickly as it began, the image faded to darkness and a low whisper from Wahkan, "You are mine..."

Alyssa's eyes closed gently until the sudden sound of gunfire shook her from her thoughts. Will had managed to pull the trigger at the creature's chest and it quickly leaped back, disappearing into the brush without a sound. The wind slowed to a gentle breeze, and the calmness returned to the forest like it had never left it to begin with. Will was still lying on his back, breathing heavily. His gun was at his side, and he stared above him at the night sky. Alyssa remained sitting on her knees, her eyes focused on the brush near the creek. Wahkan was gone, but the message left behind was not. Alyssa thought hard about the spirit's words and tried to piece together the puzzle of images that continued to play in her head.

If...I allow myself to fall for this soldier...he will be in the same boat as me. It was a warning...A warning of what might become...

Her mouth slowly dropped as she looked at Will. He released a cough followed with a heavy sigh before carefully sitting himself up. Alyssa remained quiet, watching him carefully. She examined the dirt on his face, the blood that had dried up on his arms and hands. He was a warrior. He was dedicated. He was committed. Alyssa had been blessed with him, but he could very well be the angel in disguise concealing the truth behind the traitor. This corrupted being wanted what Wahkan adored and treasured the most.

This person must be after this stone in my possession...I'm obviously not supposed to have this...So who is this person looking for?

"Are you okay?" Will's calm voice asked, interrupting her thoughts. He was sitting up, staring at her abnormal expression.

Alyssa looked at him and fought the images that Wahkan had pushed into her mind away. It was tough for her to look at him in the same way after the intimacy they had shared in her mind.

"He is not going to harm me...Not yet anyway," Alyssa said.

"What is going on, Alyssa," Will stated in a tone full of bewilderment.

"I am not the one who intended on taking this stone. Kevin was telling the truth. He was onto something. Those men that murdered my friends are obviously after what I have...and perhaps more," Alyssa said and placed her hand on her shirt, feeling the necklace behind it. "What if my father knew?"

"He could have..." Will stated and paused, looking through the brush. The forest was quiet except for the tiny stream that trickled down stones and rocks. He was becoming more anxious as the silence continued to linger around them.

"But I think we should get out of these woods. I don't want to encounter that thing again," he said. He couldn't keep the dark image out of his mind. He never experienced such fear before in his life; in his entire military career.

Alyssa carefully pushed herself to her feet, brushing off her clothing gently. She was petrified, but she had to focus so she could get them out of the wilderness.

"I can get us to the park," she stated. She wondered why Will didn't seem concerned about this killer. It made her nervous. She wanted nothing more than to have Kevin back at her side.

Will quickly stood, feeling a dull ache in his chest from the power behind the creature's leg. He remained quiet as he started following Alyssa through the woods, keeping a watchful eye on their surroundings. Wahkan's dark figure was silent and swift. He could approach them from behind so suddenly and without them being aware of it.

Will held onto his pistol carefully, unable to holster it after the nightmarish experience. He was going to be ready next time.

They continued their trek north, remaining as silent as the atmosphere, trying not to allow the slightest noise to engage the worst of their imaginations.

After traveling through the winding tunnels of the dark, humid underworld, Josh was ready to throw in the towel. The pain that ached throughout his body was beginning to take its toll.

"I can't do this...I need to rest," he gasped.

Kevin and Jessie continued to offer their support as they held onto him carefully.

"Alright, why don't you sit here. I'll try and take a look," Kevin said and he and Jessie helped him to the wall. They eased him down and allowed him to sit on the hard soil. Josh took deep breaths, the sweat dripping down his face and torso, drenching his clothing. Jessie kneeled beside him and looked up at Kevin.

"I'll stay with him," she stated.

"Okay. I'll be right back," Kevin replied and quickly shined his light down the dark corridor, jogging down it carefully. He didn't want to take too much time.

Kevin watched his footing, shining his light around the walls. He was hoping to find a way to climb out, but there were no holes or large crevices big enough for them climb through. He continued on until seeing a segment of a brick wall in the distance. He was reaching the end of the tunnel as it stretched in the distance and pushed through a part of the town's sewer system.

Kevin reached the end and looked down the corridor of the sewer. Parts of its walls had been pushed back immensely, suffering major damage. Water covered most of the flooring. A strong dingy scent congested the area as Kevin stepped into the left side of the corridor and began walking down it carefully. He continued to shine his flashlight on both of the walls, stepping over or around any pools of dark water that was in his path. He stopped once he noticed a ladder in the distance.

Just what we need...

Kevin jogged to it, keeping a watchful eye around him, fearing what could possibly be lurking below.

He grabbed onto the metal bars once he reached the ladder and shined his light above, seeing the manhole cover. He placed his flashlight into his utility belt and carefully climbed up the ladder, the soft clings echoing around him and down the corridor.

Kevin clenched his teeth once he reached the top and held on to the metal bar with one hand, the other placed firmly on the manhole cover. He pushed it with his free hand and a part of his back and shoulder with as much force as he could exert. The manhole cover slowly began to slide to the side. With one last deep breath and forceful push, he was able to move it out of the way, enough for him to take a look out.

He slowly pulled half of his body out and examined the area. There was a large pond in the distance and a few wooden benches surrounding it. A parking lot and a small restroom sat near him. It didn't take him long to recognize the area. It was a nice place to visit on the weekends with the family, Memorial Park, beside Lake Trinity.

Kevin smiled and climbed down the ladder, quickly making his way back to Josh and Jessie.

Jessie was sitting beside Josh, her hands in her lap, watching him carefully. Josh was leaning against the rough wall of the tunnel, his eyes closed. His skin was growing clammy and pale as the time ticked by.

"Hang in there, Josh," Jessie stated, hoping to keep him awake.

"I'll be alright," he responded and opened his eyes halfway. Jessie looked into them as he stared towards the ground.

"I can't give up now," Josh added.

"Did you...lose someone too?" Jessie asked hesitantly.

"No...My family left yesterday. I curse myself for not leaving with them. I've always been about business. I stayed behind and got trapped like the others who did not leave in time."

Jessie looked away. "Like me and my family," she said.

"I have a son...I need to apologize to him," Josh rambled as he stared towards the ground, grief striking him. "And...to my wife. I didn't spend enough time with them..."

Jessie placed her hand on his. "We are going to get you out of here."

Josh met her eyes and sighed heavily. Jessie took in a deep breath and glanced behind her, suddenly hearing footsteps. She could see a bright flashlight shining down at them, bouncing around. She patted Josh's hand and carefully pushed herself to her feet.

"I found a way out," Kevin stated once he was close enough.

Josh collected himself and looked at Kevin, taking a deep breath.

"It may be rough for you, but it's the only way out of here," Kevin added.

"What did you find?" Jessie asked.

"A manhole. This tunnel takes us to the sewers."

Jessie's face grew grotesque.

"Would you rather stay under here?"

"No," she quickly responded and looked at Josh. "Will you be able to climb out?"

Josh slowly nodded.

"Alright," Kevin said and knelt down, wrapping an arm around Josh's back. Jessie did the same and they both slowly eased him up. Josh's face expressed intense pain. His eyes closed tightly and he clenched his teeth, fighting at the sharp aches. His forehead was pulled down in tight lines. Jessie looked away. It was difficult for her to see someone hurt so badly.

"One step at a time, we'll make it," Kevin encouraged, noticing his pain as well.

Josh gasped, but continued to push forward until they reached the manhole cover.

The sewers were silent, but the darkness that stretched into the distance rattled Jessie's nerves. She wanted out of the underworld as quickly as possible. She dreaded the possibility of something waiting beyond the darkness.

"I'm going to help you as much as I can," Kevin stated as Josh placed his foot on the first bar of the ladder. He grabbed onto the sides and slowly pulled himself up, one foot at a time. Kevin placed his hand on his back and climbed up behind him, giving him the extra push he needed. Jessie waited until Kevin pushed Josh out before attempting to climb up. She looked down both directions of the sewers, biting her lip. Everything still seemed calm.

She carefully grabbed onto the bars and made her way up. Kevin was waiting at the top, his hand extended. Jessie grabbed it once she reached him and he carefully pulled her out. Josh was already sitting back on the ground near the manhole, breathing deeply. His pain was unmistakable. Jessie already knew that he wasn't going to make it any further.

Kevin carefully pushed the manhole cover back; using every bit of force he had remaining. Jessie looked around the park. She was very familiar with the area, but this was the first time she ever saw it so vacant and calm. There was no one in sight.

"Could you help me to the pond?" Josh suddenly asked.

Kevin stood, looking towards the water's edge before turning his attention towards the right near the rolling trails that were surrounded by trees and brush. Far in the distance, he could make out the valley's water treatment plant. Squinting his eyes, he was able to make out the object that sat near it.

"There's a helicopter..." he stated.

Jessie's face lit up. "Really?" she replied and looked towards the plant as well. She gasped in excitement and looked at Josh. He remained on the pavement, expressionless.

"We can get help," she stated and knelt down, wrapping her arm around him once more. Kevin quickly followed, and they helped him towards the pond.

"Someone has got to be there. You can sit tight and rest," Kevin said and Josh breathed deeply, not responding. He was exhausted.

As soon as they reached the water's edge, Kevin and Jessie slowly eased Josh down. He sat heavily on the soft grass, holding himself up with the last remaining strength he had left. He looked Kevin in the eyes and nodded.

"Alright, just hang tight. We will back as soon as we can," Kevin replied. He almost hated the idea of leaving him behind, but he wasn't going to be able to make it. They would have had to carry him the whole way, which was something they were not capable of doing through the hilly terrain of the hiking trails.

Jessie slowly stood up and wiped the sweat from her forehead.

"Please rest until we return," she said. She turned away and she and Kevin quickly began making their way towards the trail. They passed a picnic area and reached a small spring with a wooden bridge before reaching the tree line.

"This might be a tough hike," Kevin said.

Jessie rolled her eyes and looked at him. "You say it as if I've never done this before. I come out here every summer," she replied, smirking.

Kevin half smiled. "Sorry, I assumed that you were not much of an outdoor type."

Jessie giggled, feeling a bit hopeful after seeing the lone helicopter. It was a big relief after struggling to get through the rough underworld that they were just in.

Kevin opened his mouth, about to say something else until a low howl was heard in the distance. He quickly closed it, and he and Jessie froze in place. They had just begun their trek in the forest, the pond and field still in view.

"Please tell me that was just a dog…" Jessie stated softly.

"I don't know, but we shouldn't stop. We should keep moving," Kevin replied and they slowly carried on, watching their footing as they ascended through the wilderness.

Kevin carefully retrieved his nine, replacing the clip. Jessie watched, feeling a bit nervous. She wasn't a fan of firearms. For her, they added fear to every situation. She took in a deep breath and looked in front of her, staring through the darkness that consumed the area. As soon as they turned the bend and traveled deeper through the trails, Kevin retrieved his maglite, quickly turning it on. The thick forest hid the little light from the lamps back in the park and from the moon high above. The area was getting darker the farther they traveled.

Among the trees, the insects chirped and sang their lullabies. The owls hooted and stalked their nocturnal prey. The forest was a lively place at night. However, it kept Kevin and Jessie on their toes. The slightest noise would catch their fullest attention, striking a bit of fear within them each and every time. .

"I ah, wonder what happened to Evan," Jessie stated, breaking the long silence between them.

"I am more concerned about Alyssa," Kevin replied.

"You really care about her."

"She's been a good friend of mine since the school years, and we were also partners."

Jessie slowly nodded. "Why are you so…unsure about these men in uniform?" she asked carefully.

Kevin shot her a look as they pushed deeper into the trails. "What are you talking about?"

"Well I've seen how you look at the one that was with Alyssa, and not to mention what happened at the cathedral between you and Evan…"

Kevin cleared his throat. "That kid needed that after the comments he made," he replied and looked away. He didn't want to express his feelings about William Thompson to this woman. He was beginning to grow some respect for the man, but he was afraid that he and Alyssa were getting close…too close for comfort.

"There is anger there."

"Listen, lady, it…" Kevin sighed, "It doesn't really concern you, okay?"

Jessie looked away, feeling a bit embarrassed. "I apologize," she replied.

Kevin remained quiet. He didn't like the way this topic made him feel, but he couldn't control the anger that enraged in him towards the green berets that were deployed there. He took in a deep breath and gasped, hearing a low, spine chilling growl deep within the woods. Jessie let go of the suspicious thoughts she had and stopped, glancing behind her, her hair standing on end. Kevin held up his pistol, scanning through the trees. A few howls echoed in the distance, sending them into panic.

"We need to make a run for it," he said when suddenly, a large, brown wolf leaped from the brush behind them, landing in the middle of the path. It lowered its head and curled its lips over its sharp fangs, growling viciously at them. Jessie released a low gasp, her heart beating rapidly within her chest.

"Go!" Kevin yelled and aimed his pistol at the wolf. Jessie froze in place as it leaped at Kevin, mouth wide open.

Kevin fired two shots and the wolf yelped and fell on its side, legs kicking. Kevin fired a couple of more shots, putting a quick end to it. More howls echoed in the distance, traveling through the trees around them. Kevin glanced at Jessie. Her eyes were wide, fear stricken.

"We need to move," he gasped and he gave her a push as they started running down the path. Once they turned a bend, another wolf leaped out of the brush in front of them, growling at them. Jessie screamed and Kevin skidded to a halt, quickly firing a few rounds at the large animal. It yelped and quickly jumped into the brush, disappearing through the thick forest. Kevin took a deep breath, and they began running down the path once more.

"Keep going!" Kevin shouted.

"No, there's another one!" Jessie gasped, glancing behind her. She could hear the shuffling feet against the soil, coming directly at them.

Kevin turned around and tripped, falling against the ground. Jessie stopped and placed her hands over her mouth, her heart feeling as if it suddenly stopped. Kevin sat up and aimed at the wolf, firing at its face just when it was about to jump on top of him. The wolf barked and stumbled back, shaking its head. Kevin held his breath and fired another round at its head. A loud yelp echoed throughout the forest as the wolf collapsed onto the path.

Kevin relaxed his muscles as he rested his body against the ground, breathing heavily. Jessie ran to him and knelt down, looking at the lifeless animal lying next to him.

"Are you alright?" she asked.

Kevin nodded. "Yeah..." he gasped and sat himself up, looking through the forest as more howls were heard.

Jessie's mouth dropped as she scanned through the trees.

"We keep moving...Come on," Kevin said and pushed himself to his feet. Jessie nodded and they began to run once more down the path, traveling down descending, winding bends. After crossing a small bridge over a slow moving creek bed, they ascended through the forest, and the trees slowly began to dissipate. More grass was seen and a long chain link fence crossed their path, stretching far down the tree line before wrapping around the large, two story building of the town's water treatment plant. A gate was left swinging open, its pad lock hidden in the grass beside it.

Kevin stepped off the path and walked towards the gate. Jessie followed, glancing down the path as it veered to the left, traveling around the tree line before cutting back through it. She sighed heavily and approached Kevin at the gate.

"The lock was cut," Kevin stated and looked towards the side of the two story building.

There were a few vacant cars, cylinder buildings, and a smaller building that sat across from the plant itself. They could also see the tail end of the lone helicopter near the other side of the building. The chain link fence surrounded its property securely, and the lamps on the side of the building were on. The fence also stretched from the side of the building, extending to the fence line they stood at. The facility was dead, suspiciously quiet for a plant that operated twenty-four seven.

"Well, what are we waiting for? I don't want to get ambushed again," Jessie stated, looking behind her. She could see past the rolling forest and down into the park. She was unable to make too much out. She hoped Josh was still resting near the pond, stable.

"Alright, just follow me and keep quiet, okay?" Kevin asked.

Jessie realized it was more of a statement and kept her mouth her closed, following behind him alongside the other fence to the side entrance of the plant. Kevin approached the door cautiously, holstering his pistol. He didn't feel an immediate reason to carry it, but he wanted to be quiet and alert just to be sure the area was safe.

He placed his hand on the knob and turned it carefully, pushing the door open slowly. Jessie looked behind her while Kevin looked inside the building. The area seemed vacant with no sound to be heard.

"Alright, come on," Kevin said softly and held the door open.

Jessie quietly stepped inside the cool building. It was nicely painted with a few pictures of the valley hanging on its walls. It wasn't a common water treatment plant, one made of concrete and hideous pools. It was nicely designed and decorated with a large wetland operating to clean the building's wastewater. Rockdale Valley was proud of the new design and construction. The town was moving to a greener future, a promise to keep the valley serene.

Kevin waited for Jessie to step inside before carefully closing the side door. He glanced down the hallway they stood in, noticing a few open doors before the hall turned right around a corner. He slowly retrieved his pistol.

"Wait here," he stated and began walking down the hallway cautiously.

Jessie stood and watched him approach the first room. He looked inside the small break area, clearing it quickly. He approached the next room across the hall and glanced inside. His shoulders dropped, relaxing.

"Hello!" he shouted in the hall.

All he received was an echo. It bounced off the walls for a few seconds before slowly fading away. Silence filled the area once again and Kevin holstered his pistol. He looked at Jessie and motioned her to come as he stepped inside the room he had just checked. Jessie approached the room, stepping inside slowly. It was a small office. There was a couch, a counter with a coffee maker, and a large desk with a flat screen computer monitor centered on it.

Kevin approached the desk and leaned over it, touching a few keys on the keyboard. The computer screen awoke and a logo of the plant flashed brightly at him. There were a few icons on the desktop. Kevin placed his hand on the mouse and moved it to internet explorer, double-clicking it. He glanced up at Jessie as she slowly approached him.

"It's worth a shot...I can send a message," he stated.

"There's a helicopter here. Someone has to be nearby," Jessie replied, a bit confused.

"We need assistance. The military cannot be trusted..."

"What?" Jessie asked, eyebrows pulling down.

Kevin sighed and watched the internet explorer load a failed attempt page. "No internet access," he said and shook his head, frustration appearing on his face.

"Why can't the military be trusted, Kevin?" Jessie asked. She was deeply concerned after being around Evan.

Kevin pushed himself away from the desk, stepping around it. "Because the Army is to blame for the deaths of the Rockdale Valley police officers and personnel on duty to aid in the panic and evacuations today."

Jessie's mouth dropped as she watched Kevin's face turn to anger. He crossed his arms and took in a deep breath.

"How?"

"They walked in, asked a few questions to one of the secretaries behind the front desk, and proceeded to open fire."

Jessie released a low gasp, turning away. She couldn't look into Kevin's eyes at the moment. She didn't care too much for him in the beginning, but he had every reason to keep his distance from the two soldiers she had met. Perhaps it was too painful for him to explain earlier.

"I'm so sorry…I didn't know…" Jessie began to say and paused.

Kevin lowered his arms. "Now you should understand why I despise anyone in that uniform. I cannot trust them. It's a conspiracy."

Jessie looked at him and slowly nodded. "I understand. It's just… hard to believe. You saw their faces?"

"Yes."

"Then it wasn't Evan or…the other one?"

"No, but that doesn't mean I can trust them. They could all very well be working together," Kevin stated and thought about the group of men upstairs at the hospital, a bunch of scheming traitors. He was unable to catch everything they were saying from their extremely low, cautious voices. Then he began to think about Alyssa, Dena, and the legend.

"Why do you think they would have done that?" Jessie asked.

"Maybe they are aware of the story," Kevin replied and paused.

Jessie looked away, unsure as Kevin took a breath and continued, "These men are after someone though, and it's obviously not Alyssa, but she is the one who apparently has this *sacred* item. It's her pendant."

Jessie shook her head. "This is so confusing…" she stressed.

Kevin nodded. "Well, let's go check this helicopter and see if we can find someone. We need to get back to Josh."

"Alright," Jessie replied, deciding to let go of the possibility of Evan being a part of a conspiracy, for the time being anyway. There were more important things she needed to focus on at the moment as she and Kevin stepped back into hallway, making their way towards the large lobby and wetland.

Chapter Twenty-Two

J osh remained resting near the water's edge, cooling his face with a touch of the pond's water. He was trying to stay calm after hearing the many howls from the wolves that stalked the forest, not to mention the gunfire. He couldn't blame the residents that accused these large predators for the missing persons cases that continued to rise and shake the town. They were all over the valley, obviously on the move and in a panic due to the quakes.

Josh took in a deep breath and stared towards the water treatment plant. It was far in the distance on a hill. He could still make out part of the helicopter, but no one was moving about. This was disheartening.

Hopefully they got to it safely...The gunfire was promising.

Josh sighed heavily and sat there quietly, listening to sounds of nature that resonated through the park. He could hear the fountain in the middle of the pond spilling into the water, the frogs croaking near the water's edge, and the soft grass rustling under...

Josh's heart sank. He turned his head around, seeing an older gentleman approaching him, his face firm with no emotion. His skin, hair, and clothing were covered in what looked like ash or soot. His heavy military boots were not able to keep silent against the ground.

Josh stared into the man's eyes as he approached him. He knew this man, but wasn't sure if he should call him Captain or Smitherman.

"Well...Isn't it Mr. Walker, the little coward that ran off at the operations center," Kyle stated coldly as he stood next to him.

Josh was extremely shocked from his appearance, even more so with his tone. "Uh, yes sir..."

"And what happened to you?" Kyle asked, leaning his weight on one side, his rifle in hand, resting against his shoulder.

"I fell after the recent quake...but, weren't you supposed to be..."

"Dead?"

Josh froze, eyes wide.

Kyle smirked and tossed the sling to his rifle over his shoulder, allowing the weapon to lie across his back. "No...Not *that* easily."

Josh gulped, but kept his composure. This man scared him senseless.

"So, where are the others? I assume they're still around?" Kyle asked.

"We, ah, got split up from Will and Alyssa. The other two are searching for help elsewhere," Josh replied.

Kyle looked towards the forest. "The other two?"

"A cop and a survivor joined us. Evan left to chase the survivors that fled in a humvee. And...Will and Alyssa got trapped under the cathedral. I'm not sure if they got out yet."

Kyle stared at him for a moment. "A cop?" he asked.

Josh nodded.

"Where is this cathedral?" Kyle asked, raising an eyebrow.

"It's west from here."

"The one on the hill, I presume?"

"Yes..."

"And you're sure that Thompson and Ms. Bennett are...*alive*?"

Josh's heart began to race. He didn't like all these questions and was beginning to feel a bit suspicious of the odd behavior. "Yes," he stated and pursed his lips in a hard line.

Kyle could sense the uneasiness and smiled. He enjoyed this type of torture. "Well Mr. Walker I must thank you for that little bit of information..." he stated, stepping around him so he could face him head on.

Josh watched his every move closely.

"But...I am afraid your time has come to an end," Kyle added, his nasty smirk returning to his face.

Josh froze as Kyle retrieved the Colt 1911 he had holstered and aimed it directly at his face.

"Why…?" Josh whispered.

"You've seen and heard a bit *too* much," Kyle responded and placed his finger on the trigger.

"Are you sure we aren't lost?" Will asked as he and Alyssa continued to push through the woods. The bugs had been bothering them, and the brush had been scratching at the skin on their arms.

"Yes, I'm sorry, it's a bit of a walk, but I believe we are close," Alyssa replied.

"Those howls earlier seemed distant, but I don't want to take the chance on running into an angry pack of wolves. That's an encounter I want to avoid," Will stated, recalling the howls and gunfire earlier.

"Well someone took care of it," Alyssa stated and jumped when a loud bang echoed throughout the area. She quickly stopped, standing perfectly still.

Will stopped near her, his eyes raised. "That's a big gun."

"Yes…" Alyssa replied.

They remained silent for a moment as the atmosphere grew calm once again.

"Could be military…Come on," Will said and began making his way through the woods, pushing around twines and brush.

Alyssa followed close behind him, keeping an eye on their surroundings after the loud blast. She remained quiet, her mind constantly racing with the images that Wahkan had played in her mind. She had let go of most of them but one, the one that occurred at her parents' residence. The little hope she had for them was gone.

After traveling through the acres of trees and brush, they finally came across a road. Will jogged to it, thankful that the street lamps were on. Alyssa stepped up to the edge of the pavement and glanced to the right, familiarizing herself with the area quickly.

"The park is that way," she said, pointing to the right. She was a bit winded from the hike.

Will looked towards the rolling hills in the distance, seeing a large building. "I guess that's it," he stated, and they carefully walked down the street.

Alyssa kept her eyes on the pavement. After a few moments of silence, Will turned his attention to her as they continued forward.

"I'm sure Kevin and the others are okay..." he stated, assuming she was still worrying herself sick over her friend.

"I'm not actually thinking about them."

"Oh, I see..."

"I was thinking about my parents."

Will nodded and waited.

"I was holding on to the fact that they were possibly still alive. My father's truck wasn't there, but after what I had seen forced into my mind earlier, there was no way they could've survived," Alyssa said and paused, sighing softly. It was hard not to erase those memories from her mind.

"I saw my mother get stabbed by those massive claws..." Alyssa whispered. "I can't comprehend why he attacked them first, attacked them at all."

Will looked at her for a long moment before turning his attention back in front of him. He felt terrible for her, but he didn't know what to say. He could remember the painstaking emotions that were running throughout her and how he could practically feel them wash into his own body. It was an awful feeling.

"Once we get out of here, we will contact the appropriate authorities. There will be an investigation. What good it will do though is beyond me," Will finally replied after a moment. He took another look at Alyssa. "I am sorry about your mother and father."

Alyssa glanced at him and drew her lips into a line. She slowly nodded and looked towards the entrance of the park. She could see the small welcome sign and the bright white letters that read Memorial Park.

"We can go around the park to a small road on the left up ahead. It's a bit of a walk, but it will eventually lead us to the plant," Alyssa stated.

Will nodded and glanced at the park. It was serene and calm, but something caught his attention near the pond. "Wait..." he stated, staring towards the water's edge.

Alyssa stopped and looked at him, noticing his concerned expression. She glanced towards the park as well. It didn't take her long to spot it, the lifeless body lying on the ground near the water.

Will slowly began approaching the body, retrieving his pistol. Alyssa followed him, looking around the park to see if there was anyone else around. She took in a deep breath and looked back towards the lifeless body, her hand gently grasping and retrieving her pistol.

"Oh no..." Will stated, recognizing the man once they stepped up to him. Blood surrounded his head.

Alyssa's mouth dropped open as she and Will stared at the civilian they had met downtown, Josh Walker.

Will knelt down beside him, examining him closely, shaking his head in denial. "Why would somebody do this?"

Alyssa thought about the murderer in the precinct, and her heart started to beat a little faster.

Will pushed himself to his feet and looked at Alyssa, his face distraught. "I just don't understand," he said.

"That was the loud gunshot we heard. Kevin and Jessie could be in the vicinity. We heard a lot of gunfire earlier too," Alyssa said and felt the adrenaline rushing all over her. She was afraid. So many people...*murdered* from the hands of someone that could be amongst them. She knew there was a possibility of Kevin being amongst the dead now too. He and Josh had left together earlier...

Alyssa released a low gust of air and looked around the park. It was dark and quiet. She looked at the ground, noticing a large bullet casing. She knelt down and picked it up, examining it closely.

Will watched as her eyes slowly widened.

".45," she stated and a sudden flashback of the event that unfolded at the operations center flashed before her eyes. She had fallen into the lobby after Will shoved her through the door from the other room. The large angra had broken into the window, and Captain

Smitherman was standing right beside her, a large Colt 1911 in his hands aimed directly at the beast.

Alyssa dropped the bullet casing.

"What is it?" Will asked concernedly.

"Nothing...Let's just get to this extraction point."

Will looked at her for a moment as she glanced towards the trails in the park.

"There's a short cut. We take the trail," Alyssa said, pointing towards the forest.

"Alright," Will replied and began making his way to the bridge. He was extremely concerned with Alyssa's odd expression, but if she wasn't going to talk about it, he wasn't going to nag. He kept his nine millimeter in one hand, unable to holster it after seeing Josh's lifeless body. It had occurred just a moment ago. This murderer was still lurking around the area, able to sneak up any second.

Alyssa followed behind Will, her mind on the .45 caliber weapon that was obviously used to kill Josh.

It couldn't have been...He's dead...It could've been anyone...

She clenched her teeth becoming more frustrated with the situation, and everything pointed back to her. She was the reason for the plague, the reason for the evil presence.

Alyssa was so angry with herself, so distraught, until a firm hold took over her body, a sudden arm wrapping tightly around hers and her chest. Something cold and hard pushed against her temple, and her whole body tensed and froze in place, a low gasp pushing through her lips. It was just enough to make Will pause. He could hear the sudden fear...and the sound of her pistol falling against the soil behind him.

Will whipped around, his pistol aimed past Alyssa and directly at the one man he thought ceased to exist, the one man he looked up to.

His uniform was covered in dirt and ash, his skin and hair a mess. His eyes glared directly into his, an evil smirk curling onto his lips.

"Fast, Thompson...Just not fast enough."

Will slowly lowered his pistol. "Captain...You're alive...Wha-what are you doing?" he asked hesitantly.

"Oh I think it is quite obvious, Sergeant First Class."

Will stared at him for a long moment, feeling a bit of guilt. He looked into Alyssa's frightful eyes. She stared back at him, a look of helplessness on her face. Will looked back at Kyle, hoping he was going to be able to change this situation. "I trusted you...You wouldn't go as far as to betray your own group and the civilians in this town would you?" Will asked.

"I would do what is necessary to get my job done," Kyle responded, holding Alyssa tightly.

"What does this have to do with Alyssa? Please...just let her go. She is probably the only person who can put an end to all of this."

"No! I can put an end to all of this. And I will. Everyone will see me for who I *rightfully* am..."

Will slowly shook his head in disbelief as Kyle continued, "I should've known better than to let this former cop get involved, and for you two to get this far is an outrage! You two could've destroyed everything..."

"Who are you working for, Captain?" Will interrupted, narrowing his eyes.

Kyle smirked once more and patted Alyssa's shoulder with the hand that was wrapped tightly around her. "That's...*sensitive* information, Thompson..."

"Then was it you that corrupted Sergeant Kennedy?"

Kyle's eyes raised, the smirk still remaining on his face. "Ah... so he was alive. I assume you know the *mission*?"

"I know a lot of innocent people were murdered, and I know about the legend and the plague that haunts this valley...How many others have you corrupted, Captain?" Will asked firmly.

Alyssa remained still as she could feel the tension rattling within Kyle's body. His anger was elevating.

"Everyone else is dead. Only a few of you were able to escape the angras before they came back to finish the job. And *you*...somehow you have managed to stay alive this entire time. I misjudged you Thompson," Kyle stated.

Will looked back at Alyssa. "Captain…killing her isn't going to do you any good. It's not going to change anything," he said, looking back into Kyle's eyes.

"Who said *I* was planning on killing her…?" Kyle asked. Alyssa's heart began to race even more, her eyes widening. "She is now insurance, a guarantee. I *will* get this job done."

Will exhaled his breath in a short gasp. He didn't know what would persuade him into letting her go. He didn't care about anything else such as the truth behind the incident at the Rockdale Valley Precinct or the corruption and disappearances of the group. At this moment, he just wanted Alyssa out of his grasp and the gun away from her head.

"I'm begging you…Let her go…" he said softly, almost in a whisper.

Kyle smiled and raised an eyebrow. He noticed that there was something slightly different about the Sergeant First Class.

"So there is a weak side to you after all, Thompson…" Kyle replied and glanced down at Alyssa's hair, smiling. "I guess I cannot blame you. However, this is goodbye."

"*Please…*"

"If you try and follow us, I will pull the trigger. As you have just seen…I will not hesitate, Thompson," Kyle stated and stepped back towards the entrance of the park, pulling Alyssa with him. "Farewell."

Will breathed heavily, still caressing his pistol. He kept it at his side and watched as Kyle pulled Alyssa through the parking lot before turning around and pushing her down the street, disappearing behind the rows of trees that stood alongside the road. Will continued to stare into their direction until they were no longer to be seen or heard. The atmosphere soon grew calm. There were no voices or shuffling of feet, just the wilderness of the park.

Will's body trembled and he soon fell to his knees. He breathed deeply and stared at the ground in front of him. His heart raced with anxiety, the adrenaline still rushing in his veins.

Because I was so blind, I failed my group...I failed this town...and most of all, I failed Alyssa. I'll get her back. For now, I must continue forward with the mission...

Will sighed heavily, shaking his head. His heart rate finally slowed, but the anger was now building up within him.

Fuck the mission. There never truly was one. It's obvious that we were meant to die here. Alyssa...she is now my mission. I will see to it that the captain pays for what he did no matter the consequences...

Will continued to sit on the ground, staring towards the road. The area remained still and quiet. He turned his attention towards the plant. He noticed the forest and the trails. Alyssa had mentioned that it was a shortcut. He could reunite with the rest of the other unit and get assistance on locating her before it was too late. Will took a deep breath and pushed himself to his feet. He fought back the emotions that tried to creep throughout his body as he leaned down to pick up the pistol he had allowed Alyssa to use. He quickly holstered it and kept his in his grasp as he made his way towards the trails. He refused to look back.

The silence that surrounded the area tortured Will's nerves. He was able to handle the noise from the creatures that awoke during the night before, but now they were quiet which was odd to him. Perhaps it was the sense of trouble, the uneasiness that now lingered the area.

Will continued to push forward past the small bridge and to the foot of the trails, allowing his mind to stay clear. He had to get to this plant, to the extraction point where hopefully the other unit would be. He held onto his pistol carefully and made his way through the winding, hilly trails, refusing to get his flashlight. He didn't stop until he eventually crossed paths with a large, lifeless animal lying in the middle of the trail. Bullet casings were near it on the path and blood surrounded its body. Will stepped up to it and looked it over.

This happened not too long ago as well...It could be the others. And these wolves could be anywhere...

Will noticed the nine millimeter casings and thought about Kyle and the large gun he was able to get his hands on.

Where did he get the .45?

Will looked through the brush in front of him. Everything was calm. He glanced behind him, following the trail behind a descending bend. Hopefully whoever it was in the forest earlier was still around and was someone he could trust.

Will took in a deep breath and began to jog down the path, pushing up hills and sliding down steep slopes. Once he pushed up the tallest hill, the forest began to clear. More grass was seen and the path slowly veered to the left traveling down the tree line. Will stopped himself once he saw the large plant and the fence line. The gate was open. He walked to it, double checking his surroundings. It was too quiet for the area to be an extraction point. Where were all the soldiers and the military vehicles?

Will reached the gate and stopped, looking at the shiny metal of the pad lock. The lock had been cut.

Odd...

Will glanced towards the building, examining the parking area and other buildings that were a part of the water treatment plant. He noticed the tail end of a helicopter and felt relieved, but it was still suspicious. No one was in sight. He looked at the side door and carefully made his way to it until his radio went off, emitting a scratchy noise. Static shot out from it and then a voice. Will halted and snatched the radio out from its holster.

"...be advised...chopper dispatched to Rockdale Valley Water Treatment Plant to evacuate remaining civilians. I repeat, chopper has been dispatched," a firm voice stated.

Will stared at the radio, silence surrounding him.

What if it's too late?

He released a low gasp and holstered the radio. He had to find the others...

CHAPTER TWENTY-THREE

A LYSSA WAS PANTING BY THE time Kyle had stopped dragging her across the terrain. They had stopped near a section of the lake beside a large barn. The property sat near the water treatment plant. Rows of trees made up a barrier that split the property. A wooden fence stretched down beside the trees, separating each piece of land from the other. The entrance to the plant was also visible. It's large, double gates were open, and the helicopter was in full view. However, no one was in sight.

Kyle holstered his Colt 1911 and pulled open the barn's door. Alyssa remained silent as he removed her M4 and pushed her into the dark barn. The area smelled of hay bales, oat, and greasy tools. The floor was covered in dirt and soil. There was a tool box against the wall with many large tools hanging above it. A tractor sat in one corner, its cover lying on the ground next to it. There were two stables open, hay covering their floors. Horse tack sat on shelves next to them. The horses were nowhere to be seen.

Kyle was breathing heavily as he pulled the door shut and tossed her rifle to the floor. "You..."

Alyssa stared at him in shock as he approached her and knocked her to the ground. She yelped as the wind was forced out of her lungs abruptly. She could feel the sharp pain stretch across her side and into her chest, disrupting her breathing.

"You could have cost me everything! My title...My reputation... My *fortune!*" Kyle yelled and kicked her in the ribcage.

Alyssa screamed in pain and rolled over to her side, wrapping her arms around her stomach. The intense throbs ached throughout her torso. She was having difficulty catching her breath, her breathing short and rapid.

"And to think that I saved your life…You know, I thought it could be you standing by my side in this," Kyle added and stepped around Alyssa, watching her toss in pain and turmoil.

She quickly got herself together as best as she could, fighting back the intense pain. "So it was you…You were the one that killed all of those innocent people at the precinct, my friends…" she forced out, catching her breath.

Kyle smiled. "Yes…how unfortunate for them. I did however, get something rather remarkable out of the deal," he stated, patting the Colt 1911. "Now, where is the key to get into that damn cavern?"

The adrenaline began to rush into Alyssa's veins as the image of the gear shaped stone appeared in her mind. "I…I don't know."

"You are lying!" Kyle yelled and kicked her once again, knocking Alyssa back to the floor. The side of her face drug across it, splinters piercing through the skin of her cheek.

Alyssa gasped loudly and closed her eyes, her teeth tightly clenched. Blood began to slide from the wounds and onto the floor as tears began to make their way to her eyes.

"Brian told me everything. Your father didn't have it," Kyle stated.

Alyssa opened her eyes and breathed deeply, the name echoing in her mind.

"Who did you say…?" she whispered.

Kyle slowly smiled and knelt down beside her, staring into her hurtful eyes. "You were *used*…You see, your father wanted to hide the truth from you. I heard about your brother…what a shame. And it's all your father's fault."

Alyssa released a low gasp and shook her head. "No…My father was just trying to protect me…"

"So you *do* remember…"

Alyssa stared at him for a long moment before he grabbed her arm and pulled her up. She couldn't remember everything, but she knew it wasn't going to fly by him. It wouldn't matter what she told him. Kyle stared into her tearful eyes and moved the hair away from her face.

"Such a beauty. I'd hate to keep scarring up that face..." he said and Alyssa suddenly felt enraged, a burning sensation erupted within her chest. It felt as if another power consumed her. She felt stronger, more willful. Alyssa clenched her teeth and slung her fist up, punching Kyle under the jaw. The force made him lose his grip and stumble a few feet back. Alyssa stared at him, her eyes narrowing, the pain subsiding. The heat was rushing all throughout her body, and then she began to feel the rumble of breath deep within her chest. Alyssa's eyes widened as she stared at Kyle.

"You've got some fight in you..." Kyle said and smiled. "Why look at you, you've become one with it...haven't you?"

"I don't know what you are talking about," Alyssa said firmly. Her eyes felt as if they were on fire, burning intensely.

"Oh you know exactly what I am talking about."

Alyssa remained unresponsive. She could practically feel the evil presence within her. Kyle must have known a lot more than she thought he did.

"You are going to *regret* what you did, Kyle," Alyssa stated angrily, her body trembling.

"Am I?" Kyle asked and before Alyssa could lunge for her rifle, he quickly grabbed her and backhanded her against the side of the face, busting her nose. Alyssa fell back to the floor and caught herself with the palms of her hands. She spit out a little blood from her lip, and she could feel the warmth flowing from one of her nostrils.

Kyle grabbed her arm and pulled her back up. She coughed heavily and allowed him to drag her to one of the walls of the barn. A long metal bar protruded from it and extended a few feet across it. There were a few shelves beside the bar that contained grooming buckets full of brushes and shampoo.

Alyssa watched as Kyle snatched a lead rope from one of the shelves. He pulled her to the bar and pushed her back against it, knocking the wind out of Alyssa's lungs yet again. Alyssa choked and coughed while Kyle pulled her arms up above her head and proceeded to tie them tightly with the lead rope. Her hands were bloodshot as he turned to tie the rest of the rope tightly to the metal bar. He allowed no slack. Alyssa breathed deeply once she caught her breath and looked back into Kyle's eyes as he turned his attention back to her.

"Do you honestly believe…that you can get away with all of this?" Alyssa whispered, the blood continuing to trickle from her nose and onto her shirt.

Kyle patted her cheek. "The curse has taken a hold of *you*…as well as your family. Now it is our time to go in. No one will ever know…" he stated and smiled. "The plague has already consumed this valley. Soon, this place will be a molten wasteland. The rest of the world will see that it was just a large underground volcano."

Alyssa shook her head and watched as Kyle turned his attention to her shirt. The blood had dropped onto something that was behind it.

"What do we have here…" he stated and pulled the pendant out from behind her shirt. He caressed it gently, and his eyes slowly widened.

Alyssa's heart began to palpitate and her breathing became heavy. She watched as Kyle snatched the necklace from her neck, breaking the clamp. The back of the chain tore into her skin, leaving a small, irritating cut. Blood slowly seeped out from it and accumulated around the small wound. Kyle looked back into Alyssa's eyes, his face full of anger.

"You had it this entire time…Everything that we did when you had it in your possession this whole damn time!" he shouted and hit Alyssa once more in the face, whipping her neck to the side.

Alyssa groaned heavily and remained still, refusing to look back at Kyle. The pain stretched across her face and cervical spine, aching sharply.

"I don't care if Brian wanted to keep you safe…I'll see to it that you *rot*…" Kyle stressed and froze when he heard a low growl coming from the darkness in the barn. He turned around and scanned the area thoroughly. He became a bit frightened, but hid it well. The barn seemed clear. Nothing was in sight.

Kyle let out a light laugh and turned his attention back to Alyssa's weakened and exhausted state. Her eyes were heavy, and her body was growing limp. Kyle smirked and took a step back, still caressing the red stone.

"Or...I'll let one of the beasts take care of you. Farewell, Ms. Bennett. It's been a pleasure," he said and smiled, quickly turning and making his way back to the door of the barn. He didn't want to cross paths with another angra.

Alyssa watched as he retrieved his .45 and disappeared behind the door. Silence quickly filled the area, and Alyssa realized how dark it was inside the barn. There were a few windows, but the dark, gray clouds were beginning to hide the stars and moon. She noticed a few bright flashes of light illuminating the area and fading away every few seconds, but there was no thunder. The storm was soon to arrive.

Alyssa was growing weaker by the minute. Her wrists and hands began to tingle from the lack of blood flow, and her knees began to tremble with fatigue. She didn't care what was about to happen next. She recalled the low growl and knew who and what it was, but she wasn't too concerned with it. She was ready to go.

We were set up...

Alyssa's body broke down and her knees finally gave way. She gasped as her arms hung tightly within the knot above her, her body slumping over. Her head slowly hung down and faced the floor. A few tears crept into her eyes and eventually fell from them, splashing onto the floor, separating the dirt from it. Alyssa breathed deeply and allowed her eyes to close. She was full of pain and despair and for some reason all she could think about was William Thompson.

Will had stepped into the side entrance of the water treatment plant, his nine millimeter still in hand. He slowly walked down the long, cool hallway, examining every room he came to. The atmosphere on the inside was just the same as it was on the outside, too calm and quiet. The plant's employees must have evacuated just before it had become catastrophic.

Will stepped around the corner and began to walk down another long hallway. There were a few offices and a pair of bathrooms as well as another hall on the left. He ignored them and the pictures and décor on the wall as he continued forward, his mind becoming fuzzy and boggled with images and flashbacks from everything that had occurred. His chest was becoming tight, his breathing becoming heavier. He could practically hear his heartbeat in his ears. He couldn't control the images that crossed his mind or the anxiety that began to flood throughout his body.

Alyssa had her suspicions....And I denied them. Kevin warned me, threatened me even, and I denied those accusations. Smitherman deceived us...

Will released a heavy gust of air and stopped once he passed the other hall. He slowly turned and leaned the back of his body against the wall, closing his eyes and placing his hand over his face. The anger trembled throughout him.

The one person who could possibly put an end to this is gone... because of me. We just learned what was truly taking place here... And I failed...yet again.

Will clenched his teeth and slowly slid his body down the wall until he sat on the cold floor. He had to process everything and get himself together before making another move.

How could I have been so blind? The clues were there in front of me this entire time. So many of the group dead, missing...And I ignored it. I don't deserve to still be alive.

Will took in a deep breath and lowered his hand. He closed his eyes and attempted to relax his mind. He knew he could be stronger, but something was interfering with him.

I will unite with the other unit and assist them until extraction. I will fight this as long as I can...

Will opened his eyes, feeling a new emotion building within him as he thought about the young, former cop he had paired with after his arrival into the valley.

That's just it...I care about her...

And suddenly his thoughts were shaken when a low, painful gasp was heard down the other hall he had just passed. He quickly pushed himself to his feet, clearing his mind. He slowly stepped up to the corner and looked down the hall. There were two large rooms in the area and only one door was open.

Will carefully stepped down the hall, readying his pistol as he took steady breaths. He approached the room with the door that was open. He was able to hear the noise clearly from the other hall. He knew it had to have come from this room.

"Is anyone there?" he asked.

No response. Will stepped up to the room and held his pistol out, aimed and ready. He peered inside, examining all the large cylinders that were lined up in the center of the room. A few pipes extended from them and into neighboring pipes that wrapped around the room. He looked to the right, his gun following him as he noticed a figure on the floor from the corner of his eye. He took in a deep breath and slowly approached the older gentleman, his gun lowering halfway.

"Sir?" Will asked cautiously.

The man was breathing heavily and blood was smeared across the floor. Will could tell this man had pulled himself across it. He looked extremely exhausted.

"Excuse me, sir...I'm here to help," Will added and knelt down beside the man. His eyes were open halfway, and he was staring at the floor. Blood covered his clothing.

Will examined him, surprised at the man's injuries and how he was still alive.

"You...must be here to finish me off," the man slowly stated and looked into Will's eyes.

Will could not only see the pain, but the sadness. "Uh, no, sir... Who are you?" he asked.

"It doesn't matter anymore..."

"Sir, I can help you."

The man stared into his eyes, reading Will's body language. He glanced at his uniform and insignia. "No you cannot...unless you can find my daughter for me."

Will stared at him for a moment. He hadn't crossed paths with anyone since they met the survivors at the cathedral. "We should take care of these wounds first, sir..."

301

"No…I am done for."

Will took in a deep breath and slowly nodded. He wasn't going to pressure the issue, and he had nothing on him that could help save his life. The only medic that was still alive had joined the other unit.

"I haven't seen anyone else in this facility. Who is your daughter, sir?" Will asked.

"Alyssa Bennett."

Will eyes suddenly widened. "James?"

James looked at him, confusion plastering his exhausted face. "Who are you?" he asked.

"My name is Sergeant First Class William Thompson. I met your daughter when my group and I were deployed in the southern valley to rescue and relocate survivors and civilians for evacuation. She assisted my group, Mr. Bennett," Will said, completely awestruck that he was in the valley after what Alyssa had claimed to see.

James looked away and back towards the floor. "My daughter wasn't supposed to come here…"

"She thinks you are dead," Will stated.

James gasped lightly and took in a breath, sighing softly. "She must have come by the house. Her mother didn't make it. I tried to save her, but I didn't have enough time. I don't want my daughter to see me like this…Where is she?" he asked.

Will's heart began to beat a little faster. "We were betrayed…by my very own commander. He took her away thinking she could be insurance to him."

James closed his eyes, clenching his teeth. "It's all my fault. I never wanted to tell her the truth. I got her involved in this when I was only trying to protect her and keep her away from it," he said, tears filling his eyes.

"I just learned about the legend, Mr. Bennett. Alyssa confessed to having trouble recalling her past, but it was coming back to her upon arrival to the valley. We've realized what was truly going on here. The legend exists," Will said, recalling Dena's statements and the journal Alyssa had found.

James opened his eyes, nodding his head. "I didn't want to believe it, even though a part of me knew it was real. I failed her...I failed everyone."

Will knew exactly how he felt. He was experiencing the same emotions. "Did a green beret do this to you, Mr. Bennett?" he asked.

"Yes...but from orders," James whispered and Will remained quiet. He didn't know who else Smitherman had gotten involved other than Sergeant Brad Kennedy, and he knew that he was deceased.

"Alyssa and I were also betrayed by a very close friend of mine, an agent with the government, the one barking the orders. His name is Brian Hall. All he cared about were these rare gems he claimed to exist in the cavern. After Alyssa's brother found it and shared what he had seen and witnessed twelve years ago, the only thing this man could think about was the money potential, the power...regardless of whose lives he would possibly destroy. He was unable to locate the cave entrance for many years. If you know the tale, than I'm sure you know what cavern I am talking about," James stated.

"I do..." Will replied.

James sighed heavily. "These men are after this *one* stone in particular and the other gems. I gave Alyssa the one she had taken the night of her accident."

"Why?"

"Brian knew Alyssa suffered amnesia. She'd be the last person he would try to interrogate. But...I was still in denial. I was trying not to believe in the possibility of this sacred cavern existing. When the earthquakes hit, it didn't dawn on me that it could possibly be related, but when that monstrosity burst into our home, I knew then..."

"Mr. Bennett, you gave Alyssa this one particular stone...It's a rare diamond. Dena told her everything at the cathedral earlier. This stone was the most sacred," Will stated, surprised at how blind James had been, but then again, so had he.

"Dena?" James asked.

"Yes. We also found the journal regarding the true story behind the legend. Alyssa is possessed by the spirit, this monstrosity that burst into your home. She was given an option...to destroy the one who really wanted what she took. It seems to me that this spirit believes Alyssa is protecting the stone. Perhaps that could be why she has been able to recall the accident lately. He is helping her to remember..." Will stated. He even feared the spirit's name. His heart was beginning to race once more as his mind whispered it.

"Oh no...You must find her...Please...I need you to tell her...how truly sorry I am," James forced out, his body weakening quickly. "Perhaps if she would've known the truth. I tried to hide it all for so many years. She eventually forgot about it. I forced her to believe that her brother was mentally ill."

The tears began to fall down his cheeks as he took in a deep breath. "So many good people got involved...and it's all my fault. I could've prevented this. Please, Sergeant..."

Will placed his hand on his shoulder giving him a reassuring nod. "You can call me Will...I promise, I will do everything I can to find Alyssa," he said softly, knowing James didn't have much time left.

"Please, she doesn't have anyone left..."

"No...she does. She has me...if she accepts that now," Will replied.

James looked into Will's eyes, reading the message behind them as he carefully pulled an item that was behind him. "You seem... like a very good man, Will, one with a good heart. I know I can trust you...I can see that. Here," he stated and held out his hand. "This is what Mr. Hall is looking for. We were trying to give him the run around to buy us some time to get more reinforcements..."

Will gently took the item in his hand and examined it, quickly realizing what it was. "This is the key..." he said, recalling the picture in the journal.

"Yes. Alyssa had found it. I buried it after the death of her brother, but somehow...she located it," James said and sighed. "Brian denied telling her, but I only told him and the police chief, a good friend of mine."

Will nodded and looked down. He refused to tell him about Robert's fate.

"Brian must not get this. Use it to seal the door. I just hope that it is not too late for Alyssa," James added.

Will placed the stone in a vest pocket and watched as James took a slow, deep breath. He reached out and gently grabbed Will's arm. "Get Alyssa...and get out of here..." he whispered and Will placed his hand on his shoulder, nodding. James's grip was soon lost and his arm slowly fell to his side. His eyes closed halfway and his head slumped over, his body resting against the wall.

Will stared at him for a long moment as silence filled the room. He could feel deep within his body the emotions that were trying to erupt. His anxiety was elevating, his heart was racing. He had to go after the captain. He had to find Alyssa.

I promise Mr. Bennett...I will get her back...

Will slowly pushed himself to his feet, staring at James's lifeless body that was slumped against the wall. He was hurting for him and for Alyssa, for their family and friends that were affected by the catastrophe. He took in a deep breath and shook from the sudden startle as his radio spit out a little static. Will grabbed the radio and took a step back. He examined the room he was in to make sure that it was still clear as he brought the radio to his ear.

"All units abort mission...I repeat, abort the mission and rendezvous to extraction point immediately! We suffered a total loss, everyone else remaining in the area abort mission and evacuate immediately! I repeat, evacuate immediately! U.S. Air Force has received intel and will be dispatched to location to release TNW. Get out now!"

Will's body froze. He couldn't believe what he had just heard.

They are actually going to nuke the town?

His hand slowly lowered the radio and his eyes widened.

Alyssa...

Will quickly brought the radio to his mouth and pushed the button. "This is Sergeant First Class Thompson. We have a very valuable source trapped in Rockdale Valley that has extremely important information regarding the incident that has occurred here. I repeat we have a very valuable source trapped here that has the item on hand that can tell everyone what has occurred here! I need immediate assistance to locate her position before extraction."

Will waited.

"Negative, Sergeant First Class. I repeat, negative. This is an executive order."

Will lowered the radio and took one last look at James.

Where are the others! I cannot leave anyone behind...I've got to find Alyssa!

Will holstered the radio and quickly left the room realizing that the town was counting down its final hours.

CHAPTER TWENTY-FOUR

"THIS PLACE DIDN'T SEEM SO big from the outside, goodness..." Jessie stated as she and Kevin stepped into the lobby of the facility. They had wandered the winding halls for a few minutes, getting turned around a couple of times before stepping into the large lobby also known as the wetland. There were plants everywhere. They were able to see the second floor and more offices and winding hallways.

Kevin remained silent after Jessie's comment. He walked past the rows of plants and approached the metal double doors that led out front. The two small windows on the doors were no larger than portholes on a ship. Kevin peeked out one and grabbed the handle, attempting to pull the door open. It rattled, but the door wouldn't budge. Jessie paced around the area as Kevin tried to push the door open. It continued to rattle in place. He could feel something forceful on the other side.

"This doesn't make any sense..." Kevin stated and examined the door, looking for a lock.

Jessie approached him, continuing to check behind them to make sure the area remained safe and clear. "What's wrong?" she asked.

Kevin took in a deep breath and tugged at the door some more. "It won't open...It feels like something is keeping it closed."

Jessie looked away, feeling hopeless. "We traveled all this way just to find no one, and no way out?" she asked.

Kevin acknowledged her question as a statement and looked through the small window in the door. He could see the lone helicopter and now a couple of humvees, but the area still looked vacant.

"Where the hell is everyone?" he asked. He was becoming angry and impatient. They had to get back to Josh with or without help.

"You see why we cannot trust these men in military uniform? This makes no sense at all," Kevin stressed.

Jessie shook her head. "There could be a reason for this, Kevin. Think about it…"

"Oh I know. It's a conspiracy."

"No, that's not what I mean. There could be a reason for this place to be vacant. Something could've happened…"

"Well we can't wander around this maze trying to find someone who can help us. We need to go back to Josh, and we need to get back to Alyssa."

Jessie slowly nodded.

Kevin sighed and turned away from the door, walking back through the rows of plants. He was trying not to allow the anger to get the best of him. He was fed up.

Jessie followed behind him, keeping quiet. She was afraid to go back in the park. She wanted to hang tight for a moment. Someone could possibly show.

"Um, you sure you don't want to sit around for a moment? I don't believe they would have just abandoned the helicopter," she stated, hoping Kevin would reconsider.

Kevin stopped and turned to face her. "I don't think we should waste too much time. Josh is dying, and Alyssa and Will are still trapped under the cathedral. I'm going back."

"Alright," Jessie replied and Kevin turned back around, looking towards the hallway. He didn't move as he stared into it, alert.

Jessie looked at him concernedly and glanced at the empty hallway, hearing a faint sound of feet shuffling against the floor. Her eyes suddenly widened, and her heart went into overdrive.

"Get back," Kevin whispered, retrieving his pistol.

Jessie quickly ran towards the double doors and hid behind one of the rows of plants. Kevin walked back, his pistol up and ready.

The footsteps got closer and louder. Someone was in a hurry. Kevin stared, unable to blink, the sweat now pushing out onto his forehead. And then the person turned the corner, quickly stopping in his tracks. His eyes were wide, his face full of alarm, but there was something else wrong with his expression.

Kevin's eyes grew wider, becoming more confused. "Will?" he stated, lowering his pistol.

"Kevin..." Will said, returning the confused glare.

"Oh God, I'm so glad you two got out. We were on our way, but there was an accident. Josh got injured..." Kevin paused, looking into Will's eyes. He sensed something was off and became alarmed. "Wait...Where is she?"

Will was breathing heavily, his face flushed. "You were right..." he said and took a few steps into the lobby. "It *was* my group."

Kevin's eyes slowly narrowed. "What did you do?" he asked firmly.

"It was my commander. He took her away after we found Josh in the park..." Will stressed, overwhelmed with dejection.

"You lying sack of..."

"Kevin!" Jessie quickly interrupted, jogging to him. "*Look* at him...My goodness he obviously cares about her as much as you do. Let him talk!" she stressed. She had no reason to feel any animosity towards Will, and he seemed sincere. The look in his eyes said it all.

Kevin glanced at her before looking back into Will's eyes. He slowly lowered his pistol to his side, relaxing himself, but his body remained tense.

Will sighed. "I'm so sorry. Captain Smitherman and a few others are behind this, and they were all a part of my group. I couldn't have been more blind. You were right. You were right this entire time."

Kevin holstered his pistol, watching him carefully.

"I didn't see it coming, but the signs were there, and I didn't think twice about them. I denied the possibility of it. I've known these men for quite some time. I wouldn't think for a second that they would ever do something like this," Will added.

"We could have prevented this," Kevin said. "You better hope they do not hurt her."

"I know this could have been prevented...I *will* find her, Kevin. I don't think they will harm her. She has what they need," Will said and took in a deep breath, approaching Kevin. He didn't feel a need to keep his distance any longer.

"You found Josh?" Kevin asked.

"Yes...He's dead. Smitherman killed him," Will responded and watched Jessie cringe and turn away.

Kevin clenched his teeth.

"And...Alyssa's father was alive as well," Will added, stepping around Kevin. He approached the door as Kevin turned to face him.

"What did you say?" he asked.

Will reached the door and tried to open it. Kevin watched as he slammed his fist into it before slowly resting his forehead against it. Jessie watched him and became saddened. She never witnessed a man break down in this manner.

"James was alive...He didn't make it either. Smitherman is working for a man in the government, a Mr. Hall. He is the one giving out the horrendous orders," Will stated, keeping his head rested against the cool door.

Kevin slowly approached him. "Brian Hall?"

"Yes."

"I can't believe this...He was there after Alyssa's accident in the hospital room. He..." Kevin released a low gasp, shaking his head. "He must have known..."

Will took in a deep breath and pushed himself away from the door, looking back at him and Jessie.

Kevin stared at him for a long moment. "Where did he take Alyssa?" he asked.

"I don't know. He said he was going to kill her if I followed," Will responded.

Kevin groaned and paced around the floor. "Damn it!" he finally shouted. He had no idea what to do now.

"There is more..." Will said.

Kevin and Jessie stared at him as he continued, "I just received word that the U.S Air Force will be dispatched here."

"Why? There is nothing the military can do to stop this," Kevin replied.

"They think they can. They are going to release a tactical nuclear weapon."

"What?" Jessie asked. All she could see in her mind was a large mushroom cloud.

Kevin stared at Will in pure shock. "Why would they do that... There are still people here!" he stressed.

"Our mission was a total failure. We were able to evacuate some survivors, but the military has suffered greatly. They received enough information about the incident here to help them make this decision. We've been given strict orders to abort the mission and prepare for extraction. There is nothing that I could've done...I tried," Will replied, recalling the tone of the message he had received.

Kevin sighed heavily and looked away.

"What does this mean?" Jessie asked.

"It means that they are going to destroy the town and all that is in it," Kevin said, looking at her frightful expression.

Jessie's eyes widened and her mouth dropped. "But what about us?"

"We can get out...The extraction point is here. A helicopter has been dispatched," Will replied.

Kevin shook his head. "These doors are locked from the outside."

Will looked back at the double doors and approached them. He placed his hands on the handle and tried to pull and push them open. It rattled in place, refusing to open.

"They've been barricaded..." he said.

"We can go back around," Jessie suggested, still fearing about the wolves that lurked around the trails, but there weren't many options on the table.

"No, I'm sure there is another way around. We may have to get back into the sewers, but it's probably safer than the forest. Those wolves are crazed and there are probably packs of them out there," Kevin said. "But why the hell would anyone barricade those doors?"

Will looked back at him. "I don't know, but we'll probably find out soon enough. Kevin, why don't you lead the way? We need to get out of here…If this Mr. Hall is aware of an immediate evac operation than I'm sure he and his corrupted followers will be trying to get out too. Smitherman was just in the area, they couldn't have gone too far. We could still find Alyssa."

Kevin nodded. "Alright. Let's go," he said and made his way to a hallway on the far right.

Will and Jessie followed.

"I'm so sorry…" Jessie whispered, walking alongside Will.

He glanced at her. "For what?"

"Alyssa."

Will looked away and trailed behind Kevin as they stepped into the hall. He felt bad for not catching the girl's name at the cathedral. "I'll get her back," he replied.

Jessie half smiled. "You really care about her, don't you?"

Will watched Kevin ahead as he slowed his walk. They had passed one large room and were approaching another on the right.

"You can say that," Will replied.

They passed a couple of rooms before Kevin stopped and looked into one. It had a few desks and computer terminals. There were a few pipes protruding from the wall and a small staircase sat in the back, leading down to a metal door.

"I believe this is it," Kevin said and stepped into the room.

Jessie followed, but Will remained in place. His vision was becoming a bit fuzzy and his hearing was slowly fading as Kevin's voice became muffled. He felt an awkward sensation wash over him and his heart rate began to race. He remained calm until he heard it, the familiar low growl that awoke his and Alyssa's deepest fears. It came directly behind him, whispering into his ear.

Will turned around, glancing back into the hall and towards another room across from him. Nothing was out of place. Everything was calm. He turned his attention towards the others as they approached the staircase. They must not have heard it. Kevin stopped and suddenly glanced behind him as if he sensed something was off.

"You coming?" he asked.

Jessie looked back at Will as well, remaining silent.

"Yes...You two go ahead. I'll catch up," Will responded.

"What is it?" Kevin asked, noticing Will's frightful expression.

"I think I heard something...You two keep going. I don't want you to witness this," Will replied and stepped back into the hallway.

Kevin watched him disappear and looked at Jessie.

She shrugged. "Let's keep going like he said."

Kevin took in a breath and turned around, stepping down the stairs towards the metal door. A part of him was urging him to turn around and go back as each step he took closer to the door caused his anxiety to rise...

Will stepped back down the hall and turned the corner, slowly passing a room, scanning it thoroughly to make sure it was vacant. He approached another room, a large office with a round table centered on the floor and a small desk. There were shelves lining the walls containing scientific instruments. Some paper was lying on the table and a few pens on the floor near the chairs.

Will looked around curiously, examining the room closely. It seemed calm, but the light above was flickering wildly, casting shadows across the floor each time it flashed. It caused the atmosphere in the room to be an unpleasant one. Will couldn't remember the light being faulty when they passed the room just a moment ago. He stepped inside it cautiously, slowly retrieving his nine millimeter. All he could think about was the evil presence and the awkward sensation that had begun to crawl throughout him earlier. He knew *he* was here.

He approached the other side of the room, glaring towards the back, scanning the area carefully. He didn't want to miss anything, but all remained calm besides the light above. Will sighed and lowered his pistol. Perhaps he was now hearing things. He turned around and glanced back at the door when suddenly, the lights above went out. Darkness filled the area. Will's eyes widened, taking a few seconds to adjust when something large stepped into the room swiftly and quietly. It was a bit blurry, but his eyes finally adjusted and he took a few steps back, eventually pushing his back against the wall.

A low growl exited from the large creature he and Alyssa had met in the forest, rumbling out from its lungs and into the room. Its eyes were surprisingly bright, and it slowly curled its lips over its teeth. Will released a low gasp and turned his head to the side, closing his eyes tightly. Pain began to spread throughout his head, intensifying with each step Wahkan took towards him. Another growl rumbled from its lungs, and it sounded as if the wicked creature was directly in front of him. Will slowly slid his body to the floor and dropped his pistol, an image creeping into his mind...

He could suddenly see Kyle knocking Alyssa down onto a wooden floor. Alyssa appeared to be choking, saying something, but Will couldn't hear anything. He watched as Kyle kicked her in the ribs before snatching her back up to her feet. He couldn't control the anger that began to brew within him, the lust to kill this man that commanded him. And then he watched as Kyle pulled Alyssa's battered body across the floor and tied her arms up. Blood was dripping down her nose and the side of her face, dripping onto her shirt. Will's heart ached tremendously as he watched Kyle retrieve the pendant and rip it from Alyssa's neck. Alyssa was obviously in a lot of pain from her expression and before Kyle would take a step back, he struck the side of her face once more, whipping her head to the side. Will watched as Alyssa's body slowly hung in place, helpless and weak...and there wasn't a thing he could do but watch. He hurt for her. He hated to see her like this. He could only blame himself...

And then the image slowly changed to a dark view of the valley. He could see familiar landmarks and a destroyed landscape. The earth and pavement were split open throughout the area when suddenly, the earth began to erupt from those pits. Lava spilled from all the large tears in the valley, spewing from the very core of the earth. Fires began to consume the buildings and vegetation. The valley became a burning wasteland, a graveyard...

Will could feel himself clenching his teeth and he could hear a low, wicked whisper within his ear, "You will die..." followed by a loud, sudden bang, and the image quickly vanished...

A few more loud bangs were heard and Will opened his eyes. Wahkan was gone, but Kevin was now standing near the door with his pistol in his grasp, a look of pure shock covering his face.

"Were you just going to let that thing kill you?" Kevin gasped, lowering his pistol and approaching Will's stunned state.

Will slowly lowered his hands away from the sides of his head and looked around. His eyes were wide from the sudden shock and it took him a moment to collect himself as he took in a deep breath, sighing heavily. He eventually allowed his body to rest against the wall as he sat on the cool floor.

Kevin kneeled down next to him and picked up his pistol that he had dropped on the floor.

"Are you okay, Will?" he asked.

Will stared at the ground. "Yes..."

"What was that thing?"

Will finally looked at Kevin, wearing no expression. "Evil...in its purest form. Just like Dena had described."

Kevin looked around the room before turning his attention back to Will. The large creature that had Will pinned against the wall practically vanished in thin air, a black blur whipping out of the area in the blink of an eye.

"Alyssa and I had come across him in the forest after running into the other unit. I didn't want to say earlier, but we believe Uktena has been destroyed. We didn't see it, but we heard it. We were trying to cut through the forest to get here," Will stated.

"Hmm," Kevin mumbled, looking to the side. "But you called this creature here a *he*?" he asked, glancing back at him.

"That was Wahkan. He seems to have multiple forms. He is able to communicate telepathically, but if he comes to you in spirit like we have also seen, he can actually speak. He possesses Alyssa, and it seems like he doesn't want to cause her harm because he has only attacked me," Will replied and sighed. "I saw what Kyle did to her…"

"How?"

"I was shown…"

"Is she still alive?"

"I don't know."

Kevin took in a deep breath and handed Will his pistol. "Maybe we shouldn't sit here any longer and wonder. That thing could come back. Besides, I left Jessie in the other room. We need to move now…"

"I saw what's going to happen to this place, Kevin…What if we cannot find her in time?" Will asked and looked into Kevin's eyes.

"We will think about that when and *if* the time comes," Kevin stated and held out his hand.

Will grabbed it and Kevin helped him to his feet. He stared at him for a moment, his lips in a hard line.

"Why Alyssa, Will? Just tell me how you can deploy here and suddenly…" Kevin began to say and sighed, shaking his head. "I've seen the way you look at her…Please promise me, if we find her, you will *not* hurt her. I can see that she has become quite taken with you as much as I disapprove."

Will half smiled. "Let's just get the hell out of here, Kevin. We need to find her."

Kevin sighed and nodded, turning away to lead them back into the hallway and towards the room where Jessie waited. He knew this wasn't the time to talk about feelings, but it was a painful thorn in his side that continued to bug him.

Will hoped that Wahkan would stay at bay. He would do what he could to keep the menace from showing its wicked face towards the ones that Alyssa cared for the most even if it meant his death.

CHAPTER TWENTY-FIVE

J ESSIE WAS PACING AROUND THE room, her arms crossed when she suddenly heard Kevin and Will in the hallway. She sighed in relief and lowered her arms when they stepped into the room.

"I heard the gunshots...I was so scared..." she stated and paused.

"Everything is okay," Will reassured her.

"You seem so shaken," Jessie added, examining Will's strained expression.

Will took in a deep breath. "Wahkan has resurfaced. Alyssa and I encountered him in the forest earlier. He's here. That's why we shouldn't be here any longer. We have to move and get out of this facility."

Jessie's eyes rose. "Wahkan? How do you know...?"

"Trust me," Will replied and approached the set of the stairs in the back. All he could think about was the first encounter in the forest, and Alyssa's painstaking scream. How could they be rid of such an evil spirit? The plague was something beyond their control. They had to get out until it passed...

Kevin followed Will and Jessie quickly jumped to his side, stepping down the flight of the stairs. She was beginning to breathe heavily as the fear built up within her.

Will grabbed the handle to the door and pulled it open. It made a loud, bothersome screech as it echoed throughout the room. He carefully stepped into a short, brick corridor. It stretched to the left and into the sewers. Water flowed slowly down the sewer corridor in between sidewalks that stretched alongside it. The area was quiet except for the trickles of water pushing down its path.

Kevin and Jessie carefully stepped into the corridor, and Jessie's face grew grotesque. The area was warm and smelled of wastewater.

"Do we really have to go this way?" she asked.

"I know you don't want go back in the forest with the wolves," Kevin said and glanced at her. Jessie looked down as he continued, "If I remember correctly this should lead us to the control room. Hopefully that area isn't barricaded." He stepped around Will and continued forward.

Will approached the water's edge and examined down both sides of the sewer. The earth had shaken not long ago, but just for a few seconds.

Maybe just an aftershock...

He hoped just that. He carefully turned away and followed Kevin down the walkway.

Jessie held her nose and followed behind Will as they made their way down the tight path. Electricity had made up this segment of the sewers. Bright lights hung above and shined down on them, illuminating the path ahead. Jessie glanced behind her every few seconds or so. She dreaded being back in the sewers after traveling through them earlier. She was thankful that there was lighting, however. No dark shadows to excite her fear in the worst ways imaginable.

They carried on cautiously, remaining as quiet as the underground as they traveled further down the warm corridor with just their constant playback of images to keep them company. Kevin led the way, eventually halting once they reached another corridor that stretched to the right. A small bridge went over the water that flowed into the new area as it merged into the corridor in which they stood. The dark, murky water moved down the path slowly, pouring into the other system.

Jessie gulped and kept herself together as she watched Kevin examine the other corridor. It stretched into the distance, but what caught his attention was the flight of stairs on the right.

"Yea, that's it. That should take us up to the control room," Kevin stated.

"Good. I can't stand to be down here another minute," Jessie stated.

Will cleared his throat and began to follow Kevin to the set of stairs. Jessie followed close behind, continuing to keep a watchful eye behind them.

"Let me secure it first," Kevin stated once he stepped up the stairs and into the other corridor. It stretched towards a second flight of stairs. A metal door awaited them at the top.

Will nodded, holding onto his nine millimeter. He glanced back at Jessie and placed his finger to his lips. Jessie nodded and followed them towards the foot of the stairs. Kevin held his pistol close and carefully climbed up the stairs as quietly as he could. Will and Jessie waited at the bottom.

Kevin took in a deep breath and held it once he reached the door. He looked back at Will and nodded, motioning that he was ready. He gently placed his hand on the door handle and pushed down, slowly pushing the door forward. It opened slowly and made a soft screech. Kevin peered inside the small room, releasing his breath slowly. The area was cool and the floor and walls were made of concrete. A few pieces of mechanical equipment sat on the left with gauges on the side of them, and there was a hall on the right. The small room was quiet. Kevin relaxed himself and opened the door. He took a few steps into the room and lowered his pistol. He felt safe at the moment.

Will and Jessie were still waiting at the bottom of the stairs when Kevin peered down at them from the top.

"It's clear," he said.

Will lowered his pistol and allowed Jessie to go up first. He watched her for a moment before turning his attention back into the corridor he was in.

Alyssa...I will get you back. Smitherman will pay for what he did to you.

319

Will took in a deep breath and carefully climbed up the stairs. Kevin was standing near the corner of the hallway when he stepped into the room.

"Alright, let's get the hell out of this place," Will stated. He carefully closed the door behind him and nearly jumped out of his skin when he heard a loud gunshot burst into the room they were in. Kevin dove towards the floor, and Will quickly grabbed Jessie's arm and pulled her behind the wall near the mechanical equipment. Kevin crawled to where they were and aimed his pistol towards the dark hallway. His heart was racing away, his eyes widened in shock, and then he began to feel the sudden burn in his shoulder. Will held his pistol close, quickly switching the safety off. Jessie hugged the wall closely, tears making their way to her frightful eyes.

"Oh, shit...I'm hit," Kevin said and kept his composure as they heard a little snicker within the shadows of the hall.

Will's eyes widened even more. He was afraid to look down at Kevin below him, afraid to take his eyes off the hallway.

"So we run into each other once again, Will," the familiar voice said.

The sudden anger and burning adrenaline quickly washed over Will as he clenched his teeth. "Kyle," he stated firmly and paused, thinking about Alyssa. She had to be close.

"How dare you address me so informally, Sergeant First Class," Kyle stated casually and remained hidden within the darkness.

"You are no longer in command."

Will could practically hear the evil smile rise upon Kyle's face after that comment. "Is that so, Thompson?"

"Where is Alyssa?" Will asked and held his breath.

Kevin was breathing heavily, ignoring the constant burning in his shoulder. He continued to hold his pistol out, aimed and ready as steadily as he could.

"I wouldn't be so worried about Ms. Bennett, Thompson. She's already dead," Kyle responded.

Will felt his heart drop deep within his chest. His body began to tremble, but he held his ground. Jessie released a low gasp as the tears began to fall onto her cheeks.

"Oh, Thompson, you've broken one of my most important rules. You should've just carried on with the mission and..."

"Bullshit! There was never a mission. You just came here to set us up for failure so you could accomplish your own task. How could you, Captain...How could you kill all those innocent people at the station?" Will interrupted, his heart aching heavily.

"And Tidwell and McCallion as well as a few others? Simple. I put them out of their misery sooner rather than later. Don't you get it, Thompson? No one can relay the message regarding the true events that has taken place here to anyone. Therefore, no one can make it out of this town alive...*No one.*"

Will released a heavy exhale of breath, completely speechless.

Kyle laughed lightly. "And I'm afraid you have reached the end of the road as well. You have already lost this *war.*"

Kevin carefully pushed himself to his feet, his body shaking. "I'm tired of hearing this. He's a dead man..." he said under his breath.

Will placed his hand on Kevin's unwounded shoulder and quickly responded, "Wait. It's what he wants..."

"I don't care," Kevin said and before he could lunge towards the hall, a loud, blood curdling scream was heard within the shadows.

Will's eyes raised even more and Kevin held his ground as the painful cry suddenly subsided, followed with a haunting, scratchy growl. It sent chills down all of their spines as they remained hidden behind the wall, wai0ting, dreading the apparent monster that lurked within the darkness...

Alyssa remained hanging from the tight ropes that pinched and pulled the skin on her wrists. The pain was incredible, but she didn't have much fight left or the motivation to do anything about it. She felt her body continue to weaken. Her muscles were tight and sore, fatigue settling in. She had given up...

I'm going to die here...

She had allowed herself to accept this fate, but she was afraid that it wasn't going to change the outcome of the haunting plague that cursed Rockdale Valley. Captain Smitherman now had the red diamond.

Could it be true...We were actually set up by someone so close to the family? Brian Hall...Why...Why would you do this to us?

A tear crept into Alyssa's eye as she sighed, staring at the floor. Her heart was aching and her chest was tightening from the strain and stress of it all. But then she heard it once again, the scratchy growl coming from the darkest shadows in the barn. Her body tensed, her mind froze, but she slowly allowed herself to relax. Maybe she could end this...

Alyssa slowly moved her eyes away from the floor and looked around the dark barn. The bright flashes of lightning continued to stretch across the sky, flashing through the open windows, allowing her eyes to see through the shadows in the back. She scanned the area slowly, her eyes catching a glimpse of a dark figure as the lightning brightened the area again. Alyssa took in a deep breath and slowly lowered her head, staring back at the floor that was spotted with her blood. She closed her eyes, still able to see the bright lightning flashing continuously behind her eyelids. Another deep, low rumble of breath was heard, now closer than the last one. She knew Wahkan was approaching her. She could sense his presence clearly.

Alyssa took in a deep breath and released it heavily. She knew he was in front of her. "I know now...why you led me here...To punish me...to *corrupt* me...for what I did. So please...let us end this now. I don't have the heart to fulfill your task...Therefore, I sacrifice myself to you," she said softly, her eyes still closed.

Wahkan released another low growl and it seemed as if he was stepping off into the distance as it grew faint. Alyssa slowly opened her eyes, continuing to stare at the floor.

"We were set up..." she whispered and began to feel the similar immense pain erupt within her skull. Alyssa gasped and her body hung tightly from the rope, her muscles not willing to hold herself up as an image crept into her mind quickly...

"Ms. Bennett...I thought that was you," an older man stated as he approached her near the patrol car she stood by. She was just about to go inside the precinct as she watched Kevin disappear behind its doors.

"Um, do I know you?" she asked.

The older man stopped and stood near the curb, relaxing his appearance. He was wearing a nice business suit with a white shirt and tie. Alyssa had never seen him before. She was trying to figure out who he was.

"No, I'm afraid we never met. I do however work with a mutual friend. I'm Mr. Russell. I, ah, came across a case file and I thought you would like to take a peek at it. I think we could use your help."

Alyssa looked at the file he had in his hands and took in a deep breath, forgetting about this mutual friend he claimed to work with. "What is it about?" she asked curiously. She had never done detective work before, but it was something she was always interested in.

"This is classified information. It wasn't released to the public or the media. Please keep that in mind," Mr. Russell stated and handed her the manila folder.

Alyssa took it carefully and opened it. After reading the first sentence, her eyes widened and she quickly looked back at Mr. Russell. "This is about my brother?" she asked.

"Yes. It became a cold case after investigators were informed that Richard Bennett died from self inflicted wounds. They didn't find a letter, and investigators were told that he was suffering tremendously from depression and sleep deprivation."

"So why did it become a cold case? I know my brother was sick. I remember that..." Alyssa replied.

"Because we were given the coordinates of where your brother was before falling ill not only from a reliable source, but from the friend that was with him the night of May 7th, 2000."

Alyssa stared at the gentleman and looked away, trying to recall the memories before her brother committed suicide. She thought of the night he came home one evening, panic stricken. He had given her an odd gear shaped stone and told her to get rid of it. And she could remember when he had begged her not to go down there, which was confusing because she wasn't sure exactly where he and his friend had gone to that one weekend in the mountain, but she did have an idea.

"Why are you bringing this to my attention now?" Alyssa asked hesitantly.

"Your father wanted nothing to do with this after the investigation was closed, but...we believe we found the location in the mountain just recently. The entrance was hidden rather well. Someone barricaded it with rock and thick shrubbery..."

"Entrance to what exactly?"

"I think you already know, Ms. Bennett. You were the one that tried to persuade your father into believing, correct?"

"How do you know all of this?"

Mr. Russell smiled. "That is beside the point. You have a decision to make...whether to join your dad on this excavation next weekend and learn the truth to your brother's death, or turn your head away never knowing what truly happened. Your father is not aware of where we are going and its significance. You could be a very wealthy young lady...and you can finally live at peace with what happened those many years ago. You decide."

Alyssa's heart began to beat faster. She wanted to know what happened to her brother because she never felt that he was depressed back then. She began to feel after her father's persistent denial that he was right and that her brother was just obsessed with a story and got lost in his own world. Something obviously did happen that night when he and his friend went out there. Perhaps this would allow her father to see that she and her brother were right all along.

"So...this has something to do with...the legend?" Alyssa asked cautiously. She hated to even bring the term back up after forgetting about it. It was just an old, classic tale...

Mr. Russell smirked and remained silent. "Go...to your father's house. In the backyard there is a cherry blossom tree that you helped him plant long ago. To the left of it, not too deep within the earth,

*you will find the item your brother had given you before he passed...
Use it..."*

*Alyssa stared in shock and the image slowly faded to one at her
parents' house. She was standing on the back porch, her expression
strained, her eyes saddened. She was staring at the cherry blossom
tree in the backyard. The rain was sprinkling lightly on the lawn, but
it wasn't going to stop the determination that had built up within her.
Alyssa stepped onto the lawn and started walking towards the tree,
her stride quickening the closer she got to it. She eventually kicked
her feet and ran the last few remaining yards and collapsed to her
knees once she reached it. The tears were slowly making their way
down her cheeks, mixing with the rain that drizzled onto her skin. She
gasped and quickly began digging with all the strength she had in
her arms and hands, pulling up the grass and dirt and slinging it to
the side. After minutes of back straining labor, Alyssa felt something
hard eventually touch her fingertips. She continued to dig until she
was able to pull the rock out, the gear shaped stone. Alyssa held
it up, examining it closely, remembering the night her brother had
given it to her...*

Alyssa's eyes were wide from the scenes that played within her
mind as the barn slowly came back into view. It took her a moment
to realize where she was as she looked around, completely frozen
with shock.

"I lost so much of my memory...Oh my God, I remember
everything now..." Alyssa said and released a low gasp. "I was so
angry with my father for keeping it from me for this long. I wanted
to finally prove it to him after the case file I was able to read. And
Brian..."

Alyssa's jaw slowly dropped as her final vision flashed before
her eyes...

*Alyssa was standing at the entrance to the sacred cavern not too
deep within the cave. Her heart was beating away as she stared at
the makeshift keyhole carved within the stone wall. Alyssa carefully
placed the key within the keyhole and turned it, hearing a low click
and the sounds of gears turning. The door slowly opened halfway,*

allowing enough room for her to squeeze inside. She quickly removed the key and held onto it as she stepped inside the chamber. She carefully looked around the area, hearing the trickle of water washing through the small stream in the middle of the cavern. Colorful rocks lay embedded within the walls, glimmering brightly from the light she had in her other hand. She slowly made herself across the chamber and stream, approaching the rectangular rock. The only thing that ran through her head was the statement Mr. Russell had made before she took the file and left. "Get the prized stone, avenge your brother's fate..." And the image quickly changed...She could feel her father running out from the cave's entrance, carrying her closely. Her eyes flickered open. She could see Robert Armstrong and Brian Hall standing in the small meadow, their faces distraught.

"Damn it Brian! What have you done!" Robert shouted.

"Did she get it?" Brian asked.

James grit his teeth, shoving the two items he found near her in his pocket quickly. "No."

Brian stared at him for a moment as James continued, "If anything happens to her, you will pay..."

And the image quickly faded to one in the hospital room. Alyssa was resting, but she had already woken to the sound of her father's strained tone. Robert was there in the room with them. He was deeply saddened. His voice was shaky.

"I'm so sorry, James...I hope you understand. I didn't want to get involved in this, but I didn't have much of a choice. I...received threats that I couldn't ignore. I had no choice," Robert stated.

James sighed heavily. "I understand."

There was a brief period of silence before James said any more.

"I...I just hope she forgets all of this. I don't want her to follow in her brothers footsteps. I don't believe in that ridiculous story...I just..." he sighed and continued, "Never mind that...I just don't want my family to have any part in it. This place has been very peaceful for many years. We shouldn't have anything to do with this ancient Native American tale."

"I'm sure it's just a story, James. This will all blow over soon... and perhaps we should cut off all ties with Mr. Hall if we can help it. It will be difficult, but we cannot trust the man," Robert said.

"Yes," James agreed and the image slowly faded to one of Brian and his familiar face, yet his smile was morphing into an evil smirk, his eyes narrowing into a wicked stare...

The image quickly vanished and Alyssa was left staring at the dark barn, her eyes wide in shock. A low whisper was heard into her ears as she realized the playback was over.

"You...can live...forever..." the whisper stated and the dark shadow, the evil image of Wahkan, was gone.

His monstrous form was one thing, but his communication power was more than fearsome. It was painfully terrorizing.

Alyssa already knew what Wahkan wanted from her. Brian Hall must die...by her very own hands. If she allowed herself to enter into this evil world that Wahkan existed in, perhaps she could live forever, but in a way she didn't agree upon. She wanted to be rid of this man she and her father trusted in so much it hurt but not to join this evil realm.

Alyssa could practically feel her insides burning, erupting into hot flames. The pressure was building within her chest, tightening the space around her lungs, and suddenly without warning, the earth slowly began to quake. It was a sensation she thought she would never have to experience again.

Alyssa gasped and looked around as dirt and dust fell from the ceiling of the barn. It rained down upon her, dusting her skin and falling into her eyes. She closed them tightly and looked down until she felt the metal bar she hung from give way and fall down towards the floor. Her body fell towards the floor as well and she lied there, gasping for air. The adrenaline was already pumping steadily into her veins. Her heart rate had jumped into high gear, pumping rapidly.

Uktena? No...she's gone. I got to get out of here. I've got to find Will!

Alyssa clenched her teeth and sat herself up, carefully sliding the rope down the bar and pulling it off the end that had fallen. She brought the tight knot to her face and grabbed it with her teeth, slowly pulling it to loosen the grip from her tingling wrists and hands. She pulled and gripped with all of her might and finally loosened the knot just enough to pull it from her wrists. The blood quickly began pumping through them, and it didn't take too long for her to feel relief. The tingly sensation slowly began to dissipate. Alyssa breathed deeply, feeling her body and face ache from the beaten she had taken from Kyle earlier. She wasn't going to let it slow her down, however. She glanced at her rifle, sighing in relief that he hadn't taken it with him.

Alyssa crawled to it, pushing herself towards the one thing that could protect her from the traitors and monsters that lurked around this place. She grabbed the M4 and tossed the sling onto her shoulder, allowing the rifle to rest against her back once again. She slowly pushed herself to her feet, and walked towards the barn's doors. She fought back the agonizing pain and aches. They spread throughout her body like wildfire.

Alyssa forcefully pushed open the barn's door and stumbled out of it, examining her surroundings once again. The dark clouds were now rolling over the valley, the lightning stretching throughout them continuously. A hazy fog was now hovering over the lake in the distance, coating it thickly and stretching throughout the few rows of trees that stood near its banks.

Alyssa glanced towards the water, barely able to make much of it out from the fog as she slowly approached it, her body trembling uncontrollably. She breathed heavily and pushed forward until she made it to a section of Lake Trinity. A part of her urged to keep moving, but the other half wanted to collapse. And that was what she did. Her knees fell to the ground and she sat upon the back of her legs. She stared into the water and allowed her body to unwind and relax a moment. She couldn't believe that she was still alive…

"Will…" she whispered and closed her eyes, the sudden wave of emotions hitting her instantly. The tears were quickly making their way to her eyes and onto her checks as she sat there in immense pain, suffering…praying…

CHAPTER TWENTY-SIX

WILL WAS STILL FROZEN AGAINST the wall in the small room, the blood curdling cry still echoing throughout his mind. Silence had returned to the area, but the threat of danger lingered.

"We need to check it out," Kevin whispered.

Jessie gasped. "No..." she whispered back and remained kneeling against the wall, hugging it for comfort.

Will looked down and took in a deep breath. "We have to. We can't stay here, and we can't back track either. Just wait here, Jessie... unless you know how to use a gun."

Jessie quickly shook her head. "I...I don't feel comfortable around firearms."

Kevin glanced at her. "Wait here then," he stated. He slowly took a step around the wall and held his pistol out, aimed steadily towards the dark hall. Will gently placed Alyssa's pistol beside Jessie, carefully retrieving his rifle. He looked back at her and then back at the pistol. "Just in case," he said softly and turned away, stepping around the wall as well.

Jessie stared at the gun, becoming more terrified as she remained alone in the small, cool room.

Kevin was inching closer to the darkness and carefully retrieved his maglite. He turned it on and shined it towards the floor, witnessing the aftermath of a brutal death. Blood covered the floor, smearing down the hall and around another corner of the large control room. Will followed Kevin into the hallway and together they inched towards the large room. Their breaths exhaled slow and steady and their bodies moved quietly and swiftly. The anxiety was pulsing through their chests, and the closer they got to the control room, the more it elevated.

Kevin gulped and held his arm out, motioning Will to stop. A strange sound was coming from around the corner, and the strong scent of blood grew stronger. Will carefully retrieved a grenade and slid it in the chamber. The soft sound sent the hairs on Kevin's arms standing straight up as the strange gurgling noise stopped. It didn't take long for the heavy footsteps to start echoing in the control room, coming closer to the hall they stood in.

"Steady yourself..." Will whispered.

Kevin was breathing heavily, but kept his composure as the large beast stepped around the corner. Its head was lowered and its nostrils were flared. Its thick hide contained a few injuries. Blood had dried around one side of its body.

Will released his breath quickly and aimed the grenade launcher towards the angra. It slowly raised its head, glaring at them with its bright eyes. A low growl echoed from its lungs and out between its lips as it continued to stare at them.

"Now!" Will yelled and fired the grenade at the vile beast.

The loud explosion and wave of energy pushed against Kevin and Will as they began firing their firearms. The angra had been knocked to the ground from the force, screaming ferociously as it squirmed and jumped back to its feet.

Kevin pointed the light back towards it and pulled the trigger to his pistol repeatedly until it clicked. He quickly replaced the clip as Will slid another grenade into the launcher.

"Get back!" Will gasped and aimed his rifle at the angra as it released another piercing cry and bolted towards them. Kevin pushed himself back and continued to fire, his eyes widening in fright. Will fired the grenade and the explosion pushed the angra back to the ground. The wave of energy from the blast pushed against Will forcefully. He closed his eyes and fell back, catching himself with the palm of his hand. Kevin reached out and grabbed his arm, pulling him back to his feet as the angra squirmed and wailed.

"Finish it," Kevin gasped.

Will reloaded his launcher with the last grenade he had and slowly aimed it at the beast. The angra thrashed its body, continuing to scream. Its large teeth glistened from the light shining from Kevin's flashlight as he continued to hold it steady. Will took in a deep breath and pulled the trigger, firing the grenade at the beast. The explosion pushed the angra a few feet, sending a wave of heat in their direction. Its cry was loud, but it faded fast. Silence returned to the room, and the angra lay motionless against the floor of the hallway. Will released his breath heavily and glanced back at Kevin. His light continued to shine on the lifeless beast, his pistol still aimed directly at its hide.

"It's dead," Will stated.

"Are you sure?"

"Yes."

Kevin slowly lowered his pistol. "Jessie?" he called out.

The sounds of feet shuffling and scurrying to the hallway were heard as she hurried around the corner, stopping short from the blood. Her eyes were wide, her face full of fright.

"It's alright now," Will said and looked back at the angra. He slowly began making his way towards it, stepping around all the blood.

Kevin followed slowly, keeping a distance as Jessie quickly stepped up behind him.

"Oh my…" she whispered, staring at the large, monstrous beast on the floor.

Kevin remained quiet and watched Will stand over the beast, examining it carefully. Will slowly nodded and looked towards the left. His mouth dropped halfway and he began making his way around the corner slowly.

Kevin assumed the body of Kyle was lying around the corner. He kept his flashlight facing towards the control room as he and Jessie approached it, stepping around the body of the angra.

Jessie's heart was beating at a fast pace as she pushed herself up against the wall, getting as far from the monster as she could. She slid carefully around it, keeping her eyes on it as she took a few steps into the large room. There were many monitors and terminals with dials on them rowed in the room neatly. Towards the back were a couple of offices and bathrooms.

"Damn..." Kevin stated, approaching Will as he stood over the mutilated remains of his former commander. "This was him. I could never forget this face."

Jessie glanced at them and towards the body on the floor. Her heart sank and she quickly backed herself towards one of the computer monitors, watching closely.

"He got what was coming to him. Why I couldn't see his twisted plot, I don't know. But I'll never deny the possibility of it again," Will said and kneeled down beside the body. There were large wounds and tears through his torso and smaller wounds across his shoulder. His eyes were half open, a glassy appearance to them.

Kevin watched as Will gently removed a chain from his torn vest pocket. He brought the pendant to him, carefully standing back up.

"Is that..." Kevin asked and paused.

"Yes. Alyssa's pendant."

"She could be here. We have to look around this control room," Kevin said and shined his light around the area.

Will looked around as well, noticing Jessie's grotesque expression. He took in a deep breath, placing the pendant into a vest pocket. "Why don't you wait for us by the door. We need to clear this area."

Jessie quickly nodded and approached the small door, resting her body against it.

Kevin hurried to the back and scanned the offices while Will checked the bathrooms. After a few moments of searching, Kevin stepped out. "All clear," he stated and looked at Will.

"It's clear. She's got to be around this area though," Will replied and approached the door where Jessie waited. Kevin carefully followed.

"The helicopter should be here any time now," Will added and pushed open the side door.

It opened with ease and he stepped out onto the pavement, facing the front of the water treatment plant. Jessie and Kevin followed him and examined the vacant lot. The helicopter was to the right. There were only a couple of cars near the fence line, abandoned, and the gate to the plant was open. Its gravel road stretched alongside a large field and veered to the right, stretching over a hill towards the street. A lake was now in view. It was barely visible from the large rows of trees that surrounded a section of the field near an old, wooden barn. A fog was hovering over it, thickening as the night progressed.

"Where the hell is everybody?" Will stressed and took a few steps towards the lone helicopter.

Kevin remained quiet, examining the area. The lights outside were on and the lightning was stretching across the sky brightly. A couple of drops of rain fell against their faces and the wind brushed against their bodies gently.

"I'm going to check out this helicopter," Kevin said and began walking towards it.

Jessie followed, stepping around Will as he stared towards the trees. Something had caught his attention. He glanced at Kevin as he reached the helicopter and opened its door. Jessie stood beside it and watched him. Will approached them and stood at the back of the helicopter. His anxiety was rising.

"Are you alright?" Jessie asked, her arms crossing.

"Yea...I just need a moment. I'll be right back," Will said and began walking to the gate. Jessie watched him and sighed.

"What's going on?" Kevin asked after a moment.

"Nothing," Jessie replied and looked at Kevin as he stepped out of the helicopter. "I think Will just needs a breather," she added.

"He better not be gone for too long..."

"He looks to be in pain, Kevin."

Kevin carefully sat down and looked around the area once more. He sighed heavily and placed his hand over his face. "Well I'll let him be."

He was in pain too. He hated being on borrowed time with the fact that they may not find Alyssa. Jessie nodded, deeply saddened. She hoped that the helicopter would arrive soon so that they could finally be free from the disaster as the rain continued to drizzle down upon them.

Alyssa had dried her tears, but she remained sitting by the water's edge. Her mind and body were relaxed, but the pain was still there. She took in a deep breath and released it slowly. She knew it was time to get moving, but she dreaded traveling alone once again especially with the approaching storm. The rain had already begun, but the real storm had yet to arrive. Alyssa groaned and suddenly, her body shook in fright from the sound of a twig snapping. Something wasn't too far in the distance from behind her.

This is it...I'm finished...

Alyssa's heart began to jump once more as she carefully pushed herself to her feet. There was no way she could stand up to Kyle and survive this time around.

Alyssa slowly looked behind her, turning her body halfway around. The fog had spread through the trees near her, but something was standing in the distance, and the only thing she could focus her attention on was the barrel of a pistol staring back at her. Everything else was a blur. Alyssa released a low gasp, and the gun slowly lowered to the side. She began to breathe heavily as she moved her eyes away from the firearm and towards the eyes of the man that held onto it. Her eyes began to tear up as the sudden rush of relief washed over her. There, standing amongst the trees was Will. It was a face she didn't expect to see again.

"Alyssa..." he said, completely shocked.

The tears began to fall as she turned her body to face him. "Will," she said, her voice shaking.

Will didn't hesitate. He quickly ran to her and Alyssa was unable to take too many steps forward before Will dropped the pistol in his grasp and threw his arms around her, holding her tight. Alyssa placed her arms around him and buried her face into his vest, allowing the tears to fall heavily. Will breathed deeply, continuing to hold up her weary body.

"It's okay...I got you. You are safe now," Will said, comforting her for a moment before gently pulling away to examine her injuries. Her face was bruising in areas, and the rain had rinsed some of the blood away from her cheeks, chin, and neck. Her body trembled from pain and fatigue.

"Goodness...Look at you," Will said, placing his hand under her chin, moving her head side to side. "Please forgive me...I should have listened to you."

"It's okay, Will. It's over," Alyssa replied and took in a deep breath, looking back into Will's calm eyes. She didn't want to relive the pain, and she didn't want to speak of the past.

"He will never hurt you again. That I can promise you," Will said.

Alyssa looked confused.

"The angra finally finished him off."

Alyssa slowly nodded and watched Will's expression change to sadness. He sighed, shaking his head. "Alyssa, we are now on borrowed time, but there is something that I need to tell you."

Alyssa was quiet and patient, waiting for his response as he looked into her eyes the same way he had done in the chapel at the cathedral. There was some urgency behind the statement that made her a bit nervous.

"I ran into your father. Alyssa, he was alive," he said.

Alyssa's face lit up. "My dad..." she said and looked around Will, a bit of hope exciting her. She looked back at him and the wonderful feeling quickly faded.

Will's expression was remorseful as he stated, "I'm sorry, Alyssa, he didn't make it..." and before he could finish, Alyssa collapsed, sobbing heavily as her body fell limp towards him. Will struggled to keep her up so he allowed himself to fall to his knees with her. He pulled her back into his arms, feeling the strong emotions releasing from Alyssa's body. She closed her eyes and cried, resting her head against his vest once again. Will felt completely helpless. There was nothing he could do to stop the pain that she was experiencing in and out. So he waited. He closed his eyes and released a heavy sigh. After a few moments, he took in a deep, steady breath.

"I'm so sorry, Alyssa…There was…there was nothing that I could do," he stated and waited for her to calm down. Her tears continued, but the painful cries eventually ceased, and she was able to calm herself.

"I was able to talk to him for a bit," Will added and waited as Alyssa gently pulled herself away. Her face was flushed, and it hurt him to see her in so much pain.

"What did he say?" she asked.

Will rubbed her shoulders and took in a deep breath. "You were betrayed by a close family friend."

Alyssa sighed and looked away, nodding. "I know…I remember everything now," she said. "I was paid another visit from Wahkan. I know now what I must do."

Will watched her carefully as she looked back into his eyes. "It *was* Brian. I denied the possibility of that. We were set up. We were *betrayed*. Now I must find him. But Kyle…he took the diamond. They have won," she said.

"No…" Will quickly replied and pulled an item from his vest pocket. He didn't want to tell Alyssa the awful images he saw when Wahkan had cornered him earlier.

Alyssa watched Will caress the pendant and hand it to her. She took it, examining it closely.

"I found it on Kyle. And your father also gave me this. It's what Mr. Hall was looking for," Will added and pulled the key out from another vest pocket.

Alyssa's eyes widened as she took the gear shaped stone and looked at it. "It's the key," she said and looked into Will's eyes.

"They haven't won yet. We still have a chance," he said, reassuring her. He looked away and retrieved his pistol from the ground. He carefully handed it to her as she took it, looking back into his eyes.

Alyssa slowly nodded, holstering the pistol and taking in a deep breath. "Well…what are we waiting for? Let's get out of here," she said and before she could attempt to move, Will held her tightly.

Alyssa rested on her knees once again, looking back into Will's eyes concernedly.

"Alyssa...I thought I wasn't going to find you in time. I thought I was never going to see you again...just when you were beginning to grow on me," he said and paused, hoping she wouldn't turn away.

The bothersome anxiety began to spill into Alyssa's gut, but she refused to break the gaze. She was unsure what to say, though she could already tell that Will was reading her body language, the words hidden behind her eyes. There was nothing more he had to add to his statement. He slowly placed his hand on her cheek, caressing it gently as he leaned towards her and pressed his lips against hers.

CHAPTER TWENTY-SEVEN

THE RAIN CONTINUED TO DRIZZLE softly onto the northern valley, the dark clouds pushing northeast at a slow pace. The area began to cool quickly, and the lightning began to intensify near the mountains, the low roll of thunder echoing in the distance. Kevin was still sitting in the helicopter, his patience wearing thin. Jessie remained standing nearby as she watched the approaching storm.

Kevin looked towards the road that was located just over the hill. His sense of hearing was keen. The sound of a fast approaching vehicle was faintly heard. Jessie was oblivious. She continued to gaze towards the mountains of the west.

"Do you hear that?" he asked, quickly standing up

Jessie looked back at him, uncrossing her arms. She had allowed the rain to drench her hair as it lay heavily against her shoulders.

"What is it?" she asked and followed his gaze towards the street. She listened carefully and her expression lit up. "It's a car..."

"Yes, it is!" Kevin said and took a few steps towards the gravel road that led away from the water treatment plant and towards the street below.

Jessie was about to follow until something disrupted their footing. A soft quake was felt deep below the earth's crust, shaking and rattling the ground underneath their feet. Kevin quickly became alarmed and stopped. Jessie held herself steady, arms out, watching everything around her.

"Okay, where the hell is Will?" Kevin asked.

"He, ah…" Jessie stuttered and looked towards the field. "He went towards the lake I believe."

Kevin pushed forward, stumbling here and there as he approached the gravel past the gate. Jessie carefully followed and watched as lights appeared over the hill. A large humvee soon rolled over it, pushing gravel and rock out from beneath its tires.

"Over here!" Kevin yelled and stopped, waving his arms.

The earth slowly stopped shaking, and Kevin glanced around him and back towards the oncoming humvee. Jessie quickly met his side and looked towards the lake, watching two figures appear out of the fog that blanketed the area. They were jogging towards them. Jessie immediately recognized Will from the uniform, but it took her a moment to recognize the other. She had wounds and bruises on her face and her clothing was extremely battered.

The humvee quickly came to a stop once it reached Kevin and a familiar face was seen. A young soldier quickly jumped out of the passenger's seat and jogged to him. His skin and clothing was smothered in dirt as if he had crawled out from beneath a pile of rubble.

"Well, isn't it Officer Headley."

"Evan…" Kevin stated and looked at the two soldiers that got out of the humvee. Their faces were unrecognizable and full of exhaustion.

Jessie looked back at the soldiers about to say something, but she paused, awestruck to see the soldier that had gotten her out of City Hall.

"Evan…I thought we would never catch back up with you," she stated.

Evan took in a deep breath. "Glad to see you are still in one piece, ma'am."

"Watkins!" Will shouted, as he and Alyssa jogged to them.

Kevin turned around and felt his heart almost jump out from his chest. "Alyssa!" he gasped and quickly met her at the edge of the gravel.

Evan watched as Jessie approached him, looking back at Will and Alyssa, smiling.

"Goodness...Are you alright?" Kevin asked, looking at the wounds on Alyssa's face.

"I'll be fine, I promise," she replied.

Will patted her shoulder and approached Evan, extending his hand. Evan grabbed it, shaking it firmly. The two other soldiers grouped with him.

One nodded towards Will. "Sergeant First Class, the name's Private Bevins, National Guard."

Will nodded towards him and looked at the older soldier next to him. "Cooper," the soldier said, his face flushed.

"What happened?" Will asked, turning his attention back to Evan.

Evan glanced at Cooper. "We are all that is left, I'm afraid. The Major was able to radio it back in before he passed. He had requested an airstrike. The angras are everywhere and a part of the valley has already collapsed. It has begun..." he said and looked behind him, pointing towards the south. Dark smoke was raising high towards the sky, barely visible in the darkness.

Will's eyes widened and he glanced at Alyssa as she and Kevin spoke.

"Do we have an ETA for the evac chopper?" he asked and looked back at Evan.

Jessie watched carefully, trying to keep her composure.

"No, but it should be any time now," Evan replied.

Will took in a deep breath and looked at Alyssa. She glanced at him, seeing the concern from her peripheral vision. Kevin looked at him as well and followed Alyssa as she approached Will and the soldiers standing near him.

Alyssa nodded towards Evan. "Good to see you again," she stated.

"You too, ma'am," Evan replied.

"What happened?" Alyssa asked, looking at Will.

Will hesitated and before any words could exit his mouth, the sounds of blades chopping the air were suddenly heard far in the distance. He looked towards the east across the field, seeing a small light coming towards them.

Jessie gasped and brought her hands to her face. She couldn't be happier to hear that sound. Will's heart fluttered, and he sighed heavily in relief. Alyssa and Kevin stared towards the chopper.

"This is it..." Will said and looked at Alyssa.

She smiled and took a place by his side. Kevin watched as she gently grabbed Will's hand and waited for the helicopter to make its landing. As the helicopter slowed to a hover above them, a look of confusion began to form on Will's face.

"That's not one of ours..." Cooper stated, watching the helicopter slowly lower itself to the pavement.

Alyssa's heart began to beat faster, her anxiety level rising quickly. Kevin stepped up beside her.

"It's a Blackhawk," Will said and glanced at Cooper.

"We were expecting a Lakota for the evac."

Will looked back at the Blackhawk as it touched the ground in the field near them, its blades rapidly spinning.

"Isn't a helicopter a helicopter? These guys can still get us out of here, right?" Jessie asked.

No one looked at her or said a word. Everyone stared as the engine turned off and the blades began to slow from their rapid spin. Jessie sighed and crossed her arms, waiting nervously.

As soon as the blades came to a stop and the engine was silenced, the door to the Blackhawk slid open. Two soldiers stepped out of the vehicle, rifles in hand. Will squinted his eyes, examining their uniforms closely. One was injured, but was holding his ground steady. Will immediately recognized him from the hospital. He was one of the young soldiers in the conference room with Sergeant Brad Kennedy. How he escaped from the collapse is miraculous. The other soldier he did not recognize. Both took a few steps forward and stopped. Kevin slowly retrieved his pistol, keeping it at his side. And then someone else slowly stepped out of the helicopter. His nice business suit was sharp and easily recognizable as Will's eyes widened.

341

"I ran into this man at the hospital..." he stated and heard a low gasp from Alyssa. He quickly looked at her, seeing her eyes widen in shock.

"Brian..." she whispered and retrieved her pistol, quickly aiming it at him. The two soldiers suddenly aimed their rifles and held their ground.

"Do not fire," the man said firmly as he stepped in between the two soldiers.

Will retrieved his rifle and carefully aimed, shaken at the fact that he had to aim his weapon at his own brothers. Cooper and Bevins retrieved their weapons but refused to aim, completely shocked from the situation they were witnessing. Jessie slowly stepped back and away from the tension, claiming a spot beside the humvee, terrified.

"What's going on!" Bevins shouted.

"You do not understand! Keep back!" Will shouted, staring directly at Mr. Hall.

Evan kept his footing and retrieved his nine, refusing to aim it.

Brian stood casually, examining their faces, smiling. "Ah... Sergeant First Class Thompson, I see you have found someone I have been looking for," he stated.

Alyssa looked at Will, recalling his comment a moment ago.

"Alyssa...my dear, come with me so I can get you out of this place," Brian stated and held out his hand.

Alyssa could feel the rage building within her, the sudden wave of energy washing over her. Her eyes began to burn once again, and she could feel her strength intensifying, but she held her ground nice and steady. "I'm not going anywhere with you, Brian."

Brian slowly lowered his hand. "Alyssa, you've been like a daughter to me. I meant no harm to you..."

"You lie...You didn't care what was going to happen to me or my family!"

Brian sighed softly, shaking his head. "This cavern outside Rockdale Valley is...supernatural, mysterious...Imagine the possibilities. We wanted to study its power, but it seemed as if a certain *family*, a certain *bloodline* could safely enter this forbidden chamber..." he said and paused, smiling. "Yours."

Alyssa breathed heavily, her pistol shaking in her grasp. Will gulped, continuing to aim his rifle at the soldiers next to him. Kevin was speechless, but steady as he held onto his pistol tightly.

"Why my family?" Alyssa asked hesitantly.

"You share a descendant of the tribe. I assume your father left that little detail out too."

Alyssa gasped.

Only a native could open this door...That's why my brother and I were able to get in...Wahkan isn't trying to harm me. I took the stone, which resulted in the plague and the reason why Wahkan has possessed me. My brother was not depressed, nor suicidal. He couldn't handle the torture...the same torture that I have endured in my dreams...

"So...this power and these stones were so important to you that you would allow a family to be cursed? A family so close to you... Do you remember what happened to my family when my brother killed himself?"

"Your brother's fate definitely shook this town...Unfortunately, he wasn't as strong as you, my dear," Brian replied.

Tears began to accumulate in Alyssa's eyes. "You...do not know what this has done to me. You lie. I bet you were the one that got my brother to go there, to become involved with this legend. You thought he could get you the red diamond. Of course you or anyone else couldn't go in, you'd die! You selfish pig...You didn't realize that you were going to open the gateway to hell, did you?" she asked and clenched her teeth, feeling the rage boiling within her.

Brian stared at her for a moment and slowly smiled. "We already have what we came for...I'll give you one last chance. Leave them. I will get you out of this valley before it erupts."

Evan slowly raised his nine. He was beginning to see the truth.

"No...You don't have anything, Brian," Alyssa said.

Will smiled, continuing to aim steadily. "Kyle is dead, Mr. Hall," he stated firmly.

Brian stared at them, his smile fading. Alyssa, Will, and Kevin held their ground. Evan slowly stood by Will and took in a deep, steady breath.

"You lost this war, Brian," Alyssa said and the earth slowly began to shake.

Brian smiled once again. "No my dear, I'm afraid you and your friends have," he replied and looked at the two soldiers beside him, nodding towards the helicopter. He glanced back at Alyssa. "You had your chance."

Alyssa remained in place and watched as Brian and the two soldiers quickly got back into the helicopter. She lowered her pistol and watched as the engine roared to life and the blades started to spin. Will lowered his rifle and kept his footing as Kevin and Evan holstered their pistols.

"It's happening again, and they are going to leave us here!" Bevins shouted.

"What the hell was all that about!" Cooper gasped and the engine to the helicopter got louder as it slowly began to lift itself into the air.

Kevin turned and watched the Blackhawk carefully, making sure no one was going to fire down at them.

"A conspiracy," Alyssa stated and looked at Will as the earth began to shake violently, the wicked whispers returning to their ears.

Will's eyes slowly widened. "It can't be…"

Jessie stood up and held onto the vehicle as she watched Evan and the other two soldiers lean against it. Will carefully grabbed Alyssa and held her steady. Kevin looked away and towards the field, watching the earth tear apart.

"It's happening…" Will said. "After the waning crescent rises… the land will be taken by the pits of the earth, the valley will burn."

Alyssa felt a wave of emotion rush through her as she looked into his eyes. Will stared back into hers and heard a gasp from Kevin.

"It's not over yet!" Evan yelled and Alyssa glanced towards the field as the earth pushed upward, and the large head of Uktena came out from beneath it.

Alyssa's eyes widened, her mouth dropping. Will still held onto her tightly as they watched Uktena pull most of her body out from the gap in the earth and grab a hold of the tail end of the Blackhawk, crushing it with her jaws. They watched, immobilized with shock and fear as the helicopter erupted into bright, hot flames. The fire and pieces of the helicopter came crashing down onto the field, and the dragon slowly turned her head towards them below. Her thick hide had changed to red hues and her eyes were glazed a milky white.

"The end is here..." Alyssa whispered and Will shoved her towards the gravel road.

"Everybody go!" Will yelled and they began running towards the street below. Cooper and Bevins quickly leaped into the humvee with Evan taking gunner. Jessie jumped into the humvee before they sped around, moving towards the street. Kevin ran behind Will and Alyssa, gasping for air as the dragon released a loud, painful cry. The scream echoed throughout the valley, and Alyssa ran and leaped onto the pavement, quickly turning around to look at the beast that remained partially in the ground. Its arms and hands gripped the grassy terrain, its head lowering to stare at them below. The humvee stopped beside the street, and Evan turned the mini gun towards the dragon, holding down the trigger.

"Don't stop now!" Will shouted.

Alyssa looked at him and Kevin and nodded as Uktena released another ear piercing cry. "Go...I'm right behind you!" she said and watched as Kevin and Will began running down the street towards the park, the humvee quickly following. Evan released the trigger and watched as Alyssa turned herself to the dragon, reaching into her pocket.

She glanced back towards Will. "Goodbye..." she whispered and looked back at the dragon. She pulled the pendant out and held her arms out, staring deep into the dragon's white eyes.

"It's over..." she whispered and closed her eyes, hearing the sounds of jet engines now roaring in the distance, coming closer with each second that ticked by.

Alyssa kept her eyes closed and she could feel the tears pushing against her eyelids when a sudden relief was lifted from her shoulders, a soft whisper echoing in her ear, "Restore the sacred stone..." And the heavy burden was lifted away, washing away from her very soul. Her heart skipped a beat and she released a low gasp, keeping her eyes closed.

Richard...

But then she heard something unfamiliar, the sounds of something swooshing into the air at a fast pace. Alyssa suddenly opened her eyes as a strong forced suddenly knocked into her, pushing her over the hill the road curved around. She gasped and watched as two missiles propelled into Uktena's side, erupting into large flames. Two F-16s suddenly flew overhead, turning around for another shot. Will was holding onto Alyssa after pushing her over the edge. They fell onto the grassy hill and began rolling uncontrollably to the bottom. Alyssa gasped and eventually rolled to a stop. She gasped for air and pushed up on her arms as she looked towards the sky. Uktena's loud cry was different. She was dying...

"What are you doing!" Will yelled and crawled to her, grabbing her arms, looking deep into her tearful eyes.

"I can end this, Will...I heard my brother..."

"You don't understand Alyssa...The word has gotten out. The U.S Air Force is in route to release a tactical nuke. They are going to blow this place to hell!"

Alyssa's eyes widened. "Will, Wahkan is gone..."

Will stared at her and looked towards the sky as the F-16s returned, releasing more missiles. They propelled rapidly through the air, slamming into Uktena once more. The explosion brightened the atmosphere, a sudden wave of heat pushing against their skin. The two jets quickly flew by and continued around the valley, soon disappearing from view. Alyssa clenched her teeth from the loud, painful cry and watched as another humvee drove over the hill and through rows of trees before reaching them on the bed of grass.

"Get in!" a soldier yelled. Will quickly stood and pulled Alyssa to her feet. She glanced behind her, staring towards a few trees as she could feel *his* presence. The dark shadow, barely visible, stood there, silent and still.

"Come on!" Will gasped and Alyssa looked away, nodding. They both pushed towards the humvee and Will opened the back door, allowing Alyssa to take a seat. He jumped in next to her and closed the door, looking at the unfamiliar soldiers in the front.

"Where the hell did you two come from?" Will asked.

"We were on our way to the extraction point, saw the other humvee on the side of the road with a civilian standing by it. The soldier at gunner said that you two were down here and to grab you guys. We have a pilot. That's our helicopter up there," the driver said and quickly sped up the hill.

Will sighed in relief and looked at Alyssa. "We are going to get out of this hell after all," he said.

Alyssa was breathing heavily, staring into Will's eyes. Her body was experiencing a wave of emotions. She turned and looked towards the beast as they drove over the hill and across the street. The dragon was slowly slipping into the bottom of the pit, wailing, thrashing. Her loud cries shot through the humvee, bouncing through the glass. Will took Alyssa's hand and squeezed it. She looked away from the window and at Will, recalling the time she met him and what they had endured together. The sadness of losing her father just recently pained her, but it made her feelings for Will stronger. He was there at the time of his death, and he was still standing by her side.

Alyssa looked towards the water treatment plant, seeing the blades to the lone helicopter spinning away. The relief she felt now was like no other. They were about to be on their way out of Rockdale Valley.

Alyssa followed Will out of the humvee once it stopped in the large parking lot. Kevin was waiting near the helicopter, motioning them to come. Jessie and the others were already inside. Kevin grabbed Alyssa's shoulder once she reached him and squeezed it. "We are finally getting out of here," he said. She could see the relief in his eyes, the happiness, but she could also see the sorrow behind it for the fallen.

347

As Alyssa pulled herself into the helicopter, Kevin met Will's gaze and extended his hand. Will grabbed it and held onto the frame of the helicopter, putting one foot in.

"I was wrong about you…You're a good man. Thank you, Will," Kevin said and Will nodded, pulling himself inside so the others could get in.

Will carefully claimed his spot beside Alyssa and waited as the others climbed in and got situated. Kevin sat beside Evan and across from Will and Alyssa. The helicopter didn't waste any time as its blades spun rapidly and lifted them into the air. Alyssa took in a deep breath and looked out the window. Uktena was gone, but the large tear in the earth was bubbling. Red and yellow liquid pulsated around the tear, spewing upwards.

"Good God…" Evan said, noticing it as well.

As the helicopter reached a safe height, it began to push away from the valley, moving east. Alyssa continued to look out the window as she stared at the fires that were consuming the southern valley. The land had torn even more so, and the lava was already making its way to the surface, eating everything in its path. Alyssa slowly looked away and sighed heavily, resting her head onto Will's shoulder.

"The Air Force has arrived," the pilot called out and continued out of the valley. Alyssa refused to look out the window as she closed her eyes. She didn't want to see what was going to happen next. Will rested his head against the back of the seat and glanced out the window, looking at the oncoming B-52.

"Why did the F-16s come when they were already planning to use the nuke?" he asked, glancing at Evan.

"They were made aware about the large beast under the valley… They were going to attempt to destroy it before destroying the town just to be certain," Evan stated.

"I see," Will replied, thinking about the secrecy regarding the legend.

"Major Lyle was able to get it back to command. The government is now involved."

"I'm not surprised," Will replied and looked away, thinking about Brian and his unexpected death. He took in a deep breath and released it slowly. He was thankful for being one of the two surviving from his group, surviving from the treacherous plot. He released a heavy gust of air through his nostrils and looked back out the window. He wasn't sure what was next for them as they fled to Bethesda, Maryland.

The helicopter pushed away from the valley getting to a safe distance once the B-52 released its nuclear weapon. The large bomb slowly dropped towards the center of the valley and erupted just above the ground. The wave of energy stretched out for miles, pushing against the helicopter, shaking it for just a few seconds as the valley crumbled from the shockwave, fire erupting throughout it. Within eight seconds, Rockdale Valley was quickly erased from the map.

CHAPTER TWENTY-EIGHT

ALYSSA'S EYES WERE FLICKERING OPEN to a familiar scent, one she truly dreaded. She was trying to recall the dream she was having as her eyes slowly opened. She could remember Kayla being there with her, but the area was dark. She recalled seeing a beach with small waves and the feeling of sand beneath her feet. Will and Kevin were there also, but the sight of a hospital room made her stomach cringe after the serenity she was experiencing. She looked around and her eyes finally met Will's. He was standing beside her with a few bandages around his arm and head.

"You fell asleep on the way over here," he stated and smiled.

"Where are we?" Alyssa asked.

"Walter Reed National Military Medical Center."

Alyssa absorbed the information and looked away.

"It's going to be okay, Alyssa. The nightmare is over."

"Where are the others?" she asked.

"They are okay. Some have already been discharged. But you have a few broken ribs and many contusions. You also need stitches," Will stated and placed his hands on the bed, leaning against it. "They want to keep you here for a bit."

Alyssa sighed heavily. "I don't like hospitals."

"Me neither, but we need to make sure you're okay."

"What about you?" Alyssa asked, looking at the bandage on his head.

"A concussion. I'll be fine," Will replied and looked towards the door as it opened.

Will immediately recognized the Secretaries of Defense and Homeland Security. A few of their security agents squeezed into the room as well, one closing the door behind them.

"Mr. Secretary..." Will stated, looking at the Secretary of Defense, Damian Bashore.

"Sergeant First Class William Thompson. I was told you were in command of the 9th Army Special Forces Group deployed to Rockdale Valley. I need to know exactly what happened," Damian said.

Alyssa breathed deeply and glanced at Will as he looked back at her. "Mr. Secretary...I'll do my best to explain this. There is a lot of information."

"Understood."

"What occurred in Rockdale Valley was the work of an ancient curse. A plague consumed that town, releasing hellish creatures. The plague would've never occurred, however, if it wasn't for one of your agents, Mr. Brian Hall," Will stated.

Damian's eyebrows rose as the Secretary of Homeland Security, Allison Jennings, crossed her arms.

"A *curse*? We were made aware of possible terrorism, and that is why we sent your group armed just in case. The National Guard as well as the Army assisted with the search and rescue and the evacuations. We were also informed of the instability of the land, and that there was a magma reservoir under the valley. It suddenly had some sort of effect on certain electronic devices which is why we ordered the no fly zone," Allison stated.

"Well, this magma reservoir was going to be the cover up once the valley collapsed and burned Madam Secretary..." Will stressed.

"So the reports about certain monstrous animals were indeed... *accurate*?" Damian asked.

"Yes. I'm sure you can do some research regarding the legend of Rockdale Valley," Will replied and Alyssa carefully pushed herself up in her bed.

"I can tell you everything you need to know about it Mr. Secretary," she said.

"And your name is?" Damian asked.

"Alyssa Bennett."

"And can you tell me how your information will be credible?"

"Because I share a bloodline to a descendant of the tribe of Native Americans that this story is about. Rockdale Valley was my home."

Damian looked at Allison. She nodded and looked at Alyssa. "Tell us everything you know," she said.

Alyssa nodded and glanced at Will. "All you need is the journal."

Will carefully retrieved the journal and handed it to Allison.

"This journal was written long ago. It was protected by a Native American in the ancient cathedral of Rockdale Valley. Read it…It will tell you everything."

Allison took a breath and opened the journal. "You know anyone can write an interesting story…" she said.

Alyssa held her breath as she and Will waited patiently. They watched Allison's many facial expressions until she closed the journal and handed it to Damian. She looked at Alyssa carefully.

"Do you know why one of our agents would get involved in this?"

"He was seeking the red diamond that was located in that cavern. He also claimed that there was a supernatural power within this sacred chamber. What I learned is that he needed a descendant to get in there and retrieve the stone. My father was a very close friend of his…" Alyssa replied and looked away, trying not to get upset. "He set us up using a friend of his, an Agent Russell. I had no idea. I suffered amnesia after the incident occurred when my father and I met Agent Hall at the cavern. My father is dead now because of him. Some of the residents of the valley not to mention the tourists are dead now because of him…"

"My *group* is dead because of him as well as other countless soldiers that were sent there," Will pitched in, thinking about his close friend Alex.

"I realize you two are feeling betrayed. There *will* be an investigation. Do you have any other evidence in regards to this legend?" Allison asked.

Alyssa took in a deep breath, releasing it slowly. Will looked at her, wondering what she may be contemplating.

"No Madam Secretary," she replied.

Allison slowly nodded.

"A Captain Smitherman was able to get his hands on the diamond, but…he was killed in action. Mr. Hall is also amongst the deceased as well. I have a letter here from my former partner. He witnessed the murders that took place at the precinct that I feel you should know about. They were committed by the ones working under Mr. Hall," Alyssa added.

Allison took the note and carefully read it. She slowly nodded and looked back at Alyssa. "And this is all you have?" she asked.

"Yes," Alyssa replied.

Will nodded and looked at Allison and Damian. They were silent for a moment before Allison spoke up. "We'll have someone look into this further. For the time being, this information remains classified. I will have our lawyers come by soon with the non-disclosure agreements. I need you two to sign them. Thank you Ms. Bennett and Sergeant First Class Thompson. We will get to the bottom of it to make sure our Nation is still protected," Allison said and turned away.

One of her security agents opened the door and they stepped into the hallway. Damian stepped up to the door and looked back at them. "Thank you again Sergeant First Class, Ms. Bennett. We will be in touch," he stated and quickly stepped out into the hall, closing the door behind him.

Will took his place by Alyssa's bedside and leaned against it. "So do you mind telling me what you have in mind?"

"I heard my brother's voice. That's what I was trying to tell you when Uktena reappeared. I can end this…another way. I just need to get the diamond back to its resting ground and seal the door. I cannot trust anyone to do this but myself. It needs to be me," Alyssa stated.

Will nodded. "I understand…But we need to give this time and a lot of it. It will take a while to heal," Will said and paused, taking a deep breath in. "Once we put this all behind us, I would like to be a part of *this* …If you'll let me. I will never forgive myself…"

Alyssa half-smiled. "Will, please…It's over now. I cannot blame you for standing beside your brothers. I would've done the same."

Will nodded. "I...had an experience where I misjudged a situation overseas long ago. I failed the people I was trying to save. I told myself that I would never let anyone down again, ever. I was never able to let go of that..."

Alyssa stared at him as he continued. "Out of the dozens of people we were trying to rescue, only three made it out alive."

"Goodness...I'm so sorry," Alyssa replied softly. She didn't want to get the rest of the details. She had heard many war stories in her past. They always had a way of hitting a soft spot in her heart. She couldn't imagine being placed in a situation like that.

"And that's also why I was so determined to help you," Will added.

Alyssa placed her hand on his, patting it softly. "I understand." She leaned back in her bed and carefully retrieved his challenge coin and the picture of her and her father. "I guess I should give this back to you now," she said and held out the coin.

Will shook his head. "Hold on to it for me."

Alyssa smiled and put the coin back into her pocket and looked at the picture. Will leaned in to take a closer look as well.

"I remember this as if it happened yesterday. I will never forget all the things he taught me," Alyssa said.

Will nodded. Alyssa sighed softly and sat the picture on the table next to her. She looked back at Will and the door to the room suddenly opened once again.

"Oh, sorry for not knocking," Kevin said and closed the door. "You got to see this...It's already on the news."

Alyssa's heart skipped a beat as she sat up in her bed. She didn't want to know what they were telling the world regarding the incident.

Kevin quickly grabbed the remote and turned the small television on. He switched it to Channel 9 News, and there was a reporter with news cameras miles away from the valley, situated on the neighboring mountains. The fire was consuming the remains of the town, dark smoke and ash hovering in the sky.

"...And we haven't had the chance to speak to any survivors, but what we are being told at this moment is that the volcano situated under Rockdale Valley has indeed erupted. Many were not aware of the magma reservoir under the valley, but we are being told it was discovered not long ago. The residents' claims of mysterious, large animals attacking have been verified. Bears and wolves have been spotted in the area, traveling after the recent and frequent earthquakes that have occurred these past few days," the reporter stated and the view changed from one at the studio with a small clip of the view of the valley at the top right. "So far, the total number of people missing and/or deceased has increased to seven hundred and thirty one, that including Mrs. Cathy Woods from Channel Six News and her news crew. We send our condolences to their families as well as to Channel Six News..."

Kevin turned the volume down and glanced back at Will and Alyssa. "It's already begun."

Will remained quiet as Alyssa gulped. "Well, we were just questioned from the Secretaries of Defense and Homeland Security. They have the journal I found, but that's it."

"Clearly someone saw that B-52," Kevin stated.

"And they will find a way to cover that up too. Maybe the truth to what occurred cannot be known to the world which is why we cannot speak of it to others. We have to forget about this and move on," Will replied.

Alyssa slowly nodded. "Think of what would happen...especially if the black market was made aware of this rare diamond. That is why I must be the one responsible for putting this stone back in its rightful place. We can't put too much trust into the government."

Kevin placed the remote down. "Agreed. I'm going with you when you decide to do this."

Alyssa nodded. "I don't believe the nuke reached that location, but if it did, hopefully the damage isn't severe," she said.

"We'll just have to see. Alright, well I'll be back in a moment. You two need anything?" Kevin asked.

"No thanks," Alyssa said and Will shook his head.

"Okay," Kevin stated and left the room, closing the door gently.

The news was still on and Will glanced at it. He reached for the remote and turned it off, looking back at Alyssa, smiling.

"We start now…" he said and Alyssa nodded, returning the smile.

Will placed his hand on hers and patted it gently. A smile curled across Alyssa's face as she leaned back against the thick pillow behind her. She knew it was going to take a lot of time for any of this to blow over, but when it did, she could already see the possible future she was going to have no matter where it was going to lead her. Will was going to have a big part in it.

The valley burned for many days and many nights after the incident. The media was left to report the only information given, the sudden suspicious earthquakes and the recent find of the magma reservoir located just under the valley. The death toll and the missing rose just over eight hundred and the nation was shaken from the natural disaster. Wahkan and his loyal tribe however, were now lost to the darkness once again, becoming a forgotten tale once more, never to be resurrected again. It was a hope that would always linger in the back of their minds.

EPILOGUE

ALYSSA WAS STANDING AT THE foot of a small meadow, staring towards the thick brush that had grown around the mouth in the mountain. Rocks and boulders sat on the side of it, some crushed into smaller pebbles. The forest they climbed through was thick, hiding the sun's afternoon rays, but the small meadow she stood near was open, allowing the gentle rays to shine down on the obscured cave entrance. A few weeks had passed since the incident in Rockdale Valley and since she had stepped foot out in the wilderness. It felt nice to be back near the area she adored the most, but it was also difficult.

"So this is it?" Will asked as he stepped up beside her, his backpack full of supplies and canteens weighing heavily against his back.

"It is."

Will stared towards the cave entrance and took in a deep breath. Kevin was standing next to him, his arms crossed.

"There will never be justice done for any of the people that were killed. This will remain in the government's little black book," Kevin said, staring towards the cave.

"But they didn't get away with it. This was all Brian's doing. He failed...Now we can make sure that this never happens again," Alyssa said and glanced at Kevin. "We can't dwell on this any longer...We have to let it go. We'll never forget the ones we lost."

Kevin nodded and retrieved his maglite. "Let's do this."

Alyssa and Will retrieved their flashlights, and they carefully approached the brush. Will pushed the limbs to the side, allowing just enough room to squeeze through. Alyssa pushed herself between the limbs and waited as Will and Kevin carefully followed. She turned her attention towards the darkness and pressed on the switch to her flashlight. It beamed brightly ahead and at all the rock of the passageway as it stretched far into the distance before curving to the right. Will and Kevin turned their flashlights on, and they carefully began making their way down the path. Alyssa led the way, her nerves beginning to strike a little fear deep within her. She had to do this quickly.

They slowly pushed forward, watching their footing, until the area began to open. Their lights shone brightly in the cavern they stepped into, shining through the many crystals that hung in the area.

"I remember this place...I remember it very well now," Alyssa said and approached the large crystal that was lodged in the middle. Will followed, staring at all the crystals while trying to keep a close eye on their surroundings. Kevin trailed behind, examining the area thoroughly.

"I remember looking at this. There should be a path over here," Alyssa stated and walked around the large rock and towards the back. A small passageway was carved into the cavern, veering to the right as it wrapped around the back of it. Alyssa stopped and touched the walls, noticing the etchings, taking a deep breath in. Her heart suddenly began to race.

This is it...

"Wait here..." she said and looked at Will and Kevin who were now standing close behind her.

"Be careful," Will stated.

Alyssa nodded and looked at Kevin. "I have to go alone from here."

"Just be quick...I don't want to be here too much longer," Kevin replied and crossed his arms. The dark cavern kept him on edge.

Alyssa gave a nod and turned around, slowly making her way down the passageway. As she turned the corner, her light shined on an open door and into a dark, secluded chamber. Her heart thumped heavily within her chest, her breathing becoming rapid. She approached the door and stopped, touching the makeshift keyhole.

Of course...I ran out and left the area open...

Alyssa carefully pushed herself into the sacred chamber, shining her light towards the rectangular rock that sat just across the small stream. She retrieved the pendant and caressed it gently, slowly making her way towards the rock, gazing at the etchings carved into it. After pushing past the stream, she approached the large rock Wahkan claimed and gazed at the small bed, the diamond's resting place. Alyssa carefully placed the red gem back into its rightful place and looked back at the carefully carved etchings. She slowly placed her fingertips on them, slowly sliding them down to her side. She could hear the whispers of the Native tongue enter her mind, but she cleared her thoughts and took a deep breath.

"It's over. The secret will be safe with me," she whispered and turned away, making her way back to the door to seal it...forever.

Melissa Sharman

A Special Thank You...

Tim Poole, Kevin Moore, Gil Gonzalez, David Coleman, Debbie Arbelo, Cindy DeVaughn, Lynn Blackburn, Vicki & Bub Akins, Brittany & Michelle Akins, Audrey Freeman, Jennifer Davis, Michael Coleman, Hasan Fersner, and Lisa Clendenen. Words could never describe my gratitude. You helped make my lifelong dream a reality. Thank you!